SYNOPSIS

An uncompromising thriller set in the last decade of the 20th Century. Criminality is reaching epidemic proportions. The combination of a vociferous liberal lobby, the breakdown of family and school disciplines over three generations and a weak judicial system have produced a society living in fear.

A seemingly average rape murder case sets Detective Sergeant Phil Queen on an apparently straightforward investigation, when the suspect is swiftly apprehended. For Gary Hart, the wheels of justice begin to turn.

In the country at large, a series of random assaults and deaths are occurring. However, due to their sporadic nature, they merge into the general crime figures and, therefore, no connections are made.

Detective Sergeant Queen is congratulating himself on the progress of his murder investigation and his burgeoning friendship with the victim's mother, when his satisfaction in his work is rudely shattered by a senior colleague who accuses him of dereliction of duty during a top-brass visit to Police HQ. Alarmingly for Phil's career, this escalates into an enquiry and, frustrated by petty injustice, Phil resigns.

That night, he is contacted by a stranger who arranges an appointment to meet him. Phil is then led into an intriguing new concept of natural justice and the part he could play in a dangerous, but ultimately effective, new form of retribution on the criminal elements in society.

Even as he becomes increasingly aware of the many strands of depravity and duplicity amongst his new associates, nothing prepares him for the final denouement...

Vanguard I

They sat around a large white marble table, impeccable in their dark suits. Glasses tinkled as a large decanter was passed from hand to hand. Each filled his own glass as the young waiter left the room.

At the head of the table sat their leader. His hair was black and sleeked with expensive oils. His alpaca suit gleamed softly in the subdued lighting; its cut emphasising the lean strength of his body. His long manicured hands held a large cigar from which the smoke swirled in wreaths around his head.

A large grandfather clock ticked gently in the shadows. 'The Ten' waited, sipping at their expensively cut wine glasses. A dog barked in the distance; a large dog. You could tell from the sound.

Suddenly, the clock slowly chimed. On the eighth chime the leader stood.

"Welcome gentlemen!"
Murmurs arose from the assembled company and heads nodded in agreement.
"This, my friends, is the third meeting of 'The Ten'," the leader spoke with clipped authority.

"We are turning the tide."
More murmurs and nods greeted these words.
"Our small legion of conscripts has secured numerous victories in recent weeks. We are beginning to see the fruits of our labours. With the aid of future recruits, and with careful management, you can be sure that we can continue to cleanse our country of the scum that our justice system seems unable to control or refuses to punish. The police are being very helpful and we will now hear the reports from our area organisers..."

Fifty minutes later, 'The Ten' had spoken. Incident after incident, victory on victory, were recited and approved. Society at large was weary of the abrogation of justice which seemed to favour the perpetrator at the expense of the victim. The much vaunted get tough policies of the government had proved to be totally ineffective and crime was spiralling out of control.

It was the murder of his daughter at a fairground that had prompted the leader of 'The Ten' to act. The killer was given a three-year suspended sentence. During his spell in a young offenders' prison, prior to the court case, he had openly enjoyed the television, games of pool, comfortable beds and regular meals. It's all so different from his life in the sink estate on the fringe of the city. On his release, his comment 'thanks for the holiday mate' was widely reported in the press and noted by the leader of 'The Ten'.

Not good enough, he said to himself. He had waited for the young bastard to walk free and recruited three friends, one of whom was a highly respected but disillusioned prison officer who had no connection with their target, on whom they wrought a natural justice some weeks later when his body was found on a local railway line.

The leader stood once again.

"Good work gentlemen," he said confidently. "Our next meeting will be in three months' time. The usual coded message will be in The Times' Obituary column," he continued.

'The Ten' rose from their seats as one, raised their glasses and intoned, "To the innocent! To justice!"

The clock chimed eleven as they filed out of the room. The dog barked again as the engines of limousines sprang into life in the forecourt of the shadowy mansion. It was another meeting and another success. They had only just begun...

PART ONE

Chapter One

The boy hid in the bushes. He was 13 two weeks previously. He didn't play football much with his mates but he liked to watch kick-boxing on Friday night TV. None of his friends did what he did because they had to be indoors by nine o'clock every evening.

It was ten-fifteen p.m. on a Monday. The damp ground ate into his cheap second-hand denims; some of his mates owned Levi 501s. He wore his baseball cap back to front because he was streetwise and could handle himself. Five foot eleven and already twelve and a half stone. He was 'a big lad' or so his uncle said.

Gary Hart waited for tonight's target. Normally, it would be young kids who wouldn't retaliate or old men or women who were too weak to fight back; animals sometimes 'cos they couldn't understand much until it was too late. He smiled a self-satisfied smile. He whistled the latest rave tunes through his teeth, patiently watching the pathway ahead. Dusk was falling and shadows disappeared into darkness.

Then, he saw the figure. Female, five foot, knee length skirt, high heels (*good!*) and carrying a briefcase. She walked briskly but shouldn't have chosen tonight to take the short cut through the park...

"Stupid cow - time to die," whispered the hidden hero.

****

Janice Lee didn't have to work late but didn't mind when David did too. She liked to help him clear up. She was very late tonight though because David had cornered her in the store room and she'd thoroughly enjoyed it. She had only ever seen an erection twice. Three times now and she hoped the pill had worked. Her mum said sex before marriage was a sin. Upper class twaddle, she thought and chuckled.

She didn't see much of her attacker. He had come from behind and grabbed her roughly around the throat. She was too shocked to react. God, he was strong! The smell of rotten leaves assailed her as she hit the ground. The man wore very old training shoes and faded denims. She wanted to see as much as she could of him. As she struggled, adrenalin fed her fear but also charged her brain. They would ask questions later at the station. She watched 'Crimewatch' and now it was happening to her!

"What do you want? Just take it all!"

There was a Sun newspaper and a bag of cheese and onion crisps in the briefcase. Big business!

"Money, you cow!" spat the man.

"I only carry a plastic card you prat!"

"Bitch!"

The kick to her solar plexus winded her. She felt nausea sweep over her whole body. As her hair was pulled back, she saw his face. So strong for a youngster! Crew cut under the baseball cap, acne and he was chewing gum. There was a short silence. What next? Surely he'd run off?

Gary didn't know what tits felt like. He'd seen pictures under his dad's bed. Time to find out. She felt his hands go under her jacket. The colour drained from her face. She could feel the afternoon's coffee welling up in her stomach. Her tits felt nice and he could feel her nipples through the lacy material. He worked his way down. Janice began to panic. How far was he going to go? His breathing was getting laboured and he had an odd feeling in his stomach.

"You scream and I'll kill you!" *(Sounds good!)*
She thought he meant it, as she scrabbled around in the stinking bushes. She should have been home feeding the cat by now. It was pitch black.

"Bastard! Does your mum know where you are? Bet you've never seen a girl's bits before have you? Enjoying it? Got a hard on yet?"

"Shut it!" The slap caught her cheek and her tears stung her eyes.

"Take your pants off!"

"You do it - I'm quite enjoying myself!"

This caught him off guard. She kicked out and caught him in the groin. The groan sounded so good, she nearly laughed. As he lay retching, she grabbed the briefcase and smashed it against what she hoped was the boy's head. His gasp told her it was.

In two seconds, she came to her senses - RUN! FAST! It was quite difficult emulating the four minute mile in Lycra tights. Was he following?

Gary watched the figure run diagonally across the field. Oh shit! That was fun, he smiled to himself. The darkness enveloped him again. His erection was almost painful... It had all lasted about three fun-packed minutes.

****

The girl spoke animatedly behind the glass partition. She was pretty, dressed in jeans and a baggy jumper with flowers on it. No make-up. It was eleven fifteen and Sergeant Phil Queen had seen rape victims before. They all looked the same. Wide-eyed and babbling. The girl had phoned the station at ten forty and was in the office by eleven. Very strong-willed too. It took her five minutes to shower and get into a change of clothing. Oh, and she worked at Brandgate's, the new supermarket on the outskirts of the town. Sad. Pretty though.

"I saw his face. He looked about twelve years old and wore a baseball cap," Janice said confidently.
"Cigarette?"
"No ta, my dad died from the things."

Jackie Gleason sat opposite the latest victim, immaculate in her uniform. Fifteen years in the screws and still interviewing whining rape victims. She tried hard to sound sympathetic.

"Why did you go through the park at this late time?"
"Why not? Done it a thousand times."
"Want a cup of tea?"
"Please, two sugars."
"Did the attacker take anything?"
"No."
"Where was he from?"
"Local - definitely. Had the accent."
"Would you recognise him again?"
"Maybe. It was getting dark. He was very young and his voice hadn't broken yet."
"Were there any distinctive features?"
"He had acne on his chin and it said 'Spurs' on his baseball cap."
"It was a blue baseball cap - Spurs play in blue and white. Correct Terry?"
"Yeah. Blue and white and they're crap, ha ha."
"Yeah, OK."
"White!" Janice interrupted.
"The cap?"
"Yeah - white with blue letters – capitals."
"Now we're getting somewhere..."
"Can't be many Spurs fans in this area. Mainly Rovers or Townies," Sergeant Terry Wicks observed.
"Mmmm..mm."
"Any other features Miss Lee?"
"Skinhead. He had very short hair."
"Short or skin?"
"Crew cut."
"Good! I think we've got a lot to go on here lovey."

"I watch 'Crimewatch' all the time. I like Nick Ross."
"I wish all our customers liked Nick Ross..."

It was eleven-forty-five. Janice was led out of the interview room to give a few more particulars to the good-looking Sergeant Queen. He had a good tan and a moustache. 'RMP' was tattooed on his left forearm. It was a mistake during a drunken spree in Chichester, early in a short Army career.

"Right. Miss Lee is it?"
"Yes."
"Can I have your full work contact address and number?"
"Brandgate's - I work in the stores."
"Telephone number?"
"53462 - Mr Stokes is my boss. I do nine 'til five, six days a week."
"OK. Thanks," Sergeant Queen smiled. "We'll be in touch. Should have the photo-fit ready in a day or so, once we've got the artist's impression. Could you come and give it the once-over?"
"Yeah, great."
Phil noticed she was shaking. Delayed shock probably. She seemed so confident yet so vulnerable. Just like the majority of victims. They hardly ever cry these days.

"Fancy another cuppa before we take you home?"

"Lovely – thanks."

Janice sat in the foyer for another ten minutes, staring at the posters on the opposite wall. So depressing! She was glad she worked at Brandgate's. The people were nice, especially David, especially after tonight. He'd been a friend for months but there was something beneath the surface, until eight o'clock this evening in the storeroom. She finished her tepid tea and threw the paper cup into the plastic bin. Time to tell mum...

"Ready?"
"Yeah, fine."
The constable ushered her outside, down the steps and into the waiting vehicle, all orange and white stripes. The car disappeared into the night at a respectable speed. Someone was watching...

****

Gary knew the cow would go to the police. That was why he hadn't gone home straightaway. He had simply brushed himself down, took a stroll to McDonald's, had a late-night burger and went to stake out the station. He sat on the wall next to the Four Star taxi rank. He had an unobstructed view of the entrance to the police station but his position was in shadow.

The cow had arrived at eleven, escorted by two officers, a girl and a male.
"Go on then, tell them if I care," he sniggered to himself. Three quarters of an hour was all it took. "I didn't even touch her fanny," He chuckled as they descended the station steps and as the car pulled away he hailed a taxi. "Follow that car," Gary uttered. He'd always liked that in the films on the telly. He felt a surge of pleasure and power. The driver of the taxi regarded him in the rear-view mirror and wondered what a young lad was doing tailing a police car at this time of night. The games

people play, he thought. It was his last fare of the night, all two pounds and fifteen pence of it...

****

"Thanks, that's my flat," Janice pointed and the car pulled up opposite the brick-built three-storey building.
"Twelve o'clock - past my bedtime," she laughed as she slammed the door of the Ford.
"Goodnight love, see you again," the constable murmured with a smile.
"Take care," the WPC cautioned in farewell.
"No probs. Thanks for the lift," replied Janice and she leant on the car roof. She turned and jogged up the steps and disappeared into the flats.
"Pretty lass; had guts," the constable remarked as the car went into first gear.
"Yeah, they're always pretty," agreed WPC James.

****

The taxi dropped its occupant off eighty yards up the road, behind the police car.
"Cheers mate," grinned the spotty youth as he threw the loose change on the front passenger seat. All one pound seventy pence of it...
"Oi! Come 'ere you little bastard!"
Too late. Another duff fare.
"Sod it!"
Charlie pulled away from the kerb cursing.
"Little bastards don't know they're born..."
The scruffy youth was nowhere to be seen.

****

Phil Queen hung his uniform tidily away. The basic grey cabinet had a cold look to it. Functional, cheap and nasty. He dressed in his civilian attire - jeans, sweatshirt and hush puppies ('desert wellies' as he called them in his military days). His Barbour jacket had seen better days but he still looked the part.

The end of another shift; another night on the front desk. It was one o'clock in the morning and he was knackered. He'd go up to the kitchen area for a quick coffee, then head for his house for a good night's kip.

"See you Kev," he said to the oncoming Sergeant Keeley. Five years more experience in dealing with lost dogs and petty theft. "Have a good one!"

"Cheers Phil, see you tomorrow I suppose. Any hassles today?" Pete Keeling queried.
"Two car thefts, a GBH and a girl attacked in Glebe Park. Not much..."

"As scintillating as usual eh?"

"Yeah, see you."

He had joined the police as a last resort. After five years as a Royal Military Policeman it seemed a natural progression. One uniform to another. The Army was good while it lasted, but he had bought himself out after two years in Belfast. Only his second posting. After Belfast, anything else would have been boring. He'd seen people bombed, abused and slaughtered all in the name of religion but could do little about it. His military qualifications meant he'd little choice on civvy street. The family had been supportive and helped him get a job driving trucks for six months but the boredom soon put a stop to that.

The police welcomed him with open arms and he had risen quickly through the ranks to sergeant, six years as a constable, exams were passed and now he was a desk sergeant. Cushy!

He sat in the canteen, sipping thoughtfully at his coffee. The evening paper lay on a chair nearby. The same old headlines: **OLD WOMAN IN STABBING HORROR, TEENAGERS IN VIOLENT WRECKING SPREE, BODY IDENTIFIED AS FOUR YEAR OLD GIRL** and **WE SHALL OVERCOME SAY LABOUR.**

It's the same old stories; week in and week out. His mind wandered back to the girl he'd seen earlier, the pretty one in tight jeans that got attacked in the park by a youth. Nothing new in that. It was happening every day now, somewhere or other. The criminals were younger than ever but where was the deterrent?

The girl was a tough little cookie though, not the usual hysterical type. She had nice eyes and a nice smile too. Nice everything really! Twenty three and lived alone according to the notes they'd taken. Trainee manageress at Brandgate's. Very normal and obviously bright with good prospects. She would be back in on Wednesday to look at the artist's sketch of the assailant. Maybe she might like to go out for a drink? He hadn't had a girlfriend in three years, not since Sally had elbowed him after an argument over a holiday destination. He wanted Torquay and she wanted the Seychelles. No contest!

He went to Torquay with Trev instead and they had a whale of a time!

Oh well, he would see her again on Wednesday. He would be on day shift and he was looking forward to it. They would sit and chat about the artist's impression on the table and drink coffee. Then, he would ask her out and she would say '*yes please*' and they would live happily ever after, in Torquay of course. Phil chuckled to himself, mocking his tangential daydream, stood up, stretched and ambled downstairs into the cool night air. He was very confident in the knowledge that they would catch the kid in the baseball cap. Very confident indeed...

****

The figure hugged the dark recesses of the street. He crept along the footpath silently, his ragged trainers making no sound on the concrete as he made his way stealthily up to the gate. The flats were cheap conversion jobs within the old house which had seen days of affluence and propriety. He weighed up the position of her flat. He had seen the light come on thirty seconds after she had entered the room two hours previously.

It was two o'clock in the morning - time for her to be settled for the night, he thought. He felt powerful. All his mates would have been in bed for eleven-thirty but not him! He had made his mind up when she had escaped from his frenzied attack that he would follow her and scare her even more this time. Boys were stronger, weren't they? No school for him on Tuesday. His mum would call the doctor when he said he had a stomach ache and sore throat. Easy!

Gary Hart was in the mood for some serious fun now. The adrenalin was pumping. The street was silent. The girl's light had gone off an hour ago, twenty minutes after she had let the cat out - a nice little Persian thing. He could always play with the cat, if all else failed. Ho... ho! He felt his back pocket. The flick knife was still there. Good stuff. He opened the gate. Not a sound. Scurrying up the path to the front door, he was aided by bushes on either side. You could hear the silence as he sat on the steps. Gary tried the door knob, twisted it to the right and pushed.
Bingo, he thought...

The door creaked open and Gary entered the building, closing the door behind him.

****

She must have been half asleep when she heard the scraping on the flat door. Janice looked at the clock on her dressing table. *01.25am* it read. She had been in bed for over an hour. Was she dreaming? There was no sound at all; just the silence. The clock clicked onwards to *01.26am* (in BIG red digits).

There it was again! It sounded like rats or mice; unlike any noise she had heard before in her flat. She had gone to bed with a hot drink and her book. Her half-eaten toast lay next to the bed on the floor.

She lay still. Listening...

Nothing!

Her breathing was slow. She listened again. Not a sound - go back to sleep.
She closed her eyes and drifted off...

Miaaoow!

Her eyes shot open!

"Polly!" It was Polly, the cat!

The scraping started again.

Janice lifted her legs out of bed. She was naked. As she put on a T-shirt, she flicked on her bedside lamp and breathed a deep sigh of relief at the same time. The cat was her only companion since she bought the flat. She loved Polly!

The key was in the lock. She turned it once to the left.

"Come on in, my little..."
The force of the door knocked her backwards. She hit her head on a wooden stool. The concussion was immediate and painful.
"Cats can't open doors, you crazy bitch," hissed the figure in the doorway.

Janice Lee looked up through blurred and tear-filled eyes. Her last thought was that she was right about the crew-cut...
Gary Hart felt for his flick knife once more.

****

AN OXFORDSHIRE VILLAGE – 11.15PM

The village was quiet. Quiet, apart from the crowd departing from the Black Horse public house. Laughter mingled with noisy teenagers singing a medley of Take That hits. The pub was situated on the corner of the High Street, opposite the Post Office and Mrs Greenall's trinket shop, which was popular with people passing through on holidays or at weekends.

There were three youths leaving the bar, obviously the worse for drink. Two tall ones and a smaller stocky one. It was the stocky one they wanted. They wanted the stocky one, a certain Keith Harris. He was known as 'Orville' to his mates and he'd been released from Long Lartin prison two days earlier after serving six months of a paltry three year sentence.

Three years for the beating and rape of old Missy Jackson from Bleasdale Gardens. Missy never recovered. She died three weeks later in hospital and gave up the will to live, the doctor said.

There was national outrage and sympathy in the press and her photo appeared on page seven of The Sun. **THE FACE OF BRITAIN** was the headline. There was no condemnation strong enough, said the local Liberal candidate for the area. There were seventy plus mourners at the funeral, mainly relatives and villagers. There was no media coverage of the service on page seven of The Sun. On the day Missy Jackson was buried; it clashed with another royal scandal. Not enough space for a picture of the scene inside the Norman church so not a mention.

But the village did not forget! Orville and company made their way across the road and into the darkness of the village park. They didn't see the six figures standing at the rear of the Black Horse car park. Two of the figures held baseball bats and one had a rope. The other three just stood. All six had woollen hats on their heads.

"Let's go," murmured the leading figure.

There was the sound of feet on gravel at a slow pace. In the distance, they heard drunken singing in the park.

"Glory, glory Man United...and 'The Reds' keep marching on... on... ON!"

"Wankers," murmured one of 'The Six'.

They walked on into the park.

"We only want Orville," one of the figures whispered. "Remember that!"

Orville and his two cohorts lounged next to the statue in the centre of the park. The sound of opening lager cans broke the singing.

"This is cheap shit!"

"Can't afford Heineken. Anyway, it all tastes the same so drink it," slurred his sidekick.

"Bollocks!" retorted Orville, spraying him with a stream of cheap booze.

"You bastard! They should have locked you up and threw away the key!"

"Behaved, din' I?" laughed Orville, "Yes sir, no sir, eight bags full sir. No hassle!"

"She died - the old slag. Left twenty grand an' all," added the tallest one.

"Tough shit - she'd never have spent it anyway."
The three amigos inebriated laughter overflowed into the darkness.

'The Six' stood in shadow thirty metres away and they were hidden by a clump of bushes.
"Got a sense of humour have we? You'll need it!"
Fingers tightened around the bat as he clasped it in his right hand.
"Give it five minutes," whispered number Three.
Laughter drifted across the park. They were rolling about on the grass.
"Delinquents," a voice whispered.
"That's too good a description - they're scum!"
The laughter died.
"They're shit-faced..."
"Good," said Four.
"Split 'em up. We only want Orville."
"They'll run like buggery when we show up."
The big man with the bat nudged number Two.
"You make sure Orville stays put!"
"OK."

Two more minutes passed as the circus by the statue continued. Orville lay on his back looking up at the stars. It was a warm, silent night. "Creepy innit?" groaned Orville as he looked up through the giant oak tree.

None of the three noticed as six shadowy figures approached around the statue. Not until it was too late to run. They stood over their target.

"What the..."

The man with the bat was huge and he fought the tall one as he tried to scramble to his feet.
"You two - fuck off!" spat number Three.
Number Two already had Orville in an armlock. The two tall youths sprinted off into the night. They looked like rabbits in the sights of a very big gun, thought number Five giggling inside.
"Who the fuck are you?" screamed Orville!
"We're your worst nightmare," said Six slowly. He liked that saying and he'd rehearsed it.
"Piss off, we're only havin' a drink!" whined Orville; his eyes rolling in his ashen face.
Orville thought the baseball bat looked nasty. Why did they have a rope? He couldn't see their faces; the torch saw to that. All he saw were five, no six men, stood over him in judgement.

Number Two had a vice-like grip. A black belt in Tai Kwon Do helped.

We've come to punish you Keith," said number One.
Orville's eyes widened in disbelief.
"Wha', I've been in nick! Thass enough innit?"
"Eye for an eye is what we think Keith."
"How did it feel hitting Missy with the chair leg?"
"Bet it felt good eh? Hard eh?"
They were all talking at once...
"WELL?" shouted all three suddenly!
"SPEAK!"
"I...I...didn't mean to... All I wanted was a bit of fun! It got out of hand and she scr'..."
The bat came down on Orville's left leg, just below the knee. The pain was incredible.

"This is FUN Keith!" spat the huge man.
"It's getting out of hand don't you think?"
Orville couldn't speak. He threw up on the grass, moaning.
"Tut, tut - can't hold your beer eh?" commented Two.
The other bat came down on the other leg above the ankle. Another scream but it was louder this time. Orville's sobs were the only sound for a moment.

"ROPE!"
The word registered with Orville in spite of his agony.
"Wha'...!?" He stared incredulously into the torch's beam.
He tried to scrabble away. He can't get far with two broken legs thought number Six. Screams broke the night air.
"No use - the villagers know who's screaming," said Five. His country drawl was unnerving.
"Who heard Missy's screams Keith?"
"You did Keith because you caused them."
"I know it's painful but you did it to Missy so it must be OK, eh Keith?"
Orville was hysterical now.
"I'M SORRY!" he shouted in a high pitched pleading wail.
"Sorry is too late. Sorry is not enough. Sorry is just SHIT!" pursued Six.
"I know who you are!" cried Orville through gritted teeth.
"Oh me, oh my, are we crapping our pants boys?" replied one of the Six.
"Yeah, I must run away, the police might come," sneered Two.

"I'll sue! Then you'll be in nick like I was!" Desperation tinged Orville's voice.

"Sue!?" Six laughed. "The thing is, Keith, you have no grasp of this situation."

"Remember what I said," drawled Five. "An eye for an eye."

Three threw the rope over the thickest branch of the giant oak tree. It had given shade and shelter for over seventy years.

The glare of the torch blocked Orville's view. His legs were on fire.

"Get me an ambulance you wankers! You've had your fun!" grimaced the writhing figure on the grass.

The huge one with the bat nodded to the others.

"Get him up!"

"Cheers lads," the relief was evident in Orville's tone.

The rope was now noosed. Number One stood on the plinth of the statue.

"Are you sure?" he asked Six.

"Very."

"Fucking hell!" screamed Orville as he saw the tree. "You can't! I'M SORRY! I've said I'..."

A damp rag was stuffed unceremoniously into his protesting mouth and masking tape wrapped around his wrists.

"Not his legs because I want to see them kick," said Six.

Orville's last muffled pleas did not reach the night air.

Four brawny arms lifted him off the ground. A good three foot gap was needed. Kicking legs flailed in the warm, night air. The noose was looped over his long hair, the head was all over the place and it wouldn't keep still. A swift punch to the stomach took the last fight out of Orville. The noose was tight and four hands let go. The tree creaked... The rope stretched to its full length and the tree took the weight well. Two looked away.

Four stared at the writhing legs. "Dance you wanker," he said grimly.

It took two minutes for the last movements to fade. Orville's eyes were wide. He had wet and shit himself. A pool of urine wet the grass under the swaying body. The rag had nearly left his mouth. The figure swung slowly in the summer breeze as the creaking tree held the weight.
"Say '*Hi*' to Missy," whispered Six.

The figures walked slowly away from the scene. One of them softly whistled the Neighbours' theme.

****

Chapter Two

"Are you getting up this morning or what?"

Brenda Hart was fat. Very fat! She was a good looking woman once, before he left her for that slag up north.

"You're going to be late for school!"

She went back into the kitchen and sat at the small wooden table.

Tuesday's edition of the Daily Mirror stared up at her as she ate her bacon, eggs, sausages, beans and toast.

The headline read **'DI'S STOLEN KISSES'** with a picture of a demure Princess of Wales. They always chose a picture to fit the story. This one was at least two years' old, thought Brenda, because her hair was in its old style. Brenda snorted, "Stupid cow, she's ugly."

There was still no movement from her only son upstairs.

"Bollocks!" Brenda angrily pushed her plate away.

"GARY! Get down here NOW!" she screamed while leaning on the bannister.

She had started to sweat already but she'd showered first thing.

"If I have to come up, I'll tan yer arse!"

She gave him ten seconds.

"Right, that's it!"

Brenda heaved herself up the stairs barefoot. Her breathing was laboured and her cheeks flushed as she threw open the bedroom door.

Gary had not got in until half past three. That was nothing new though, so no questions were asked. His clothing was strewn all over the floor: jeans, T-shirt, Y-fronts, socks, trainers, hair brush and numerous CD boxes and record covers.
His bedroom walls were covered with posters, garish colours, fluorescent rave adverts and pictures of Gary Lineker and Paul Gascoigne, taken when England was a good team in the last World Cup in the early 1990s.

"Get up when I tell yer."
"Maa-arm, I've got a sore throat and my tummy hurts!"
The low voice came from somewhere under the duvet. It was a Thomas the Tank Engine duvet.
"What did you eat last night?"
"A burger and chips - must've been off," Gary moaned.
"Have you had a crap this morning?"
"Nah, not yet."
"Well, it's not food poisoning then."
"I just feel sick mum."
"Well, I'll phone for the doctor, but you can deal with him when he gets here 'cos I'm off to work."
"OK ta - I'll see him."
"Stay in bed and drink some water. I'll get you a tablet."
"OK."

Brenda disappeared slowly down the stairs. A fist punched the air in the bedroom.
"Yee-ssss!"

Gary Hart relaxed and went back to sleep. His mum didn't notice the dried red stains on her son's T-shirt and jeans. If she'd looked closer, she'd have seen a pair of women's knickers amongst the squalor that he slept in. Brenda had long since given up noticing or nagging about her son's lifestyle.

Brenda left the house at eight thirty and Brandgate's opened at nine. She had to be on the checkout at five to.

The doctor arrived at eleven o'clock. Just a stomach bug he said. No problem. A day in bed with plenty of liquids and no rich food.

"Easy, cheers Doc!"

****

Phil felt knackered. On entering the station, a severe hangover started to set in. He liked a drink during his days off. Normally, he would only touch the stuff at weekends but when a friend called with free booze, who was he to argue? He had been planning on an early night just before Jeff's arrival. Jeff was his old school mate. Jeff was still a good mate. Trouble was, he liked a drink too. A couple of beers had turned into a couple of crates and now it was too late to say, 'Sorry mate, no can do.'

Phil went straight to the 'Coffee-Now' instant vendor. He inserted his 25 pence. Extortion, he thought but he could smell the whisky on his own breath. (*Shit!*)

Easing himself into his uniform, he tried not to think about the next eight hours of missing cats, lost cars, stolen cars, complaints, questions and never-ending paperwork. He should have been a bloody lumberjack! Still, it paid the bills. His still glassy eyes scanned last night's occurrence book.

"All quiet then Joe?"
"Yeah, very little action bar a fight in the Red Lion."

"Shock! Horror! Probe!" responded a stricken Phil.
"Two pints and they can take on the whole fuckin' world these days. I remember when I started drinking..." started Joe.
"Yeah, yeah, OK Joe, I've heard it all before. OK?"
"Who twisted your bollocks then?" laughed Joe; nudging Phil in the ribs.
"Oh sorry mate, I've got a bit of a hangover. Had an old friend round last night for a few jars, you know."
"Old friends are the worst matey. Take it from me," Joe said with a faraway look on his face.
"Yeah, cheers Joe." Phil tried to sound bored.
"You'll regret it today. Looks like a scorcher outside."

With the sun was already beating down through the windows; the heat would be intense later.
"Hope you've got some money for the ice-cream man!" Joe laughed uproariously as he disappeared down the corridor to the changing rooms.
"Fuck off, Mr Funny!" Phil retorted. He wasn't feeling very well at all. He sat at the desk with his head in his hands.
"Mornin' Sarge!" shouted a young constable.
"Oh, hi Mark. Nice morning isn't it?"
Phil looked up at Constable Perry. He was a nice lad.
"Christ Sarge you look like shit!"

"Thanks for the memory."
"Heavy session was it?"
"Er... yeah, you could say that."
"The Super won't be pleased will he? You've got that visit on today ain't cha?"
"Visit. What visit?"
"You know, that big-wig government minister. What's his name? Garrett? That's it! He's coming today to look at the local community policing crap."
"No, that's next week you prick!" Phil replied.
"Sorry Sarge but you're wrong. Look, you've even circled it on your Man United calendar up there," Perry said as he pointed to the picture of Eric Cantona.
A small red circle surrounded the number 15.
"March 15th... Damn, you're right!"
"It's my job Sarge. See ya. Oh and have a nice day!"
"Cheers Perry," said Phil slowly.
He let out a long, exhausted sigh. He had to get things ship-shape and fast! The Super was a stickler and only gave out gold stars once or twice a year. He wanted at least silver today.

The office was a tip. He needed assistance. He walked hurriedly towards the side offices. Laura should be in, he thought. He pushed open the door to the typing pool. Gwen was in. Oh no, he thought to himself.

"Hi Gwen, where's Laurie today?"

"Day off Phil," replied Gwen.

She had her favourite dungarees on. Fifty-two and she was still wearing dungarees and trainers. Gwen was the resident hippy. She was chewing something too. Probably an ancient herbal remedy, thought Phil.

"Want a Wrigley's?" Gwen asked with her glasses tilted on the end of her tiny nose.

"Oh cheers love. I need it."

"Looks like a heavy night eh?"

"Er,... yeah... Look Gwen, could you give me a hand? The office is a mess and..."

"Before you even ask, NO!"

"Oh come on Gwen. Just ten minutes... please?"

"Sorry Phil, but this report must be done before Commissioner Garrett's arrival."

"Commissioner Garrett?"

"Yes, Deputy Police Commissioner Garrett no less," Gwen chuckled.

"Deputy Commissioner ... Christ!"

Gwen tousled her greying hair and typed on.

Phil was gone.

He always had to tidy up himself. Never anyone there to help, he thought. He started on the bins: half-eaten apple here, sticky yoghourt carton there, a banana skin, crossword puzzles half-solved and a copy of 'Mayfair' - stained. He laughed to himself, dirty bugger Joe.

He emptied all the bins into a black plastic bin liner and left it lying by the entrance to the station. He would chuck it later. He had ten minutes. A wet cloth saw to the desk tops. Dust half an inch thick lay on the cabinets. He wondered if the private industrial cleaners did their job every Monday night. There were no carpets, thank God. Hoovering would be too much of an embarrassment. The office looked habitable now. He even cleaned all the mugs. One had a picture of Prince Charles and Di on it. Happy families, he thought.

Phil sat back in his chair; a look of contentment on his face. No problems, no problems at all. He didn't even need Gwen...

****

The minutes ticked by.
He felt like he was at the dentist. (*Two fillings and an extraction, cheers pal!*)
How could he forget such an important appointment? He castigated himself silently.
Nearly a wooden star mate, he thought. Wooden spoon more likely.

He heard a car, two cars, pull up outside the front of the building. The sound of slamming doors. Voices low. Laughter. Footsteps now, coming closer... louder.
Then, he saw the bag of rubbish by the entrance. He couldn't take his eyes off it. They widened; his stomach lurched. His hangover was back with a vengeance!

No gold stars for me today... Phil thought with resignation. Two fillings and eight extractions were preferable to what happened next.
"It happened in slow motion, as if in a dream sequence," Phil told his workmates later.
The Super had entered the building first; all wore dark suit and brogues. He led the group of dignitaries who were laughing too much; too apologetic by half (*grovelling in any other language*) thought Phil.

"Do come in Sir," the Super said.
The Deputy Police Commissioner entered the station. Two very attractive ladies behind him, they looked like lawyers, were smiling at the way they were being feted by his boss.

As Superintendent Clive Badger pushed the swing doors open, the black plastic bag lurched to the ground on impact due to being top heavy with the half-eaten fruit, yoghourt tubs and porn magazines! One of the apple cores had a mind of its own and bounced away along the polished floor, finally landing at the feet of Phil Queen. He looked down between his legs, sheepishly picking up the offending object. He placed it on top of the occurrence book. Phil looked up slowly.

The face of the Super was comical. A cross between the winner of the Eurovision Song Contest and a heart attack victim. Speechless really. The copy of 'Mayfair' lay open at the centre pages. Trudy from Cornwall really did have a lovely arse, thought Phil.

'If looks could kill, they probably will...' bubbled up from his sub-conscious mind.

The two female lawyers had spotted the 'Mayfair' lying on the floor. They whispered and giggled in the background.

The Deputy Commissioner had obviously been to 'Charm School'. He was grossly overweight and was sweating profusely. He dabbed his forehead with a handkerchief, which probably had his initials on it thought Phil.

"I'm sure there's an explanation Clive," he blurted embarrassed.

"I'm sure there is," replied a very grim-faced Super looking directly into Phil's eyes.

"Sorry sirs, ladies erm... Can I get you all a drink? Tea? Coffee? A cold drink?" Phil stammered.

"You certainly can Sergeant," The fat one spoke.

"We shall be in my office Sergeant Queen!" The anger was not suppressed.

"Kindly clean up and proffer us some sustenance."

Proffer us some sustenance; should be playing bastard Hamlet thought Phil.

The Superintendent led his entourage past the duty desk into his inner sanctum. The two women skirted the yoghourt tubs and grinned surreptitiously at Phil.

"Sorry ladies..." Phil stifled an answering smile as they passed him. One of them winked and blew him a kiss as the door closed.

A kiss before dying thought Phil as the voices diminished. One poxy black bag had probably binned his entire future.

Gwen appeared from the office.

"Trouble?" she smirked as she took off her horn rims.

"No - just the end of a very short career," Phil moaned. "Forgot the crappy bag didn't I? Super only knocked it for six, all over Garrett's feet! Think I'll go for the cyanide capsule right off."

"Poor love…" murmured Gwen unconvincingly.

"Yeah, yeah..."

"Would you say you're in the pooh then?"

"Sinking fast I should imagine."

"Need any help?" Gwen volunteered.

Phil glanced at her; his thoughts only too evident. If looks could kill, he thought bitterly.
"Oh - perhaps not..." said Gwen.

****

Brenda Hart sat at the check-out. Her bottom hung over the edges of the small stool. She chewed gum.

"That'll be forty-nine pounds fifty-three pence love, please."
She punched the till and it buzzed as it produced the receipt.

A small girl with her mum pushed the groceries into individual plastic bags. Another customer began to lay various objects on the conveyor. A bag of peas, bread rolls, crisps, bottle of wine, milk, chicken, dips, Branston pickle etc., etcetera - ad infinitum...

Brenda, or 'Big Bren' as her workmates called her, stared into the distance waiting for the next two hundred shoppers. God it was a pain, but it was a job as her mum had always said. She did it in her sleep so her husband used to say. After seven years it was second nature. She pressed the attention bell.

"Flo! Can I have some change please?" she shouted.
Flo nodded and scurried off.

The uniforms they wore were crap she thought. Too tight by half. Losing weight wouldn't help either. They would never fit her. It was all the fault of the nobs at the top. It's OK for them sat in their offices in their nice suits. That young Janice Lee never had to wear these shitty costumes. Oh no - she had 0-levels and was in 'management'. She didn't have to sit on an uncomfortable stool all day did she? Too much hard graft that was.

Brenda saw Flo returning with Stuart Barnes, the manager. Oh dear, something's up!

Flo gave her the bag of change. Brenda opened it and distributed it into the till.
Mr Barnes looked concerned. He was only twenty-seven but looked eighty-seven, she thought.
"Mrs Hart, isn't it?" the manager asked.
"Yeah, so what?" Brenda replied defensively as she glanced in slight panic at Flo.
"Oh, it's nothing really. I just wondered if you had seen Miss Lee this morning - you know Janice?"
"Yeah, I know Jan," said Brenda while she quizzically looked at the young man.
"Only - it's just that she hasn't turned in today, or yesterday, and we haven't heard anything. You live near her don't you? I wondered if you knew anything?"
"Well yes, she does live about a mile up the road. Not really near. She lives in the flats - I think..."
"Oh I see. I'm sorry, I thought you were neighbours."
"Not within spitting distance, no love," Brenda replied. Flo looked on.
"Oh fine, OK Mrs Hart. Thanks anyway," muttered her boss.
"Anytime," said Brenda shrugging.
Flo moved off since there seemed no news of any interest.
"See you Bren."

"Ciao," answered Bren automatically settling back on her stool.
"Next!" she shouted into the throng of people, hypnotised by the displays, as they pushed their trollies slowly along.

****

It was lunchtime and hot. Phil was hungry but too nervous to eat. The boss was still in his meeting. He hadn't said a word since the bag had tumbled. A cursory glance was all Phil had got when he took in the tea and biscuits two hours ago. He was living on borrowed time after the ghastly incident earlier.

What would happen? He had spent the last hour mulling over possible punishments. Clive Badger was a bastard of the highest order. He didn't like him and the feeling was mutual, Phil reckoned. They had merely tolerated each other from day one. Badger had zero charisma. The sense of humour of a used tea-bag and the self-satisfied look of someone who had just won the pools twice.

Why me, thought Phil. Why was it my shift? Why not Joe's? If only Gwen had helped, if only the cleaners had emptied the bins, if only... "Bollocks to it!" he cursed. It wasn't his job anyway to empty bins. (*It was today, a little voice reminded him!*) He stared out of the window while the traffic sped by; oblivious to his doubts and fears.

The phone on his desk pealed. Three rings later he picked up.
"Thornberry Police. Sergeant Queen speaking. Can I help you?"

The voice at the other end of the line sounded apologetic. "Oh... er hello. I'm sorry to bother you officer, but we seem to have a problem here. Erm... it's to do with one of my staff. It may be nothing but I just thought I should phone," said the man's voice.

"Fine. Could I please have your name sir?"
Oh, of course, how silly of me. I'm Mr Barnes, Stuart Barnes. I work as Area Manager of Brandgate's - the new supermarket. You may know it?"
"I certainly do, Mr Barnes. Nice cold meats are sold there, aren't they?" chuckled Phil scribbling on his pad.
"Er yes, of course. We do our best..."

"What seems to be the problem then?"
"Well officer, we have a young assistant manageress working here, Janice Lee and..."
"Did you say Lee, Mr Barnes?" Phil knew that name.
"Yes, Janice Lee. She's our store's assistant."
"Right, what's up?"
"Well, she hasn't been in to work for two days. I've phoned her flat and there's no answer. I wondered if you had any ideas about tracing her. She lives alone in the flat and I'm a bit concerned as to her well-being."

"Phil was trying to recall where he knew Janice Lee from. Then it hit him!

"Christ!" he exclaimed.
"Sorry officer?"
"Er nothing Mr Barnes. Look, leave this with me and I'll follow it up immediately. I can assure you I'll get on to it right away."

Thank you very much officer. It may be nothing but you never know do you?"
"No, you've done the right thing sir. I'll be in touch."

Phil put the receiver back on its rest.
He suddenly darted across to the current records cabinet, delved into the top drawer, searched through the alphabetical card sections and stopped quickly at Section L.
"L for Lee," he murmured.
He lifted out a sheet of typed paper. A small photograph on the top left hand side caught his eye. She certainly was pretty.
"Bingo," he whispered.
The accompanying text told of the attack in the park two days previously. It had her description of the attacker, the location and time. He turned the page. There, in his own writing, was Miss Lee's address and telephone number. Then, he remembered.
"Shit!"
She should have reported this morning! Phil picked up the phone and dialled.
"Hello Mick. Good? Any joy on the picture of the Lee attack? Done? Brilliant! I'll be down in twenty minutes. See you..."
He was no longer hungry. He rushed into Gwen's office. She was eating an apple. Mind where you put the core thought Phil.
"Gwen, can you sit out front until Constable Green returns? He shouldn't be long."
"Sure," said Gwen. "I owe you one anyway." She smiled.
"Cheers, you're a darling! Tell the boss something's come up and I'll speak to him later," he instructed and hurriedly put on his jacket.

"Bit warm for a coat innit?" Gwen commented.
"Smart as ever.." Phil grinned and winked.

He lurched out of the station as he put his hat on and searched for his car keys.
The station was quiet. Then a voice from down the corridor...
"Sergeant Queen, more tea please!"
Gwen smiled to herself, throwing her apple core in the bin to her left.

****

Phil took ten minutes to get to his destination. He knocked at the door. The door opened and a large bearded man stood holding a piece of A4 paper.
"It's the best I could do," Mick said looking grim.
"It's perfect!" said Phil.
He was looking at a picture of Gary Hart, although he didn't realise it.
Time to visit Miss Lee...

****

HIGHGATE SECONDARY MODERN - NEAR NOTTINGHAM

The boy was scared. He hated lunchtimes. Lunchtime meant going it alone. He didn't have friends who he could spend the time with. Most of the class played football or cricket. Colin hated sport of any kind. His parents had made him take up the violin instead. However, there were not many world famous violinists as unfit as Colin Seymour.

The bell had sounded at the usual time - *12.30pm* on the dot. The melee of schoolchildren filed out of the buildings into the playground and on to the playing fields, happy in their little groups. Girls skipped or just ate their sandwiches and chatted obliviously to the podgy boy strolling alone across the grounds to the exit gates.

They would be after the podgy boy in a minute. Laughing at him. Pushing, kicking, poking and shouting too. Colin speeded up. They usually caught up with him by the bus stop. He stared straight ahead as his stride lengthened. His breathing came in fits and starts while his cheeks were reddening with each passing second.

Then he heard the footsteps and whispers. He knew they were behind him again. Tears began to well up in his eyes. Why hadn't he taken up self-defence or boxing?

He was hot. His school tie constricted his breathing as usual.
His feet were kicked from beneath him.
"Gotcha!" a voice spat rejoicing. They had their prey.
Colin hit the pavement with a thump.
He could still hear the sounds of children playing in the distance.
No games for him. He was in the same old game of survival.
"How are you today fatty?"
There were only two today thank God.
"Leave me alone will you?"
"No chance. Give us your dinner money!"
"I haven't any. I've got sandwiches today."
"They'll do. You eat too much anyway."
"Yeah, you fat puff!"

Colin's lunchbox was gone in a flash. Harvey Jones and Ian Broad were the worst two of the group. They had bullied him incessantly from day one of the new term.
"How's mummy's little darling then?" sneered Ian contemptuously.
"Fine thanks." Colin always tried to sound tough but it was useless!
"Don't get funny with me tubs, else we're goin' to get you all dirty aren't we Harv?"
"Yeah."
"Hope you can swim!"
"At least he'll float!" said 'the two comedians' as they laughed at their joke.

No one saw the figure sitting on the wall opposite. A large man with broad shoulders wearing jeans and sneakers. He watched the little circus opposite, as he had done for weeks. Every day, the boy was left in a heap crying with no help at hand. Every day, the figure saw the same things happening to Colin that had happened to him when he was younger and a lot fatter.

One of the bullies now had the victim in a head-lock. He hated head locks because of the way your hair was pulled. Tears pricked his eyes as he watched the scenes before him. He felt his anger again as it welled up inside.

"Time to turn the tables," he whispered inaudibly.

He slipped down from the wall and casually walked parallel to the scuffling figures across the road. He carried on walking.

By now, Colin was getting scared as usual. As usual, the pain was interminable and he didn't fight back. The grip that Harvey had on his neck was like a vice. He couldn't breathe and he felt his legs go weak. Panic began to set in, when suddenly he was released. He fell to the ground as Harvey's grip relaxed.

Colin saw another pair of legs! He gasped in mouthfuls of oxygen, as the sound of another new struggle diverted his gaze. He looked up through tear-filled eyes.

Colin watched as Harvey Jones and Ian Broad were beaten up. The man was very big, adult even. It was like slow motion. The thuds of fist on body rang out. Grunt followed grunt as the hulking figure waded into the helpless teenagers. The figure spoke as he struck.

"That's for you! This is for you! One for you... and another for you!" Kicking and thumping, one at a time, the shadow took about one minute to reduce the two boys to their cowering knees.

Then it was over.

The figure brushed himself down.

Colin suddenly found his voice. "Who are you?" he asked in amazement.

"Someone who went through the same as you son," was all the stranger said.

The two bullies were motionless. Not a sound came from their bloodied faces.

Colin stood up. "Thanks," he said retrieving his lunchbox.

"Should keep them off your back for a while," said his rescuer.

Colin could see him clearly now. He had a smiling face and a moustache.

"If it starts again, just say you've got my name and number. I'm not Superman but it should make those idiots think twice. OK?"
"Er yeah, sure. Thanks mister."
"See you around..."

The figure walked away across the road, into the park and out of sight.
"Christ!" Colin looked down at Harv and Ian.
Not a whisper. Just silence. He stifled a chuckle.
He started to walk. He hadn't walked this slowly during a lunchtime for weeks...

Chapter Three

Phil knocked on the door of the flats again. Nothing.

He stepped to the side, lifting a hanging basket aside and peered into the basement window. A large spider crawled over his left hand. He didn't mind spiders or snakes. The Army training helped. No fear!

It was pitch black inside. Grimy curtains, lacy and unwashed, hung on either side of the grey window frames. There was a transistor radio on the sill next to a box of Swan matches. He could just make out a load of dishes in the sink but nothing more.

He tapped on the glass.

"Anyone home? Police!"

Zilch.

He heard footsteps. They were coming up the path.

"Hi," the youth acknowledged Phil.

"Morning sir. Do you live here?"

"Unfortunately, yeah. It's a shit-hole but it's got a light and a bed."

Phil smiled at the lad's sarcasm. The boy's sharp northern accent was a surprise.

"Do you know a Miss Janice Lee?"

"Is she the horny one with the cat?"

"Cat? Er ... I can't say for sure but she was due at the station this morning."

"Prostitute eh? Nice one," the youth joked.

He wore spectacles, an AC-DC shirt and cords. His lank hair needed some conditioner, Phil thought.

"I'm afraid it's more serious than selling her body sir. Do you know her?" Phil was getting a little impatient.

"Oh, sorry officer. Well yes, she always says hello. We never socialise here. Just hello, goodbye, nice weather - that sort of thing. Come to think of it, I haven't seen her for a couple of days. Normally it's every morning. My name's Neil by the way. I'm a student."

What a shock, Phil thought.

"OK. Do you mind if I go up to her room? I don't have a warrant or an ulterior motive."

Phil smiled. He quite liked Neil, even if he was unclean.

"Fine by me. I'll let you in here." He opened the front doors.

"How many residents in this dump Neil?"

" 'bout six. Mainly single youngsters. Office people you know."

"Yeah, I get the picture. No all-night raves then?"

"No, everyone keeps things to themselves really. I've a girlfriend up north. Just got back from a long weekend."

"Does she like AC-DC?"

"Nah, the classics, Mozart 'n' crap like that."

"Cultured eh?"

"Nah, she's a mechanic!" Neil laughed aloud.

The pair had reached the second floor by now.

"That's hers," Neil said as he pointed to the door opposite the top of the stairs.

A dish lay by the door.

"Cat's milk dish. Makes you want to cry dunnit," Neil chuckled.

"Very homely," murmured Phil.

A newspaper was stuck in the flap.

"Today's Independent," said Phil.

"She ain't at work then. Must be in bed or something."

"Perhaps she's got flu?"

"Probably got a client!" Neil sniggered.

"Yeah, yeah OK. Cut the crap mate."

Phil knocked at the door.

"Miss Lee? Police. Can we talk?"

Neil sat on the stairs picking his nose.

Silence.

Phil felt something wrap itself around his ankles. He cried out.

"Shit!"

The cat looked up at him, purring.

Neil smiled.

"Wants its milk now."

Phil knocked at the door but harder this time.

"Miss Lee, it's the police. Will you please open your door!"

"Have a look through the flap," Neil suggested.

"One more knock. Third time lucky."

No response. Phil got down on one knee. The cat purred louder.

He peered into the flat beyond.

There was a bed. All flats have beds...

The curtains were drawn, making it very difficult to distinguish the body lying on the bed. A table was the object nearest the door. Phil could see an open handbag and there was a flat, smooth book next to the bag.

"Chequebook," whispered Phil. One eye closed, grimacing in concentration. At that precise moment, Phil saw Janice Lee's left foot. To the left of the handbag, about a metre further on, Janice's motionless foot dangled from underneath the duvet.

"She's in but she's asleep," Phil reckoned.

"She don't work shifts officer. No way."

Neil's face looked confused. He took his glasses off and fingered them.

"She's up every day without fail. Even on Sundays. She jogs too. Fit cow!"

"You know a lot about her, don't you?" commented Phil.

"Well, I do live opposite. You can hear an earwig fart in here in the mornings," Neil smiled.

Phil was puzzled. He banged the door a fourth time. "Miss Lee!!"

"What the fuck!" he spat. "I'm going in... Problem?"

"You're the boss officer. Go for it. I'm your witness."

"Good lad."

Phil stood back and kicked his right leg at the wooden framework.

The door swung open with a crash, rotten to the core.

"First time! What a star!" Neil jumped up from the stairs; putting on his spectacles excitedly.

Phil didn't want Neil to see this.

"Go to your room Neil!" Phil instructed and he pulled the door shut.

"Eh?"

"I said, open your flat and make two cups of strong coffee, milky with two sugars. OK?"

"Yeah, sure. Whatever."
Neil fumbled with his keys and entered his own flat.
Phil was perspiring; his breathing laboured.

He re-opened Room Six of Pear Tree Flats.
He followed Janice's left foot from left to right. The duvet only covered her lower torso. A bluebottle fly buzzed in the humidity of the enclosed room. A curtain flapped apologetically. Sunlight glinted through the parting across a chair which lay on its side.

Janice lay on her back, arms slayed as if on a cross. A pillow covered her face. She had a blue T-shirt with 'Give Peace a Chance' in green lettering. A clock radio was playing very quietly.

This would be his first real corpse, thought Phil. A song by 'Wham' played on the radio. He switched it off. "Bastard!" He swallowed hard as he removed the pillow from the face of Janice Lee.

She stared blindly at the ceiling, eyes wide and glazed. She looked like she'd just been told her winning coupon hadn't been posted.

Phil tried to look away. Forensics will love this, he thought. A false fingernail lay next to her head. Red polish. Didn't they call it varnish? Another one lay by her clenched right hand.
Put up one hell of a fight, didn't you love?

His eyes moved down. She didn't wear a bra. He resisted the urge to lift the T-shirt.

Her legs were apart. Something between...?
He looked closer; the darkness parted. There was blood on the sheets between her crotch and something shoved inside her vagina. He looked intently and stared.
Phil pulled out his handkerchief and gagged. A TV remote control's last two inches protruded at an angle between the victim's thighs. The red ON/OFF button could be seen, but only if you looked closely.

Phil went into the kitchen and threw up. As he wiped his mouth and forehead with a damp wrist, something caught his eye. His mind whirled. Beside the bed where Janice Lee had met her violent death lay a small white cap with 'Spurs' printed neatly in the centre of its peak.

"Bingo," Phil whispered as he turned on the cold tap with a sharp tug.
He stared out of the window.
A voice at the door of the flat startled him.
"Coffee officer? Oh my God!"

The sound of breaking crockery alerted Phil. He ran out to the sound. Neil knelt on the floor, staring at the bed... Hot coffee settled into the cheap carpet; steam rising from the floor.
Phil thought he looked like a yoga freak.
"Didn't really want coffee anyway," he murmured.

****

It took fourteen minutes for the back-up circus to arrive. The big nobs, forensics and constables with white tape jostled by ghouls hoping to see the body. TV crews, journalists, press and kids on bikes. It was bedlam!

An hour ago, nobody had even heard of Janice Lee. Two days from now, a whole nation would know her upbringing, her favourite teddy, her Uncle Bill from Rochdale, how she died, where she worked, who she liked, disliked, etc., etc., ad infinitum... Janice Lee would become media fodder.

Phil leaned on the gate with his hat in hand.

"Morning Sergeant," mumbled a senior nob.

The plain clothes' mob walked up the path. A young constable guarded the building. He jerked to attention as the circus ambled in, briefcases in hand and cameras at the ready.

A man, in his early fifties, came down the path. He wore the uniform associated with the nitpickers - Forensics. Phil stepped out.

"Hi! Phil Queen," he introduced himself. "I found the body." He showed his warrant card.

"Bill Neat, Squad Eight Forensics."

They shook hands. Bill wore washing up gloves.

"Nasty bastards these days," Bill looked at Phil. He looked his age.

"How did she die?"

"Slowly."

Phil baulked. He pictured her at the station.

"He - or she - enjoyed it," Bill remarked. He had a soft Scottish accent.

"It's the first time I've seen one of those shoved up a lassie."

"Why do that?" Phil asked; remembering his own nauseous reaction.

"For fun probably. Sexually repressed or inexperienced."

"Was she suffocated then?"

"Yes, but after the fun and games with the monitor, I think. She put up a game fight. Must have been a strong bastard though."
"The killer?"
"Or killers?" Bill lit a cigarette.
"Two of 'em?"
"I'm not sure... maybe she was concussed when he did... you know..."
Bill stared at the ground.
"Yeah," Phil nodded thoughtfully.
"The Yorkshire Ripper - Sutcliffe. He did that sort of thing... hammers. Nasty!"
"Quite a copycat then?"
"Oh no, I don't think so. This was probably just off the cuff, nearest thing to hand probably."

Phil thought of the park attack. The kid.
"Could a youngster have done it? Say, a fourteen or fifteen year old?
"I suppose anything's possible in this day and age. Little bastards are evil. Look at those two at Liverpool - eleven for God's sake!"
"True, true," murmured Phil.
"But I'm pissed off Bill. My only possible witness was away for a bloody long weekend - her neighbour."

Bill said his farewells and headed for his van. A second and third gloved man came out of the flats. One carried a plastic bag, full to the top, on which Phil could see the white peaked cap.

A voice broke into his thoughts.
"Oi Queenie! You're in deep shit!"

A burly figure ambled over to him from a parked panda car.
"What's up Kev?" Phil asked as he buttoned up his jacket.
"Super's going ape! Wanted to know where you were."
"I told Gwen to tell him I was on this job!"
"I know, but it doesn't look good when you leave the civvie manning the desk during a hectic schedule does it?" laughed Kev meaningfully.

"Constable Green should be there!"
"Well, he ain't and you are 'Public Enemy Numero Uno' mate. I suggest you get back there and pronto!"
"Shite!" Phil got into his car and put it into second gear right off.
"Shite again!"
He was perspiring much more when he entered the car park at the station. He went straight to the front desk. A young woman constable regarded him over her coffee mug. She didn't speak, but her eyes went to the right and her eyebrows rose. This meant 'You are wanted and are in deepus shittus!'

"Cheers," Phil said quietly while he headed purposefully for the Super's office.

****

Chief Superintendent Clive Badger sat at his large mahogany desk. He felt powerful today. He smiled a self-satisfied smile and looked at the photograph propped up in front of him. His wife (Hilary) and two offspring (Gregory and Shanice) smiled back, secure in the knowledge that their husband/daddy earned loads of money and would keep them in bread and water until they felt they'd had enough.

God you're ugly, he thought looking at Hilary. Her buck teeth grin had always pissed him off but her body was fantastic. For a stuck-up cow, she knew how to use it when they had courted years ago.

She had a father big in politics so Clive went after her. He never went for the Tracys and Sharons of this world. They had met at an inaugural ceremony somewhere - he couldn't recall. He was an up-and-coming police sergeant and she was a local councillor.

It was her bottom and breasts he liked most. He never looked much at her face. She didn't smile much but had a laugh that would break glass at four paces. People spoke to her 'cos she was on the Council.

He had wanted her immediately but she made him wait a few weeks before he got his paws on her 'parts', as he called them. The sex was great, so he married her after three years of fumbling about in car parks or country hotels. She had got very ugly around her forty-fifth year. It was then he started going to the massage parlours of the city. It was a release. He spent his hard-earned cash on Yvonne, Sharon, Excelsior (the black one) or Carole. Nubile young women with bodies and faces to match. Gorgeous! He told Hilary the reason he couldn't come anymore was pressure of work and she believed him. Stupid cow! Sex happened at Christmas and birthdays now. Four minutes of fantasising over Yvonne, just to get hard enough to satisfy his pig of a wife. Then a cigar, then sleep. It would soon be her bloody birthday again. Worse luck!

A knock at the door caught him off guard.

"Who is it?" Badger called impatiently.

"Queen sir. Sergeant Queen."

"Come in Queen!"

Phil thought Badger sounded weary.

"Sir!"

Phil stood before the superintendent. Beads of sweat appeared on his forehead.

He wasn't offered a seat. Trouble in t' store, he thought with a frown.

"Sergeant Queen..." A pregnant pause.

"Sir?"

"Do you enjoy your job?"

"Very much sir."

"You've come a long way in a very short time, have you not?" Badger peered at him.

"Well sir. Yes, I suppose so."

"I think someone who has got to your rank so quickly deserves a pat on the back," said Badger unsmiling.

"Thank you sir."

Silence...

Speak you prat. Phil stood ramrod straight.

Badger stood up slowly and looked out of the window. The sun was still beating down. He puffed on his cigar.

"However... your behaviour today leaves a lot - a hell of a lot - to be desired..."

"I can expl'..."

"Quiet please Queen!" There was contempt in the Superintendent's manner, Phil thought.

"Let me speak. Speak only when you are spoken to Sergeant."

"Sir." The collar of Phil's shirt felt tight.

"I have watched your progress of late Sergeant Queen and I have come to some conclusions."

Here we go, brace yourself. Phil felt as if a noose was being prepared.

"It took me nine years to get to the rank you now hold. I was good. Still am."

Modest or what, thought Phil.

"I was patient. Went by the book and always did what I was told. Never questioned my superiors. And yet... it took nine years!" (*Who's feeling sorry for who here?*)

"Now, I am a Superintendent looking down on people like you, Sergeant. People who cannot keep a tidy and efficient station. People who leave untidy and inefficient stations in the hands of old lady typists, chewing gum."

Phil snapped.

"I had to go! I had a lead..."

"Shut up Sergeant!"

Phil shut up.

"What if there had been an emergency Sergeant?"

The last emergency had been four months ago. A hit and run in the local precinct, Phil recalled silently.

"Who could I call on? Mmmm?"

Phil blinked. Confused. He was getting pushed into a corner.

"Sir. With all due respe'..."

"Wait!"

Phil waited.

"Gwen, the typist! Brilliant!" Badger stubbed his half-smoked cigar out on the side of his rubbish bin then stood up.

When the commissioner decided to leave, he said he wanted to thank my staff for the refreshment provided. 'Good' I thought. But when he entered the foyer, he was greeted by Gwendoline, bless her cotton socks, chewing gum and doing The Sun's crossword!" Badger's voice rose.

Phil said nothing. He swallowed audibly...

"How do you think it made ME look Sergeant?"

"Sir, I can explain if you'd just let me."

"I looked a prize penis, if you must know. It's probably cost me my next job." Sad, Phil thought.

"I found a dead body this morning sir."

Badger stopped ranting.

"I was following up a lead, like I said sir."

Badger sat down.

"The flat - Fanshaw Villa. The girl who was attacked the other night. She's dead sir."

Clive Badger had never found a dead body. Never got there in time. Spent most of his formative years on the football terraces breaking up fist fights. Now, this young whippersnapper had found a body in his first fucking year in the rank of Sergeant. He felt the jealousy rise and well in him. As he spoke, he tried to control himself.

"Oh right," he whispered.

Phil looked at Badger, expecting the pat on the back.

"So I suppose you think that makes it all right?"

"Sorry sir?"

"I said, I suppose you think it's fine just to leave your desk on a whim to go and find bodies."

"Well sir, I did have good reason to leave. You see..." Phil attempted to speak again.

Wrong move.

"No! YOU see Sergeant Queen!" Badger was on his feet again. "I'm going to see that your little misdemeanour will not go unpunished."

"But sir," Phil began to feel his frustration rising.

"No buts!" *(It's got to be butter..)*

"I am putting you on report Sergeant. I take a very dim view of your behaviour today. I shall ensure that it doesn't happen in my station again."

Phil was dumbstruck.

"I... er, I'd like to be heard sir. With all due respect, you don't know all the facts," Phil swayed.

"Oh, I think I do Sergeant."

Phil closed his eyes and swallowed. His palms were wet with perspiration. Janice Lee's face, the baseball cap, the foot dangling out of the duvet. Image upon image flashed before him. He forced his eyes open and came back to reality.

".... I said, that will be all Sergeant Queen."

Clive Badger watched as the young officer left his office. The smug grin returned. He leaned back in his large leather swivel chair and pressed the intercom switch.

"Gwendoline darling, coffee, black with no sugar thank you."

Phil went to the ablutions. He splashed his face with cold water. He threw up for the second time in a day. It was usually too many shorts; today it was his job. He stared into the large mirror opposite. Kev was right. You are in deep shit...

****

Gary Hart felt good today. He'd got out of bed without complaint, made his own breakfast and attended school. His mother was perplexed. He had never shown any initiative domestically before. He'd even kissed her on the cheek as he departed!

Stupid cow, Gary thought as he ambled down the stairs of the tenement building. Graffiti was sprayed everywhere. Meaningless comments in garish colours. The obligatory **"PIGS OUT"**, **"JOBS NOT DOLE"** and **"KEEP BRITAIN ENGLISH"**. Gary liked that one, even though he didn't understand it.

Early morning in the flats was a depressing scene. Unmarried mothers pushed prams containing their screaming offspring and shrieked expletives at anything or anybody in their path. Unsmiling faces; the same old routines. A trip to the shopping precinct was their highlight of the week. A chance to exchange the same old tired gossip to the same old neighbours.

Gary made his way across the car park. Broken bottles, empty cans, newspapers, food scraps, broken bicycles and broken homes. Even the traffic lights were out of order. The council had put wire mesh over the lamps. Within two days, the vandals had trashed them again. Another victory, another job well done and another waste of tax-payers' money.

Nobody gave the lights a second glance. Traffic swarmed everywhere with horns blaring. Six year olds dodged vehicles on their way to school while pensioners hovered at the kerb, deprived of a chance to cross.

Gary entered the newsagents. Mr Patel sat like a Buddha behind the counter.
"Good morning Gary," he said recognising the boy.
"Hi!" grunted Gary scanning the magazine rack. (*Black bastard!)*
"Nice morning for school?"
"Yeah." (*Keep the boring Paki sweet.)*
"That's if you're going to school today - ha ha."

Gary took a can of Coke from the fridge.
"Thirty-five pence please," Mr Patel held out his hand.
Gary fumbled in his pocket and handed over forty pence.
Mr Patel turned to the till for the change.
"Cheers," said Gary. (*Wanker!*)
"Thank you Gary. Have a nice day."

Impassively, Mr Patel watched Gary depart as he contemplated the divide between their cultures.

Gary took the Mars bar out of his pocket. He had it taped. Every day the same routine. Get the Coke, the Paki turns away for change. One Mars for breakfast - helps you work...No problem! Act nice. He must have nicked sixty bars in the last couple of months. Coke and Mars to start the day right. He entered the school gates for the first time in two weeks.

****

Phil woke with a jerk. It was a bad dream. Not surprising, after the nightmare of yesterday. He had dreamt about Janice Lee. They had gone out for a meal and kissed but the face he saw when he opened his eyes was Gwen. Gwen, the typist, and Clive Badger behind her. Clive was wagging his finger and saying, "Who's for the high jump then?" He said it over and over...

He hauled himself off the bed. His duvet was on the floor, kicked away in a fit during the night. He looked at the clock. Eight-forty. An hour and a bit to get ready for today's shift. The pit of his stomach ached with apprehension. He loved his job so why worry? I'll tell you why, nagged a small voice in his mind, because you (my son) are in deep shit that's why.

He exhaled deeply, stretched arms above his head, inhaled deeply and stretched again, then shrugged and headed for the bathroom.

He leaned over the sink facing the uncompromising mirror. You're still a good looking bastard Phil, he thought. Tall, muscular, tattooed, dark moustache, dark eyes and skin. Everything a woman, or man, could wish for! Everything except a nice, friendly boss who liked and respected him. Instead, he had a jealous fifty-something with an inferiority complex the size of the Sahara.

The sink gurgled as he brushed his teeth. He mentally mapped out the day ahead... Distribute photo of attacker, visit relatives of deceased, haircut and worry about my future... SHIT! He couldn't get Badger's face out of his mind.

The shower jet was invigorating. He could have been modelling for the latest smelly gel on the market (with Janice). He saw her lying on the bed; eyes wide with wonder. Whoever did it was sick and deserved the same fate. He was sure it was her attacker from the park.

But why? No reason. Most murders these days had little motive. He had read about a hanging in a public park yesterday. A revenge killing apparently. A man released early from prison had been viciously beaten and hung from an oak tree in the centre of his home village. No witnesses. No assistance. He should have stayed in prison, playing table tennis and watching videos, Phil thought. Three square meals a day, a gym, TV and no restrictions – except freedom. Easy life! Just like being on holiday. These days the criminals came first. What about the victims?

There had been countless debates by the faceless councillors in suits, pontificating about rights about liberalism. What about the '*Mrs Smiths*' left bereft at home because of her son, daughter or husband - murdered, robbed, injured or scarred for life? There are no ears for their stories...

Snap out of it Phil! Christ! He was beginning to sound like the blinking Pope! He snapped the shower switch off and dried himself with his favourite Tom & Jerry towel.

****

EDGEHAM PRISON - SUFFOLK

The wardens watched without emotion as he made his way along the brightly lit corridor. He wore his uniform; the clothes he had worn for the last twelve years: light blue, like a pair of pyjamas, he had often thought. His name tag read 'HILL' in green letters. As he walked, he could hear the voices of the other prisoners.

"Rot in hell, you mother-fucker!"
"Hope you die!"
"I'll see you in hell Hill..."

Insults, insults, tut tut, he thought. He smiled inwardly. Don't let the elation show, thought Geoffrey Hill - child molester extraordinaire.

He entered a second corridor, then a third. The thick-set warden's large bunch of keys jangled as each door to the *'outside'* beckoned. The shouts and taunts of those he was leaving behind became a distant memory.
"Bye, bye me lovers," he whispered.

He was led into a long room. Behind a desk sat Quinn, the Head Warden.
"So, you're out Hilly? Thirteen years inside. How do you feel?"
"Heartbroken sir. All my friends are in here."
"Bollocks! You're lucky. If I had my way, you'd rot in here and public opinion agrees."
"Yes, yes Mr Quinn but society has improved with age... I'm not a bad man really."

Hill had always reminded Quinn of Fagin, as depicted by Ron Moody in the film of Oliver Twist. Always so bloody theatrical, he thought. God - he even sounded like him when he spoke.

"I'd like to thank you and your wondrous staff for looking after me all these years. So caring, so kind, so..."
"Oh, shut up Hill!" Hill did so.

Quinn beckoned a burly warden whose forearms resembled those of Popeye.
"Give him his belongings, take off his prison kit and burn it."
"Oh, Mr Quinn can't I keep it as a memory of such a lovely time?"
Quinn ignored Hill's sarcastic comment. A slight northern accent gave him a faintly comedic persona.

Hill was as bald as a coot. He stood five feet seven and barefoot. Only his underpants remained. His blue eyes darted everywhere. A tattoo on his back bore the legend 'Mother' on a scroll beneath a snake. A short stubble covered his chin. Was it an attempt to change his appearance? Quinn observed the prisoner pensively.
"Put this lot on."

Quinn handed Hill a plastic bag containing a tweed suit, brogues, tie and socks. The brown shirt reminded Quinn of a Nazi uniform. He couldn't conceal his distaste of this man before him.

"You must have spun quite a yarn to get out this early," he remarked.
"Oh no, Mr Quinn. The lady was very understanding. My mother is very ill and she's in need of my attention. <u>My</u> attention."
"I don't think the general public will think much of us when they learn that you've been let out."
"I've done my time sir. I was just beginning to enjoy it actually. Just the other day..."
"Shut up and fuck off. I've heard enough!"

Geoffrey Hill finished dressing himself. Softly, he whistled 'My Way'. He was led down the final corridor to freedom, carrying a bag containing all his worldly possessions. A toothbrush, his wallet containing seventeen pounds in one pound notes and change, but most of it obsolete. A bunch of keys on a Mickey Mouse key ring. He was going home.

The front double doors confronted him. An officer stepped out to open the small door set in the side and he stepped through into freedom. He was OUT!

He stood motionless; staring at the distant hills beyond.

Geoffrey, my boy, you've some catching up to do. He still had his address book hidden at his mother's bungalow. Names and addresses of countless friends with the same tastes and ideas. Tasteful and distasteful. Wonderful!

He would call Hans in Germany as soon as he got home. Mother could suffer. She was the least of his concerns...

He crossed the road to the bus stop. He had no idea of the timetables and his mind wandered as he waited. Thirteen years ago, he'd been the ring-leader of the largest paedophile group in Europe. He deviated from one messy relationship to another. Any child under the age of fourteen would do. Have 'em and leave 'em was his philosophy.

He'd met Hans in The Star, a club just off the main Soho network in London.

Hans and his wife (Brigid, a Dutch model) had been lovers for seven years after the first introduction. They cultivated a following in England, Zurich, Amsterdam and even Australia for a time. Hans had not been caught though. Heaven only knew what he'd missed in the wasted years inside. He would make contact with Hans as soon as he got home. It shouldn't be too difficult.

The killing of the two kids in Oxford had been his downfall. Buried alive in a box and the police found the bodies eight weeks after they went missing. Partially decomposed and naked. The case had shocked the whole nation and he could still recall the faces of the parents in court.

He smiled and breathed deeply. "Que Sera Sera," he whistled with his eyes closed. The bench he sat on creaked as he lay back. His mind was drifting...

His eyes suddenly opened. He could hear a car. He looked left - nothing. Right -there it was. Its droning engine got louder as it approached and the Vauxhall's powerful engine scared the birds out of the trees.

Geoffrey Hill's eyes closed again. He thought it was the bus, oh well...

As the car drew nearer, the engine noise lessened. Geoffrey's eyes opened to see the car slowing down about twenty-five metres away. He smiled at the occupants as they drew level.

"Good morning sir."

"I don't suppose you know the area?" asked the driver. He wore a neat beard. Hill leaned forward. *(Time to lie!)*

"Oh yes! I'm from Ipswich, just up the road."
"Great! Just visiting then?" the driver said.
"Er - yes! My brother's in for burglary," answered Hill with a wry smile.
"Oh, got caught nicking videos did he?" The driver laughed; so did his passenger.
"Yes, he got three years' hard labour," Hill lied confidently.
"Tough shit I say. Should've been ten!" *(Just agree.)*
"Yes, I couldn't agree more. It's costing me a fortune in fruit and bus fares!" Hill joked.
"Want a lift? We're off to Sudbury."
(Suckers!)
"Oh, sure. If you don't mind. The buses are so infrequent round here aren't they?"
"Crap! Should be privatised I say."
"Good idea... Shall I get in the back?"
"Yeah, no probs. Hop in mate."
(Spot on Geoff, old son. Such nice people!)

Geoff sat back in the unexpected luxury. What a stroke of luck! He could phone mother from Sudbury and find a bed and breakfast or hotel to stay in for a day or two.

"Cigarette?" the bearded man asked.
"Don't mind if I do." The old catchphrase. The two men in the front of the car exchanged glances.

Terry Clark knew Geoffrey Hill straight away. The tip-off was spot-on. His beard was a good cover. Bobby Clark didn't know Geoffrey Hill. He was only sixteen, after all. His dad had told him everything though. He would have a brother and a sister, if it hadn't been for the man sitting in the back of the car.

The driver and the front passenger exchanged small talk as the car wound its way through the beautiful countryside...

"What do you do for a living?" Hill broke the silence after a ten minute pause in conversation.
"Oh, I'm in the hospitality business," said Terry.
"What sort of hospitality?"
"Hotels, catering and stuff like that," Terry lied.
"Oh, lovely... I haven't been in a hotel for years being cooped up..."
(Shit!)
"Sorry?" Terry glanced in the rear mirror.
"Oh, nothing. Just a slip. I've been living with my mother all my life. I've never needed to use a hotel much".
"Lucky sod!"
"You sound as if you're form up North?" asked Hill.
"Yeah, Halifax, Yorkshire."
"Near Leeds?"
Terry glanced at Bobby.
"Not far, yeah."
"Oh, I know Leeds quite well," Hill said.
(I bet you do, you bastard!)
"Lovely people, just like yourselves. Salt of the earth, friendly..."
"We like to think so..." Terry's grim expression belied his words and was lost on Hill.

Hill had taken little interest in the car's route. It weaved through the tight country lanes, sun shone and birds sang. (Freedom! Freedom! What joy, thought Hill in the comfort of the back seat of the luxury estate car.)
"It's here," Bobby pointed.

Hill looked to the right. A track led through an open gate into a field. Cows grazed, moving lazily in the heat. At the end of the track was a large, shed-like building. Bales of hay were stacked and tied with rope.

"Where are we boys?" Hill asked, suddenly mystified.

"Just a piss stop. A man's gotta do... You know." Terry smiled and got out of the car.

"You want one?" Bobby turned round to look at the bald creature on the rear seat.

"No ta. Strong liver. Good livin' you see."

Bobby nodded and stared straight ahead.

The sound of running water. The sound of a man having a piss, Hill thought. He closed his eyes relaxing slowly. Soon be home... He then heard a sharp click! The rear passenger door was thrown open suddenly. Geoffrey Hill was staring down the barrels of a very large shotgun.

"Out wanker!"

"Eh?" Hill's face gawped in amazement.

"Are you deaf too? OUT!"

The barrel was two inches from his forehead.

"You'd better get out, Geoffrey old son," Bobby said dully as he stared intently at Hill.

"Wha'... How d'you know my...?"

Terry was grinning.

"I've waited thirteen years for this, you cunt!"

Geoffrey Hill's bowels lurched as he crept out of the car; his eyes never leaving the gun.

"Walk up the hill to that shed," rasped Terry. "Don't even think of running 'cos I can hit a clay pigeon at two hundred yards!"

"Fine, fine. Please... I have money..." Geoffrey pleaded, stuffing his hand into a pocket.

He was in trouble. He knew it.

"Hilly old chap, you can shove your poxy money where you normally shove your cock," Terry said triumphantly. "Oh and stay there Bobby. You don't need to see this."

"OK," replied the youth. His arms were crossed and he gave out a long, deep sigh.

Bobby put a cassette into his personal stereo and sat back in the car. He was singing as the two figures made their way up the grassy hillock past the indifferent cows to the barn. Hill was finding it difficult. Years of inactivity in prison had sent his leg muscles to mush so he panted as he walked.

"I'm Terry Clark."

"Terry Clark?"

"Yeah, recognise me? You would without the beard."

As he walked in front of the madman, realisation dawned upon Geoffrey Hill.

"Sally and Paul were my children. Remember them all those years ago? When they dug up their bodies, you were probably shagging some other unfortunate kiddie!"

Hill's eyes widened in terror. The barn beckoned him, like the jaws of a wild beast. He could smell the cow dung; flies buzzed in the sultry heat. They entered the barn.

"Stop... Kneel!"

"Yes, of course - certainly... Er... surely you're a man of reason sir? I've got thousands and the cash is yours... Just..."

"Money can't buy you love...."

Terry pointed the barrel at the back of Geoffrey Hill's bald head.

His finger lifted the safety catch.

Geoffrey Hill defecated into his underpants.
"You stink..." murmured Terry as his finger tightened.

They were the last words Geoffrey Hill would ever hear.

As Bobby listened to his music, he saw a large flock of birds rise as one from the roof of the barn on the hill. They silhouetted against beautiful blue sky.

A few moments passed and his father appeared at the entrance and made his way down the bank to the car. He opened the door and eased himself into his seat, placing his gun in the opposing footwell. He turned to his son.

"It's done," he said as he clipped on his seat belt.
A tear tickled down Bobby Clark's cheek. Terry clasped his son's right hand tightly, turning on the ignition in one swift movement.

As the car slowly moved off down the track, the birds settled again on the barn roof.

Silence hung on the summer air...

****

Chapter Four

Phil's first job was to distribute the artist's impression of the suspect to the press. He faxed a copy to six of the local rags, one to the television network and one to the printers at Police Headquarters. Copies were needed to place at strategic points in the locality.

The picture showed a young man, early teens, spotty chin and brow, sallow complexion and a crew-cut hairstyle. The baseball cap with the 'Spurs' motto was mentioned in the attached information brief. Janice had given a remarkably precise description. However, she was in no position, sadly, to give a second opinion as to the accuracy of the finished sketch.

Once all the necessary business had been finalised with the posters, Phil left the station, plain-clothed, to pay a visit to the parents of Janice Lee. The address was traced to a village about an hour's drive away - an isolated spot on the coast. It was a nice day for it (in other circumstances) he pondered. He took care to make sure, prior to leaving, that there was double cover on the office. Gwen smiled at his conscientiousness. About time too, she had joked.

He went alone with his notebook in hand. The route was very picturesque. Blue skies and the wind in his hair. How poetic.

The newspapers had been sympathetic to the murder enquiry. The usual coverage. Ghoulish references to the murder scene, empty anger and over the top headlines.

"TV MONITOR KILLER!" The black headline enticed the purchaser.

They needn't have mentioned that, thought Phil. "I support it attracts the voyeur and gives 'him' a lift over his bacon sarnie and first fag," muttered Phil.

The usual 'expert' psycho-analytical viewpoints were propounded at length: '... has been experienced by other victims. Scenes like this are commonplace with murder in this day and age....'

'The killer is obviously traumatised.... possibly due to his hard upbringing... no father figure.'

Or '... trying to make a statement, a cry for help...'.

A cry for help, indeed! Who heard Janice Lee's cries for help, thought Phil bitterly. Same lame old excuses for what Phil had found at the flat.

He drove carefully through the heavy traffic. It was high season for the resorts and as he entered the village of Knotton, the familiar tourist bustle was evident. People on bikes, girls in shorts, tanned legs, howling babies and retired men and women strolling arm-in-arm. It felt good to be alive. He thought of Janice again...

It wasn't difficult to find the cottage. He parked his unmarked blue Ford Sierra opposite the beautiful fenced-off garden. As he crossed the road, a magpie flew over his head. 'One for sorrow' so he hoped he'd spot a second one soon.

****

She approached the front door, the lock was secure and the chain engaged in its slot. More bloody reporters I suppose. She stifled a sneeze as she opened the entrance door on its chain.

"Who is it?" she enquired shrilly.
"Good morning madam, police, Sergeant Queen." Phil offered his identification.
"Oh, of course. Sorry, please do come in," she replied in a low voice. She sounded only just in control of herself and her sorrow coloured her voice.
The door opened very slowly.
My God, she's beautiful! (*Was Phil's initial reaction.)*
Chloe Lee stared at the stranger on her doorstep. Phil gawped back.
There was a silence then they both spoke at once.
"Please forgive me officer."
"I'm sorry I... Just call me Phil."
"Er... Phil... It's just that I've been plagued constantly by callers, reporters and TV folks for the last day and a half and..." her voice trailed off.
She had blue eyes and long brown hair. Her flowered print summer dress ended at her knees, her legs were deeply tanned and she was barefoot. Phil paused, taking in this gorgeous creature. His mission momentarily suspended. (*Snap out of it man!)*
"I'm Chloe," She tried to smile and turned away. The silence was broken.

Phil stepped into the cottage and followed her down the tiny hallway into the living room. The fresh smell of her perfume led him.
"Your cottage is beautiful, Mrs Lee."

"Thank you. Thank you very much," Chloe replied.
"Would you like a drink? Tea? Coffee?"
"Do you have anything cold?"
"Fresh orange juice? Coke?"
"Anything, thank you."

He couldn't take his eyes off her. She was exquisite! Whoever was the husband had struck lucky.
Chloe left the living room. His eyes expertly scanned the room. It was tastefully but comfortably furnished.
He sat on the sofa, smoothing back his dark hair. His attention was diverted by a photograph on the sideboard. He stood up to take a closer look. Chloe and Janice, a mother and daughter, on a seafront with their ice creams in hand. Her husband must have taken the picture, thought Phil. Chloe was the taller one, about five-six. His eyes scanned the walls. A large framed picture of a castle hung above the open fireplace. It looked Celtic, very moody. Small antiques lay everywhere. A man on a horse with a sword in his hand took his eye.

"It's Conan the Barbarian," Chloe returned softly. She handed him a glass of Coke. The ice tinkled.
"Thank you. I was just admiring your beautiful home."
"Yes, I am rather proud of it actually."
"You have quite a taste for things," remarked Phil.
"Well, I'm a lover of historical, medieval type things. I've Scottish ancestry and I love anything to do with olden times."
"The castle in the picture, is it Scottish?"
"Irish. My third cousins were from Larne, in the north," Chloe replied.
"Fascinating." Phil was getting side tracked.

"I also love astrology, herbal remedies, anything out of the ordinary really. People think I'm a bit of a weirdo," She said as she rolled her eyes and she shrugged her shoulders.
"Oh no! No way," Phil cried. "I'm an Aries."
"That's the ram isn't it? Ruled by Mars, so you're a fiery one eh?" quizzed Chloe.
"Now and again, I'm pretty stable though," Phil laughed.
"I'm a Gemini, pleased to meet you," Chloe gestured.
"Is that the water bearer?" enquired Phil.
"No, that's Aquarius. Gemini is the twins."
"Of course, my dad was a Gemini," Phil said with a grin. "He's dead unfortunately..."

The atmosphere changed. Chloe sat down slowly.
"I suppose you're here about Jan?" Chloe said as she looked up and spoke sombrely. The lightness had gone from her voice. There was a deep sorrow in her manner now. The clock chimed suddenly. Two o'clock already. Phil sat down opposite to her in a chair.
"Yes," Phil paused. "I found her... I was following up information we'd received from her boss at Brandgate's. She hadn't turned in for work for two days."
He stared at his feet. "She didn't suffer," he lied.
"Good... good, thank you for telling me. The detectives were very nice," Chloe whispered. "I was told about an hour after she was found," she continued quietly.
"They do a good job," Phil said looking up.
"They sent a female officer and she was in tears too," said Chloe.
"Yes, we're all human underneath all the uniform. Some folks don't always think so but it's part of the job."

Chloe looked directly at Phil. She sipped her cold coffee and grimaced.
"Please catch her killer. It mustn't happen again!"
"I know. We're following all leads. We've made a good start and your daughter gave us a good description of her attacker."
"She would. Our Jan is as bright as a button," Chloe murmured with a faraway expression on her face.
"Yes, that's the impression I got when I interviewed her after her first attack."
"She said you were wonderful when she phoned me on the night of the attack," said Chloe.
"Just doing my job." The old clichés always came in useful.
"She said there was a sergeant who was very caring. It must have been you eh?" Chloe's eyes met his.
"I was going to see her but you know how it is, it was late... If only I'd bothered," Chloe explained.
Then the tears came. Quietly at first, then in great racking sobs.
Phil hated to see a woman cry. He got up, went and sat beside her on the sofa and placed his arm around her tiny shoulders.
"Shsssh, it'll all work out," comforted Phil. He found himself welling up too. He fought off the sensation, biting his lip and squeezing his eyes tightly shut. (*Get a grip man!)*
"I'm so sorry, we're so close and almost like sisters," Chloe sobbed.
"We really bonded when her daddy died. She was very close to Pete and we've been inseparable these last two years," Chloe said. She sighed as her tears began to gradually subside.

"I'm sorry, I didn't realise," said Phil.

"You weren't to know. My husband died in a hit-and-run accident. He never stood a chance and they never managed to convict the drunk driver."

Chloe blew her nose. She sniffed.

"I apologise for being like this." Chloe smiled weakly at Phil.

"Don't fret, I can assure you that I won't rest until we get this all sorted."

"Good! He should be locked away. It's evil what he did. The papers said she was injured prior to her death," Chloe said. Her voice was almost inaudible now.

"No, that just helps them sell papers. The more the gore, the more they score we say."

"You would tell me if she did suffer?" Chloe asked. Her eyes were like saucers with tears still evident.

"Yes, of course," Phil lied. He bit his lip unnoticed.

Chloe sat motionless. Exhausted!

"More Coke?" she asked suddenly.

"No, no relax Chloe."

Phil still held her hand reassuringly.

"God, I must look awful. I do apologise," Chloe uttered as she crossed to the mirror and fingered through her hair.

"You look absolutely fine to me," assured Phil.

"I've got to reopen the shop tomorrow," Chloe stated without much conviction.

"You have a shop?" enquired Phil.

"Yes, it's in the village. Bric-a-brac you know. Typical tourist dross," expressed Chloe.

"I'm sure you make a mint," said Phil.

"Yes, I do in the summer. Like now - it's a madhouse. I can't really afford to be closed." Her voice held a country lilt.

"Do you have an assistant?" asked Phil.

Chloe lowered her head.

"Well, Jan used to help at weekends and especially in the summer. We had such a laugh... Still, don't worry because my neighbour, Doris, has promised to stand in. We rally round in the village. They're all very good people and I'm very lucky," She picked up the glasses. "Are you sure you don't want another drink?"

Phil thought yes. He did want one. It would delay the moment he would have to leave this lovely creature. Just being close to Chloe was all he wanted. *(Don't push your luck chum!)*

"Er... no. I must go actually. I've loads to do concerning Jan." (*Good boy!)*

"Yes, of course," Chloe led him towards the door. "Please Philip, let me know what's happening."

Phil nodded. She handed him a small card.

"Here's my number for the shop. My home number is on the back but you already have that."

"Yes, great thanks. I'll be in touch very soon."

They stood on the doorstep; Chloe was wiping her eyes. "Sorry about the theatrics," She said and smiled her lovely smile.

"Don't worry, I understand," assured Phil.

The gate creaked at the end of the path. (*It needed some oil.)*

"Yoo hoo!" they heard.

Phil turned as Chloe looked past his shoulder.

"Ah, it's Doris!"

Doris looked like Miss Marple, thought Phil. (*Wonder if she has her talents too?)*

He smiled as the old lady approached.

"Hello Chloe. Everything all right?" Doris asked.

"Yes Doris. It's only the police again," Chloe replied with a sad smile.

"Good afternoon. Sergeant Philip Queen," announced Phil and Doris' hand met Phil's firmly.

"Hello Sergeant, glad to see you. What a terrible, terrible business this is!"

"Yes, indeed. I'm leading the enquiry and I'm keeping an eye on Chloe," said Phil.

"Well, we all keep an eye on each other you could say. If there's anything I can do to help at the moment - I'm only too glad..." Doris' voice tailed away.

"I'll remember that. I'm sure your support for Chloe is the best help you can give at this time," Phil assured her.

"Doris is my fairy godmother." Chloe smiled.

"Only the best for you my girl," Doris chimed in.

The hanging basket on the porch swung gently as Phil said his farewells. When he shook Chloe's hand, they squeezed in unison. He felt a thrill run through him and 'Miss Marple' looked on approvingly.

"Bye, I'll phone you," Phil promised as his eyes meet Chloe's.

"Thanks for your visit, I really appreciate it." Chloe watched him as he ambled off down the path. At the gate, he turned for one last look at her but Chloe and Doris had already gone off inside the cottage.

Phil settled in his car. The heat was oppressive. He checked he still had her card. He studied it carefully. 'Chloe's Cabin. Bric-a-brac'. He smiled and inserted it carefully into his wallet.

As he switched on the ignition, the rhythms of Dr Hook filled his car - 'When you're in love with a beautiful woman... it's hard...'
Phil laughed out loud. He saw Chloe in his mind's eye and smiled at the memory.

The car pulled out into the village, the sun bent down on Knotton and one magpie flew directly over Phil's car unseen...

****

THE OUTSKIRTS OF LEEDS, MID-AFTERNOON
They had easily stolen the car fifteen minutes previously. Stevo and Moby sped through the country lanes at high speed. The cabriolet had been parked in the upper class area of Leeds. The roof had been conveniently lowered due to the midday heat. It had taken two minutes to gain entry and start the engine. They were experienced in the art of joy riding.

"Nice motor eh?" Stevo screamed as the wind rushed through his mop of hair.
"Not bad, prefer the Ford version." Moby laughed, chewed his gum and concentrating on the road ahead.
The fuel gauge registered FULL so they had a whole afternoon to play with. The world was their oyster!

Neither of the occupants of the bright red car had a job or wanted one. The state paid for their well-being. They lived in a squat with ten other young, unemployed down-and-outs but they enjoyed it. Freedom! They got up when they liked. The only day they exercised any modicum of responsibility was when they had to rise early to saunter down to the 'Social' to sign on. Otherwise, the giros would dry up. It wasn't much but who gave a shit? 'No future', the Sex Pistols once sang. Stevo still had the album and it was their anthem. After ten cans of cheap cider, they would sing-a-longa Johnny Rotten. Life was a breeze.

Today, they had managed only five cans. A bit of Dutch courage prior to some petty thieving. A wonderful life...
"Wonder what the owner's doin?" shouted Stevo above the screeching engine.

The sharp gear changes every few hundred metres was a great sound.
"His fucking nut, probably," retorted Moby prominently; showing the gaps in his teeth as he grinned with his pal. He spat his gum into the onrushing slipstream.
"Get some vibes on Stevo."
"Yeah, OK."
The four speakers crackled into life. A classical violin concerto blasted out of the panels.
"Shite! Get something else on," drawled Stevo above the din. Moby pressed the search button.
'...the war in Bosnia has once again...'
"Nah, crappy news..."
'...tomorrow's guest on Desert Island.....'
"Cack!"
The sound of Huey Lewis and the News blasted out. 'That's the Power of Love!'
"Got it! Keep it on mate."

The car continued to weave its way through the green, lush countryside. Cows grazed lazily; raising their heads as the vehicle shot by at speed.

"Let's head back to town, this is borin'!" said Stevo.
Moby nodded sagely as the car approached a busy junction. The car skidded to a halt behind an old green Mini. A woman driver awaited her opportunity to move on.
"She looks tasty in front. Follow that Mini!" quoted Stevo with his eyes gleaming. He blinked frequently; a nervous tic inherited from his father.
"She's going into town. Perfect!" answered Moby as he flicked his hair out of glazed eyes.

The road fanned out from a single route into a dual carriageway. A tune by Slade now belted out from the stereo.

"This is your old man's era Mobe!" mocked Stevo as he grinned sideways at his companion.
"Bollocks, at least I've got a dad!"
Stevo was silent. That one hurt!

The Mini in front was struggling into fourth gear. Moby's speedometer showed thirty-six mph. He banged the small steering wheel in frustration.
"Fuck me, get a soddin' move one girl!" shouted Moby.
A blue Ford Sierra sped past in the outside lane.
"Must be doin' ninety at least!" bellowed Stevo as the car revved up to sixty-two mph.
"I'll catch him up!"

In Moby's inebriated condition he was finding it more and more difficult to control the monster. He thrust the gear stick from fourth into fifth gear and pushed his foot down hard on the accelerator.

"Geron-i-mooooo!" he screamed as the car slewed into the fast lane; instantly leaving the green Mini for dead.

Claire Jackson watched dumbstruck as the cabriolet sped past her. She'd been observing the car to her rear for the past five minutes.
Idiots she had said to herself as they had pulled up behind her at the junction. The two youths in the car, gestured and grimaced wildly. She could hear the thud, thud, thud of the stereo even above her own car's engine.

"Charming gentlemen, just charming," she whispered as she waited to pull out on the main road. She occasionally looked into her rear mirror to check on their childish antics. People like that were everywhere these days. The car was probably stolen. Either that or it's daddy's.

As the cabriolet went past her at speed, her initial shock at the rate it was moving was compounded by an additional scene. The occupant of the passenger seat had lowered his trousers to his ankles as he stood on the seat. He then leaned on the windscreen frame with his white buttocks swayed from side to side. Whoops of delight at this obscene act floated back to Claire as she retched slightly and slowed down. As they gathered speed away from her, the driver raised his left hand and pointed his middle finger in her direction. The moonie demonstrator turned briefly and blew her a kiss.

Claire slackened her speed, staring straight ahead until they disappeared into the heat haze.

"She's a pig anyway!" screamed Stevo as he hitched his trousers back up.

"She loved us!" shouted Moby, delighted at their exhibition of male virility.

They'd caught up with the blue Ford Sierra.

"Flash him. Go on, flash him!" shouted Stevo.

Stevo's eyes were wildly staring. The cabriolet's full beam momentarily blinded the driver in front.

Keith Hurst, an insurance salesman from Derby had not even been aware of the car behind him until the bright light distracted him. He was concentrating too much on the day's edition of The Archers. He glanced again in his mirror.

"Oh, do piss off!" he spat.

He hated joy riders nearly as much as his boss.

The cabriolet was inches from his bumper. He looked at the dial on the dashboard.

"Eighty? Christ!" Hurst slackened his speed and his tie.

Moby's foot engaged the accelerator once more.

"Come on old chap – faster," he whispered.

Hurst was now sweating. He was unfit and overweight. The doc was always ticking in the box marked 'high' on the blood pressure section. He looked at the left hand wing mirror for a gap in the traffic. There was no space to enter the slower lane. He increased his speed slowly. The two wankers behind were still flashing wildly.

Anyone watching the traffic from a bridge above the carriageway could have been forgiven for thinking they were watching an old Keystone Kops movie.

Two cars were matching speed at about ninety to a hundred miles per hour on a seventy mph section of roadway. The vehicles in the left hand lane, mainly huge container trucks were chugging along at a comparatively sedate sixty. This enhanced the speed of those in the right hand lane even more.

Hurst didn't see the **REDUCE SPEED NOW** signs, as he approached the roundabout ahead. However, Stevo did.

"Slow it Moby!" he shouted as they approached the distant junction. The cabriolet whined as they decelerated swiftly.

Keith Hurst didn't brake at all. As he hurtled onwards, still trying to shake off his pursuers.
Christ! Even the trucks in the left hand lane were flashing him now! Even their horns were blaring as he shot past them.
"What the fuck's up?" he yelled. "Have I got bells on or what?"
"Look at him go!" Moby gloated as their two crazed faces fixed on the large roundabout about seventy metres ahead.

Keith Hurst did not have time to brake. The last thing he saw was the face of a young hitch-hiker holding a sign pleading '*Midlands*'. The Sierra left the dual carriageway at ninety-four miles per hour, clipped the verge slightly, keeled into a double somersault and just missed the hiker by inches.

There was a silence followed by a crumping sound as the car came to rest on its roof. In a pregnant pause, all the traffic came to a standstill. Two wheels flew crazily away in different directions as the explosion came. Acrid smoke billowed into the sky as flames licked from beneath the shattered metal mass.

Panic pursued!

Drivers left their stationery vehicles and some lay in the middle of the road.
Hazard lights flashed all around! The hitch-hiker sat on the side of the road, incredulous at his survival, and stared at the smoke.
A burly lorry driver ran across the dual carriageway to an emergency telephone and frantically scrabbled at the door.

Two young men ran on to the grassy roundabout and shielded their faces from the heat of the wreckage. They peered inside the smouldering heap, but backed off helplessly and collapsed on the verge with their heads in hands.

Stevo and Moby stared ahead while sitting in the cabriolet stationary at the roundabout.
"Oh shit! Look what's happened!" Moby chuckled.
Silence from Stevo. He leaned over the side and threw up.
"Wanker!"
The sound of retching was very unpleasant. The stereo was still playing.
Traffic had stopped for a distance of about half a mile back from the scene of destruction.
Moby looked at his pal.

"We'd better leave I think," Stevo heaved; his eyes watery, "What's up? It was fun wasn't it?"
"Bleeding 'ell Mobe, I didn't want this!"
"Tough! It's happened. Got any cider left?"

As the pair argued, they did not see the group of about fifteen large men approaching the cabriolet from behind. Their feet were silent on the tarmac. The two in the car noticed far too late.

"You two get out!"
"Moby turned in an instant, eyes wide. Stevo was still being sick.
Moby watched the men of all ages, about twenty to fifty he thought.
The group halted and surrounded the car.
"Oh dear," sniggered Moby still high on cider and the thrill of the accident.
Suddenly, his hair was being tugged and another arm grappled with his shoulders.
"Should've worn a seatbelt," muttered the big, thickset trucker. Moby noticed a tattoo on his tanned forearm. It read 'Don't mess!'

Strong arms heaved the two from the car mercilessly.
"Gerroff!" Stevo protested and struggling wildly. His right eye closed with pain as a fist struck. He doubled up in terror.
Someone from the group leaned into the cabriolet and turned off the engine and the stereo faded into silence.
The only sound was the crackle of the flames around the wrecked car and shouts from horrified onlookers.

The ignition keys jangled as the trucker dangled them in front of Moby, "These yours?"
Moby was defiant, "Yeah, course they are!"
"Oh, then why does the tag mention a Miss Julie Smythe?" He spoke deliberately.
Moby felt his head torn backwards and his hair was pulled at the roots.
He winced in pain.

"It's not their car!" A woman's voice cut the silence.
The group turned.
Claire Jackson approached. Stevo, kneeling on the grass, could only make out her black stilettos and long brown legs between the dungarees of the group assembled above him. He heard her speak again.
"They passed me five miles back! They're bloody joy riders but thieves don't bring any joy though do they?"
The atmosphere was heavy with a dull anger.
Moby spoke, "You're quite tasty actually."

Claire tossed her long blonde hair and approached him. She took off her sunglasses as she stood inches from the youth's grinning face.
Moby wasn't prepared for the kick to his testicles.
"And you're fucking useless!" she spat and he doubled up gasping.
"Want another? Eh?" she shouted loudly with tears in her eyes.

A tall youth touched her shoulder. "Leave it love; come on."
He led her away; arms wrapped round her heaving shoulders. She sobbed as they walked away. Suddenly,

Claire turned back. "Murderers!" she screamed. "He's dead, isn't he? You're scum!"

The mood was getting nasty, Stevo thought. He rose slowly.

A large fist appeared from nowhere, knocking him back to the ground.

"Come on lads, let's teach 'em a lesson!" shouted one of the group. "The police will be here soon!"

Murmurs of approval emitted from the surrounding crowd.

Moby and Stevo had lost the energy to struggle. Moby's crutch was killing him. Stevo began to retch again.

They were led down a steep embankment and into some lush, green grass.

"Me first," Moby heard through his pain, as the first blows rained down.

Every kick was accompanied by an expletive.

Thud! "Bastard!"

Thud! "Wank stain!"

Thud! "Cunt!"

Whack! "Eat this!"

Others were dealing the same to Stevo, who lay moaning and twitching.

It lasted ten minutes. People on the roundabout heard the screams and blows but they did not intervene.

Police sirens wailed in the distance...

The group of men silently made their way back up the embankment, brushing seed heads carefully from their working clothes. They each went back to their individual vehicles and sat, impassively waiting. Some read their newspapers and some turned on their stereos. Claire Jackson bit her lip as she drifted off to sleep in the hot sun.

The police arrive a few minutes later and they moved around the scene. They had three deaths on their plate and not one witness!

****

Chapter Five

The droning voice of the teacher was getting on Gary Hart's nerves. He hated maths. What the fuck was algebra supposed to mean? A equals B plus 2 equals 2AB. So what! How was that likely to help footballers, chemists, bus drivers or even famous criminals?
"Hart!"
Gary's eyes shot wide open.
"Wake up boy!"

Mr Watling was a pale forty year old man. He always wore corduroy trousers, sensible shoes, a shirt and tie. Gary detested the teachers. All except Miss Gray. She wore short skirts with stilettos and looked like the girls in the magazines he used to find under his dad's bed. Gary looked forward to Geography. He never learned much but he always sat near the front where he could look up Miss Gray's skirt. (*Paradise!*)

Mr Watling droned on, "... therefore challenging the tangent at thirty degrees... correct?"
Yes sir, the class acknowledged.
(*Bollocks!*)

Gary looked out at the playground. He had a view of the whole entrance to the school. The playing field beyond was dotted with rubbish left by careless or playful pupils. A lean dog sniffed at an old yoghourt tub; his tongue investigating the interior feverishly for any scraps.

Gary's eyes looked further. Afternoons were the worst; he always felt tired. His eyelids drooped, then snapped wide open!

A police car had pulled up at the school gates. Two young constables stepped out putting on their peaked flat caps. They strolled along, in step with one another, up the path to the main doors of the school.

Gary's eyes followed them.

Enquiries of course. The papers were full of it. One of the policemen carried a roll of paper. They entered the building and disappeared from his view.

Gary fell asleep. The teacher mentioned cosines or something ...

****

Robert Jenkins sat at his desk, studying magazines with a cup of tea to his left. He was a large man wearing spectacles, collar and tie. (*Must maintain standards!*) He had a double chin caused by too many committee dinners. His hair and bushy eyebrows were jet black. Mr Jenkin's upheld authority in bundles and his long thin stick lay beside his desk. The bookcase was stocked full with Roget's Thesaurus, Oxford dictionaries, Wisden Cricketers' Almanack, Warnock Report, magazines and manuals.

The window to Mr Jenkin's office was open and a breeze wafted in. He loved his job as headmaster of the most notorious school in the town.

A knock at the door startled him.

"Yes?"

The school secretary entered. Maggie Gardner was in that time of life when the opportunity of a school job had been like manna from heaven. Her children were in school, her husband's work provided for them quite adequately but the extra pennies, plus school holidays free from working, meant some luxuries were occasionally available to her family. Also, she liked the feeling of being part of the world again after seven years of domesticity.

"Excuse me headmaster, there are two policemen here and they would like to have a word if you can spare the time."

Policemen?! The calm of Robert Jenkins' afternoon rippled.

"Certainly," he replied, handing Maggie his empty cup and saucer while hastily scanning his desk and gathering some scattered papers and books. "Send them in."

"Hello, Mr Jenkins isn't it?"

"Oh yes, come in. Please take a seat," replied Jenkins shaking the hands of PCs Low and Cole.

"You got our call sir?"

"Yes, this lunchtime. Do you have the pictures?"

"Yes, we feel they're quite detailed and distinctive."

The other constable took the elastic band from the roll of papers. His radio crackled with static in his shirt pocket. He smoothed the picture flat on Robert Jenkins' desk. Jenkins leaned over and looked at the face. Gary Hart stared back.

"Mmmm... Quite young eh?"

"Yes sir. The young lady - the er, murdered lady, quite clearly stated that her assailant couldn't have been very old," said PC Low.

"And you have reason to think it's the same person who had attacked her earlier?"
"Almost certainly. The evidence seems to point that way," suggested PC Low.
"Evidence?" Jenkins looked up.
"Yes, a hat which she described was found at the murder scene."
Jenkins read the accompanying text.
"Oh, the baseball cap - they're fairly common aren't they?"
"Yes, 'Spurs'."
"That's a bit strange. We're nowhere near London, are we?"
"True sir, but football fans support anyone these days. After all, who'd want to support Rovers at the present?" PC Low laughed.
"Oi watch it!" PC Cole interjected.
"Oops, sorry I forgot mate!"
Jenkins smiled, "Fine, I'll put the picture up today. Maybe we'll be lucky."
"Hope so sir. Nasty little bastard, whoever he is."
"If he's local, this should sniff him out. If he's a wanderer, we'll disseminate the pictures nationally and we'll do that if there's no response immediately too."
"Good!" Jenkins was concerned about the pupils. The town did not often have to deal with murder.

"Well, we can only hope there's a satisfactory outcome and fairly soon," remarked Jenkins as the two constables stood up.
"Thanks for your co-operation. The picture should be everywhere tonight: newspapers, in town and on the TV. The net is closing in," P.C. Cole declared as he rolled up his remaining copies.

They all shook hands.
"Please phone if there's any news or if we can help any further," urged Jenkins and he opened the door.
"Will do! Cheers sir."

The police left by the same door at which they had arrived. If they had looked back, they would have spotted a lone figure at a window staring down at them.
Gary Hart watched. The pigs were off. Good! No arrests and he was safe. He was too sensible to make mistakes. They wouldn't have found any prints because he was no fool. He watched 'The Bill' all the time anyway.

****

The photo fit was put to the public. The pitted face of Gary Hart stared out at shoppers, business people, bus drivers, the famous and the not so famous. Everyone had their chance to win the lottery. (*Simply phone in your answer, don't write on a postcard!*) The police stations dotted around the area were inundated with calls of help and hoaxers flourished as usual.
"It was my brother!"
"I know him, he lives above me. He's a right nutter!"
"He doesn't support Spurs, it's Chelsea and he's got a tattoo on his left arm."

Even the clairvoyants got in on the act, as always.

"I see a railway embankment..."
"His mother owns a fish and chip shop."
"He's evil... He'll strike again..."
Eighty per cent of the calls were followed up.

It may have been mere coincidence, but the winning caller in the lottery chose Phil Queen's station only three hours after the picture and description went on public release. WPC Carol Mills took the call.

"Good afternoon. Can I help you?"

"Yeah, I know him. The boy. Him in the picture."

It was Carol's seventeenth call.

"Yes sir?" It was a young boy's voice on the line.

"Could you give me a name?"

"Yeah, it's Gary. Gary Hart. I go to school with him. He's a right bastard! Only last week he beat up..." the voice rambled on.

"Hold on, hold on. You say he goes to your school?" Carol's eyes widened.

"Yeah, Conford Secondary and he's in my class. I hate him!"

"Fine," replied Carol. "Could I have your name and address please?"

There was a click as the line went dead.

"Great," Carol muttered to herself. Road to nowhere. Another hoaxer wasting my time.

Someone getting back at a bully? She jotted down the name Gary Hart and that of the school.

She rose and went across to Phil Queen's office.

"Phil?"

"Yes. Hi, Carol - nice day. Are we keeping you busy?" Phil folded the newspaper he was reading.

"Hi. Yes, well... it might be something or nothing but I've just had a phone call from a young lad. Left no name and he's just hung up, little brat, but still you never know..." Carol handed Phil the note.

"Let's have a look. 'Gary Hart' and his school is just around the corner. It's about two miles away."

"Yes, I know. Fancy a visit?" Carol asked.
"Tomorrow 'cos they'll all be away by now."
"Surely we could trace this lad's home address, can't we?"

Phil looked pensive, "Yes, where there's a will I suppose... Get me the headmaster's name. You can check the records as well and see who we sent round there. We've done all the schools with the picture today."
"Fine, I'll get on to it!" Carol's enthusiastic response reflected her personality, Phil thought. He liked her. She was not too attractive but just nice. Her small features reminded Phil of a small bird that was always on the go. Busy, keen, blue eyes and a neat bobbed, brunette hairstyle that's feminine but efficient. Her brain was always razor-sharp too! If she had a fault, it was that she's somewhat lacking in the sense of humour department. She was always on the case with no time for banter. She would go far.

Carol returned, interrupting Phil's musings, "Greg and Mick went..."
Phil took the buff folder from Carol. He found the head's private address. "Phone him up and ask him if he knows this kid, Hart's address. He may know him well. It's worth a shot."
"Right away!" Carol saluted and smiled.
It took Phil by surprise. He had not associated Carol with off-the-cuff remarks or light-hearted behaviour. He must revise his assessment, he thought, as he went back to his newspaper.

****

Brenda Hart recognised her son immediately. The picture had been put up at the entrance to the supermarket where customers had to pass it and, hopefully, notice it.

She had been on her break as she passed Kelvin, the Jamaican store man.
He was placing the black and white photofit alongside the Choccy-Chip Ice Cream advert.
"What's all this then Kelv?"
"The bastard who knocked off Jan." Kelvin had fancied the pants off Janice Lee. C'est la vie - there were more dogs in the kennel, he reasoned.
He was a very big man, twenty years old and played basketball for the Colts. Kelvin was rarely without a smile. Today, his frown was unnerving for the people who knew him.
"Terrible. She was great, was Jan," said Brenda as she waddled up to the window.
"He looks a right one," commented Kelvin staring at the face.

Brenda was silent. The toffee she'd been chewing stuck in her throat.
Her eyes were wide and she sucked in great gasps of air as she tried to dislodge the sweet.
"You OK?"
Kelvin looked down at big Bren. She presented an unappetising picture.
"Yeah, yeah," she spluttered with tears in her eyes. "Went down the wrong way, that's all."
Go on a diet you fat slob, thought Kelvin.
She read the text, even though she already knew.
Height - 5' 10''. Complexion – spotty. Hair - short, crew cut.

Distinguishing features - wore a white baseball cap with Spurs in blue capital letters on it. Jeans, training shoes and a T-shirt.

Brenda's eyes closed for a couple of seconds.
"You sure you're OK?" Kelvin frowned.
"Yes fine... fine," she murmured. Gary was out late most nights.
She didn't know and didn't even care what he got up to - but this?
She cared now.

****

Chapter Six

Mr Jenkins had been more than helpful. Phil now had Gary Hart's home address.

As he drove towards the sprawling council estate, Phil was filled with a burning sense of achievement. (*All my own work*!)

He had single-handedly taken on this case, and now he was maybe fifteen minutes away from solving it. He bristled as he manoeuvred the blue Sierra into the forecourt.
"Hats on!" he told his aide, WPC Jo Long.
He took the key from the ignition and looked up at the imposing slab of ugly flat lets. The two officers wore full uniform. Imperiously, they walked across the rubbish strewn concrete. Small children played games and shrieked wildly. The odd expletive which also emanated from the group did not shock the two adults.
"Little horrors..." Jo gave Phil a sideways glance.
"Lovely, aren't they?" he replied. "They get their tuition at home."

An orange football bounced across their path.
"Sorry!" said a small boy, about six years old, as he scurried away clutching the sphere of battered plastic like a trophy.

Phil smiled, "Not all bad though."
He pointed to the concrete steps and said, "Up here."

Jo followed behind him. She felt safe with Sergeant Queen. All the girls fancied him. He oozed wit and self-confidence. She eyed his shapely bum as he preceded her up to the first level. (*Some lucky girl.*)

"Number twenty-two isn't it?"
"Yes Sarge, twenty-two."
They negotiated the next platform, and then headed towards their target.

"Let me do the talking. You keep your eyes and ears open for anything interesting OK?"
"Sarge!"

He braced himself as he knocked on the scruffy pale grey door. Graffiti smeared every available flat surface. A radio could be heard on the other side of the door. A cheap tranny, thought Jo.
Phil banged again, louder this time.
They heard voices.
"Comin' - hang on."
Phil looked into Jo's eyes. "Bingo!" he mouthed silently and smiled, putting Jo at her ease. She was nervous.

The door flew open and Brenda Hart sagged in the doorway. She wore jeans and a baggy sweatshirt. A cigarette hung limply from the corner of her podgy mouth.
"Yeah?"
It was early evening and dusk was setting in. The theme from Eastenders drifted from the interior of the flat.

God! You're a mess, thought Jo.
"Good evening madam. Mrs Hart is it?" asked Phil calmly.
Brenda squinted at him through the smoke.
"Yeah, so?"
"We're making enquires about the murder of Janice..."
Phil was cut off in mid-sentence.
"He's here. In the living room."
"I'm sorry?" Phil was caught off guard at the sharp sudden outburst.
"My wanker of a son. It's him you want innit?"
"Well... er."
"Stop pussy footin' Sergeant. Come in."
She stepped aside as the two police officers entered the flat. A waft of curry hit them. Yuk, thought Jo.
Brenda whispered and pointed, "He's watchin' that poxy cockney show."
Phil nodded as he removed his cap. The three figures entered the living room.
"Oi! Someone 'ere to see you," snapped Brenda. A figure sat watching the black and white portable television set, legs sprawling over the sofa motionless.

"Gary Hart?"
The figure shifted slightly, turning to look at the two uniformed intruders. He tutted petulantly.
"What yer want? I'm watching telly. Come back in half an hour."

Jo regarded Gary Hart with distaste. A plate of curry, half-eaten, lay on the floor beside the sofa.
Phil's reaction mirrored Jo's but he was too professional to show it.

"I'd like to ask you some questions as to your whereabouts on Monday evening Gary."
"And...?"
"Well, let's say where were you at about ten o'clock that night?"
"Down the town with some mates."
"Can you name them?"
Silence.
"Gary - can you name your friends so that they can corrobor... er, back up your story?" asked Phil slowly.
"I ain't done nothing."'
Jo studied Gary silently. He wasn't exactly Mel Gibson in looks. Large frame for his age though, crew cut, adolescent acne and the normal teenage dress sense. She spoke. Phil listened. The photo-fit had been spot on!
"Gary, we have reason to believe that a description given to us by a lady who was murdered on Monday night matches your description."

Gary stared at Jo. She could almost hear his mind ticking. He looked at the floor.
"Answer the constable Gary."
Brenda leaned on the door frame and puffed at her cigarette.
"I've told ya!" His voice rose in pitch. "I was in town!"

Phil changed track.
"Could I have a look in your bedroom son?"
Silence.
"Go ahead make our day. It's the second on the left out there," Brenda moaned as she pointed along the hallway.
Jo stayed put, trying not to gag on the stale smell of curry.

Phil opened 'Gary's Room' (as it proclaimed on the ceramic plaque bearing a teddy with a balloon).

Phil's immediate impression was one of distaste at the chaos which greeted him. There was no order at all. Clothes were tossed carelessly aside, unwashed, judging by the pong. Half-eaten food and unwashed mugs covered a bedside table. There were magazines of all shapes and content. Even a surprising copy of Woman's Weekly lay next to the cassette player. The bed was unmade and a blue and white toothbrush lay on the duvet. His eyes wandered to the walls where a large picture of the Tottenham Hotspur team caught his eye – 'SPURS 1990-1991'.

The grinning players stared back at Phil. They seemed to be saying 'He did it. He did it!' like manic ventriloquist dummies.

There was a sudden crash and a shout, "Come here!" screamed Jo's voice.

A dark shadow shot past the open bedroom door. Phil's reaction was sharp and automatic. As he emerged from the bedroom, he saw Gary Hart scrabbling at the front door.

"Bastards!" he was bawling.

Phil grabbed his shirt and yanked him back. Big lad, he thought. The arm lock was swift and immobilising. He pushed the youth's face first on to the floor and reached for his handcuffs.

"Fuck you pigs!" Hart screamed.

Phil had engaged the door latch as he had entered the flat. An old trick from the college. It had slowed

Hart down just enough to grab him. He grinned with satisfaction as the restraining metal cuffs clicked into position.

Jo stood in the living room rubbing her shoulders.

"You OK?" asked Phil.

"Fine Sarge, yeah," she grimaced.

Brenda stood beside Jo.

"Serves you right you little devil," she whined while looking at her prostrate son.

"Bollocks the lot of you!" Gary's head twisted on the floor.

Time for the spiel. Phil relayed, "Gary Hart, I am arresting you..."

As he read the youth his rights in the hallway, Jo turned to Brenda.

"Thanks, Mrs Hart."

"No bother. I'll be glad to see the back of 'im. Takes after 'is bloody father does that one."

"... you don't have to say anything but what you do say may be used as evidence..." Phil continued. The figure struggled still.

"Nice lass Janice," Brenda remarked, ignoring the scene behind her.

"You knew her?" Janice eyes widened.

"Yeah - worked with her at Brandgate's." Brenda's eyes were distant.

She stubbed out the cigarette in an overflowing ashtray.

"Would you like to make a statement Mrs Hart?"

"How can I help?"

"Oh, you could state that Gary was not at home on Monday evening. That would be to our advantage."

"Yeah sure," Brenda said and nodded sullenly.

"Bitch! You're my mother for fuck's sake!"

Gary Hart now stood at the front door. Phil was at his side holding his arm. "Yeah, but you're no son of mine you evil little toe rag!"
Hart lunged forward, a terrifying sight, suddenly the child factor submerged in his expression of vicious hate. Phil retained his vice-like grip.
"OH NO you don't Gary!" he spoke through gritted teeth.

Jo radioed the station to prepare a cell. The normal static crackle masked the response.
"Let's go," Phil motioned Gary outside the flat. Small children stood on the walkway, their eyes like goldfish.

Gary Hart's legs felt like lead weights as he said, "I didn't do it."
"Tell us at the station Gary," Phil countered.
"Fuckin' 'ell!"

They ambled towards the Sierra. The night was closing in. The strains of the signature tune of 'The Bill' followed them across the forecourt from an open window. The remaining children playing in the fading light did not even notice the four figures climbing into the car. Brenda and Jo had reached the common female bridge of small talk as they approached the vehicle.
"How old is your son Mrs Hart?"
"Thirteen. Fourteen in November."
"Do you think he would be capable of such a thing?"
Jo looked at Brenda Hart sympathetically. (*Who'd be a mother?)*

"Oh yeah. No hassle. He could do it," she said and she heaved a shuddering sigh, as if she was relieved of a long-felt constriction.

Jo shivered.

Gary sat in the back of the car, staring silently at Jo as his mother joined him. His eyes seemed to bore into her very soul. She looked away quickly and slid into the passenger seat, next to Phil.

Brenda felt the contact of her son alongside her, but no sense of warmth was transmitted between them. No word was exchanged. Both looked at on the passing scene in different directions.

As the car moved off, the bright orange football bounced across the bonnet of the vehicle. In the rear view mirror was reflected the tiny figure giving a malevolent V-sign...

****

KENSINGTON, LONDON

The large grey Mercedes crawled along the busy High Street, sandwiched between a scarlet, open-top tourist bus filled with mewing foreign visitors and a van advertising rubber tyres. This was cosmopolitan London after all, where the rich, the poor and the poorer all mixed freely. The pavements were packed with people from all denominations: Jews, Arabs, Asians, Chinese, Japanese and even the odd Englishman. They rushed like ants to an unseen rendezvous. Kebab shops, shoe shops, newsagents, carpet sellers, butchers, candlestick makers as they all plied their trades. Screams of marketers mingled with laughter from people seated outside the many cafes and bars interspersed between the shops. A group of West Indians conversed on a corner in their uniforms of baggy jeans, T-shirts and baseball caps. None of the clothes seemed to fit, frowned Judge Vernon Meek as he listened to the classical music emanating from his huge German-produced car stereo. He pressed a button on the space age console. The window to his right lowered slowly. Immediately, the music was drowned out by the roar of the city traffic.

He stared at the rear of the bus which had moved in front of his car. An advertisement for an Opera Gala at Covent Garden caught his eye. He could go to that, he thought, because he could afford it and he loved the music. He would take his wife, Lucinda, and his younger daughter, Charlotte. Lottie hated classical music but it did her no harm to socialise in his circles. Politicians, financiers, and media moguls would all attend such a social coup - Pavarotti and Domingo. It was a full house but he had the right connections. It was a chance to see and be seen and Lucinda loved the ambience. Her dinner parties were always popular with the same people. They were rich beyond their early dreams, thanks to his salary, his expertise on the Stock Exchange and his finance contacts in the city.

The two o'clock news interrupted his train of thought:

'...criticism was levelled at the judge who freed a convicted rapist. Police in the Metropolitan force claim that Judge Vernon Meek is totally out of touch with public opinion and should be struck off.'
Vernon frowned.

'... The man in question, Paul Cross, had been charged with assault, robbery and rape on a sixty-five year old spinster. She is now in a home. In his summing-up, Judge Meek stated that Cross had now become a devout Christian since the attack and was of sound character, regretting the indecent totally.'

Vernon nodded.

'...the daughter of the victim had to be restrained in court, causing the Judge to warn her for contempt...'

"Too right...too right," Vernon murmured and nodded furiously.

'Sports news... England lost the Third Test against Sri Lanka by three wickets.'

"No!" Vernon Meek snapped off the radio in a flash. "Bloody useless!" Cricket was not what it used to be. He was a Lords' Taverner and a friend of Mick Jagger no less. Even Lottie was quite impressed by that cache. He whistled softly to himself, as he drove slowly towards his evening gin and tonic. A big man, horn rimmed spectacles and his thick greying hair was slicked back. He tanned easily and at the age of sixty, he felt good. The holiday in Brazil with Lucy had helped him relax. He loved making headlines. Out of touch indeed!

Twenty years as a Royal Marines officer had given him a disciplined outlook on life. He still attended Naval Association meetings in Portsmouth and drank whisky until the early hours with his old shipmates. He had studied law whilst in the forces, gaining all the necessary diplomas on the ladder to Lieutenant Colonel. Lucy had been secretary to the defence attaché in Kuala Lumpur when his ship was docked there.

A whirlwind romance ensued and she returned to Arbroath with him for his final tour of duty. He loved Lucy with a passion. She was fifteen years his junior and still had the body and skin of a thirty year old. She devoted a good deal of time to supporting animal rights and worked in their office in Harlow from time to time. Vernon's salary meant that she didn't need to work now.

The Mercedes came to a halt in the interminable jam. He slipped off his blue blazer with its unmistakable badge of the Royal National Lifeboat Association. He was sweating now. The hot afternoon sun blazed down through the sun roof. He placed his horn rims in a spectacle case and replaced them with his Rayban's. Thoroughly modern Verny, he chuckled to himself. He slackened the tie around his thick neck. It was Friday afternoon in the centre of London. Total chaos! He'd been in the car for fifty minutes and had travelled one and a half miles. Typical!

Lucy would be at home, probably in the garden in her bikini reading the latest Jilly Cooper. He felt the old urges in his loins. He was proud of his ability still to satisfy Lucy. She was very athletic which helped. All he had to do was lie there and think of Plymouth...

They were going to Henley regatta this weekend. He loved it. All the old faces, royalty, TV and the press. He breathed out deeply; looking to his left. He watched as a vagrant searched in a litter bin for scraps.

"Get a bloody life," he whispered scornfully.

****

The sun was beginning to dip perceptibly in the west as he turned with relief into the long exclusive road where he had lived for the past eight years. The Mercedes inched along the leafy avenue. The parked cars on the gravelled drives reflected the affluence of their owners. A Porsche here and a top of the range Honda there.

Judge Vernon Meek manoeuvred his vehicle into the driveway of his detached mock Tudor residence and parked behind his wife's Nissan Sunny. The passenger window was still wide open.

"Tut, tut," Vernon commented at his wife's carelessness. The heat was oppressive as he locked his car and walked back along the drive and around to the front door. His feet scrunched on the gravel as he noticed that the front windows were open and the net curtains were floating out in the sultry breeze.

As he approached the house, he could hear the sound of a radio. God it was loud! She must have been doing her aerobics again, he mused.

The front door was standing ajar. Vernon frowned as he replaced his keys in his pocket.

As he entered the hallway, the music from the front room blared in his ears. It wasn't her usual station - she liked Radio Two. Unless Lottie was home early. Yes, of course...

He switched the radio off. Total silence.
"Lucy! I'm home darling," Vernon called. Not a sound. No reply at all. (*Try the garden...*)

He entered their modern kitchen. (*It cost a bomb but Lucy loved it!)* Looking out at the expanse of lawn, he could see a deckchair, a radio and a book just as he had predicted. The small transistor played on. But there was no sign of Lucy so a small frisson of alarm crept into his brain.
"Lucy?!" he shouted quizzically.

A carton of milk stood on the fridge. He took a slug and left the kitchen, wiping his mouth with the back of his hand. The garden lay serene and shimmering in the heat. Birds twittered sleepily in the shrubbery but the silence was unnerving. Something did not fit with the calm scene. He looked up at the house. The bedroom windows were shut. Lucy always kept them open on warm days.
The curtains were drawn...
"Pull yourself together you idiot!" he muttered while his mind simply whirled.

He heard a scraping noise to his right.
"Hi!"
Mr Green from next door was busy digging.

"Oh, evening Tom. Er, lovely day for it."
"Yes, yes, it is Vern. I was only saying to Lucinda earlier, what a good summer it's been."
Vernon started, "Lucy. You've spoken to her?"
"Oh yes, about er... an hour ago. She was sunbathing as per usual," smiled Tom. "I like her new hairdo. Suits her."
"Ah yes, it does," Vernon mumbled.
Tom continued to dig methodically. "See you later then," he said as he glanced up from his labours. Vernon Meek was gone.

****

An hour earlier, Lucinda Meek had been relaxing in her Harrods' deckchair reading about sex in the suburbs, as described so amusingly by Jilly Cooper. The sun was very hot but she refrained from the desire to go topless. Didn't want Tom having a heart attack. The lecherous old sod. Sipping on her iced lemonade, she scanned the garden. Tom was digging again. He always dug when she sunbathed. Sheer coincidence of course. She smiled to herself as she heard him grunt with every thrust of his spade.

"Morning Tom!" said Lucy as she stood up and brushed her dark hair back.

The digging stopped.
"Lucy! Hello my love. How's life?"
"Hot and bothered. Lovely day."
"Yes – I reckon it's the warmest yet."
Tom was bare-chested. For sixty-seven he was a fit man. His balding head and grey sideburns gave the game away. He had retired from the city three years earlier. His sharp wit was a constant source of amusement for Lucy during her lonely days at the house. He often came round for coffee. Tom's a real gentleman.

Tom's wife had died in a plane crash just prior to his retirement. All of his energy, from that tragic event, was centred on his garden. Even the winter snows didn't deter him from the pruning and grooming of the rockery or the pond.
"I'm planting some begonias," said Tom with a smile.
"Lovely. I like them," Lucy replied. "They always add a splash of colour around the lawn."

"Your tan is coming along nicely," Tom remarked approvingly.

"So's yours!" laughed Lucy. Tom didn't tan but he often looked like a ripe tomato during the summer.

"Very funny. I'm using Factor 80 today, especially on my head!"

Tom grimaced as he patted the scarlet patch covering his skull.

Lucy laughed out loud and turned away. "I must get a refill," she said as she held up her empty glass. The melting ice tinkled. "See you later on."

"Of course Lucy. Keep up your liquid intake. Have fun."

Tom continued to dig feverishly as his breathing laboured. Lucy headed for the kitchen and more refreshment. Vernon would be home soon...

****

Vernon rushed up the stairs and panic gripped him like a vice. He tried to control it. There WAS something wrong. He felt sure of it.

Then, he screamed aloud in utter shock when he opened their bedroom door.

"Oh my God!"

Lucy lay sprawled across the floor. The bed was a mess. The television was on showing an afternoon soap opera. Lucy was gagged and bound. She was unconscious. An enormous wave of nausea swamped Judge Vernon Meek.

"Lucy! Lucy... Lucy!"

He was on his knees in seconds, trying desperately to undo the knotted nylon stocking which held his wife's hands together. Tears of rage rolled down his face.

She was naked too, apart from her black stilettos.

"Christ almighty - who did this?" Vernon gasped as he fumbled with the other stocking which restrained his loved one's ankles. Beads of sweat arose on his forehead. His hand touched something wet on the carpet. He recoiled. Sticky and wet.

Not blood... Cold, sticky and wet. His eyes widened in horror as he smelt his fingertips. He gagged, wiping his hand on his trousers as he recognised the aroma of sperm.

"Jesus!"

Bile rose in his throat. His vision blurred.

Judge Vernon Meek vomited up his packed lunch on the Wilton pile.

Shuddering, he looked at his wife. Her face was red from her tears. Her hair was matted; there were marks on her breasts and scratch marks on her thighs. Vernon checked her breathing.

She was alive, though her pulse was extremely faint. He carefully listed her onto the bed. The tears subsided, replaced by cold reason as his professional instinct surfaced.

Phone the Police NOW!

He rose from the bed, picked up the phone and dialled 999. There was a small moan from the bed. Lucy moved as the call was connected.

"Hello, which service do you require?"

His eyes never left the prostrate figure of his wife as he replied.

"Police and emergency ambulance! My wife has been attacked!" he blustered.

A female voice came over the line.

"Yes sir, can I have your name and address please?"

They were so detached from my terror and professional but it's their job, thought Vernon.
Calmly he replied, "8 Friary Avenue."
The girl answered in that curious monotone.
"Is that Friary Road in Fulham or Kensington?"
Fuck!
"I said Friary AVENUE. Are you deaf?"
"Please calm down sir. Help is on its way."
"For God's sake! My wife is at death's door and you ask me to calm down!"
"Can I have your name, please sir?"
Vernon was losing it.
"You've got my bloody address so send something!"
Lucy moaned again and stirred on the bed.
"We must have your name sir. It's for our records, in case of hoax calls."
Vernon gritted his teeth and spoke as calmly as he could manage.
"My name... is Vernon Meek! Got it?"

Then he saw the envelope on the table.
"Is that Vernon with an 'O' sir?"
It was white and it looked like a birthday card envelope.
"Hello sir," the girl's voice was insistent. "Are you still there?"
It had something written on it in large, red capital letters.
Vernon slowly put down the receiver and he picked up the envelope.
It read: "BIG VERN - SUPER JUDGE" in red lipstick.
Vernon opened the envelope. The phone crackled. He ignored Lucy's faint cries as she regained consciousness.
He began to read the letter enclosed in the envelope.

'Hi Vern. How's it going? Me and my pal have had such a fun afternoon with your lovely wife. She really suits those black high heels. She moaned a lot when we got her on her knees. Missionary's a bit boring!
Of course, you don't mind women being raped, do you? Rapists are such good people. You'd rather see them on the streets than locked up.
Hope you can see the fruits of your convictions, or rather lack of convictions, Verny old boy. How does it feel to be a victim?
Oh yes, I'm a devout Christian believer and I really do regret what's happened here today. I'm sure you're happy in this knowledge.
Regards to your daughter. She looks great too.
Sincerely yours,
'The Enforcer'

Vernon Meek raised his blurred eyes from the paper and stared at the mirror. There were more red smears. They read 'How does it feel Vern?'

In the distance, he vaguely heard a police siren getting nearer and nearer. He began to sob uncontrollably.

****

Ernest Moore was late, a habit he'd frequently been accused of lately. The desk sergeant observed him in a cool, detached manner. He reserved this demeanour for dealing with defence solicitors.

Moore placed his black briefcase on the high counter and cleared his throat in an attempt to attract the Sergeant's attention. A balding, forty-something, Moore had always had a timid personality and he still lived with his mother. He resembled the comedian, Charlie Drake.

Sergeant Amos Oates looked up at the squat, nervous man before him.

He carefully placed his pen on the counter and leaned forward.

"Yes, can I help you sir?" His tone implied that any information would come as no surprise to him.

Ernest Moore tried to sound authoritative but he failed abysmally.

"Er... Morning Sergeant," he began, quietly thrusting a clammy hand forward in readiness to receive a handshake from the giant Negro. He didn't receive one.

"I'm Ernest Quinlan Moore, defence solicitor for Gary Hart."

Oates smiled. "Oh right. You've come to try and bail the arrogant little sod, have you?" he queried nasally.

Moore recoiled immediately on the defensive.

"Of course not! Well, you and I know only too well Sergeant that man, or in this case a boy, remains innocent until..."

"...until proven guilty. Yeah, yeah," interrupted Oates and nodding his head.

"I find your attitude most disrespectful officer!" snorted Ernest in a high-pitched whine.

Oates leaned forward with his large face inches from Moore's.

"Listen Mister Moore," he purred. "I have seen too many rapists, murderers, thieves and wastrels go free because of do-gooders like you. Excuse me if I am being, er, disrespectful. Now, do you want to see your client or do I have to listen to your bullshit all morning?"

Moore was beginning to sweat a little. He eased his collar and nodded.

"Er, no officer of course not. Please direct me to Mr Hart's cell. I have little time for small talk."

"Good!" Oates replied sarcastically. "Please come this way."

He called through to the adjoining office. "Constable Tibbetts! Please take over the desk for a few moments while I escort our visitor."

"Sarge!"

Oates opened the door to the cell corridor.

"Follow me," he motioned to Moore.

"Thank you officer," murmured Moore keeping a safe distance from the huge, bristling policeman. He glanced at the chalked names on the cell doors.

"We're empty, apart from superman here," Oates explained and he put the key in the lock. "Do you want an escort to sit in with you?"

"I don't think so. He's only a kid, isn't he?" Moore answered a hint of sympathy in his voice.

"The kid, as you so quaintly put it, has so far been the most disruptive little shit we've had in for months. But on your own head be it," commented Oates as he opened the door. It swung inwards.

"I'll leave the door open anyway. I'm just down back there if you need any assistance," he said pointing down the way they had come.

"Oh, I'm sure I'll be fine thanks," said Moore confidently.

He entered the cell. Oates whistled softly as he returned along the corridor. "Have fun," he replied smiling and keys jangling.

Gary Hart sat on a plain wooden bench. An empty plastic beaker lay at his feet. He looked up sullenly at the small, bald, suited man at the door.
"Who're you then?" he asked in a lazy tone.
"Hello, Mister Hart. Gary isn't it?" said Moore weakly.
" 'course it is. You ought to know my effin' name. It's been in the papers all week."

Moore sidled up to Hart, putting his briefcase down and taking a pen from his inside pocket.
"You're my brief, ain't ya?" remarked Gary, picking his nose casually.
"Spot on Gary!" Moore replied in cheerful tones whilst opening his notepad.
The words spilled out shocking the solicitor.
"I didn't do it you know! She was asking for it! Naked she was.
I only meant to put the frighteners on her!" blurted Hart.
Moore's body went rigid and he recoiled.
"Hang on, hang on! Let me see... You are going to plead 'not guilty'. You do know that all the evidence points at you?"
Moore sat down warily alongside Hart.
"What evidence? A poxy hat?! Wearing a hat means I did it, does it?"
Moore scribbled on his notepad. He continued, "Blood samples taken at the scene matched yours. O Positive. Are you O Positive?" He leaned towards Hart.

"Yeah, twelve million others and me! Common as muck!" spat Hart. "Proves nothing!"
He leapt suddenly to his feet and kicked the plastic cup across the cell. It smacked against the wall. The noise echoed.
"I'm just a scapegoat! She screamed so I ran off! I only wanted to scare the cow. Serves her right!"

Moore was getting nervous and wished he'd got an escort after all. Hart was a big and powerful lad by the look of him.
"Now then, calm down Gary. I'm here to help you."
"Help? The last thing I want is help! I'm piggin' innocent! They're out to get me. I bet the bloody school kids are lovin' this! Gary's in nick. Hurray!"
Moore frowned. Gary gesticulated wildly.
"What do you mean? Are you saying you have no friends?" he asked in a tone of concern. (*Appeal to his better nature to calm him down.*)
"Yeah, everyone hates my guts! Never let me join in. I'm always last to be picked for anything."
"Oh, I see. So you're not a very good team player? You don't like sports?"
"I'm brilliant but they just don't like me!"
Moore stood up to his maximum five foot three height and squared Hart's shoulders.
"Let me ask you something Gary."
Hart stared at the floor with his shoulders hunched in silence.
"What?"

Moore knelt in front of him and looked up into the teenager's acne-ridden face.
"Are you? No. Were you... a bully?" he whispered.

The kick came from nowhere, catching Moore full in the chest. He reeled backwards. His notebook and pen flew from his hands as his shocked scream resounded through the adjoining corridors. As he struck the tiled floor, an excruciating pain shot up his spine.

"You're all the same! Bastards!" screamed Hart. He stood over Moore spitting wildly, "SCUM!"

Another kick caught Moore in the groin. He had never experienced pain like it. He tried to curl up in a ball as the blows rained down. Tears filled his eyes and he retched violently.

"Bastard! Bastard!!" shouted Hart.

The words echoed around the cell as running footsteps and shouts mingled with the violent screams.

Amos Oates hurled himself at Hart, backed up by two constables. Their bodies joined in a mass embrace.

"Get off him!" yelled Oates. They struggled for what seemed an eternity. The body of the victim shook in sheer terror. Oates gained a restricting hold on Hart and the two supporting policemen transferred their attention to the figure curled up on the floor.

"I warned you Mr Moore," Sergeant Oates' voice penetrated Ernest Moore's semi-consciousness. He opened his eyes fearfully to see Oates frogmarching Gary Hart out of the cell. The struggling youth's eyes were wild and his face contorted with fury.

"Wanker, I don't need you!" he shrieked at Moore.

"Shut it!" Oates hold tightened as he led the youth away.

Moore was coughing violently as he slowly uncurled his body. The dull ache in his crotch slowly subsided.

A stream of spittle and phlegm flowed from his lips as his breath gave in intermittent gasps.

"Can you stand sir?" One of the young officers held his arm.
"Yes. I think so," groaned Moore wincing at the sharp pain in his back.
"Nasty piece of work that one," volunteered the other constable.

Moore stood up and sat on the bench.
"Please pass me my notes and my pen. They're somewhere..."
The officer bent down and collected the pathetic tools of Moore's profession. He sat with his head bowed.
"I'll get you a cup of tea sir?"
"Thank you."
Footsteps could be heard along the corridor and Sergeant Oates reappeared in the doorway. He leaned on the door jamb, with his arms crossed, and looked at the crestfallen figure of the solicitor.
"See what I mean?" he asked softly.
Moore looked up slowly.
"Yes Sergeant, I do. I'm sorry, I was far too trusting," he admitted pitifully.
"You'll know better next time. That is, if there is a next time," said Oates knowingly.

Moore wiped his mouth with a paper towel offered by the constable. He shrugged. "He's all I've got. He says he's innocent so I have to defend him. Someone has to no matter what. It's what I'm paid for," he spoke wearily.

Oates raised his eyebrows. “I admire your confidence Mr Moore. However, don’t you think after today’s little episode, you may be fighting a losing battle?”
The young constable looked down at Moore.

“No, I stand by my principles. He’s an angry young man Sergeant and, at the end of the day, I have to do my utmost to help in any way I can.”

Oates tossed his head. “Listen to him - can you sort that out?”
Hart’s ranting could still be heard from the depths of the station...

Moore placed his pen in his pocket and sighed deeply; picking up his briefcase.
“He’s not the first one I’ve dealt with and he sure won’t be the last.”
Oates did not answer.
Moore continued, “The funny thing is, and think what you like Sergeant, I reckon he’s telling the truth. That boy is innocent of <u>this</u> crime, make no mistake.”

Sergeant Oates shook his head slowly and turned away. His footsteps echoed dully on the tiled corridor floor. Hart’s protestations could still be heard.

Ernest Moore stood up and looked at the young constable. “Now, what about that cup of tea young man?”

****

Chapter Seven

For the second time in a week, Phil Queen approached the village. It was raining today though and the wipers moaned as the rubber squeegeed the droplets from the windscreen.

It was mid-afternoon. He couldn't wait to tell Chloe the news that they had HIM! Gary Hart, thirteen years old and a murderer.

It would read as a chilling precise CV for any prospective employer, thought Phil. The interview had taken an hour and needed all Phil's persuasive patience. He was a tough little bastard for his age. Eventually, Gary had confessed. It all tied up neatly: the cap, the timings and the look in the youth's eyes. She was like a frightened animal. He wasn't as clever as he thought he was. He had stepped out of his league when he attacked an adult female. His usual victims were smaller kids.

Phil's thoughts turned to Brenda Hart. She'd been a godsend to the investigation. How can a mother hate her own son? Sad, but in this case patently true. She had given her side of the story, even down to the stomach upset scam Gary had concocted the following morning. He'd even conned the medic too.

Hart's headmaster had sounded as shocked as was possible in their telephone conversation. However, a quick check of the attendance records had proved an embarrassing moment for him.

"Truanting? I'm sorry, but I'm afraid I've missed all of this officer. It seems Gary had only attended school twice in two months."

Phil had forbore to comment on the efficiency, or otherwise, of the situation but had suggested mildly that the headmaster should undertake a total check of all his pupils in the circumstances. Apathy was usually the beginning.

"Yes, of course officer. Please don't let this matter become public knowledge. I'm sure we can keep the situation under control."
Phil had agreed. He had enough on his plate.

He drove past Chloe's cottage and continued down into the High Street. He spotted the shop next to the pub. He pulled up outside, checking for restrictions. People milled about in the drizzle. As he locked the car, laughter and voices reached him and the sound of the juke box in the bar.

He approached the shop, noting the tasteful window display of a few choice items guaranteed to attract the passer-by. As he pushed the door open, a wind chime tinkled above his head. He noted a 'Mind The Step!' sign. It was a fair old drop down into the shop.

Phil closed the door carefully. He was alone; there were no other customers. A clock ticked to his left. It looked valuable as did all of the items on display. The shop was chock-full of antiques and objects d'art, books, china, old bottles, furniture. An Aladdin's cave for the collector, whatever his or her fancy. Antiques Road Show would have a field day here, he thought. He picked up a leather bound book (Great Expectations by Charles Dickens) and opened the front fly leaf. The pages were sallow and turning brown at the edges. This wasn't any old tat.

A voice broke the silence. "It's an early edition so take care with it," Chloe smilingly chided him.

Phil jumped and turned round to face her. "God do you creep up on all your clients like that?!"
"Only the suspicious looking ones," she laughed.
Phil's heart skipped a beat. She stood about a yard away, her black dress blending into the shadows. She wore black stilettos and a small crucifix hung from a fine chain around her slender neck. She looked stunning.

"I must look like the wicked witch of the North all dressed in black?"
"No, you look..." Phil stammered; realising he was staring like some gormless imbecile.
"I usually like black, but I feel as if I'm wearing it for a purpose today. I've been thinking about the funeral," she said with her head bowed. She put down a mug of coffee near the till. Its last registry was £85.00, a payment for some treasure.
"Oh yes, I should have known you'd be busy with the arrangements. Shall I come back tomorrow? Do you need time, you know, to think things through?" (*Stop gibbering, he told himself.*)

"No, no - it's all right but I feel that I can't really start to get myself together until that's over," she murmured, toying with her small cross.

"Do you have any news yet?" She stared out of the window at the drizzle with unseeing eyes. She was unsure whether she wanted to know whether she could face the actual prospect of seeing her daughter's killer.

Phil couldn't say it fast enough but he controlled his feelings and sat down on an elegant chair opposite Chloe. "I have good news. We reckon we got him!" Phil said confidently.
He watched her reaction carefully. Her eyes flickered momentarily. She sat motionless, staring ahead.
"Chloe, we arrested a boy yesterday," Phil repeated.
"A boy?" she whispered.
"Yes, he's only thirteen."
"Thirteen?!"
"Yes, sadly."
Phil lowered his eyes. Chloe closed her eyes and breathed a huge sigh.
There was a moment of silence, then a small tear escaped down her cheek.
Phil rose from his seat.
"I'm sorry, so sorry Chloe."
"Thirteen," she whispered in disbelief at the news.
Phil saw shock setting in. He walked across to the entrance door, turned around the card to 'Closed' and forcefully pushed across its lock.

Returning to Chloe, he saw a very sad figure. She looked empty, he thought. With her daughter gone, what had she left?

Phil sat down and pulled his chair closer to Chloe's.
"Thank you for catching him," she murmured.
Phil leaned forward.
"It's not over yet Chloe. I want to see him put away for good. Life should mean life!"
Chloe looked up and said, "Will we get justice though? He's only thirteen."
"We shall push for the highest possible sentence Chloe. I assure you."

Phil's mind wandered back to the scene at Janice's flat. He thought of Janice's pleading and sightless expression, then abruptly snapped back into the present.
"How did you find him so soon?" Chloe asked, sipping at her cooling coffee again. Her tears had subsided.
"The photofit was superb. It was one of the kids at Hart's school."
"Is that his name? Hart?" Chloe enquired.
"Yes, it's Gary Hart."
"Sounds like a politician's name," she said unsmiling.
"Anyway, one of his school mates recognised him and phoned in. We went to his flat and according to his mother he was out all Monday night. He had followed Janice from the station back to the flat and he had attacked her in the park after that."
"<u>He</u> attacked her in the park?" she asked with her eyes open wide.
"Yes, it looks that way. Janice described her attacker so well for the photofit. Then, when she was found..." Phil hesitated.
"There was evidence in Hart's flat that tied him to Janice's description." Phil nodded.

"So, he must have followed her after she reported the assault as well?"

"Yes, Hart must have. But he's only admitting to the attack but he's denying that he killed her. To be honest, I'm certain that it's Hart because it all points to him."

"What happens now then?" Chloe asked.

"We have him in custody until tomorrow then he goes in front of the magistrate to be charged."

"Then what?" Chloe queried.

"Then it's circus time. He'll be given notice of when his case will come to court. I imagine he'll be held in custody. I shall be the main witness. I don't know how you feel about attending the hearing but you can if you wish," Phil waited as Chloe considered this suggestion.

Finally, she sat up defiantly and said, "Yes, I do want to attend. I want to see this monster for myself!" her eyes flashed with sudden decision.

"Good, I'll get in touch and let you know the court date as soon as it's all set."

Phil had not noticed but they were now holding hands, as if in the midst of some strange kind of ritual. Chloe's face was inches from his and he was held by her gaze.

"Thank you Phil," She said and leaned forward to gently kiss Phil's forehead. Closing his eyes, he let out a deep sigh. Her perfume was intoxicating and the black dress accentuated her graceful figure.

Chloe sat back, blushing profusely.

"Oh Phil, do forgive me. How stupid of me!" Chloe declared.

Phil was in heaven!

"Coffee please," Phil teased as he tried to cover his feelings to give her time to regain her composure.
"Don't worry, I'm just try to unwind a little now you know he's in custody. If there's anything I can do - you know I'm around."

Chloe stood up with a jolt and said, "Yes, of course. Do you take sugar?"
"Two please."

Chloe disappeared through a bead curtain into the rear of the shop. Phil heard the tinkle of cutlery and a kettle being filled. He rose and followed her. She stood at the sink with her back to him, putting instant coffee into two mugs. Phil leaned on the wall and observed. The black dress came to just below her knees. She had kicked off her high heels and was now barefoot. Her back was tanned above the scooped neck of the dress and her hair was looped up into a chignon. Phil had preferred it loose and long.
The kettle came slowly to the boil.
"You said two sugars?" Chloe shouted.
"Er... yes," Phil replied.
The sugar bowl she was holding fell to the floor with a crash, scattering tiny shards of glass on the brick floor.

"Sh - ugar!" she exclaimed in anger.
They stared at each other for two interminable seconds. Phil laughed and Chloe followed suit. The absurdity of the situation suddenly struck them both.
Phil reached out and Chloe came into his gentle embrace.
"Chloe," Phil whispered as she looked up at him.
"Yes Mister Policeman?"

The moment lasted.
"I knew... the first time..." he said tentatively.
"So did I..." The couple resumed their chairs in the living room.

They considered this amazing turn of events.
"When will I see you again?" asked Phil.
"I've always like that song," she teasingly replied, "But it's still a good line!"
"I'm not giving you a line! Can we meet - go out for dinner perhaps?"
"Perhaps..." she responded thoughtfully.
"Sorry, I'm rushing things. It's not the time while this is all going on."
"No, it's not that. It's just - there's been no one since..." her voice tailed off.
"Since Pete?"
"Yes, I guess I'm a bit out of practice."

Phil couldn't believe his luck. She wasn't rejecting him. She was considering the possibilities. He stood and drew her close. Suddenly his whole body responded to the sheer sexuality of the woman in his arms.
"I'm sorry..." he said hurriedly, releasing her.
"That's all right," she giggled, "It seems I haven't lost it after all!"

Phil realised with relief and joy that he was actually being encouraged. "Aries and Gemini!" he reminded her, "What a combination!"
"What a memory!" Chloe exclaimed and pushed him away, "Did you say you'd like two sugars in your coffee?" as she wandered back to the kitchen.

She then knelt down and began to collect the shards of glass.
Phil reached across and switched the kettle on again...

****

Gary sat hunched in the cell. He stared at the opposite wall. He could hear the scrape of metal as doors opened and closed. The cell was as big as his bedroom. It contained a bench with a blanket, a sink and a bucket. It was a real home from home for the famous thirteen year old.

He studied his feet. The cheap training shoes were two months' old but looked as if they might disintegrate at any time. The anger simmered just below the surface. Resentment at his mother, the police and the world. He picked at a festering pustule on his chin. Studying the core of pus on the end of his finger, he happily slipped it into his mouth. In a couple of hours he'd be out on bail awaiting the next part of the game - juvenile court. He had no qualms. He would get off without charge. His solicitor would see to that. It always happened like that on TV anyway. Then, he could get back to his favourite pastimes of truancy, bullying and the odd petty theft. The death of the slag had been a surprise to him. He had no part in that he told himself. If only he hadn't dropped the bloody Spurs' cap when he panicked. Her eyes had rolled up and she'd started to go blue and he'd run off...

The hatch in the door shot back.
"Five minutes Hart and you're off!"

The policeman's eyes watched him through the narrow slit.

Gary nodded slowly while constantly staring at the wall. The latch slammed shut again.

They came for him, just as they'd promised. Two burly officers flanked him as he left the cell. Gary tried not to look smug but he didn't quite master it.
"Where're we goin'?" he demanded.
"Somewhere the sun don't shine sonny," remarked the bearded policeman.
"Where?" Gary looked stunned.
"It's a night in the detention centre for you matey!"
"No, I'm goin' home. You've got it wrong!" Gary protested.
" 'fraid not. You won't see home for a while Gary."

They entered the rear car park. A large white van with blacked-out windows waited for them with its doors open at the back.

"Get in!"
Gary climbed in sullenly. He could hear voices in the distance as the doors closed. Shouts and curses.
The two police officers sat opposite him as the vehicle pulled away.
Gary looked out of the dark windows. After just thirty seconds, the van stopped and he could hear louder shouting. Something slammed against the side of the vehicle causing it to lurch. Gary licked his lips and blinked sharply.
Wide-eyed, he turned to the big man with the beard.
"What was that?"
His escort smiled.
"That's one of your fans Gary," he replied nonchalantly.

Gary could hear the screams of women.
"Hang the bastard!"
"Scum!"
"You're dead!"

The police van suddenly lurched forward at speed, weaving from side to side. Gary had to hold on to the seat. Another series of thuds struck the vehicle in quick succession. The voices drifted away as the van picked up speed.

"You are flavour of the month, aren't you," commented the younger policeman sarcastically. He stared hard at Gary; his eyes were black pits.

"Proud of yourself , are you?" asked the bearded one.
Gary's eyes darted from one officer to the other.
"Didn't do it, did I," Gary spoke defiantly.
"Oh, we think you did Gary," said the young one.
"Prove it then!"
"I think we'll leave that to the court."

The bearded officer yawned, stretched and said, "Down to the pub later for a nice lager and a bag of salt and vinegar."
They totally ignored Gary but he listened.
"Of course, 'Mr Big' here won't see a pub 'til he's thirty-five. Such a shame!"
The two officers silently glared at Gary.
The van continued on its way and its engine grinded with every gear change.
Gary tried to look in control. His face was a mask and it hid his real feelings well. His stomach lurched and his

head ached. He was panicky. (*What if they're right? What if I'm proved to be the killer? I attacked her, yes, but will they believe me if I say I didn't kill her? She was still alive when... God! I'm in trouble!)*

One of the policemen farted loudly.
"Sorry, I'm just excited," he said staring at an unsmiling Gary.
"Soon be there, don't worry mate," said the younger copper. (*He didn't mean don't worry, he really meant tough shit Gary!)*
The vehicle stopped. Gary heard muffled voices.
"Is he in here then?"
"Yeah, little wanker!"
"Let's be 'avin' you then!"
The doors swung open. Three large prison officers stood outside.
"Come on, get out!"
Gary rose from his seat with wary eyes.
"Don't be scared. The beds are very comfortable and the eggs are delicious!"
The group of big men laughed approvingly.
Gary wanted the lavatory badly. The script was all wrong! He should have been out on bail!

****

Sergeant Phil Queen stood once more in front of Superintendent Clive Badger. He'd been looking forward to work today. His liaison with Chloe, coupled with the capture of Hart, had put him on cloud nine. At this moment, though, the clouds were fast turning into a storm.

"I've spoken to District headquarters Sergeant Queen." Badger looked at his notes.

"Sir?"

"They're of the same opinion as myself. I gave them the facts and they agree that disciplinary action is the only course to be taken."

Phil was stunned!

"You'll appear in front of a tribunal in a week's time. The sooner we clear this little matter up, the better mmmm?"

Phil mustered speech, "With all due respect sir, surely this, er little matter, can be kept 'in house'? Does it really warrant a tribunal? It isn't as though I've..."

"Silence, Sergeant Queen!" Badger bristled. Phil wavered visibly.

"I feel you've transgressed. You're to be punished for this negligence.

I sincerely hope it will be a fair punishment. I'd hate to lose your undoubted talents from my office."

Phil gritted his teeth. (*You fucking hypocrite he thought to himself!)*

"You will have ample opportunity to defend your actions next week. Until then, I don't want to hear another word from you. Is that clear?"

Phil was silent.

"I said, is that clear Sergeant Queen?"

"Yes sir!"

"You may leave."

Phil turned immediately. As his hand held the door handle, Badger spoke again.

"Oh by the way Sergeant, very well done on the Lee case. Very well done indeed!"

Phil left the office without deigning to reply, slamming the door in exasperation, but he was not called back for a reprimand.
Clive Badger picked up his phone, "Gwen? Get me District H.Q. I'd like to speak to Deputy Chief Constable Ellis. Thank you my love."

He stared out of the window. Queen wouldn't get off this one, he smiled to himself as he placed his feet on the edge of his desk. He doodled on the pad as he waited for a reply from District. As he began to speak to DCC Ellis, he unconsciously drew a gibbet and a hangman's noose...

****

REQUIEM

Chloe's face was a picture of concentration. She sat in the front row of the church, silently staring ahead towards the plain wooden cross above the altar. In front of the altar stood the brass wheeled bier carrying the plain wooden coffin. The same wood, she thought inconsequentially. She felt totally numb!

The vicar's mouth moved but she didn't hear the platitudes. All she could see was Janice: Janice on her bicycle, Janice in the swimming pool, Janice doing a jigsaw...

So many funerals, Chloe thought, and it didn't get any easier. The first had been her father, Eric. He'd died following a stroke in his second year of retirement. His life of heavy lifting work had taken its toll. His last words to her had been 'see you' as he set off down the narrow country lane to the small pub near the village green. She'd rarely ever told him that she loved him and this made her feel very sad.

Her mother, Rhiannon, was her mentor and best friend. She was always ready to listen but advising only when asked. She had been the only stable support in Chloe's life when Pete was killed. She shivered as she remembered the desolation she felt at the death of her husband. She would never have revived her life if it had not been for her mother. She was always available, supportive and never demanding. The cancer had been massive and the end was swift. Rhiannon had been granted a merciful, quiet release and Chloe had sat with her that last rainy Sunday.
She did not forget this time...
"I love you mummy," were the last words her mother heard, as the frail hand lost its grip for the final time.

From then on, Chloe had told Janice constantly that she loved her. It was sometimes an embarrassment to her daughter, especially at parties when she had drunk two vodkas too many.

Now she was alone.

She had the shop and friends in the village, but the evenings and weekends lay ahead without Janice. It was so bloody unfair! A tear escaped and she closed her eyes as the service rolled on. She gritted her teeth, trying to gain control of her emotions. She held her handkerchief tightly, as if it was her last possession. The droning voice of Reverend Ablett cascaded down from the lectern.

There were only a few mourners present. Most were too shocked to attend and some didn't have the money to travel. She had numerous sympathy cards at home from well-wishers, people she'd never met and local friends. They all expressed their support and concern.

But, now she was alone.
The vicar was announcing the final hymn and the congregation joined in the well-known words, "The Lord is my shepherd..."

Chloe did not sing. She looked at the coffin again. Flowers of spring decorated the cross which lay on its top. Chloe had chosen cremation. Burial was so depressing, especially if it rained. She wanted no rain on Janice's memory.

The organ played the last verse and she mouthed the words remembered from school assemblies. She was thankful there was a small choir in attendance or the music would have been superfluous.

A stained glass window over the altar coloured the sunbeams shining through. It had a depiction of the Virgin Mary holding a baby Jesus and six tiny lambs frolicked around her feet. Mary's expression was, as always, serene and gentle. Behind her head was a star. Chloe saw Janice in the star. She was smiling. As Chloe's eyes blurred with tears, she was sure she heard Janice's voice saying I love you mummy.

****

Chloe shook hands with the priest.
"Thank you, it was a lovely service," she smiled wanly.
The Reverend Ablett held her hands in a firm grasp.
"Be strong Chloe. I know it's a difficult time for you."
"Yes, I know but I can cope," she replied, "I have to for Janice's sake."
"Don't hesitate to call me if I can help you in any way," the priest said reassuringly.
She nodded as he handed her a small white card.
"This is my number and I'm always available."
"Thank you vicar, I'm grateful for that."

She turned and walked down the narrow gravel path head bowed to where a long black limousine waited. A gust of wind caught her black dress.
The priest's gaze followed her until she was out of sight.

****

MOUNT SNOWDON, WALES

The three figures made their way steadily up the mountainside. A fine drizzle fell, covering their faces with a thin viscous film. The surrounding hills reared up on either side of the path, the summits shrouded in mist. The three men could have been spotted at some distance in clearer weather, their colourful wet proof suits clashing gaudily against the brooding shades of green, grey and brown of the hills. On some days, when the sun broke through, hillwalking became a physical test.

Thousands climbed Mount Snowdon's peaks every spring, summer and autumn. It was enjoyed by families, scout groups, charity fundraisers, school trips and the armed forces. Everybody and anybody came to beat the hill. Some took the easy route, wearing the kit associated with the hill walker: cagoule, woolly hat, boots (the most expensive of course) and carrying packs on their backs. Others, less hardy souls, chose to climb it on the tram. Easy life, no sweating. Just climb aboard at the bottom and clamber off at the top. They'd look at the views, take snaps to show back home, have a cup of tea and buy the all-important 'I've climbed Snowdon' badge to add to their collection.

Today, though, the three intrepid walkers who made their way over the shifting shale paths and the occasional wooden stile were here for a different reason.

Craig Pearson, a social worker, was twenty-eight years old. Six years of toil with Luton Social Services had made him a thin, gangly man with a ready wit. He was bearded (*weren't all social workers bearded?*), pissed off and knackered. They'd come miles, or so it seemed in a constantly upward direction of the mountain. They had to be near the top soon.

Perry Willis, Craig's partner, puffed and panted. He was a stone overweight from too many Saturday night curries and not enough exercise. Social worker, minus the beard (an individualist!). His ruddy cheeks made him look like Santa Claus. He was well hacked off with this. Five years of dealing with irate families, screaming kids, illiterate teenagers and fatuous councillors was beginning to grate on his normally reserved demeanour. He pulled up sharply.
"Where the hell are we Craig?"
His partner stood with his hands on his hips, regaining his breath and gazing at the surrounding walls of

prehistoric rock. He took out a map and mentally compared it with the salient points around them.
"Nearly there. It gets tougher soon though because the paths change to a softer shale for the last half mile. I climbed this four years ago. It's a killer so be prepared for three steps forwards, two back, I'm afraid."
"Fuck, that's all I need!" spat Perry. He stared hard at the third member of the merry band.

Trevor Beckinsale was a car thief and petty crook of the highest order. Thirteen charges to date ranging from aggravated burglary to GBH. His designer stubble, imitating one of those young, hip pop groups and far from enhancing the image of youth culture, only served to exaggerate his insalubrious appearance. Perry drew on a cigarette and eyed their charge distastefully.
"What's up fat boy, can't hack the pace?" sneered Beckinsale.
"Oi, calm down Beckinsale. If it wasn't for you, we wouldn't be here," Craig butted in sharply.
"Tough, I'm enjoying it! I'd rather be kicking ass on the estates but it's just as much a workout!"
Perry grabbed him roughly by the collar.
"Listen to me Beckinsale, I don't like you! Fucking social services indeed. You should have been locked up. We're not here to have FUN!"
"Listen fatty, this is part of my being accepted back into the community innit?" chortled the sullen youth.
"That's bollocks! It just keeps you away from the poor buggers you terrorise week in, week out."

Craig tried to interrupt.
"Lads, lads - come on. We're nearly there. Let's not spoil it. We've done very well so far, haven't we?"

"Done very well?" moaned Perry, "I'm absolutely fucked and it's all down to this little snotrag here."
"Diddums den," sneered Beckinsale, giggling at the contention he had generated.
"Come on, let's go," urged Craig, enthusiastically setting off again up the winding path.

Perry's anger simmered as they clambered slowly on upward. The mist that covered the tops of the mountain now began to engulf them, eddying around and mingling with their visible breaths as they gasped in the thinner air. He was at the rear of the group. Craig led, carrying the plastic-covered map and guide. Trevor Beckinsale tramped in the middle of the group. The gravel gave way to the softer shale Craig had mentioned earlier.

Perry thought about the meeting he had attended two nights earlier and the job he had to do today...

****

Perry had joined 'The Brothers' two months previously. It had been a chance meeting in the local library. The conversation he had had with Pierre Miller had changed his life forever. They had accidentally bumped into one another in the crime section. Miller had been reading a book concerned with social injustice, a subject which matched Perry's own strong ideals.

Two hours and a gallon of black coffee later, he was embroiled in a completely new world; a world where wrong would be righted and where the innocent would defeat the perpetrators of crime.

Miller was a lawyer, big in the London area, and part of a new underground movement calling itself the 'Brothers of Justice'. The movement had been in force for just under a year and its leaders were always on the lookout for new 'disciples', as Miller put it.

Perry was a member within three weeks. The oath held all of his ideals and summarised how he felt totally. The cheque he had received on his recruitment was a godsend. £15,000 on the spot! He couldn't have dreamed of such a fortune a month earlier. It was like his ship had come in, docked and been dismantled all in one fell swoop.

It was at the second meeting he was given his first 'tasking'.
The leader of the 'Brothers' spoke, "This youth is of no real use to society. He has singlehandedly terrorised a small, middle-class estate in Loughborough for over five years. His reign of terror began at the age of eleven. By the age of fourteen he could drive high performance cars and in spite of being caught and cautioned he was released on no fewer than twelve occasions! His latest offence was grievous bodily harm. He beat and robbed a seventy-two year old man, a veteran of the first world war. He was given a supervision order and told to pay six hundred pounds compensation. Of course, he won't pay and his age means he can literally get away with anything short of murder. The man he assaulted and robbed is now frightened to unlock his front door, especially at night. Brother Willis is tasked to eliminate Mr Beckinsale."

Perry recalled the surge of adrenalin as he was given his first task.

"He will be aided by Brother Pearson," continued the leader, as they both hail from the same area.
Murmurs of approval from the committee gave Perry the confidence he required. Each and every member shook him warmly by the hand and gave their approval to the plan.
"Do it Perry!"
"Good luck young lad. Eliminate this idiot!"
"We're all on your side. Get it done!"

****

The climb was getting more arduous by the yard. The shale shifted under their feet, as they pushed onwards and upwards, and it was almost vertical in the mist.
"Piece of piss," whispered Beckinsale hoarsely.

Perry felt his anger rise again. Soon. It will be soon you piece of shit, he thought.

Craig came to a halt.
"What's up?" asked Perry.
"We've got to be careful. There's a sheer drop coming up in about two hundred metres. One false move and it's curtains in these conditions," declared Craig.
The fog was thicker than ever. The two 'Brothers' looked at each other knowingly. Trevor Beckinsale was too busy retying his bootlaces to see the wink from Perry. Craig nodded his affirmation. The three shadows moved off again, into the chilling mist.
Perry's breathing was coming in fits and starts. Every time he took a step the shale shifted like sand beneath his feet. It was like climbing up a downward escalator. His calf muscles screamed in pain at the effort of it all.

What the hell am I doing here, he thought. I'm a bloody social worker, not an adventure training expert, for God's sake!
Luckily, Craig had all the qualifications necessary for the trip. He was also twice as fit. This was like eating strawberries for him.
That smug bastard. Beckinsale hadn't a clue what to expect. Perry grimaced with a certain pleasure as he pulled himself onto level ground at last.

Craig spoke calmly, "This is the bit I meant. It's about a four hundred metre drop either side so be very, very careful OK?"
He looked at Perry, then Beckinsale intently.
Perry leaned outwards, peering into the blackness below. His vision was impeded by the swirling mist. He could see about ten feet but beyond was a dense cloud.
"Spot on!" said Beckinsale cockily.
"Let's go," Craig motioned the other two to follow along the narrow level path. He walked with the utmost caution, Perry bringing up the rear and watching every step that Beckinsale took.

After about twenty metres, Perry started whistling and Craig joined in.
"Fun or what?" Craig shouted to his rear.
"No sweat," murmured Beckinsale slowly.
He had literally taken only three more steps when he felt the hand on his shoulder. An instant frisson of dread overtook him. It was the feeling you have when someone feigns to push you off a bridge or into a canal.
Only this time, he sensed this was no game. It was for real!

Beckinsale was tripped and pushed at the same time. His balance was lost in an instant. The heavy rucksack on his back shifted to the left, taking him with it. He left the pathway and his figure arced through the foggy void. He had no chance to speak. White with terror, he disappeared over the precipice and into oblivion. His thin screams lasted about four seconds. No impact was heard.

Perry looked at Craig and no emotion showed on his face. "Well, you did say be careful," he drily observed. A faint smile played on his lips.
"The boy who could fly! We just met Peter Pan!" chuckled Craig.

They moved towards one another. They embraced.
" 'Justice to the innocent," Craig said in a whisper.
"We must report this," said Perry flatly.
"I know. Just an accident. It happens all the time up here. Stupid bastard slipped. Where are the witnesses?" Craig smiled at his deductions.
"He had the fucking coffee flask too..." murmured Perry with a wry grin.
"Little bastard!"
The two men turned and began the slow descent into the valley; their mission complete. They whistled shrilly in time with their steps. They nodded intermittently at walkers coming up from the other direction.

The fog followed them down the mountain and a beautiful silence descended once more on Snowdon...

****

Chapter Eight

Phil Queen was on edge. Today was the day his future would be mapped out in front of him. Trial by his own. He hadn't slept at all well. He felt physically drained. The ochre colour of his skin gave it away. He sipped an Alka-Seltzer – his life saver. All day yesterday a steady stream of well-wishers had phoned him or tried to boost his morale.

"You'll get off no problem."

"Should never have come to this."

"We're all gunning for you Phil."

He'd smiled an embarrassed smile for all his fans and tried to get on with his job, just like any other day. However, the self-doubt and anxiety kept gnawing away at his gut. He felt like a schoolboy again; waiting to turn over the examination paper, only to see questions he couldn't answer. Or like the time he took his Army swimming test. He hated jumping in the deep end. The same pit of the stomach feeling as he stood on the edge of the pool. The jump. The splash. The coming up for that gasp of air.

Today, all he could see was the Super's face across the table leering at him. He was a lamb for the slaughter, make no mistake.

Chloe had phoned him last night. Her reassuring voice was small comfort.

"You're too good a policeman to be treated this way," she said.

Phil had tried to agree but he knew that he'd cocked up. But did it really warrant the Chief Constable of the division and two independent observers to sit in and dissect his career? All this for forgetting to empty a sodding rubbish bin! That's the bottom line, he thought. A poxy waste bin!

He dressed in a suit. The tie was knotted tightly and it made him feel more nauseous. He paused before the full length mirror on the wardrobe and his wry smile looked back at him. "Morning gorgeous..." he murmured softly as he squared his shoulders. Picking up his grey overcoat, he headed for the front door.

The telephone rang.

Phil retraced his steps and lifted the receiver.

"Hello," he spoke impatiently.

"Mr. Queen is it?" a low voice enquired.

"Yes, who's speaking?"

"You don't know me but I've heard about you. Can we meet?"

Phil frowned. The disembodied voice had a north east accent. Phil pictured Jimmy Nail in his minds eye. "Who are you?" His eyes caught the clock on the mantelpiece. It was eight o'clock. Going to be late he thought...

"You don't need to know yet. Meet me tonight. I shall be at the entrance to the Redmond cinema complex – seven-thirty sharp. Please be there."

"But..." The phone went dead with a click.

Phil slowly replaced the receiver, his frown deepening. "Interesting..." he muttered.

He wasn't working this evening so he could go or he could say stuff it. There was a knowing tone to the person's voice, as if he knew Phil would appear. He knew of Phil but from whom? It didn't sound like a hoax. Things were getting rather strange.
He headed for the door once more. He paused - silence.

With a sharp intake of breath, he slammed the door behind him. It was raining as he pulled away from the kerb in the blue Sierra.

He didn't see the figure across the road, leaving the telephone kiosk. The man limped to a waiting vehicle, entering the passenger side. A nod of the head and the car slowly pulled away with its windscreen wipers intermittently clearing the steady fall of rain.

****

Gary Hart toyed with his breakfast. The sausage was only half cooked, the egg watery and the bacon could have been used to sole the boot of a navvy. "Shite, shite, shite!" he shouted while throwing the metal tray across the cell. He just missing the waste bucket.
The viewing hole in the door opened with a click.
"Temper, temper Gary!" said the officer.
"Fuck off, I ain't eatin' this crap!"
"Fine, you can starve then."
"I want cereal!"
"Want?"
"Yeah, want!"

You can want as much as you like. Whether you'll get it is another matter, diddums."

The officer's eyes glared down at the malevolent boy.
"I'm hungry," Gary whined.
"Then eat your breakfast honey," drawled the officer, imitating a southern American sneer.
The hole slammed shut.
"Bollocks!" screamed Hart as he kicked the wall.

The laughter of the officer drifted back down the corridor.
"See you later alligator..." came the distant reply.

****

Phil sat outside the division conference room. He could hear the tinkling of glass and laughter. The joke must have been a good one.

The door opened. A rather pretty WPC appeared, carrying a coffee jug and an empty tray.
"Vultures! Two packets of McVities gone in an instant!" she said with a smile.
Phil tried to smile back but he failed miserably.

He sat opposite a wall of notices: a Drink-Drive campaign, Know Your Local Bobby competition forms and a variety of pro-police advertisements. They danced before his eyes. He leaned back and closed his eyes and swallowed hard. The next hour could be the most important of his life.

His eyes followed the WPC as she walked down the corridor. Very nice, he thought. At least she's not in the shit.

It was five minutes to nine. His mind drifted back to the earlier telephone call from Jimmy Nail. It had sounded like something out of an old B movie or a James Bond story. This sort of thing happened in America with the FBI or CIA.
'I've heard about you...'

He tried to think of an answer. Perhaps someone had seen him play football and wanted to recruit him for a team. But why the cloak and dagger bit? Maybe the Samaritans were desperate for new blood and this was their new gimmick?

The door opened again. A head poked out.
"Sergeant Philip Queen?"
"Yes," replied Phil standing up.
"Please do come in. Have you waited long?"
"Only for ten or fifteen minutes."

Phil entered the lions' den with his coat in hand.
The long table could have staged a medieval banquet. Three figures sat at the table. The man who had opened the door scurried over to a separate table where a typewriter sat. Secretary, presumably, though Phil.
A single chair was positioned opposite the three wise monkeys. (*See no evil, hear no...*) Stoppit!

"Sergeant Queen, please do sit down," the central figure indicated the chair.
"Thank you sir," said Queen.
"Feel free to drink." A carafe of water and a glass had been provided on a small table near to Phil.

Phil nodded nervously.
"Now, let's see... I think introductions are in order, don't you?" Phil nodded.

The man in the middle was of a wiry physique, sharp eyed with a moustache. He played with a pen as he spoke. This made Phil uneasy.

"I am Chief Constable Whittingham. To my left is Superintendent Charles from Kent and to my right is Superintendent Lewis from Cumbria."
"Good morning," Phil nodded to each of the men sitting like lords in front of him.
"Now, the case in hand..."
Phil fidgeted nervously. He poured some water into the glass. He needed something to hold.

"Sergeant Queen, I have read the report from your superior. I'm of the view that you behaved in a negligent and undisciplined manner regarding both the hygiene of your station and the smooth running of the administration. However, your previous record is exceptional and you appear to have come a long way in a short time. This may have been a factor in your behaviour. Over confidence perhaps? Certainly, your slackness has not been seen before."

Phil listened intently. The only other sound was the tap, tap of the secretary's typewriter. (*He's a bloody fast typist, Phil thought)*. As the Chief stopped speaking, the tapping ceased not a second later. (*Ten out of ten!)*

"I realise that you had certain other things on your mind that day, but a rather cavalier attitude clouded your judgement, I feel. You may well have left the station for richer pickings but this does not, in any way, mean that I should condone your actions."

Phil whispered and nodded with wide eyes, "Yes sir."
The Chief Constable shifted in his seat. Leaning forward, as if to emphasise the words as he spoke. One of the other figures coughed.
"Excuse me," he mumbled. (*How would the typist spell a cough, Phil thought stifling a smile.*)

"... Do you have anything to say Sergeant Queen?"
Phil placed the glass on the table.
"Well sir, I can understand the anger of certain people over my actions that day. However, I never intended any embarrassment for anyone. It was heat of the moment stuff really. I wanted the kid, Gary Hart, brought in as soon as possible. Finding the body of Miss... the young lady in question would probably have been delayed by days if I had not followed up the call from her boss. I put two and two together when he gave her name because it was the same name as the girl who had reported being attacked. It all fell into a piece and I left the station to make the enquiry at the flat. The fact that since that morning, I single-handedly captured the young man responsible should, I feel, outweigh anything that happened in the station that morning. I do apologise unreservedly for my behaviour but I'm more concerned that the situation in the station, by comparison, seems trivial in the light of the subsequent events. We do appear to have solved a murder here."

Phil felt good. He had said his piece without interruption. His body was visibly relaxed as he awaited the reaction of the three stooges.

"Trivial?!"
The tone of the Chief Constable shocked Phil.
"Did you say 'trivial' Sergeant?"
The two observers shuffled in their seats and Phil suddenly felt very uneasy.
"Well, er... yes sir... I suppose..."
"You suppose nothing!"
The secretary's tap, tap, tap ceased again.
"I think you fail to see my point Sergeant Queen! You're not here to... to trivialise a disciplinary hearing! You're here to be punished! Your attitude here this morning leaves a lot to be desired young man! I was hoping that you'd have seen the error of your ways. However, quite contrary to this, you seem to be proud of your misdemeanours."

Phil's eyes drifted from one man to the next. The two observers had hardly said a word. One cough was all he had heard from them. (*Thanks a lot*!)

The Chief Constable droned on, "...satisfactorily... I'm going to recommend that you're unfit to hold your current rank. You'll be demoted to Constable!"

Phil blinked incredulously.
"Demoted?!"

Whittingham was unmoved. He silently scrawled on a notepad.
"Sir, did you say 'demoted'?"
The Chief looked up slowly and stopped writing.
"Yes, I said demoted. Sergeant." he flatly replied with his voice brooking no argument.

Phil's mind whirled. A hundred emotions flashed through his brain.
Surely he didn't mean it but He'd said so. Demotion to Constable!
The bastard was demoting him for not emptying a bin! Catching a murderer meant nothing!
Paranoia took over.
"You're all in this together, aren't you?" Phil blurted out, as if in a nightmare.
Whittingham stopped writing again.
"What did you say?"
"You heard sir! I said, you're all in it together. I could have found Lord Lucan that day and I'd still have been stitched up. Badger put you up to this, didn't he?"

The two Superintendents shifted uneasily again in their chairs. The wood creaked as they nervously changed position. One of them coughed again.
Phil rounded on them both.
"You two have been a great help! What an inspiration to any young, aspiring policeman!"
He stared coldly at Lewis and Charles. Lewis was open-mouthed. This pleased Phil.
"Thanks for your undiluted support. Nothing I could have said would have helped, would it? I was guilty before I even sat down!"

"BE QUIET!"
Whittingham's eyes were like black holes. Phil continued. He was enjoying himself.
"Quiet? You must be joking!"
Whittingham recoiled as if he'd been struck physically.

"I RESIGN!" blurted Phil standing up sharply. He didn't care now.

"It'll save you a lot of paperwork."

The three officers looked as if they'd witnessed the second coming. Phil turned to leave.

"Where are you going?" Whittingham's voice sounded choked and he had a panic-stricken look on his pale face.

"To get another job of course!" replied Phil wildly.

He looked across at the secretary and said, "Did you get that on record matey?"

The typing stopped.

"Yes... yes, of course..." his eyes were wide with amazement at this turn of events.

Phil glowered at the shocked conspirators.

"Give my regards to Clive old chap and I'll pay him a visit when I've got time."

Phil turned and opened the door to leave. The young WPC stood there with yet another tray of luxury biscuits. Phil chose a chocolate digestive, winked at the startled girl and made his exit, slamming the door on exit.

"More biscuits sirs?" the WPC enquired as she crossed the room, blushing profusely...

****

Phil spent the afternoon sitting in the park watching the world go by. It was a simple activity, one in which he had not indulged for some years. He watched strangers walking dogs, children playing with Frisbees and lovers strolling hand-in-hand. He contemplated his own reaction to his outburst of the morning. He realised it had been a knee-jerk response to being treated so shabbily by his so-called superiors. He smiled wryly to himself as he recollected the expression on Whittingham's face. He likened it to being slapped in the mouth with a wet fish.

But he'd done it. Resigned. Finito. No job; no future. From Sergeant to dole queue in five seconds. A new world record?

A young child sped past on a bicycle. Phil saw himself on the bike. The bike his Dad had rescued from the skip in 1974. It was his pride and joy. It wasn't a Raleigh 'Chopper' like his friends had. It was a bog-standard bike. The chipped paintwork and faulty left brake was fixed and Phil rode it with pride doing his errands. Bert, the corner shop keeper, would always comment on it. Said he could hear him coming by the squeak of the wheels. Phil smiled at the memory...

Then, he saw Gary Hart. In his mind's eye, he was sitting in his cell staring at him.

"Come and get me Mr Policeman..." Hart whispered.

Phil jerked back to reality. He would have to go in tomorrow and explain the reasoning behind his shock decision. He knew, deep down, that he really didn't want to leave. Personal pride was the primary factor. To go back to the routine of being a beat constable after tasting the full life of the higher rank and the responsibility that went with it, would be too much to bear.

The back-stabbers and snipers would have a field day. Phil could see himself sitting with his tea and toast in the canteen, hidden behind his newspaper, shielding himself from the stares and whispers, nods and winks that came to anyone who was in the crap. He wouldn't get many sympathy votes.

The sycophants would be there too. Platitude after platitude.

"Well done Phil, you stood up to the bastards, eh?"

"Sorry to hear about your leaving."

All they really meant was tough shit, sucker Queen! Two faced bastards.

He needed to speak to Chloe again. He wouldn't be needed at the Hart hearing now. Not as a policeman anyway. He could see it now...

"Mr Queen has since resigned from the force."

So be it, he thought.

Then he recalled the strange phone call that morning.

"You don't know me, but..."

Who was it?

He could find out tonight if he chose to keep the appointment to meet the caller. He was both puzzled and intrigued. Someone wanted him for something but what? A pool's win? A long-lost cousin from Newcastle? He didn't feel threatened by the call though. Go for it! There may even be a job in it for God's sake!

Phil stood up and stretched. It was five o'clock. Three hours to the showdown at the Redmond cinema complex with his mystery caller. Time to go home to freshen up, phone Chloe with the day's news and have a bite to eat.

It would soon be time to meet the 'tall, dark and handsome' stranger...

He walked towards the exit gates of the park. He didn't notice the tall figure near the bandstand. The man limped away in the opposite direction to a waiting black BMW.

****

Chapter Nine

Chloe poured herself a sherry and sat at the large desk. A hard day's trading in the shop brought its rewards. She had sold an antique chair for five hundred pounds to a Swedish collector that morning. He had paid cash 'on the nose' as he put it in his quaint foreign accent. Chloe's Swedish was useless; not her favourite language. However, she had 'A' levels in French and German. The man was on an antique shopping trip and had spent over seven thousand pounds on his latest sojourn. He loved the English countryside, he had told her, and had even bought a small house in Brighton in order to have an English seaside break every year. Nice work if you can get it, thought Chloe.

She scanned the morning paper. One headline caught her eye. **'JUDGE'S WIFE IN RAPE PERIL!'** it screamed.

Apparently, one of London's most learned judges had come home to find his badly beaten wife trussed up after a vicious assault. A rape had apparently ensued by somebody who had left a note criticising the judge's sentencing ability.

This made a change, thought Chloe. Maybe he'd change his tune next time he was faced by a smug, smiling thug opposite him in the dock. Too often lately, the criminal fraternity laughed blatantly in the face of the judiciary. Their crimes were trivialised by liberal old lags in wigs.

Chloe shivered. She felt a wave of sympathy for the Judge's wife. No one had been caught. Even if they were captured, thought Chloe cynically, they would most likely be given a suspended sentence with a requirement to take a rock climbing holiday in the south of France. Where were the deterrents these days?

Her musings were cut short by the ringing of the telephone. She took a sip of her sherry and lifted the receiver.
"Hello?"
"Hi, it's me Phil."
"Hello Phil, how are you?" Chloe's voice reflected her pleasure at hearing his name.
"Fine, fine... Well actually I'm not fine," Phil replied, his tone betraying his mood.

Chloe slowly sat down and asked, "Why, what's happened?" She prepared herself for bad news.
"Well yes, I'm fine. I'm just out of a job that's all," Phil replied matter of factly.
"What?!"
"I resigned Chloe. This morning at the disciplinary hearing. They made me mad. They were going to bust me back to Constable so I've packed it all in."
Phil sounded at a very low ebb.
"No, I don't believe it! You did nothing wrong Phil," assured Chloe.
Chloe's eyes were wide with disbelief.

"I know that. You know that. They didn't quite see it that way. I think Badger, my boss, knew all along what the outcome would be."

"You mean you've been set up?" Chloe queried.

"Well yes, I mean... it seems that way. He must have known it would come to this. I'm not normally paranoid but I felt that this morning. I just blew my top Chloe."

Chloe took a sharp slug of her sherry.

"Can you retract your decision to resign?" Chloe asked.

"I could but I don't want to," said Phil, "I couldn't face all my colleagues' false sympathy."

"Pride comes before a fall, in most cases, not after it," laughed Chloe in an attempt to lighten Phil's gloom.

"Yes, I suppose so," agreed Phil quietly, "Chloe, can I see you? I think I need a shoulder to cry on."

He sounded totally disconsolate.

"Of course. I'm very sorry, Phil. I can't understand it. You were doing such a great job with the Hart kid and all..."

"Yes, I know. I don't know if I'll still have to give evidence because I'm officially off the case now. Hart will get a shock when he finds out I'm unemployed."

"The newspapers will have a great time too. It's right up their street."

"Yes, I can't wait. Fame at last!" enjoined Phil, his sarcastic humour making a small reappearance. "I'm going in tomorrow to clear my desk. They'll be putting up the bunting and balloons by now I imagine!"

Chloe declared, "No way, you'll be sorely missed."

"Not by everyone. There's always someone waiting their chance to move upwards and onwards. And I bet Badger's having a good gloat!"

"You may have turned the tables on him Phil. He may have some explaining to do as to how the force has lost one of their superstars," said Chloe trying to show some support.

"I never thought of that. Maybe you're right. Thanks Chloe."

"You're welcome," Chloe smiled, "Cheer up, it may be a blessing in disguise!"

"Well, perhaps. I may as well start being positive again. Listen, how about dinner tomorrow night?"

"Sounds perfect."

"Fine, I'll pick you up about eight?"

"Great, see you tomorrow."

The phone clicked off.

Chloe shook her head and stared out into her garden.

"Poor Phil..." she whispered.

She poured another sherry and went into the bathroom. She needed a good long soak to relax and time to think... It will wash away the troubles, she thought.

Unbeknown to her, however, they were just beginning...

****

Phil dressed himself carefully. He wore a dark blue suit, pale shirt and a scarlet tie. He slicked back his strong hair and he'd trimmed his moustache considerably.

He stood in front of the mirror. He looked good.

I'll dress like this tomorrow for Chloe, he thought. She'll be putty in my hands. He welcomed the return of his confidence, winked at himself and turned to leave the house.

He hadn't been to the flicks for ages. Maybe there would be time to take in a movie after his mysterious 'appointment'. The latest goodie versus baddie was showing. One man takes on a whole army, falls for the downtrodden woman and walks into the sunset, carefree and unhurt. It would be Schwarzenegger or Willis - the usual indestructibles. Five star violence for all the would be heroes in the balcony. Thirty-five baddies slaughtered in the final reel by one man wielding a six shooter and a Swiss army knife! God, I'm getting bitter and twisted, he thought.

He parked up in the short stay car park, put coins in the meter and claimed his ticket. He stuck it on his offside windscreen and locked the car.

A wolf whistle from two passing teenage girls made him grin appreciatively. Ten years ago, I'd have been in there he gloomily thought.

He walked towards the cinema. The pit of his stomach suddenly lurched with apprehension. My first blind date with a bloke, he thought. How would he know who to approach? He didn't fancy propositioning the wrong man. Could be a mite embarrassing!

As he turned the corner to the vast cinema complex, he had the familiar sensation of being watched. A sixth sense caused the hair on the nape of his neck to rise. So, it doesn't just happen in the movies he realised. It was ten past seven. He was early.
He crossed the road and entered a small snack bar. He ordered a black coffee and sat next to the main frontage

window. He scanned the entrance to the cinema for any clues as to his 'date'. It was impossible. About a hundred or more teenagers milled around, screaming, laughing and pushing. They were all there to see a remake of the remake of some obscure western. Bags of fun, thought Phil. Maybe Mel Gibson had something to do with it. He slowly sipped his cooling coffee.

A man came into the cafe, or rather limped in. He had no stick to aid him. He definitely had a military bearing, mused Phil as he saw the tall, muscular man with short, cropped hair. Only the limp seemed to hinder him.

Phil resumed his watch on the antics across the street. Still no sign of his man.

"Mr Queen?"
Phil whirled around in his seat.
The man with the limp stood behind him.
"Yes, that's me."
"Good. I'm Kenneth Jamieson. We spoke this morning," said the man with the limp as he offered his hand.

Phil stood up and firmly shook hands while making eye contact.
"Yes, right. Let's sit down..."
"No, not here. My car is waiting," said the stranger.
Jamieson nodded in the direction of the cinema. Phil peered through the glass and saw a dark BMW parked alongside the cinema's car park.
"What we have to discuss is not for public consumption," Jamieson remarked quietly as he eyed the other customers.
Phil felt somewhat unnerved by this information.

"At least tell me what this is all about. My mum always told me never to accept lifts from strangers," Phil joked. Phil's new best friend did not smile back.
"Sorry, I feel like I'm in some kind of James Bond movie at the moment - forgive me."
"Everything will become clear, once we are alone," replied Jamieson.

Phil noticed a long scar on the mans' forehead. It looked quite a recent injury. The man was obviously very fit, apart from his limp. Strangely, Phil didn't feel at all threatened by the stranger so far.

"OK, I'll come," Phil finally agreed.
"Good. You can eat with me tonight."
Phil detected the familiar Geordie accent in the man's voice.
"My friends have prepared a meal for us. Please do come, time is getting on."
Phil followed the tall figure out of the Cafe. As they emerged, the BMW approached and pulled up alongside them, after doing a sharp U-turn.
"It's not far. A matter of minutes," said Jamieson as Phil climbed into the back of the car.
"Good. I hate long journeys," Phil replied.

He noticed the driver was a West Indian of huge proportions. Jamieson turned, wincing slightly.
"Meet my chauffeur, Parker," as he put on his seat belt.
"Hi," Phil stifled a laugh.
"It's his real name - Parker Abbotsbury. He hates any reference to Thunderbirds or Lady Penelope so please remember that."

"No problem," Phil replied warily.
Parker looked like a pit bull in a suit!

Parker eyed him in the rear view mirror. Phil nodded with a smile but Parker didn't smile back.
"Parker can't speak. He's mute but his hearing is incredible. He can hear gnats fart at two hundred paces," laughed Jamieson, "He nods or doesn't nod. You'll know if he doesn't agree with you. His facial expression is his only method of communicating, other than physically."

Phil listened but made no reply. Who is this man? What does he want?
"We'll be there in a minute. Are you hungry?"
"To be frank, I'm a bit more interested in why I'm here."
"All in good time Mr Queen. May I call you Phillip?"
"How did you..? Yes, Phil's fine."
Phil frowned. Here he was with a mute guy and a total stranger being driven to some unknown location in a top of the range BMW.
Curiouser and curiouser, he thought.

The car was now in lush countryside. They'd only been travelling a matter of minutes. Then, they turned into a long drive. Trees stood on either side like a green guard of honour. A large house came into view about a half mile further on. A mansion, more like, thought Phil.

Parker pulled up beside the entrance. They stepped out onto the gravel.

"Welcome to Gardenstone Manor," the stranger said with a beaming smile - the first to cross his features since their meeting.

The front door opened. Another man; another stranger.
"Meet my brother, Maurice."

"Hi!" Phil looked up at the man at the top of the steps.
"So glad you could come." Maurice's accent was identical with that of his brother.
"Come in mate."

Phil climbed the steps. He felt like he was entering the Ghost Train at a fun fair. What next, he wondered as the door closed behind them.

He was led through a brightly lit hallway. A huge chandelier hung from the long patterned ceiling.
These boys are rich, thought Phil.
"Please - in here," said Kenneth placidly, "Don't worry, we won't bite."
This did nothing to allay the feelings in the pit of Phil's stomach.
The dining room they entered was magnificent. Massive portraits of long-dead ancestors looked down on the present benefactors.
Cancel rich. Insert filthy rich, pondered Phil as he was led to a large comfortable chair fashioned in teak.

"These chairs are very valuable. Please refrain from disposing of your chewing gum under the seat!"
"Very droll Moss," Kenneth remarked drily, "I'm sure Mr Queen can understand he is in no ordinary house."
"Of course," said Phil, "I'm on my best behaviour. Do I have to pay for the tour?"

Kenneth and Maurice smiled in unison. They liked Phil already. He had an easy conversational style and they noticed his relaxed yet confident air, in spite of his obvious curiosity and wariness about his position. They needed people like this. Cockiness would not be tolerated. Their contacts had done another good job.

Phil looked around the room again. He was a little overawed but tried not to show it. It felt rather like a job interview but without the pressure. Kenneth and Maurice sat opposite like two lords of the manor which they probably were, he mused.

Kenneth was the older, Phil reasoned. He was evidently the one in charge. Maurice 's servile attitude was obvious. The Colonel and his Lieutenant; he suppressed a wry smile.
"Welcome Mr Queen. Can we call you Phil?"
"Of course."
Phil shifted in his seat. Now he knew what the contestants in 'Mastermind' must feel!

"Please feel free to ask any questions once I have finished. You may call me Ken and you may call Maurice Mo or Moss. I hate long names don't you?"
A song entered Phil's memory suddenly. 'The Joker' by Steve Miller but he dismissed it quickly from his thoughts. He continued, trying to concentrate on the situation in hand.

Phil nodded. He was known as 'Corgi' in the army thanks to his surname. All his mates had nicknames: Smudge Smith, Budgie Burgess, Chalky White - the list could fill a novel.
"The reason you're here will become obvious later. Firstly, a few routine questions. Nothing difficult. I can't

even remember my seven times table by heart!" laughed Ken.

"Phil laughed nervously. It was bloody Mastermind! Then it started.

"We would like to know some things about you. Political leanings?" Ken raised his eyebrows questioningly.

"I buy The Sun so I must be a raving right-wing loyalist!"

"Who do you vote for?"

"I never have, to be honest, what with..."

"Fine!" Ken interrupted, "Favourite food?" He asked as he was jotting notes down on a pad.

"Eh? Oh, erm... Chinese and Italian pasta. I try to keep fit."

"Did you serve in the British Army?"

"Yes," replied Phil.

"Any weapons experience? Close protection? Security training?"

Phil waded in, "SLR, SMG, LMG, pistol trained. 66mm, grenades... I didn't do bomb disposal. I was an MP."

"I know. Close protection?"

"The basics. Nothing any other grunt didn't learn," Phil answered with refreshing honesty.

"Did you see action?"

Phil knew instinctively what was meant.

"Yes, in Northern Ireland."

"Thank you, that's all I need to know."

Phil waited for the next tirade.

"Going back to your fitness training - anything specific?"

"I run, play football and do a bit of self-defence."

Ken raised an eyebrow.

"Tai Kwon Do - six weeks when I was seventeen. Army self-defence; you know," offered Phil.

"Mmmmm. I see. Are you still much cop?"

"I can handle myself."

Phil recalled Gary bolting for the door.

"Good," Ken replied as he scribbled on his pad again. Moss sat impassively. There was a pause.

"Can you swim?" Ken continued.

"Yes."

"Do you smoke?"

"Never."

"Girlfriends?" (*Chloe, Phil wished.*)

"No."

"Do you look for women?" (*Chloe, Phil wished again!)*

"No, not really. My job didn't help," Phil commented.

"I suppose not."

Ken looked at Moss and said, "Anything else Mossy?"

Phil wondered about Chloe. Should he have mentioned her?

Ken spoke again.

"Drink? Drugs?"

"No, but I like a lager shandy on a Sunday evening," Phil murmured slightly embarrassed.

Moss spoke.

"What do you like?" he asked.

"What do you mean?"

"What turns you on in life?"

Phil answered, "My team winning, a bath after a long jog, a nice lasagne and humour."

"Dislikes?"

"Ignorance, violence, loud people, my team losing, er and a bad lasagne," Phil replied.

Ken and Moss both laughed out loud.

"Very good, thanks Phil. I think that's just about it. Moss?"

"No hassle. Excellent!"

Phil's confidence was growing.

"Do I win a teddy bear or another go?"

"No prizes tonight. Sorry, sold out," Moss said as he smiled.

He had ginger hair and wore jeans, sneakers and a T-shirt with the legend **'FRANKIE SAYS NAFF OFF'** in black letters. It showed his age of about thirty-two, thought Phil. The two brothers were about as alike as Abbot and Costello.

Ken placed his notes inside a folder which he handed to Moss and nodded.

Moss rose to leave the table.

"Excuse me Phil. Do you fancy that lager shandy?" asked Ken.

Phil replied, "Yes please, that would be nice."

Moss looked at his brother. "Drink Ken?"

"Whisky and don't forget the ice," Ken scolded.

Moss left the room.

Ken whispered at Phil as he raised his eyes, "He always forgets the flaming ice!"

Phil smiled. He felt at ease now in the strange surroundings.

"Relax! Loosen your tie. You look frazzled!"

Phil frowned, feeling uneasy again.

"Frankly Ken, I just want to know why I'm here?"

Ken let out a sigh.

"Yes, it's time you knew. I'm sorry for all the cloak and dagger shit," he said throwing his arms upwards, "The Brothers demand the utmost secrecy in all our dealings."

Phil straightened in his chair.

"Brothers? I don't understand."

Ken looked directly at Phil, his eyes burning with a new intensity.

"Listen carefully Phil. What I'm about to tell you must not be breathed to a living soul. Even your closest family must never know this information."

Phil's mouth felt dry. He wasn't far off with his James Bond theory!

"What are you getting at Ken?"

"Tonight you took the first step to becoming one of us. A unique band of men... and some women. Some very young, some as young as seventeen, who have taken it upon themselves to do something worthwhile about the rising level of crime, violence and needless misery inflicted on the innocents in our society."

Phil leaned forward in his chair, eyes widening with interest.

Ken continued, "... We, the Brothers of Justice, have seen fit to set new standards of discipline within society. For months now, we have been growing in strength and numbers. Our recruits have had success as far afield as the north of Scotland. We have cells in ten different areas of the British mainland. Ireland has enough on its plate. We intend expanding into Europe eventually. Then, who knows?"

Phil nodded as his brain absorbed this intriguing information.

"Moss and I are responsible for the catchment area you live in. At present we have forty-eight recruits responsible for four separate counties. You will be our forty-ninth conscript."

Phil interrupted, "You're vigilantes?"

"No, we aren't. Not in the strict sense of the word," Ken responded, "We are the fist of the innocent. We are not

after revenge. We are cleansing the sickness of our nation on a grand scale.
Not all the murders you read about are as random as the police would have you believe."

Ken was noting Phil's reaction. He needed to get Phil to agree with the policies he was describing, otherwise Phil was a liability within the organisation.
"You mean... you kill the killers?" Phil asked thoughtfully.
"Not kill – remove," corrected Ken.
"Phil nodded slowly. Realisation showed in his eyes and his expression.
"I see," Phil whispered.
"Not all these scumbags are eliminated. Many just get a short, sharp warning with threats of worse if they don't change their ways. Only the really lost causes are dispensed with."
"How do you rate them?" asked Phil.
"Top of the list come the really evil ones. Murderers without conscience, child molesters and rapists because they are psychopaths beyond help or reason."
Phil listened intently.
"They don't last long - outside or inside."
"You mean they're bumped off in prison?"
"Spot on! You learn fast Phil," Ken nodded.
"Christ!"
"No, he doesn't help..." Ken commented with a straight face.
Phil laughed a nervous laugh and then asked, "So, how did you get involved then?"

Ken indicated the long, snake-like scar across his forehead.

"See this Phil?"

"Yes, I couldn't help but notice it earlier."

"I got attacked on the tube in London one unfortunate Saturday evening. A gang of glue sniffers decided they were going to smear my face all over the walls. They didn't. Not mine anyway. My wife drew the short straw," his voice trailed away.

"Your wife?" Phil asked as he looked at Ken in shock.

"Yes, she was eight months' pregnant. They kicked her around like a football until she died. Our baby boy too. He would have been one next week."

Phil gasped still in shock, "God, I'm sorry."

"One of the bastards had one of those Stanley knives and he caught me nicely here," Ken pointed to the jagged scar, "But I was lucky. I'm still here."

Ken's eyes closed and he swallowed hard while his fists clenched showing white knuckles.

Phil felt useless.

"So… I thought to myself, do I need this?" Ken suddenly spoke again, "And a little voice said 'do I fuck!' I left the army soon after."

"You were in too?" asked Phil.

"Yes, Major in the Parachute Regiment."

"Para eh? Nice one," Phil remarked approvingly.

"Yes, I loved it but I loved Cheryl more."

Phil spoke again, after a brief silence.

"Your limp... Did the sniffers do that too?"

"Nope, I broke my leg on exercise on Salisbury Plain so no romantic connotations there. I was medically downgraded for my last two years' service. I still get twinges.

I ended up with a desk job in Whitehall. Fucking boring!"

"Yes, I can see what you mean Ken."

Ken rose slowly as he looked at Phil earnestly.

"Haven't put you off, have I?"

Phil thought to himself. Sounds like fun. Fun? Nobbling the scum of society.

It sounded like a privately-run army of sorts.

"How did they advertise?" Phil asked.

"Do you ever read The Times?"

"Never," Phil replied.

"Well, we use a small column in the obituary section. It's all coded. Silly little messages. It's a bit like 'Dateline'. The last one was something about champagne and roses. Beats me sometimes too. The messages are very irregular and they appear at any time. The big boys at the top get them published. The editor is in on all this too. You'd be surprised who we've recruited. Media stars and big financial cats aid our coffers."

"So, do we get paid like mercenaries too?" asked Phil.

"No, not quite. If you do join, and you'd better, you'll receive £15,000 up front. No questions asked."

Phil was stunned.

"That's nearly a year's salary in the army!" Phil interjected.

"I know. Fun, isn't it?" Ken smiled and quipped, "Where's my bloody whisky?"

Then, Ken turned towards the door and said, "Moss, get a move on!"

Phil smiled. He was thirsty after all the discussion.

"Ken, what does Moss do?" Phil asked.

Ken turned and answered, "He's deputy of our cell. I am chief co-ordinator. The big cheese is still fully employed. We all interact. You would work in tandem with us. We'll find you a flat and a secure telephone line."

Phil relaxed. He could handle this.
"Remember, not a word to anybody! That means to your mum, dad, cousin Billy... Got it?"
Phil swallowed and declared, "So I'm in then?"
"Yes, once you've been sworn in."
This is just like the army, thought Phil, and twice the excitement.

Moss re-entered like a butler carrying a silver tray.
"One question," said Phil, "Whose house is this?"
Ken sat once more. He took his iced whisky from the tray.
"This house, my friend, is mine. My wife was third in line to a very wealthy English landowner. This is legacy of her death. A sort of calm after the storm so to speak. My pension helped to secure a comfortable existence after the army. Moss is my butler. Luckily, we get on. Eh Moss?"
"Yeah, no hassles bro."' Moss confirmed.

The North East accent gave the brothers an endearing quality, thought Phil.
"I used to be a shopkeeper in Sunderland," said Moss, "God, I miss that shop. The humbugs were ace."
"Bollocks," laughed Ken.
Moss doubled up in a mocking manner.
Phil laughed out loud at their comic exchange.
"You two should be on the stage," Phil suggested.
"Nah, I prefer castrating paedophiles!" Moss screamed in feigned anger.
"Calm it mate," Ken quietly said.
Phil sensed that Moss was slightly drunk.
"Moss likes his 'home brew' but give me a whisky anytime," commented Ken.

Moss sat down and said, "I've just faxed the file on Phil to the Boss."
"Good, now we wait for a phone call. It shouldn't be long," remarked Ken.
"You're credentials are good. I don't think you'll be turned down," Moss murmured confidently to Phil.

Phil looked at the large paintings which adorned the panelled walls around the table. The room was so high the ceiling was veiled in darkness.
"Who's that?" he asked, pointing to a picture of a rotund man on a horse.
"That's Lord Mitchell Potts. He was the first owner of this fine piece of history," Moss replied with his words slightly slurred.
"Mitch, that's a funny name for a lord," said Phil.
"I bet he'd have liked any name with the money he had. Perhaps Quentin, Jeremy or fat bastard?" Moss countered.
"OK, OK Mossy, leave it out," Ken interrupted as he was looking at his watch.

The phone rang in the hallway and Ken rose and limped out of the room to answer it.
Phil and Moss listened quietly.
"Hello. Yes. Yes," responded Ken.
Moss winked at Phil. Phil sipped his lager and registered the tone of Ken's replies.
"Cheers, see you soon. Many thanks. Goodbye."

Phil watched Ken's face as he returned for some indication of his future. Ken sat down and looked Phil full in the face. He paused for effect.
"You're in!"

Moss stood up and slapped Phil on the back, "Pleased to meet you 'brother'!"
They shook hands.
Phil walked around the table to Ken. They shook hands and embraced.
"Touching," Moss slyly remarked.
"Well done Phil. Don't let us down," Ken commented.
Phil's head whirled. It was like a movie. He half expected Sean Connery to burst in at any moment.
"Thanks," said Phil.
"Time for the Oath," said Ken.

Moss lifted a sheet of paper from a folder and placed it in front of Phil, "Read, sign and shake," said Moss.

Phil began to read. It sounded like something from medieval England. The Ss were shaped like Fs and a red seal and ribbon adorned the space next to where the signature was indicated. It looked archaic, but at the same time impressive, and the wording defined the commitment he would be making to the aims which Ken had already detailed to him. Phil read the flowery prose carefully and signed his name.

Ken and Moss spoke as one, "To the victim, to justice!"
Phil reciprocated. The three men shook hands again and sat down.
"Phew!" Phil wiped imaginary sweat from his forehead.

Ken regarded him seriously, "Remember! Tell no one. Never tell a soul. You're a 'Brother of Justice'. If you break our silence you would be just as much an enemy of the brothers as the next rapist or murderer. Have you got that Phil?"

Phil gazed directly back at Ken for a moment and nodded silently.

Ken handed him a small piece of paper. Phil looked down. It was a cheque for £15,000. He was in.

****

Chapter Ten

He felt like a teenager again. It was some years since he felt like this. The butterflies in his stomach. The inability to eat anything but what was necessary. The thought of HER. Chloe.

Tonight's the night, he said silently to himself as he did his ablutions. He hadn't shaved so carefully for a while either. It was usually a quick scrape with a cheap razor and a splash of cheap cologne. Tonight, however, shaving was a thing of religious importance. One false move, a sharp nick, and the familiar depressing trickle of blood would rush down his neck. He detested it when he cut himself. It took vital minutes to stem the flow with toilet roll, repeatedly checking to see if it was still oozing. The worst part was putting the aftershave on. That was five seconds of sheer agony.

Then, the ritual putting on of the shirt. He recalled an experience when he was in the army. One morning he wasn't on the ball. It was the day of a big Freedom Parade. He hadn't done his 'final checks' and when the RSM began his inspection, it was too late. Blood had trickled down his neck onto the buff collar of his military shirt. He looked like the victim of a rather wayward vampire. He missed the parade, the afternoon party and the chance to pick up a nice young lady. They loved the ceremonial uniforms, sometimes more than they fancied the blokes in them. He smiled at the memory.

No chance of that tonight. His fastidiousness bordered on the insane. He slapped on his most expensive after shave. Something made in Paris. Must be good, he thought. He used to splash on 'Hai Karate'...

He'd pressed all his clothes that morning to forestall a rush job. The smartly tailored suit hung on the wardrobe door. Boxers or knickers? Christ! This could mean the difference between success and failure if he got that far, he mused. Boxers! No contest really. Not too over-the-top? He chose a pair with the least pattern.
Vest? Vest!? You must be kidding!
Socks? Black. White socks are a big no-no unless you're Michael Jackson of course.
Shirt? White? No pattern? No pattern!
Tie? Blue. Non-threatening. He chose a dark blue patterned tie. It would go with the dark suit he'd prepared.
Braces? No, he wasn't a bloody stockbroker.
Phil studied his reflection. Just the jacket to go.
What about shoes? Black - no problem.
Finished! The mirror presented the image. "You shall go to the ball!" Phil laughed out loud at his modesty.
The hair gel gave his hair a totally different look. He combed a large smear into his dark thatch.
Would she like him with a less bushy moustache? Of course she would!

He put his wallet into his inside breast pocket of his jacket, calmly checking for his credit card.

It was seven thirty-two.
They were meeting at a local bistro. A good meal, a few drinks, conversation and then who knows?
He was going to pick up Chloe but he needed a couple of drinks tonight. His visit to the station that morning had been a sad experience. Luckily, Badger wasn't there so he didn't have to face him. As he cleared his desk the rest of the staff had crept into an adjoining office. They had clubbed together to get him a present. Old Jimmy Dodd had given an impromptu speech. One of the younger WPCs had been in tears. Gwen hugged him and told him to keep in touch.

"We'll miss you sexy," Gwen whispered.
It had taken them all off guard.
On leaving, he had telephoned Chloe and asked her if she minded getting to the restaurant under her own steam.
"No problem, I understand Phil," she had replied, "I'll get the train in and we'll take it from there."
He was falling for Chloe. He knew it. Their first embrace had been highly charged. His erection said it all. She was thirty-nine and he was thirty-three. Two attractive, horny adults with no ties. The electricity when they touched had been almost scary.

His taxi would be here soon. He turned the TV on and tuned to the BBC Ceefax service. He'd been out of touch with the news for a couple of days.
The headlines told the same sad story: rapes, murders, political bickering, royal scandal and sport sensations. It was no different from last week, last month or last year, he thought moodily.

Phil knew that the brothers would be in touch again soon. He'd popped into his newsagent and placed an order for The Times from the next day.
His first task could come any day, any time. He'd banked the cheque. The eyes of the clerk at the bank had widened when Phil handed it in.

"Family inheritance," Phil quietly said.
The clerk had winked slyly in silent acknowledgement.

Phil had told Ken that he didn't want to move to a new flat; he was quite happy where he was.
"You may have to," Ken replied, "certain anonymity in our circles is necessary. No, it's vital! I'll see if I can swing it for you to stay where you are but don't count on it. I'll let you know."
His telephone would have to change though. Only family and the brothers could know the new number. The fact that he only contacted his family once in a blue moon pleased Ken and Moss.
"Good. You must go ex-directory," they instructed, "And we'll supply an answering machine."
Phil thought about Chloe. Surely, she could be trusted with the number? He remembered that he had said he had no girlfriends.

Then, the sound of a car horn broke into his train of thought.
Let's go Casanova," Phil whispered as he switched the TV off. He looked out of the window. The taxi was waiting for him.

****

Phil arrived at Gerry's Bistro at five to eight precisely. He gave his name and the waiter led him to his table. It was a non-smoking area, away from the entrance. His instructions had been obeyed to the letter.
He sat alone, studying the menu intently.
"Hi!"
Phil looked up sharply.
Chloe stood over him.
"Oh, Chloe. Sorry, I didn't see you arrive. Please sit down."

She looked divine. Her hair was pinned up. She wore a black strapless dress, black stockings and high stilettos. Phil was putty in her hands tonight.
"You look fabulous Chloe!"
"So do you," Chloe replied; a faint mocking smile betrayed her appreciation of their mutual attraction. She sat down at the table.
"How did you get here?"
"Taxi. I didn't fancy being on a train alone, especially dressed like this."
"Yes, I see. It must have cost a bomb," said Phil and he couldn't take his eyes off her.
"Not really. I knew the driver. He gives me discount so it only cost nine pounds."
"Bloody hell, give me his name and number," laughed Phil as he clutched his chest to fake a heart attack. He felt so secure in Chloe's company.
The small talk continued at a pace.
"How's business Chloe?"
"Great. Three big sales in two days," Chloe told Phil about the Swede and the chair, the Iranian bottle collector and the man from Liverpool who wanted Beatles memorabilia.

"I only had a musty old copy of 'Yellow Submarine' but I sold it for £35! I must get some of John Lennon's old stuff. You never know - he may come back," said Chloe.

"Brilliant, I'm so glad you're doing well after all the recent, er, problems."

"Yes, I know. It's certainly taken my mind off the murder." Chloe's eyes lowered.

Phil changed the subject quickly.

"I'm an unemployment statistic again," Phil volunteered as Chloe leaned forward.

Phil couldn't help staring at her cleavage.

"Oh, yes. Have you finally severed all ties?"

"Yes, I went in this morning as I said earlier. It was quite an emotional experience, I can tell you."

"I'm sure it must have been. I told you they'd miss you. They'll realise their mistake in the long run, I'm sure," Chloe reassured him.

"Drink?" Phil asked as he concentrated at last on the real purpose of their meeting. A waiter hovered at his shoulder. He was a tall, half-caste youth with a goatee beard. He held his pen poised over his notepad.

"Wine please. Preferably red," said Chloe.

"We have a good Rose," the waiter enthused.

"Bring it over," said Phil.

"You can do the tasting," Phil nodded at Chloe. The waiter smiled as he wrote on his pad.

"I'll have a pint of lager shandy thanks."

The waiter nodded and left.

"Well, what do you fancy? To eat?"

Chloe laughed at his subtle pun.

"We'll see," she replied slowly.

Phil was in heaven. She was the lady of his dreams, for sure.

Chloe eyed the menu intently.
"Are we having a starter?" she asked, looking at him over the card.
"Anything and everything. I'm in the money too!"
Phil immediately realised his mistake. He recalled Ken's words.
"In the money eh? And on the dole?" remarked Chloe inquisitively.
"Oh, yeah... I cashed in an insurance policy today. I don't really need it now anyway. I'm on the streets again, so to speak," he lied.
"Oh, I see. Good idea. I suppose you're in a low risk category now?"
"What? Unemployed," laughed Phil.
"No, I mean you're in less danger now you're out of the force."
"Oh yes, I suppose so."

Phil realised that he didn't, indeed, need his current policy any more after all. He would cash it in anyway. The following day, he would phone the company and sever all ties. Nice one!

"I think I'll have the fish. It's an aphrodisiac you know," Chloe teased with dancing eyes and raised her eyebrows.
Take it easy, Phil thought. Cool it... She's toying with you matey.
"Steak and chips for me," he responded.

Chloe smiled. She wanted Phil as much as he wanted her. The ritual had begun. It was years since she had been the seducer.

Anyone watching the beautiful twosome at table three couldn't fail to be impressed. They were made for each other. Two peas in a pod and in prime condition.

The waiter returned with the uncorked wine. He poured a sample into Chloe's glass. She sniffed the aroma, swirled the glass in her hand, sipped the vintage and nodded, "Lovely thank you." The waiter nodded, filled her glass and departed.

Phil sampled his shandy.
"Ready to order?" he asked.
"Ready sir," Chloe saluted in reply as she smiled with her radiant smile.

****

The meal was superb. The conversation was a mish-mash of several topics: racism, favourite comedians, good holidays, disastrous food, the state of the economy, childhood, gardening and ice hockey.

They talked and talked; they couldn't stop.

By the time the dessert was served, they were holding hands across the table. Chloe stared at Phil.
"Thank you, Phil," She sipped her wine thoughtfully.
"No problem."
"No - I mean - I know it's a cliché but I don't know what I'd have done quite honestly these last couple of weeks without your support."
"You're right. It is a cliché," Phil replied with a serious expression crossing his face.
Their laughter caused heads to turn.

Phil said, "Do you realise that we have been the only couple who have been enjoying ourselves in here tonight?" They glanced around the room.

"Yes, it's a sad reflection of society today. Everything you do seems to be frowned upon. People don't enjoy life. They're too busy or too fearful of health or money - whatever. You know, sugar is bad for you and drink less milk because dairy foods are harmful. Your bones get soft without calcium so drink more milk but not the sort with fat in it. Watch your cholesterol... It begins to get confusing so you ignore all the scares and just think - what the hell!

I've got to die of something so I might as well enjoy life while I can." Phil frowned.

"Sorry, I'm on a soapbox again," he halted his diatribe.

"No, Phil. I do understand what you mean. Scaremongering seems to have become an industry today. All it really does is confuse people. Life's too short so let's laugh a little! I've drunk gallons of wine in my adult life and look at me," she shrugged.

Phil realised she was into her second bottle! She was still coherent, however.

"I can handle it. It's my only luxury and it helps me unwind," she said with a smile.

"Yes, I agree. I've never been much of a drinker but I always have a pudding!"

"Oh, so you <u>do</u> have a vice?" Chloe laughed. "Me too, let's order!"

They laughed again, in unison. They were oblivious to the other diners sitting in comparative silence around them.

The waiter approached their table again and his pad opened expectantly. It was so refreshing to serve a cheerful, happy couple, he thought...

****

The satisfying meal ended eventually. Phil toyed with the obligatory chocolate mint and noticed Chloe's glass was almost empty again.

"You don't smoke, do you?" she suddenly asked.

Phil raised his eyebrows.

"No, why?"

"Oh, I just wondered. I hate smoking. My father smoked. The house used to reek of cigarettes so I never stayed long on visits because of it."

"Shame," smiled Phil.

Chloe smiled back, "This relationship would have been a non-starter; that's all sonny boy!" she cagily remarked.

"I reckon I would have given up for you," replied Phil, wondering if he was really being truthful with her.

"Thank you sir," Chloe laughed aloud. The wine was taking effect, thought Phil, in anticipation.

"Waiter!"

The half-caste youth sidled over to the table.

"Sir?"

"Bill please. Thank you." The youth turned sharply and nodded.

"He's been a damn good waiter, hasn't he?" Phil quietly remarked to Chloe.

"Wonderful! He's got a lovely bum too," Chloe commented as she watched the waiter's route back to the till.

"You fancy a toy boy then, do you?" asked Phil slyly, while he narrowed his eyes to tease her.

"No thanks. No need - I've got you, haven't I?"
Her eyes locked on him, as she drained the last of her wine, slowly.
"Your place or mine...?"

Phil shifted in his seat. Here we go, he thought. Don't muck it up...
He leaned forward; taking Chloe's hand in his.
"Do you think we should?" he asked, knowing full well he thought they quite definitely SHOULD.
"Should what?" Chloe raised her eyebrows, teasingly.
"Well, you know... it's late and..."
"Hang on, Phil. What do you mean? I'm not Cinderella and you haven't got a job to go to tomorrow, have you?" she teased.
"Well, no..." Phil considered the situation. He was unprepared for this shift of initiative, but surprisingly he didn't find it unattractive.
"But I think a lie-in could be in order, don't you," Chloe said as she watched his face for a reaction.

Chloe was loving this. It had been an absolute age since she seduced a man. The last time had been about eighteen years ago. She stealthily edged off her left stiletto and underneath the table, her toe teased Phil's leg.

Phil started. His mind was in a whirl. Here he was trying to be a perfect host, and gentleman, and Chloe was coolly engineering him into her bed in a most unladylike fashion. His hormones began dancing a jig!

He looked at Chloe, hoping his confused thoughts were not written across his face. Her full breasts encased in the sheer black dress could be his for the tasting! He fought the urge to climb over the table and plant a kiss on her invitingly full lips.

"Well?" Chloe pursued him with a wily smile while encouraging his wild thoughts.

"Err... whatever you want..." Phil stammered nervously. So much for being putty in my hands, he thought. Chloe had turned the tables on him.

"My place it is then?" Chloe flatly stated. Her eyes were piercing as she awaited his response.

"I'm not arguing - you're the boss tonight," Phil replied in defeat.

Chloe smiled; nibbling a tooth pick.

The waiter returned. "Your bill, sir, madam. I trust you enjoyed your meal?"

Phil studied the slip of paper and said, "Fine, thank you for your attention. Is a cheque OK?"

"A cheque is fine." The tall swarthy waiter's eyes briefly met Chloe's.

She winked. He flushed visibly and glanced at Phil.

"You're wonderful tonight!" Chloe invitingly smiled up at him.

"Oh, err, thank you madam. We do our best."

"I'm sure you do... I'm sure."

"Chloe! Leave him alone," Phil scolded.

"See what your wine has done?" Phil then commented to the waiter. The youth laughed nervously and took the cheque.

"Hang on son." Phil placed a fiver on the tray with the cheque.

"Thank you sir. Thank you very much."

"No problem. We have appreciated your service." The waiter's confidence immediately returned and he smiled at them both as they rose from the table.
Phil glanced at Chloe and asked, "Ready?"
"...and willing," replied Chloe in a conspiratorial whisper.

Phil felt the familiar sensations building in his loins. No first-night nerves now he silently told himself.
"I'll just call a taxi," Phil said.
"Right - see you in a sec' - just popping..." Phil watched her walk away to the cloakroom. He wondered how to contain his erection which was now becoming uncomfortable in the extreme.

****

The taxi drive took forty-five minutes and cost an arm and two legs. No discount this time.
Phil reckoned the £15,000 cheque he'd banked yesterday might just cover the expense of seeing Chloe on a regular basis!

The taxi sped off into the chill night air. They stood at the gate of the cottage. The silence which hung over the village had an eerie sensation. They quietly embraced. They had hardly spoken during the drive. Chloe had nestled her head on his shoulder and stared silently out into the night. Phil had his arm around her shoulders and tried in vain to fight off visions of Chloe naked. His excitement in the restaurant had been difficult to quell, but he could now feel it returning as Chloe opened the small wooden gate.
"Come on, let's get inside. I'm cold."

Her high heels tapped lightly up the path as they made their way to the front door. Phil followed slower, as he negotiated the unfamiliar path in the dim light. He shivered with cold or anticipation. He wasn't sure.

Once inside, they kissed slowly and their tongues entwined. The after-taste of the wine was intoxicating. Phil's hands were clumsy. He wanted her so much, but did not want to seem ignorant in the ways of turning a woman on.

Chloe wanted Phil. She fought the desire to rush into it. Phil's hand pulled her suddenly close and his erection stirred against her. She closed her eyes, savouring the strength of his body in the knowledge that he was hers for the taking. Her hand came round and glided between his legs. Phil's breathing was more laboured.
"Christ!" he gasped urgently.
Chloe spoke, "I want it inside me!"

Phil's hands loosened their hold on her rear and instinctively cupped her breasts.
"Oh my God Phil!"
She frantically untied his tie. His jacket lay discarded on the floor by the door. He had never unbuttoned a shirt so fast. Chloe's dress must have had some quick release gear, he thought dazedly, as it slid to the ground. She stood in sheer black lingerie and her skin was translucent in the dim hall. Phil resisted the urge to push her down on to the carpet, there and then. Where to now he wondered, but his confusion was soon solved.

Chloe fell to her knees and started to undo his belt buckle. "Now! I can't wait," she was muttering.

Phil's head was spinning. He had never expected anything like this, even in his wildest fantasies. They were only feet inside the cottage entrance. His trousers fell and he felt the exquisite release as his erection sprang from its confinement. He sagged against the wall as Chloe's lips enfolded his manhood caressing him like silk. He looked down at her bobbing head. This only happens in the movies, he thought. The sensations that coursed through his body were indescribable and he gave himself.

Chloe was an expert at giving head. She had shocked Phil. She knew it.
As she sucked, his hands grasped her head and she could hear his gasping breaths as his threshold rose. His voice was hoarse as he felt a long lost sensation building.
"Chloe! I'm ... co...co..."
Chloe responded with a murmur without losing her rhythm and the vibration in her throat sent Phil over the edge.
"...come!"
Phil's legs gave way. Chloe swallowed his seed, warm and complete. Her hands cupped his balls. Phil sounded as if his death was close at hand, his breathing laboured and his body shuddered.
"Hmmmm. Delicious," concluded Chloe, wiping her hand across her damp mouth. She looked up at Phil in the half light, smiling wickedly. Her hand still grasped his waning penis. She toyed with it, slowly licking the tip.

"More?" she whispered.

Phil found it difficult to speak. He was seeing stars. "Fuck me! That was incredible!"

"We've only just started." Chloe said. They both climbed to their feet.
She embraced him and kissed him full on the lips, a salutation after her passion.

"You're a sly one," Phil sighed.
"It's been so long since I did anything like this," Chloe whispered, "You bring out the animal in me. Have I shocked you?"

Without waiting for his reply, she took his hand and led him towards the stairs. He tripped over his forgotten trousers, kicked them free and left them in the hall, sniggering slightly.
"Let's go somewhere more comfortable," she invited. As he followed her, he could feel the blood returning to his crotch. Chloe turned him on like no woman he had known.
"My, my - you are enjoying yourself, aren't you?" she grinned, as she noted his resurgence. She unclipped her bra and her freed breasts hung beautifully. Phil kissed each nipple.

The duvet on the double bed was turned down as if in welcome.
"You planned all this, didn't you?" he whispered.
"Of course darling. How could an Aries refuse?" Chloe smiled kneeling in front of him; toying with her breasts. Her eyes closed and she lay back opening her legs, as she discarded the minute black panties. Phil's erection was ready. Chloe sucked her middle finger and moved it below her navel, toying with her vagina.
"Fuck me, now!"

He entered her. Her legs embraced him, locking around his waist. They made love urgently. Chloe was the master; turning him, this way, that way and riding him. She kneeled over him, her body warm as she bit the pillow, waiting for him. Then Phil roughly ordered her onto her knees. He lasted twenty-five minutes before he reached the point of no return once again. Silently, they came back down to earth and lay entwined, their breathing becoming steady at last.

Phil stared at the ceiling. Chloe still wore one stocking; the other had been ripped off in their sexual frenzy. She tugged at the nylon, tossing the last vestige of propriety on to the floor. Satiated, they gazed at each other in mutual pleasure.

Chloe broke the silence, "It's OK. I'm on the pill..."

There was a pause, and then they both laughed. Phil thought, just as well, too late now to regret not putting on a condom. They had succumbed to their lust so fast.
"I must say it was not my main thought," he stated with brutal honesty.
"I know - we didn't exactly indulge in any foreplay, did we?" Chloe dully commented.
"Ah, but will you respect me in the morning?" Phil plaintively asked.
"I suppose so!" Chloe mockingly spat.

They laughed again; pulling each other closer.

"Well, I reckon we're pretty compatible physically," Phil commented.

"Compatible?! Combustible more like," she laughed.

There was silence once more. Phil felt drained. He hadn't been so physically active for months. The last time was a drunken one night stand in Majorca. He had bonked a Spanish waitress on the beach and spent the next 24 hours getting sand out of his nether regions. He winced mentally at the memory.

Chloe felt a warm glow. She had missed sex dreadfully but she wasn't the one to fall into bed with any available stud or old codger. Phil was perfect. She had been struck by his calm intellect. Their first meeting had been business-like, but by the time he left the cottage she knew she wanted him in her bed. Many fantasies later, here he was. It had been worth the wait.
She had two 'cosmic orgasms' in one night. Pete had been good but this good? Never. Phil was all she had ever wanted and more. She could put her vibrator away forever. Masturbation was a hopeless substitute. Like chips without ketchup. Useless!

She looked at the clock radio. It was three-forty-five. She had to be up at eight to open the shop for nine. It was then the idea hit her.
"Phil?"
"M..mmm...?"
Phil moaned and drifted off to sleep; like all men who have come twice in an hour. Chloe smiled - the stronger sex??
"Goodnight... I love you," she whispered. A silent tear trickled down her face.
Phil didn't even hear her. His low calm breathing came in unison with the rise and fall of his chest.

Chloe pulled up the duvet over their sated bodies. She closed her eyes and drifted into unconsciousness.

The cottage was silent once more. The two entwined figures slept as one undisturbed by the early streaks of the dawn...

****

Maurice was cold. He was also bored. Late night radio was tedious. Love ballads intermingled with messages of undying love for those whose earning was done during the hours of darkness.

The car was comfortable though. The reclining seat only served to make Mo sleepier. He had followed Phil at a cautious distance following their meeting. It was just a hunch - a gut feeling. How right he had been! By his failure to mention this girlfriend, Phil had broken one of the cardinal rules of their system. He was just the type they were anxious to recruit. But now, the future looked bleak for Phil. All he needed to do was to tell the truth, but could they really trust him now? How much might he have told this mystery lady? She looked fairly classy. But was she a threat to the smooth secret running of the organisation?

Maurice drew in a deep breath and eased his aching body in the restrictive space of the driving seat. He felt the hunger pangs which had been gnawing since he had left the restaurant. He'd concentrated on his task of watching the pair of lovebirds eat their romantic meal. His concealed position behind a large pot of ornamental fake plastic greenery allowed him to observe their every move. They only had eyes for each other, fortunately, and it was apparent the relationship was mutually satisfying, judging by their animated conversation and expressions as the meal progressed at a leisurely pace.

Maurice had restricted his intake to a prawn cocktail and two coffees during his two-hour surveillance and he was now regretting his choice. His stomach gurgled and groaned, crying out for a burger and chips. At one o'clock in the morning in this quaint country village, a burger van would have looked as credible as tits on a frog! He crossed his arms and hugged himself against the cold. To start up the engine would be a mistake. The couple had only just entered the house and no lights appeared. They must have got down to business pretty sharpish, he thought. Lucky sods! She was attractive, whoever she was. Was it her house or his? Whatever, she would have to be visited and checked out.

At this moment, all he longed for was a good long hot drink and a warm duvet. A light mist had fallen on the village, giving an eerie atmosphere. In the distance, a lone bird piped a signal note. Maurice had counted only one other vehicle passing through since he had parked thirty metres from the cottage. He checked his waterproof wristwatch. It was one-eighteen. He considered the position. To stay, getting more and more chilled and hungry or to leave? He needed to make a decision - stick or twist?

If he hung about, what was the chance of seeing anything of any use? Very little. Phil obviously had things other than work on his agenda tonight. If I leave, he thought,

I could be in bed by two-thirty, outside of a cup of tea and a sarnie. He sat and pondered.

Twist! No contest, but he gave it another five minutes just to be sure.

He gently turned the ignition key and gave as little gas as he could. The car started up almost silently. No headlights yet. He peered at the darkened cottage for forty seconds for any sign of a flickering curtain.

Nothing.

He imagined Phil and his lady, rutting in wild abandon. A faint smile appeared on his tired face as he cautiously U-turned the sleek car and left the village. His job accomplished.

****

Chapter Eleven

Chloe woke at six-thirty sharp. The radio had eased her out of her slumber. A song by Jim Reeves rhythmically floated over the air waves from Radio 2. Back to reality. She turned towards Phil somnolent figure. His broad back rose and fell so his steady breathing showed that he was still well out of it.

She stretched and yawned. Her mind wandered to the previous night and she smiled to herself. God - she felt randy again! Phil had certainly reawakened her dormant sex drive. She felt her hands unconsciously wandering down her body. Her nipples stood erect on her firm breasts. Need a cold shower, she thought, and quick!

Trying hard not to disturb the comatose figure beside her, she climbed from the bed and opened the wardrobe. She slid her arms into her silk negligee and made for the bathroom. She tutted at her reflection in the mirror. Last night's make-up, so carefully applied, was a total wreck! She looked like a French tart in a burlesque show. Terry Wogan droned on the radio in the background...

The shower faucet sprayed an invigorating stream of hot water as Chloe stepped into the refreshing steam. She let the water warm her whole body closing her eyes against the flow. Her hand groped for the bar of soap as she closed the plastic curtain and began to work up a lather on the sponge.

The curtain was suddenly snatched aside. Chloe gasped out loud, "God, you scared me!"
Phil stood, equally naked, in front of her.
"I don't mind if I do, madam," he smirked as he stepped into the shower to join her with his early morning erection leading the way.
"I thought you were asleep!" shouted Chloe, above the noise of the rushing water.
"I was, 'til you got up," smiled Phil while he shook his soaking hair, "Don't mind do you?"
"Not at all, it'll save on the water rate!" Chloe laughed as she was grabbling at his taut manhood.
"No, not again. I'm still knackered from last night!" pleaded Phil.
"OK. I can wait - I think..." agreed Chloe; rubbing soap on his chest.
They kissed under the hot spray.
"Good morning darling," murmured Phil.
"Hi," replied Chloe. She wanted him again, but suppressed her urges.
She hadn't felt so secure for years. Laughter filled the cottage for the first time in an age...

****

They dried each other off, then dressed.
"Have you got a plain T-shirt I can borrow?" asked Phil, "My shirt's all creased up somehow."
"Have a look in my drawers," Chloe called from her bedroom.

"I did - last night!" laughed Phil.
"Cheeky sod!" Chloe scolded.

He found an extra-large white shirt. He put it on and admired his reflection.
Chloe stared; admiring her new-found lover.
"Suits you. I normally wear it as a nightshirt," she commented.

Phil made his way down the stairs, gathering up his shoes, socks and his discarded trousers from the hallway. He was laughing to himself ruefully, as he recalled the night's events.
"It was rape last night!" he called to Chloe.
"Yeah, but who raped who?" she countered.
"Couldn't say. 'bout equal!" Phil answered as he tied his laces.

Chloe came down the staircase. She wore faded denims and a baggy sweater.
She was barefoot. Phil kissed her on the forehead.
"Want breakfast?" she asked.
"Toast and coffee please. I'm not a big breakfast type."
"Me neither. I'm happy with just a glass of orange."

Chloe put two slices of bread in the toaster and knelt down in front of the fridge. Her hair was still wet. Phil was smitten. He loved her; he was sure. Their lovemaking was something else too. He wondered if she felt the same.
"I've got eggs, sausage, the works, if you like? You should have the appetite of a horse after last night's exertions!"
Phil laughed and replied, "No thanks, just toast in fine."

He sat at the small table, staring at Chloe's shapely buttocks. He wanted to tell her how he felt, but something was holding him back. He knew what it was. The Brothers. He had told them he didn't have a woman in his life and now, here he was, bonking the mother of a murder victim. Very unprofessional, he thought. Although, he wasn't in the profession now, was he? He knew, however, that he would have to come clean with Ken and Moss, and soon, or they would doubtless find out and then what?

"How do you like your coffee?" Chloe's voice dragged him back to the moment.

"Oh, black with two sugars thanks."

"Toast. Is brown bread OK?"

"Yeah, great."

She handed him the plate and mug and sat down opposite with her glass of juice.

"I'm out of orange so pineapple will have to do," she brightly remarked.

Phil reached across and took her hand. He clasped it tightly. "You shocked me last night," he said; his eyes never leaving her face.

"I'm sorry, Phil. It's been so long since I've - you know..." she looked down a moment, then faced him again, "... but I wanted <u>you</u> more than I wanted the sex," she said urgently.

"I'm not saying I didn't enjoy it. It was fantastic," said Phil, almost apologetically.

"I agree. It was good. Actually, it was better than good," she agreed mischievously, "And I do respect you!"

Phil joined in her laughter and they relaxed. He couldn't take his eyes off her.

"I wanted to ask you something last night but you fell asleep," Chloe began.

"Yes? What was that? I'm sorry, I was shattered. You really took it out of me and I'd had a bit of a day..." Phil's voice tailed off in his embarrassment.

Chloe smiled and asked, "I was wondering if you'd like to move in?"

She stared hard at his face. Phil was stunned.

"I know it's fast but we get on so well. It would be so much easier for you. It's such a drive from town out here. You could help in the shop if you like... Partners or such like?" Chloe watched him questioningly.

Phil took a deep breath and replied, "Well, yes... er... fantastic. I mean, I'm lost for words. I really am." His heart was beating ten to the dozen.

Chloe jumped up and jogged around the table.

"Great!" She hugged him around the shoulders and kissed is cheek and confirmed, "That's settled then!"

Phil stood up and took her in his arms.

"I love you Phil."

"Me too," he replied with his eyes closed, but in his mind's eye all he could see were Moss and Ken sat at a table. They had a small piece of paper and Ken was tearing his £15,000 cheque into tiny pieces.

He had to tell them about Chloe and fast. His whole future depended upon it.

****

The morning sun was high as Phil said his farewells. He had to tie up some loose ends at his flat. On the way back, he stopped at a newsagents and bought a copy of

The Times. The obituary column yielded nothing. No message. At least, nothing that meant anything to him. Just the usual tributes to the great and the good that had gone to their maker perhaps. A former high society lawyer's demise took up half a page. Who gives a shit bar the family and hangers-on, Phil thought.

He discarded the paper in a waste bin and drove on. He was on a distinct high with his conquest of Chloe. She was the most beautiful creature he had ever 'scored'. The age difference was an advantage in a way. She could instil a modicum of maturity into his character at last. He tried to stop thinking about their lovemaking. She had the figure of a 'Page 3' beauty and brains besides. He was a heck of a lucky ex-policeman! She made good coffee and toast too. It was all too much!

****

Phil arrived at his bachelor pad at ten-fifteen. He opened the door and stepped over a scattering of mail on the hall floor. He gathered it up with little enthusiasm. The usual: Readers' Digest competition, bank statement and a plain white envelope.

'OPEN FIRST' it read.

The single piece of paper had red writing in capital letters.

'WE CALLED BUT YOU WERE OUT. PHONE US. WE HAVE A JOB FOR YOU. IMPORTANT. HURRY. PHONE 0624 55433. RING NOW. M and K.'

Phil's stomach did a somersault. He hurried to the phone and dialled the number. Two rings out and a voice answered.

"Yes?"
"Hello. Moss? Ken?"
"Phil? Is that you?"
"Yeah. Got your note," Phil spoke quickly.
"Where the fuck were you? We called last night at eleven," Ken spoke solemnly.
"Sorry mate, I had trouble with the car. A mate was fixing it up for me," lied Phil, biting his lip and grimacing.
"Right! Is it fixed now? You'll need it."
"Yes. It was a trashed clutch," Phil lied again.

The Geordie accent sounded menacing. Phil was glad he knew the person behind the voice.
"Right! It's a weekend job, up in the Kenniton Valley. We have got to wipe out a couple of very naughty boys. You'll be backed up by three other Brothers. Go to the crime section in the library tomorrow and sit at the study table. You'll be met at nine o'clock in the morning. Got that?"

Phil's mind raced. He was just beginning to realise what he had let himself in for. What would he tell Chloe?
"There was no message in The Times."
"Of course not. They're put in for the heads of districts, for meetings.
You needn't worry about all of that yet," Ken said flatly.
"Must've got my wires crossed a bit," said Phil.
"Not to worry. Just be at the library."
"When's the hit?"
"They'll give you all the gen tomorrow. I think it's about a couple of weeks away. There's still some groundwork to be done on the targets. Don't worry; the actual hit is over in minutes - in and out – quick. No messing!" Ken spoke confidently.

"Fine. I'll be there at nine sharp," Phil nodded.
"Great! Enjoy yourself. You know it makes sense."

The phone clicked off. Phil stood; contemplating the information as he slowly replaced the receiver. He heard the letterbox flap clatter. He headed for the hall again, and found an official envelope on the mat. He opened it curiously. It was a summons.

He was bidden to give evidence at the Juvenile Court on Thursday morning. Today was Tuesday. Good. He could make it to the library tomorrow. He'd better not let the Brothers down again.

His mind wandered back to Gary Hart, then to Chloe. She had said she wanted to go to court too. He dialled her number.
"Hello?"
"Chloe. It's me – lover boy."
"Hi gorgeous! Can't keep away, hey?"
"It's about Hart - the court appearance," Phil's voice was serious, "It's Thursday morning. He's up before the Juvenile Court. Do you still want to go? I'll drive."
"Yes, of course. I'll have to shut the shop. I do want to be there. What time?"
"Eleven-thirty."
"We can go together. You could stop here Wednesday if you like," enquired Chloe.
"Great. Can't wait," responded Phil as his mind wandered again to the thought of Chloe's naked form.
"See you then. Love you."
Phil replaced the receiver.

It was all go. He was busier now than he had ever been in the police or the army! Life was looking more interesting by the hour.

****

BETTY'S DINER - 10.15am

The dingy roadside cafe had seen better days. 'Betty's Diner' was still a thriving business despite obvious neglect and it was busier than ever. The races always attracted crowds. Businessmen mingled with truckers. Betty called them 'suits and cigarettes'. When the big races were on, she employed two extra helpers behind the counter. Susie and Roz were rushed off their feet today.

"Bloody 'ell Roz! I'm knackered and it's only ten-fifteen!" Susie Bennett was seventeen years old, buxom, bright and loud. Just the type its punters loved. She darted in between the fifteen plastic-topped tables, attracting appreciative wolf-whistles, lewd comments, and a pinched bum here and there. She loved the attention. The hunky truck drivers missed their wives. (*Did they hell!*) She balanced three full breakfasts on large round plates.

She slammed the fry-ups down in front of the customers, smiling her usual 'you-can-look-but-you-can't-touch' greeting. Her stained yellow T-shirt strained to contain her mobile full bosom struggling to escape its folds. She never wore a bra on race day. Gave the fat blokes something to fantasise over as they consumed their bacon and eggs. Did no harm, as long as they paid up. Susie enjoyed race day. The compliments came thick and fast. Only the regulars treated her well; they had been eating their grease-laden swill there for years and knew Susie and Roz like daughters.

But race day was different. City gents mingled with HGV blokes. The tips were bigger too. Susie often found the odd tenner stuffed into her jean's pocket from the occasional bum-toucher.

Roz was Susie's cousin and Betty was their Gran. It was a family concern and a thriving one at that. They could make upwards of a grand on race days. Even the winter months brought a steady stream of customers.

Roz was twenty-one, buxom, bright and loud. They were a double act all right. One blonde and the other brunette - something for everyone.

The noise of the cafe was incredible. A cheap tinny-tranny radio next to the Mars bars was all but drowned out by the banter. Knives and forks clattered and scraped. Glasses and mugs slammed on tables. Laughter. Always laughter! Sometimes raucous joking and singing, especially after winnings.

Susie's blonde hair tossed as she laughed in response to the latest round of mickey-taking.
"Nice shirt Sue - give us a feel of the material!"
"Piss off Alf - you'll 'ave a bloody coron'ry!"

Roars of approval erupted from the beefy drivers and their assorted mates. "I say, Roz darling - could you pass the sauce?" shouted a rotund, suited gent from his seat by the entrance.

"Red or brown?" screeched Roz, in her blatant Cockney accent.

"Red, please darling. Super!" replied her client, winking lasciviously.

He whispered an aside to his two pals, eyeing Roz in her cut-off shorts.

"Keep your eye on your sausage lovey!" Roz warned cheekily as she passed the tomato ketchup over several animated heads.

"You can have my sausage anytime, doll!" rejoined another pin-stripe from an adjacent table.

Roz returned to the counter with a grin. She wiped not entirely imaginary sweat from her brow and commented to Susie, "Christ, what a mornin'. When's the races start?"

"Just over an hour, I think," called Susie from the rear of the cafe.

"Two coffees - one black please," a voice shouted.

"Comin' up!" Roz replied automatically, her back to the throng, "Wish Betty was here. How is she?"

She handed over the two drinks and rang up the till.

"Not too bad," Susie said, returning from the kitchen, "Her veins are playin' her up. She'll be at the doc's 'til twelve," Her concern was evident in her tone.

"If I ever get them varicose thingies, I'll chop me bloody legs off," laughed Roz. She examined her own perfect pins. She did two aerobic sessions a week and fun and fitness was her motto.

"If you chop 'em off, you won't keep this glorious job! Got to keep your looks in this profession," joked Susie. "This lot would soon move on!" Susie nodded at the male-dominated maelstrom around them.

"Fun though, innit?" winked Roz. She picked up two more steaming mugs and threaded her way through the chairs. Her bottom received gentle pats as she passed by her appreciative audience. Susie smiled to herself as she accepted more money from too well-heeled studs.

****

The worst was over. They had been going non-stop since eight o'clock. The crowd was thinning out now. A chance for a breather thought Susie, as she shovelled another load of chips into the fryer. She hummed along with the tunes from the tranny, and now its thin sound could be heard through calmer conversations. Most of the racing fraternity had dispersed to offer their salaries to the bookies, in the hope of increasing their worth. Some hope! Never met a broke bookie, did yer? thought Susie.

Another half-hour and they could have a fag and do The Sun's crossword, or at least they'd try to. She had never completed it. 'Thick cow' she thought to herself ruefully.

Roz returned with a puzzled look on her face.

"Oi, Susie. Them two over there, up the corner... Do you know 'em?"

She tossed her head in the direction of the table next to the gaming machines. Susie eyed the two men seated by the window.

"No... They're nice though," Susie commented with interest.

"They ordered the coffees. They were really short with me when I took them over. Told me to hurry up. Geordie wankers!" Roz looked hurt.

It was not often she was treated with such disdain by any punter.

"Probably their 'time of the month'," grinned Susie, "Either that, or they forgot to post the coupon. Don't worry. For every tosser, there'll always be a good couple of lads," she remarked encouragingly.

"yeah, s'pose so," Roz replied whilst chewing her fingernail.

The two girls continued their task of feeding the five thousand and their voices mingled with the assorted melee they encountered every morning.

****

"Nice idea, coming to a Greasy Joe," said the figure in the Armani suit. He toyed with his plastic spoon, stirring the black coffee and adding sugar from the dingy plastic bowl.

"Yeah, it's always busy. The mob are too busy eyeing up the two slags behind the counter to be bothered with us," Moss said. His thick north-east accent was noticeably out of place among the surrounding southern crowd.

"Yes, I can see why. Nice tits," replied his companion as he winked slyly.

Moss nodded sagely. He had come to meet his Head of District. He chose his words carefully. The head didn't suffer fools gladly. It was a well-known fact.

"Queen is our new recruit. He started yesterday."

"And?"

"He looks good. Fit. Alert. Willing."

"Who is he answerable to, at this stage?"

Moss shifted in his seat.

"Myself and my brother, Kenneth. We did the oath a couple of nights ago," Moss said. His voice was just loud

enough to be discerned above the general noise of the cafe. A tall trucker in jeans and a grey sweatshirt walked by.
"Do you think he'll do a good job?"
"Yes, without a doubt. He is an ex-copper, after all."
"Not all ex-coppers are trustworthy, my friend." The sarcasm in the head's voice was noticeable.
"No, perhaps not. But he didn't give any indication to us that he might be a liability," Moss replied. He was pleased with his choice of words.
"Are you tailing him? Has a thorough check of his movements been done since he took the oath?"
"Yes."
"And?"
"Well, er, he has a girlfriend. He didn't tell us this at the indoctrination..." Moss waited for a reaction.
Nothing. Just silence.
He continued, "We don't know who she is. We reckon it's long-term.
He speaks to her like a familiar friend."

Moss watched his companion as he drew imaginary shapes on the plastic table as he listened intently. Moss felt a shade uncomfortable.

The gaming machine exploded into life. A tall businessman fed coin after coin into the slots.

Moss spoke again, "We're going to pay her a visit. Nothing too strong; just a little hello."'

He cleared his throat, as no response came. "She owns a little shop in a sleepy village out of town. Shouldn't be too much of a problem..."

"He should have told you about her. He's lied. He could be a bad egg among the good."

"Don't worry. We shall find out as soon as we can. Let's see how he makes out on his first job, eh?" Moss suggested with his eyebrows raised.

Silence.

He could sense the disapproval. Yet, he'd liked Phil. Why hadn't he mentioned the woman in his life? He didn't seem to have anything to hide.

He'd have to find out, and soon...

****

"Here he comes, our Geordie boy," Roz said as she nudged Susie in the ribs.

Moss stood at the counter with the two empty mugs.

"Cheers love," he said as he tried not to stare too obviously at Roz's lovely twin appendages.

"That's forty-five pence thanks," she replied unsmiling.

"Cheap at half the price," he wanly smiled.

"That's forty-five pence EACH!" Roz spat.

Moss flushed visibly said, "Oh, er, sorry love. Here." He passed over a pound coin.

Susie leaned on the oven as she eyed him up.

"Are you a Geordie then?"

"Yeah, I've just driven down from Sunderland," Moss lied.

"You must be knackered. Coffee nice?" Susie asked. She liked the look of him. He seemed totally opposite to the way Roz had portrayed him.

"Er, yeah. Lovely thanks," Moss was beginning to blush. All this attention wasn't good. The cafe had suddenly quietened. He sensed somebody...

"Howay, the lads..." a voice growled over his shoulder. Moss turned sharply.

A huge man stood staring down at him, chewing gum. His blue T-shirt was at least two sizes too small for him. '**WEST HAM DON'T RUN**" was blazoned in large claret letters across the chest. Moss shivered, visibly scared. The tiny shirt made the man seem even bigger.
"Fuckin' Geordies! Kicked their arses at Newcastle last season we did," the high London drawl was menacing.
Moss could smell the spearmint overlaid with bacon and eggs. There was no visible movement or sound in the cafe. The remaining clients were all now observing the tense pair at the counter.
"I'm not a footy fan mate. Rugby's my game," Moss lied again. (*Forgive me Sunderland*!)
"Tough, you're still a Geordie wanker!"
Not a sound. Moss quaked as he watched the pitted face above him. He was a coward just like any other bloke when faced with 15 stone of angry brawn.

Susie's voice tried vainly to defuse the situation.
"Leave it out Tone. He's harmed nobody!" she screeched.
"Cocky bugger insulted me he did!" Roz spat, gleefully stirring up the situation.
Moss felt like a trapped animal. He looked over the thug's broad shoulder hoping for some assistance. The table he had recently left was now deserted.
Shit!
"Look, I don't want any hassle mate. I only came in for a coffee," he pleaded as he glanced at the two tarts behind the counter. They merely stared back dully and began to lose interest in him. (*Thanks for nowt*!)

The unexpected kick to his testicles winded him. He exhaled and fell to the tiled floor in agony. He vaguely heard a murmur from the assembled customers. As he looked up at the ceiling, a large black boot blocked his vision. It was the last thing he remembered before he lost consciousness. The pain overwhelmed him, and then blackness engulfed him.

"Fuck me Tone, you've killed 'im!"
Susie knelt beside the bloody face oozing on to the floor. Customers jostled for a look, like ghouls at a peep show.
"Nah, just giving 'im something to think about, that's all," replied the smiling trucker.
"This is awful! He didn't do nothing."'
"You fancy 'im or something'?" Roz turned to Susie.
"No, but I just don't like violence."

The thug slapped a five pound note down on the greasy counter and turned to leave.
"Serves 'im right. Should have been elsewhere. Wrong place; wrong time.
"Up the Hammers," he laughed with his fist punching the air as he slammed the door.
"You're barred!" Susie screamed after him. A two-fingered salute and mocking laughter echoed back to the cafe.
The remaining customers sullenly filed out; suddenly anxious to quit the scene. No-one wanted to get involved. No-one offered any assistance.

"Typical. Bloody typical!" murmured Susie as she regarded Moss' prostrate body.
"He's comin' round!" Roz said excitedly.

Moss had a hell of a headache. He felt like he'd done six rounds with Mike Tyson. As his vision cleared, he saw the two girls' faces mighty close-up. Their matching cleavages swam before his eyes.
"What a welcome!" he smiled as he rubbed his bloody forehead.
"Get a cloth, Roz!" said Susie in a panic, "Here, sit up." She tried to ease Moss into a sitting position. He tried to stand but he sat straight back down again.
"Cheers love. Nice clientele. I'll come here again. Do you sell tickets?"

Susie sympathetically smiled back at him and said, "I'm sorry. Tone's a bloody maniac. It's not the first time. He was in nick for five years for GBH with menaces."
"Charming," Moss moaned. He winced in pain. His bruised crotch was on fire. "My bollocks are like jelly. Any good at massage?" he felt his humour returning.
Susie laughed and her breasts rose and fell.
Roz returned with a cloth and some water.
"Here, on the house," Susie said and her attitude began to soften a little.
"Twat! He needs a good kicking!" Moss spat, wincing at the ministrations of his two nurses as they cleaned up his battered face.

Two new customers had entered and they stared at Moss in consternation.
"It's OK lads. She doesn't love me anymore."
The two truckers laughed nervously. Susie lit up a cigarette and offered it to Moss.
"No, ta. I'm a fitness freak. Baked potato and beans. No excess fat or acids in me."

Susie laughed. She liked this ginger-haired Geordie. He had sparkling eyes and a quick wit. She always went for blokes who could laugh at themselves. The poseurs in the nightclubs were not for the likes of her.

"Any chance of another coffee? I suppose a blow job's out of the question?" Moss's confidence was beginning to return.

Susie slapped him on the shoulder.

"Cheeky git!"

"At least I tried. If you don't ask, you don't get is my motto," Moss moaned comically.

"Roz, coffee for the invalid!"

"Cheers and thanks. What's your name?"

"Susie."

"Moss."

"Short for?"

"Maurice."

Susie sniggered behind her hand.

"It's me mum's fault. Her dad was called Maurice. You know what mums are like."

Susie nodded while drawing on her cigarette.

"I was lucky. Susie's nice. I like it," said Susie.

"Yeah, nice name. My brother's a Kenneth," said Moss.

"Not bad. Ken has got a ring to it."

"Lucky bastard," Moss droned. Susie laughed again.

Moss tried to drag his eyes away from Susie's ample charms.

"Sorry, I'm just admiring your T-shirt."

Susie covered her breasts and folded her arms.

"Oh, I'm used to it. It's better than advertising and it gets the clients in! No good looking like Olive Oyl behind a transport counter is it?"

Roz glared at them over the counter.

"S'pose not. I'm a bum man myself," Moss lied yet again. He loved big tits! Susie suggestively leaned forward.

"Oh, yeah. Well, go on then; have a good look. I don't care!"

"Susie, stop it!" Roz shouted.

Moss blushed furiously. He couldn't look away.

"This always works," Susie smirked at him, "Men can't handle it when it's on a plate!"

"You're right! Too bloody right."

The two men at the counter laughed at Moss's discomfort.

"Serves you right, you pervert!"

"How's your head?" asked Susie, "That's a nasty graze. Have an aspirin."

"Fine. I'll live."

Roz passed him a bottle of paracetemol pills.

"Here, I take them like Smarties. Need 'em in here. It's a bloody nightmare, especially on race days."

Moss chewed the tablet, grimacing at the taste, and he washed it down thankfully.

More customers were beginning to file in again. As the two girls picked up speed serving new plates of chips and beverages, he watched Susie. He fancied her rotten. A little rough around the edges, but good potential in different circumstances. In a mini skirt and high heels, for instance. His daydream salved his bruises, as he sat quietly and took in the busy scene. Lucky for him, The Brothers' district head had left before the fracas. It could have got out of hand, or created problems, if they'd both been involved.

****

Half an hour later, the cafe was again deserted. Moss felt disinclined to move but he had to meet Ken in town.
"Well girls, quite an eventful morning?!"
They both looked knackered. Still attractive, though, in spite of the steam-crinkled hair and flushed faces.

"Are you off then? Where're you goin'?"
"Er, Watford. Dropping off some metal," Moss lied again.
"Not far then?" commented Susie.
"No, another hour or so."
She was writing something on a matchbox.
"Here's my address and phone number to keep in touch," she said as she handed him the empty Swan box.
"Cheers, thanks. OK, I pass by quite often."
Susie stood up. She leaned over and kissed his bruised temple.
"Get well soon Maurice," she murmured in a bad French accent.
Again, a rosy flush crept up his cheeks.
"Susie, you're such a tease," Roz called as she watched the pair.
"Piss off, he's cute," Susie replied as she grinned at Moss.
"You sure you're OK?"
"Yeah, hard as nails us Jarrow lads," Moss joked. (*Except for those who blush, he thought wryly.*)
He stuffed the matchbox into his denims.
"I'll be in touch. Thanks for the coffee and sympathy."
"Anytime," sneered Roz as she turned to the crossword chewing the pencil.
Moss headed for the exit; Susie followed.
"Eight down. Angry. Seven letters," yelled Roz.
"Pissed off?" he retorted.

Susie laughed.
"Begins with F," she smirked.
Moss stared out at the parking area; his brain ticking.
"F ... Furious!" Moss shouted exultantly.
"It fits! Spot on Mossa!" Roz called back in congratulation.
Moss smiled again at Susie.
"Not bad for the thick Geordie wanker eh?"

Moss strolled across the yard.
"Don't forget to write or phone!" Susie called as he climbed into his small pickup truck.
Susie wondered why the rear of the truck contained nothing. She turned back into the cafe as the vehicle left raising a small cloud of dust.
"Roz? Didn't he say he was delivering metal?"
"Yeah, to Watford, wasn't it?"
Susie frowned.
"Lying bastard! His truck was empty," Susie moaned disconsolately.
"All men are bastards, remember?" commented Roz as she resumed her efforts with the crossword.
"Yeah, but why lie to a stranger?" muttered Susie.

****

Chapter Twelve

Phil and Chloe entered the High Street. The scenes that greeted them made the lovers catch their breath.

"Christ, is it Michael Jackson opening a supermarket?" murmured Phil as he clasped Chloe's hand firmly. They were approaching the mass of milling bodies in front of the Juvenile Court building. A heaving mass from the street up the steps to the plate glass doors, were only just being controlled by the police. Old men and women mingled with young and middle-aged mothers, some carrying children or wheeling pushchairs into the melee. Large men in donkey jackets shouted obscenities at no one in particular.

"Just lower your head and keep on walking," instructed Phil when they crossed the road. As they jostled and pushed their way up the steps, a senior police officer roughly barred their progress.

"No entry sir... Phil!"
Phil nodded a swift hello to an old friend.
"Hi, Tom! We're part of the party. Can we go in please?"

Tom Jenkins, Chief Constable, of an outlying district had been drafted in to help with the expected control needed for the trial of the 'TV Killer'; as the tabloids had so subtly described the case. He smiled a tired smile at Phil and winked at Chloe as he shouted above the raucous throng.

"No problem, I'm sorry ma'am."

Chloe smiled briefly in reply as she continued their troubled climb to the Court entrance. Phil followed and shook Tom's gloved hand in thanks.

"Good luck!" remarked Tom. Phil never heard him. As he stepped on the top step, he turned and scanned the view to his rear. There was a seething mass of people; some very young. There were women with placards bearing graffiti slogans and screaming premature judgement on the murderer.

It was hysteria and Phil could understand the feelings of the innocents. This was a public backlash demanding retribution. The Brothers have caught the public mood, he thought, and I'm part of its commitment. His brain assimilated the messages.

"SICK TO DEATH OF CRIME!" exclaimed one slogan.

"TOP THE SCUM!"

"KEEP OUR STREETS KILLER FREE!"

"JUSTICE FOR THE WEAK!"

Phil breathed a long sigh. He felt a slight tug at his overcoat.

"Come on, we're in," Chloe said as she looked like a frightened rabbit.

"It's OK love; they're on our side," he said rather ruefully as they made their way into the modern brick building. Barely had they reached it, when the first journalist sighted them.

"Mrs Lee, isn't it? I'm Carl Thomas from The Herald. How do you see the hearing going? Are you sure this kid is the killer? Can we have a photo?"

Phil snapped, "Get out of our face Thomas! Be a good boy and go away. This is not the time. OK?"

"Sir, I'm just doing my job. Who are you anyway?"

"You'll find out soon enough. Now, if you'll bear with us, we want to get inside and find our seats. Thank you."

Phil led Chloe away from the frustrated hack.
"The first of many I'm afraid love."
Chloe nodded and pronounced, "They're all cashing in on other people's misery."
"It's their job," Phil wearily replied.

They entered Court Number One in silence. They could still hear the noise from the distant High Street.
"Are you OK?" Phil looked at Chloe intently. Her face was very pale.
"Yes, I'm just a bit taken aback by the welcome," she joked feebly.

"I'm afraid 'Joe Public' has just about had enough of today's criminal fraternity. The worm is turning, Chloe. For the better, I think." (*I hope!*) His thoughts returned again to the Brothers. He had kept that quiet up to now. Sooner or later he would have to tell her.

"All I hope is that it's a just punishment," she said sternly.

They approached their seats.
"There's Mel," Chloe said pointing and Phil followed her gaze.

Melvyn Pike, celebrated solicitor, sat at his allotted position in the well of the court. He rose as he saw them approach and greeted Chloe with a warm smile.
"Chloe! Hello, are you well?" His mellifluous baritone voice resounded as it did so often in the course of his profession.
"Hello, Mel. Yes, I'm fine. This is Phil Queen."
Phil offered his hand into a firm dry grasp from the advocate.
"Hello, Phil. Nice to meet you. Chloe has told me all about you; you lucky guy!!"
Phil blushed slightly. "I think Chloe's lucky too!" he commented to cover his confusion. (*What had Chloe told Pike?)*
"Modesty, I love it!" guffawed Pike as he accepted the levity in Phil's tone.

Chloe's tone abruptly changed and brought the conversation back to the real situation.
"Can we win this case? What do you think?"
Pike's expression became serious immediately. Phil folded his arms and awaited his reply.
"All the evidence points to a quick conclusion. However, the lad has pleaded 'not guilty'. Strange that. I've studied all the available paperwork and, to me, it's a clear-cut murder. No question!"
Phil cut in. "If Hart didn't do it, then it was the bloody tooth fairy!"

Pike sat down. Phil and Chloe joined him. Their voices became muted.
"That's Hart's lawyer over there. The man's a useless little toe rag," said Pike slowly.
Phil and Chloe stared across the room at Edwin Moore.
"He looks like Woody Allen," sniggered Chloe. Phil smiled. He knew that appearances could be deceptive. The tiny solicitor was in conversation with a fat lady. Phil recognised Brenda Hart. She wore an ill-fitting skirt and sagging sweatshirt. Her hair was a mess and she held the remains of a cigarette. Chloe noticed the NO SMOKING signs at the entrance to the courtroom and thought tersely to herself, perhaps the stupid, blowsy woman couldn't read.

The clock above the bench showed ten minutes to ten.

With five minutes to go, a side door opened and the jury filed into their places. There were five women and seven men. Four black and eight white. A cross section of the public, thought Chloe, to decide the future of her daughter's killer.

The Press corps sat at the rear and busily scribbled a description of the scene on notepads. One, Chloe noticed, appeared to be sketching on a larger sheet.

Phil slackened the tie around his neck; the atmosphere was close and tense. The public gallery was packed, a whispering morass of faces, expectant and excited. The entrance door had been locked half an hour ago. Phil strained to hear any noise from outside but there was none now. The heavy wooden doors to the court room were closed. Two orderlies stood in silence on either side.

They all waited for the star of the show. They didn't have to wait long.

At two minutes to ten, Gary Hart climbed the steps into the dock and he was flanked by two burly prison officers; one female.

He stood for about fifteen seconds; silently taking in the scene around the courtroom. The silence was deafening. In a flash of recognition, he winked at someone to Chloe's left. Chloe did not turn to look but assumed it was his mother. People began to cough nervously.

Suddenly, a scuffle broke out in the gallery. A loud voice. "You're dead, you little shit!"
All eyes turned to the mini-riot in the balcony above. A large man with a beard was having an altercation with two larger police officers.

Gary Hart's eyes flickered at the interruption. A slight smile played on his lips as he watched the policemen remove the protesting onlooker. The press would later tell the world that he was a Mr Jimmy Parrish, a father of four. He was later cautioned for breach of the peace in court!

Gary Hart sat with his face immobile. His crew-cut and teenage acne served to further antagonise his audience. His total image, in black T-shirt and jeans, heightened the public's revulsion which hung like a tangible cloud in the quiet waiting courtroom.

Chloe's eyes never left the accused. Her mind whirled as she considered this murderer of her daughter. Surely such a boy couldn't be so evil. He had suffocated and mutilated her own flesh and blood and he sat barely ten yards away from her. The urge to leap up and attack him, like a tigress, raged underneath her apparently placid exterior.

Phil also contemplated the attacker he had apprehended in the course of his duty. Hart recognised him. Phil recoiled as Hart pursed his lips and mockingly blew him a kiss!

Mind games, thought Phil, don't let him get to you. Days from now, chummy, you'll be blowing kisses at four walls and porridge for life so grin all you bloody well like.

"All stand!" The clerk of the court brought the assembly to their feet as the judge entered.
A woman!
Phil glanced at Mervyn Pike. He mouthed, "She's GOOD!"

Judge Helen Coombes took her place in the focal point of the court.
The circus had begun!

****

TEMBURY MANSIONS - 10.00am
At the precise moment that Judge Helen Coombes took her seat in the Crown Court, Kelly Giles snapped.

He was thirty-four and on the dole. The odd labouring job brought in some spare cash to feed his kids, Jamie and Tammy. The dole went on essentials; the bare essentials. A staple diet of toast, beans, chips and pies had taken its toll of his physique. His sex life was virtually suspended, either through apathy or incipient impotence. He masturbated when Kim went shopping and the box of dog-eared soft porn magazines he secreted under the bed fulfilled any occasional fantasies or needs he could summon up. His life was a cess-pit of indifference, apart from the noise from next door.

The incessant bump, bump, bump of the stereo had been playing on Kelly's nerves for months. His basically easy-going nature had allowed him to grin and bear it for a time, but now he was obsessed by the intrusions. At six in the morning, three in the afternoon or five-thirty on a Sunday... He never knew when it would begin or finish.

It was happening now, again. Today!

Kelly Giles decided that NOW he'd had enough.

He got out of bed. His feet tapped involuntarily to the beat of the latest 'acid house' track. He drew his faded denims over his bare buttocks, pulled a Fred Perry shirt over his tousled head and tucked it in as he closed his fly zip. His ten year old Doc Marten boots slipped on his bare feet like gloves and shaped snugly around every toe. It took forty seconds to lace them.

He really quite liked his neighbour, Billy. Nice lad. Cheeky though. On a bad day, he got on Kelly's nerves a little. Today, he was getting on his nerves a lot.

The music had been playing since Kim took the kids to playschool; their only haven in life. Fucking playschool is paid for by the council. At least it got the kids and Kim out of the house and he got some peace. Peace until the beat began again.

Kelly went to the bathroom. The mirror reflected his mood. Shitty!

The kids had smeared toothpaste and shampoo all over the sink. Kim had scolded them in her high pitched whine of a voice.
"Tamm-eee! Stop it, you naughty girl!"
It had about as much effect as a wet sponge. No deterrents these days. No discipline!
He cleaned his teeth as the walls vibrated to the latest of Billy's collection. The tattoo on his forearm proclaimed the legend "MAM-DAD" underneath a snake. Meaningless. He'd paid 25 quid for it ten years ago, after a piss-up in Wigan. Happy days...

His headache was pounding.
As he opened the front door of his cesspit, he stopped.
(*What have you forgotten?*)
The knife of course. (*Go and get it then.)*
Yeah, silly me.

He returned to the kitchen. The cutlery jangled in the drawer. Where was the carver? On the wall?
Of course it was. He took the knife from the rack which hung on loose screws in the damp plaster. Kim wanted a special knife rack but he had no tools to plug the wall so

it was constantly falling off and scattering the knives across the floor.

He weighed the carver in his hand. Time to go.

Tembury Mansions was a misnomer for the tenement which was a crumbling warren of warring, poverty-stricken families. Noise was a way of life. Screaming parents, kids, joy riders, argumentative neighbours and always the background beat of rap, soul and country grinding out through the buildings.

Life's rich tapestry, thought Kelly. To think that seven '0' levels and a full engineering qualification had come to this.

He banged on Billy Coogan's front and only door. The music was so loud that it was obvious he could not hear the door being thumped. Kelly sat down and waited for a gap in the tracks. Minutes ticked by. He thumped the peeling wood again and suddenly the door opened.

"Yeah, what's up?" Billy stood, bare chested, with an open can in his hand.

Kelly leaned in and said in his usual monotone, "It's the noise."

"Sorry, you'll have to speak up," shouted Billy above the thumps from the interior. (*That's just it, you little twat!*)

"I said, it's the noise," Kelly flatly stated again.

"So, I'm just playing my stereo. Don't you like it?"

Kelly rubbed his tired eyes.

"It's been going on like this for two hours," he said as he sullenly stared down at his boots.

"Tough! I can play my music when I want and you can't stop me," Bill taunted him as he took a swig from his

can. He was unaware of the growing resentment of his neighbour on the doorstep. The music continued to echo out of the flat and around the courtyard. He stepped back and attempted to close the door.
Kelly's foot shot out and held the door.
"Tough is it?" Kelly repeated Billy's comment as his arm leaned on the door post.
"Yeah, piss off!"

Kelly snapped.

The ferocity of the first blow sent Billy sprawling back into the hallway. He banged his head on a low table. Kelly bore down upon him. The music drowned out the noise of the two adversaries.

Billy's head was bleeding. He gasped as his hand came away from his scalp. Kelly's hand gripped the vicious carving knife. Billy scrambled away backwards along the floor. He was shouting something but Kelly could not make out the words.

As Billy leapt up on to his unsteady feet, Kelly brought the knife down in an arc. It sliced into Billy's midriff. His face crumpled in pain and disbelief. Blood spurted across the floor. The latest Yellow Pages turned crimson. Another motion from Kelly sent the knife through Billy's left arm.

Kelly could only hear the music. The damned fucking music! His white Fred Perry was a mass of red blotches.

"Tough!?" he screamed, as he slashed at the motionless form on the floor.

A large pool of blood spread across into the kitchen.

Kelly stopped his maniacal stabbing. A job well done. Billy Coogan breathed his last at ten past ten. Kelly Giles did likewise at fourteen minutes past. The drop from the seventh floor drove the knife straight through his stomach. He had found peace at last.

Someone switched off the music at ten-forty-two.

****

Chapter Thirteen

The preliminaries were over. Phil and Chloe awaited the first confrontation of the trial. The press had been instructed not to publish any photographs of the accused due to his age. An artist was busy sketching the scene to their right.

Phil gripped Chloe's hand as Judge Coombes called for the prosecution QC to start his questioning.

Melvyn Pike approached the area in front of the dock.

Gary Hart sat impassively. Having taken the oath, he awaited his ordeal calmly, presenting an almost bored appearance to the expectant court.

"Gary, you are thirteen years old - am I correct?" began Pike, slowly.
"Yeah. Fourteen in November," replied Hart.
"Have you ever had a girlfriend, Gary?"
Hart shifted slightly in his seat.
"No. Never."
"Do you like girls, Gary?"
"'spose so. Do you?" responded Hart, enjoying the responsive laughter from the gallery.
Cocky, thought Pike.

"Never mind me, Gary. Would you agree that girls are the weaker sex?"
"Course they are. They're weak."
"I see."

Pike turned to face his audience. The jury sat in silence, staring at Hart's rough features.
"Why did you attack Janice Lee, Gary? If girls are weak, why did you choose to jump on a defenceless young woman in the park?"

Hart's head lowered. He stared at his feet.
"Gary?" prompted Pike, quietly.
"Yeah?"
"Please answer the question."
"I... I wanted to scare her, that's all." Hart mumbled, his attention still directed at the floor.
"Oh, I see. You wanted to scare her," repeated Pike.
"Yeah. It was just a laugh." Gary looked up at Melvyn Pike.
"A laugh?"
"Yeah."

Chloe's hand tightened around Phil's at these words.
"So why Gary, did you follow Janice Lee to her flat?"
"I wanted to say 'Sorry'. Honest!" blurted Hart.
"Sorry?"
"Yeah - I followed her to the cop shop first. Once she left, I got a taxi and ended up at her flat."
"At that late hour, surely you should have gone home?"
"I just wanted to say sorry." said Hart, flatly.

Melvyn Pike paused and paced back and forth, a thoughtful expression on his face. He was debonair. At fifty-four, he wouldn't have looked out of place in a Las Vegas casino with a woman on each arm.

"So..." he continued, "Do I understand that you forced entry into a young lady's flat. A young lady, who only an hour or so earlier you had attempted to rape - to say... er,... 'Sorry'?"
Hart nodded in reply and his eyes again lowered.

Pike approached Judge Coombes and murmured something unintelligible.
Chloe glanced at Phil, frowning. Phil winked.
"Gary..." Pike resumed his interrogation, leaning on the dock, "did you, on the night of 17th July, murder Janice Lee in cold blood?"

Hart's demeanour changed dramatically. He leapt to his feet, eyes wide. "NO!... NO, I didn't!" he shouted, "She fell over... she was screaming. I got scared and ran off!"

The public gallery erupted into a chattering comment on these words. Pike could smell his quarry on the run and went in for a quick kill.

"Silence in court!" Hollered Judge Coombes above the uproar.
The noise abated. Phil eyed Edwin Moore who was in conversation with Hart's mother. He was nodding frantically.
"Please continue, Mr Pike." said Judge Coombes, calmly.

Pike picked up where he'd been interrupted.

"How do you account for the fact that your cap was found under Miss Lee's bed?"

"I must've dropped it in the struggle," blurted Hart.

Gasps came from the gallery.

Pike composed himself. There was a pregnant pause.

"Did you say... struggle, Gary?" Pike's voice was silky-smooth.

Silence.

"I repeat. Did you say you dropped your hat in a struggle with Janice Lee?"

"No... Well... yeah. I suppose so, maybe I did," Hart blustered; his eyes would not meet those of the dominant lawyer.

Pike spoke almost in a whisper. He changed tack effortlessly.

"What did Miss Lee have on, Gary?"

"Nothin' - just a shirt."

"Did she wear any knickers?" Pike asked.

"No, she was bare apart from the shirt."

"Did it excite you, Gary - to see a young lady like that?"

Silence.

"Please answer me, Gary," pursued Pike.

"She told me to fuck off. She picked up a fork!"

"You attacked her didn't you?" continued Pike, "She was almost nude.

You struggled. You had to silence her, didn't you?"

"No! She screamed. She was on the floor with the fork in her hand.

I ran off when she fell down. I didn't touch her!"

Hart was shouting wildly at Mervyn Pike. His eyes roved around the packed courtroom in panic.

Chloe took a handkerchief out of her pocket and wiped her eyes. It was an effort not to cry. Several women in the public gallery were now in tears.

Pike calmly turned to Judge Coombes, "No further questions your Honour."
He returned to his seat and turned to Phil.
"Little shit's lying through his teeth," he whispered.

Phil nodded. Chloe's eyes were puffy and red but she smiled at Pike, trying to compose herself.

Judge Coombes called for the defence. People coughed and murmured during the lull in the proceedings.

Edwin Moore stood up and approached the dock. He nodded at Judge Coombes smiling grimly. At this moment, he was on a hiding to nothing, and he knew it. In the eyes of 98 per cent of the people in the court, Hart was guilty as hell.

Give it a go, Eddy, he thought. You win some, you lose some.
He cleared his throat and turned to Gary Hart.

"Gary - at this moment you are accused of a disgusting murder of a defenceless young woman," he began, "Why should anyone believe you did not kill Janice Lee? Let me get a few facts right..."
Hart stared at Moore blankly. No emotion showed in his features. He seemed almost apathetic after his outburst of a few moments before.

"You admit to the attack in the park," Moore continued. "You say that you molested the young lady just to...er... frighten her. Is that correct?"
Hart shrugged and nodded, dumbly.
"At no time did you indulge in any sexual assault? Did you, for instance, take your privates out of your trousers? Did you expose yourself to Miss Lee?"
Hart blushed furiously, "No!"

Moore could feel every eye in the court on his back. "Did you, at any time, touch any of Miss Lee's private parts?"
"No sir," Hart lied.

Phil leaned across to Pike. "That's bollocks. He touched her breasts - read her statement!"
Pike nodded.
Moore continued his questions, "Have you ever seen a woman's vagina Gary?"
Again, Hart flushed and nodded; looking at his feet.
"When? In a magazine?"
"Yeah. Some lads showed me."
Moore nodded. "Did it 'turn you on'?"
Hart shrugged again and made no answer.
"Yes or No, Gary?"
"Not really. I thought it was funny,"
"I see..." murmured Moore, as he consulted his notes. "Now, let's go to the flat, Gary. How did you gain entrance to the flat?"
"The main entrance was left open. It was easy," Hart replied watching his counsel's face, "I climbed the stairs and she let me in."
There were gasps of astonishment from the gallery.

Moore raised his eyebrows in surprise. "She let you in...?" Pike nudged Phil, also showing surprise at this information.

"Do you mean... er... you knocked - and was let in?"
Hart shook his head, slowly.
"Then how did you get her to let you in?"
"I made a noise."
"What sort of noise?"
"A cat."
Moore's excitement grew. "So, what you're saying is - you pretended to be Miss Lee's cat?"
Hart nodded in embarrassment. Laughter rolled down from the balcony.
"Crafty little shit," muttered Pike. Two jurors hid their smiles.
Hart also relaxed as he recognised that he had an interested audience.
"Yeah," he continued enjoying his little joke, "I scratched the door and made cat noises. Then she let me in; stupid cow!"
He grinned at the assembled faces.

Suddenly Chloe was on her feet. "How dare you!" she screamed.
Phil leapt up and tried to calm her. The whole court erupted in jeers and angry comment.
"Silence!" Judge Coombes restored a semblance of order again by rapping her gavel several times.
Chloe sat down sobbing uncontrollably.

Edwin Moore approached the bench and said, "I'm sorry your Honour, this is wholly inappropriate."

Judge Coombes gave him a look of disgust. She didn't need words because her expression said it all.

"Please continue," she warningly remarked and the sarcasm audible in her tone.

Moore returned to his client. "Gary, behave! You're doing yourself no favours," he whispered, almost inaudibly.

"I'm just telling the truth," Hart replied. "They can't prove nothing,"' he then scoffed confidently.

"Even so, you're not helping by antagonising the court with your flippant attitude," insisted Moore. He was feeling hot and flustered, and wiped his sweaty forehead with the back of his hand.

"I'm innocent! Now get me out of this shit!" spat Hart, despising the little man.

"Christ, Gary. You're not giving me a chance!"

The cool voice of Judge Coombes fell on their ears.

"Is there a problem, Mr Moore?"

Edwin spun round as if stung.

"Problem? No, certainly not ma'am, none at all... no problem," he blustered.

"Then let us get on."

Moore turned back to Hart.

"If you want my help you must behave. You're making yourself look guilty don't you see?" Moore almost pleaded.

Hart nodded sullenly, as Moore flicked through his notes again. He composed himself, clearing his throat. His voice rose once more.

"Now, where were we? You said... Miss Lee let you in. You didn't force the door? What did you say to her, once she'd opened the door?"

Gary shifted uneasily in his seat, "I said I was sorry and I wanted to tell her personally."
Chloe fought back her fury and Phil shook his bowed head, remembering the scene at the flat.

"So - how did Miss Lee come to fall over?"
"She was startled. Shocked to see me, I suppose."
"So you didn't touch her or manhandle her in any way?"
"Nah. She just slipped. Then, she screamed at me to get out. I panicked and ran. I must've dropped the hat then."
Moore continued, "Miss Lee had a fork in her hand. Did she threaten you with it?"
Melvyn Pike stood up and interjected, "Objection! Miss Lee is not on trial here your Honour."
"Objection sustained. The jury will ignore the last question," Judge Coombes directed the select dozen jurors, some of whom nodded.
"I'm sorry your Honour - no further questions at this stage."

Melvyn Pike stood once more.
"Gary - what did you expect Janice Lee to say when she saw you standing at her door? Come in? Tea or coffee? After you'd attacked her only an hour before - on your own admission?"
More laughter came from the public gallery.
"Did you honestly think she'd calmly welcome you with open arms at that time of night?"
Silence.
"Well?"
"I thought she'd be glad to see her cat!" sniggered Hart.
Edwin Moore buried his head in his hands, despairingly.
Chloe was on her feet, yelling at Hart incoherently. Phil

had a job restraining her for a second time. It took five minutes to calm the reaction to Hart's insolence. Mervyn Pike was becoming really hacked off with Gary Hart.

Time to put the pressure on...

"Gary!" Pike's authoritative voice rang through the court, "Why mutilate the body after you'd killed her?"

"I didn't kill her!"

Pike pressed on his advantage, hearing the note of fear again in Hart's voice.

"A TV monitor? Did you enjoy that? She was already suffocated. Why?"

"I didn't do it! I don't know who did! It wasn't me!" Hart's scream rose into the court as he leapt to his feet.

"Sit down, Mr Hart!" shouted the Judge, as a policeman leaned forward to restrain the wild figure.

"I'm NOT guilty! I've been set up!" ranted the crew-cut figure. He slumped back into the dock.

"No more questions."

Gary Hart sat forlornly between the two police officers.

"Call your next witness."

"Your Honour, I call Sanjay Mahrat," replied Pike.

Sanjay Mahrat entered the court and took the oath. His Indian origin was apparent and his cultured accent changed the atmosphere of the proceedings. He spoke with quiet authority and was heard in respectful silence.

"Mr Mahrat – you're the coroner. Could you please tell the court how Janice Lee was killed?"

"Janice Lee was asphyxiated - possibly with a pillow or cushion," he stated flatly.

"Did she put up a struggle?"

"Yes. No doubt about that. Her arms were bruised. She had sustained a cut upper lip and she had lesions on her wrists, consistent with being forcibly held down."

Chloe's eyes closed and a tear ran down her cheek.

Pike continued quietly, "Was she raped?"

"No," replied the coroner.

Chloe smiled slightly and relaxed as Phil took her hand.

"There's no significant interference sexually, apart from..."

"The monitor – yes," Mahrat answered stony-faced.

"Thank you – that'll be all."

Mahrat rose and left the witness box.

Pike turned to Phil.

"Your Honour, I call Philip Queen to the stand."

Phil stood up. Chloe followed him with her gaze. He took the oath and looked around the court. He was amazed how full it was from this viewpoint. People were crammed into every possible vantage point.

"Mr Queen - you were, until recently, a policeman based at 'Q' Division?"

"Yes," replied Phil.

"You were on duty the night that Janice Lee was attacked in the park?"

"Yes, I was and I took her statement."

"What was Miss Lee's manner when she arrived at the station?"

"Flustered. Shocked. Scared. The normal reaction. I've dealt with a number of similar cases," Phil calmly stated.

"How was she when she left the station? Had she calmed down by then?"

"Yes, she seemed fine. Well... as fine as she could be, under the circumstances."

"In your opinion, Mr Queen, was the attack sexually motivated?"

"Yes, definitely."

"Why do you say this?"

"Well, in her statement she, Janice Lee, told me that her attacker had tried to fondle... er... touch her breasts."

Muted comment came from the gallery. Hart shuffled in the dock.

"Anything else?"

"She said he got excited."

"In what way Mr Queen?"

"Shortness of breath... er.... he had an erection."

"Visible?"

"No."

"So - he was a deep-breathing, violent, turned-on, six foot menace?"

"Yes."

"Not some school kid out for a bit of fun?"

"No."

"Thank you Mr Queen. You may stand down."

Phil returned to his seat and let out a sigh of relief.

"Well done love," Chloe whispered, reaching out for his reassuring hand once more.

****

At the precise moment that Chloe Lee uttered her cry of indignation at Gary Hart; Kenneth, brother of Maurice, knew what they had to do.

Phil Queen had gone from a valuable asset to The Brothers to a distinct liability, almost overnight. The fact that Phil had kept his liaison with Chloe a secret both angered and saddened Ken. They had liked the ex-policeman. However, here he sat in court, amongst an angry public gallery, watching one of their latest recruits go into the witness stand and the nation's headlines. Bad for business, Ken thought sadly.

It was routine procedure for the recruits of the Brotherhood to be put under surveillance for a period. It was a safety clause. Just in case the odd 'bad egg' slipped through the net.

Phil Queen hadn't slipped through. The net would now slip around him and his not-so-mysterious girlfriend.

The area heads would not take kindly to this latest turn of events. Elimination of the couple was a possibility, a very distinct possibility. Alternatively, Phil would have to come up with a few watertight reasons as to why he had failed them during his initiation.

Ken slipped a Polo mint between his lips. He would have to put Phil's first 'mission' on hold; at least until he had been questioned further. There were plenty of other Brothers who could complete the task. They would have to wait until the trial was over... Or would they?

The way it was going, the whole business would be finished in record time. The youth was as guilty as hell. In the first morning, Gary Hart had dug a hole for himself the size of Wembley. If the Judge had any sense, it would all be over by close of play tomorrow. How many more witnesses are there?

Ken stared at Gary Hart. He was just the sort of person 'The Brothers' could have dealt with in a stroke. Hart was a thoroughly evil piece of work, thirteen years old and a most useless piece of humanity he'd ever seen.

The trial was a joke! The defence lawyer's feeble attempts to save Hart from certain doom had caused disgust in the gallery. Whispers of, "Should hang the little runt!" could be heard during the morning. "Waste of time and money," commented another.

Ken knew what the majority of the great British public wanted. A return of the death penalty! In today's clear-cut cases, a trial should have been the prelude to the hangman's noose for most murderers.

But no! The do-gooders were in the ascendancy. The assembly in the House of Commons did not reflect the voice of the people. The democrats were still not listening to the voice of the people. It's the opposite, in fact. "The death penalty is barbaric!" one elected representative had stated only that week.

Is cold-blooded murder barbaric? Ken cogitated long and hard over his 'for and against' argument against capital punishment and concluded that 'a life for a life' should mean just that.

The Brothers were turning the tide though. Slowly but surely, the bad and the ugly were losing out to the good and summary justice on the streets of Great Britain. The 'New Order' was emerging with monumental proportions.

In six weeks' time, an organised march would take place. it would be an opportunity for significant public outcry against crime. Thousands were expected to march on Parliament and the police had already been informed. The march would include a public flogging and the recipient would only be selected several days prior to the march.

The Brothers had been planning the demonstration for months and they would be there in force to ensure it didn't get out of hand. The police were under orders not to interfere. An agreement had been given the rubber stamp at the highest level. TV coverage is expected to be extensive and would be shown throughout the world. it would strike at the very heart of government. 'The fists of the innocents' could smash the criminal fraternity and produce the massive publicity coup for The Brothers.

Ken bristled as he pondered the march. The politicians in their cossetted cloisters will get the shock of their lives. Underground leaflets were distributed to ensure the element of surprise. Surely, the Home Secretary will then be forced to respond? The controlled attack of public opinion on such a scale meant they couldn't lose...

Ken's thoughts were interrupted by the sound of the Judge's gavel. She rapped twice and shouted, "Silence!" A man at the rear of the gallery was being manhandled out of his place. Another dismayed member of the public, thought Ken.

"This is a farce!" the man shouted, "The little bleeder is guilty as hell! Hang him!"

Ken turned as the two officers ushered the man out of court. He smiled because the man was right. He was expressing what every right-minded person in the court was thinking.

Gary Hart shuffled uneasily in his seat. Hart's position was rapidly becoming untenable and the atmosphere in the court was increasingly unnerving.

Judge Coombes appeared flustered by the latest outburst which had again interrupted the proceedings. The public were usually well-behaved. This trial, however, seemed to have touched a raw nerve in people. They were releasing the suppressed resentment at the lax judiciary which had been fermenting since the capture of Hart. He'd become a focus for the public to express their despair at the trite comments and ineffective sentencing in so many courts, where the victims and their families were given the last consideration.

Judge Coombes calmed herself and continued once more. "The court will retire," she announced loudly. She's clearly ill at ease with the air of hatred emanating from the public gallery. "We shall resume at ten o'clock tomorrow," she resounded.

When Judge Coombes stood and left through the rear entrance, voices rose and fell as the people slowly made their way out into the corridors. Phil and Chloe sat in silence as Gary Hart was led away to the cells.
"Not a bad morning's work. Hart's on a slow boat to a guilty verdict!" boomed Melvyn Pike. He then smiled reassuringly at Chloe.

"Good," Chloe responded; as Phil put his arm around her shaking shoulders. "He can't go to prison though, can he? He's under-age."

"No. It'll have to be a Young Offender's Institution until he's sixteen," agreed Pike. "Then a transfer to a more hellish existence. His reputation will precede him. Undoubtedly, there'll be a welcome committee for him," continued Pike.

"His life won't be worth living," commented Phil.

"But he will still be living, won't he? Janice isn't." Chloe's voice shook as she spoke.

"Let's hope he's sentenced tomorrow. I can't see it lasting much longer.

The apparent lack of witnesses helps," remarked Pike.

"What about the other people in the flats? Didn't they hear anything?" suggested Chloe.

"The place was virtually empty. It's summer recess for the students. People on holiday - you know the score," explained Phil.

"Oh, yes. I see," Chloe said looking grimly disappointed.

"The only other person in the house was a lad called Neil. He was there when I called and found Janice. He was at his girlfriend's pad up north at the time of the attack. He's gone abroad since then picking oranges in Spain so he's no help whatsoever," said Phil.

"This could be the speediest murder trial in history!" remarked Pike excitedly. "Two falls and a submission in two days!" he joked.

Chloe stared at Phil and Pike earnestly.

"He's not much use, is he?" she commented while tossing her head in the direction of Edwin Moore, who was deep in conversation with two middle-aged women.

"Told you so, didn't I? Still, he's fighting a losing battle anyway. Hart hasn't done his cause much good with his stupid petulance and insolence," Pike stated flatly at the same time as gathering up his papers.

Phil took Chloe's hand. "Ready?" Phil said.
"Yes, let's go and do lunch. What about you, Mel?" Chloe turned to the advocate.
"No but thanks all the same. I can get a game of golf in this afternoon since we've been let out of school early. See you both tomorrow," Mel said with a smile.

Chloe and Phil walked slowly out under the gallery. If Phil had glanced upward, he might have noticed a familiar figure partly obscured by a copy of The Times. It'd been busy observing every detail of the scene below.

As the two disappeared out of his view, Kenneth folded the newspaper in a mood of resolve. He had work to do. He limped down the stairs and followed Phil and Chloe along the marble hall, although he kept a discreet distance from them.

****

The trial captured the public's imagination. The media was in a ferment of hyperbole. Claim and counter-claim filled the columns and assaulted eyes and ears in news bulletins.
"UPROAR IN MONITOR TRIAL!"
"VERDICT IN RECORD TIME?"
"GUILTY AS HELL!"
Chloe and Phil spent the evening indoors. They watched news report after news report. Cameras followed their

every move. The long day had tired them so they headed for the quiet of the bedroom.

Their lovemaking was a disappointment and did little to ease their tension. Phil could sense Chloe's sadness. Her tears flowed freely and slowly. She relaxed and he held her in his arms until she drifted off to sleep. His own mind was still in turmoil and his sleep was fitful. The day's events were hard to shake off.

Phil awoke with a 4.00a.m. start. He gently rose from the bed; covering Chloe with the duvet. Her naked body sprawled across the bed and her breathing was slow and calm.

Phil went into the kitchen and knelt down by the fridge. In the darkness, he took out a carton of milk. After closing the fridge, he sat on the edge of the table and drank.

Then, he heard the cars. He went to the front window and peered through the fine net of the curtain into the mist-shrouded street. As his eyes became accustomed to the gloom, he saw two cars at the end of the village. They both faced the house and their headlights were switched off. Why are cars there at four o'clock in the morning? That's very strange, thought Phil. He took another swig of cool milk and watched intently.

Two men stood beside the cars. One lit a cigarette. As the light glimmered, something struck a chord in Phil's brain. An instant thought came to him that Kenneth must know everything and now he's a marked man!

Phil ducked back into the dark room. His breathing came in short, sharp bursts. He sat with his back to the window and eyes tightly shut.

Kenneth must have followed him! Them!

It was three days since the induction. They know about Chloe!

Panic gripped Phil. You should have told them, he thought over and over again!

He turned on his knees and gently moved the curtain aside. One of the figures was getting into a car. Was it Ken? The door thumped shut.

The car silently pulled away with no headlights.

The remaining figure sat in the other vehicle.

Silent. Watching. Waiting...

Phil forced himself to think rationally. Had they been on his tail ever since the induction? If so, they must also know about the trial; especially with his face on TV tonight. They must know! Why hadn't I told them everything? One thing Phil knew for certain was the he had to tell The Brothers - or Chloe! Whatever the decision; he was in the shit again. If he told Chloe about his dealings with The Brothers, he would be reneging on his promise to Ken and Maurice. If he told The Brothers of his liaison with Chloe, he may have to give her up. The choice was obvious but the decision was extremely difficult. He needed a crap. A feeling of dread filled him.

He climbed the stairs, trying to gather his thoughts. He had to leave the house without being seen. He dressed hurriedly, in silence.

Chloe slept on, oblivious to Phil's turmoil and he scribbled her a hurried note. He quietly placed it on the pillow, where she would expect to find him when she woke, and he softly closed the bedroom door behind him.

He could still see the car through the front window. It had not moved. He crawled into the kitchen, unlocked the back door and entered the garden. The smell of dew and fresh air hit him. There was a small fence between the garden and a field. He shut the door behind him, bent double, and ran across the short lawn. Scaling the fence silently, he scuttled into a small clump of trees. Looking back at the cottage, he tried to get his bearings. He felt as he used to on an escape and evasion exercise during his service days. The same adrenalin high - fight or flight...

If he went right he would eventually come out on the main road into town. He could risk that.
It would be an hour before the first bus arrived. Better safe than sorry he thought, sombrely.
He was conscious of a thin film of sweat breaking out on his forehead as he jogged down the cool, country lane dressed for dinner!

The Brothers would come for him; he was sure of that. He'd have to go to ground. He daren't go to the court again. He'd given his evidence but would he explain everything to Chloe? His mind raced as he ran.

After about twenty minutes, he saw a petrol station at the far end of the road. It was just opening for business as he casually approached it. Phil wiped the sweat from his face.

"Morning!" he called to the youth inside the station shop.

"Hi, bit early ain't ya?" responded the lad, suspiciously.

"Yeah, my car's broken down up the lane," lied Phil.

"Oh, I see. Need a phone?"

"Yes, I must ring the AA," Phil panted.

The youth opened the door.

"Thanks," said Phil as he was ushered into an office at the rear of the shop.

He flicked through the Yellow Pages and dialled. "Taxis?" he quietly enquired. "I need a taxi immediately from the petrol station in Yate-upon-Dean into town" continued Phil. "Yes, fifteen minutes is great, thanks!" Phil concluded as he replaced the receiver and breathed a sigh of relief.

"Cheers mate," Phil said as he left.

The attendant watched him go, frowning, as he saw movement outside. "First customers? Early or what?" he smiled. (*A good start to the day!*)

Phil also turned to look and froze.

The black BMW glided on the forecourt. Phil's bowels were churning again.

Chloe sat in the back seat; her face a mask of terror. A gun was held at her temple.

Ken leaned across and opened the door. "Get in Phil," he spoke softly.

Phil reckoned his choices were severely limited under the circumstances, so he eased himself on the back seat beside Chloe...

****

They were driven for what seemed an eternity. Ken's assistant thug kept a reptilian eye on them from the front passenger seat. Any attempts to speak that Phil made were met by stony silence.
"Where're we going?" Silence.
"I can explain everything..." Nothing.

Chloe was dressed in a jersey and jeans. Her lack of make-up only accentuated the pallor of her face. The latch on the back door had been left off when Phil sneaked out, giving Ken and Co easy access to the cottage. Chloe was unharmed physically but it was obvious she was on the verge of breaking down. Phil drew her close in an attempt to reassure her.
"What's going on?" she mouthed at him; her eyes like dark pools.
Phil pursed his lips and put an index finger to them.
"It'll be fine," he mouthed back. Lip reading was not one of her greatest talents.
He saw the desperation in her eyes. She didn't deserve all this, he thought ruefully, and it was all his fault. He should have honestly told Kenneth and Maurice everything about her. Maybe it wasn't too late now? He pondered but he was unconvinced.

Ken's silence was unnerving. Days earlier, after his 'induction ceremony', they'd been the best of pals but it was all in tatters now.

Daylight was just breaking when the car pulled up near a small farmhouse. Birds twittered in the trees to greet the new day, as the foursome clambered out of the car. The farmhouse's front door opened and Maurice stood with his arms folded. Phil smiled weakly as he was escorted into the building. Chloe followed, stifling the urge to ask questions about these grim strangers.

"Please sit down," motioned Maurice. His Geordie accent was clipped. Gone was the friendly tone of three days before.

Chloe sat on the leather sofa and Phil joined her. Kenneth stood by the open log fire. The clock on the mantelpiece read six-forty.

"So, here we are again!" Kenneth began loudly.

Phil shifted uneasily. The leather squealed in protest at his writhing.

"I can explai..."

"Listen to me Phil," interrupted Kenneth gruffly, "You were an extremely impressive recruit to the organisation."

Chloe frowned at Kenneth. She was more confused by the minute. (*Organisation?*)

"We took you at your word. We believed you when you said you had no, shall we say 'extra-curricular activities on the go' when we last spoke."

"Phil stammered, "I...I... didn't want Chloe to get involved. She..."

"Chloe is it? Pleased to meet you," Kenneth officially greeted and leaned forward offering his hand. Chloe shook it, tamely.

"Hello... er..."

"Kenneth Jamieson. This is my brother, Maurice," he motioned in the direction of his brother who stood, barring the exit from the room.

"Hi!" Maurice eyed Chloe with evident pleasure. He waved a lazy hand.

Chloe nodded and waited.

"Did you really think you could pull the wool on this one Phil?" asked Maurice. "Surely you must have realised you were under the microscope from day one. Ours is not the type of organisation that suffers fools gladly. We didn't take you for a fool," he continued.

"I'm afraid I'm not with you on all of this gentlemen. Could someone please tell me exactly what's going on?" Chloe found her voice at last.

Kenneth nodded. "All in good time my dear."

Phil clasped her hand. "It's all my fault darling. I'm sorry; I've been a bloody idiot. Maurice is right."

"What have you done? Who are these people? I'd like some answers and quickly!" exclaimed Chloe; her eyes blazing as she regained her confidence.

Maurice glanced across at his brother.

"Wait. Let's calm things down a little," Maurice suggested. "I apologise for the cloak and dagger way in which you've been treated, Mrs Lee, er... Chloe," he continued.

"There's a reason for this and we'll try to make it clear very soon," Kenneth interrupted.

Phil licked his lips nervously and wondered if they were in any immediate danger. He couldn't discern any obvious anger from the two brothers; merely a very heavy feeling of dissatisfaction at being deceived.

"Are you part of the military?" pursued Chloe.

"No - far from it," replied Kenneth. "Let's say we are Phil's new employers."

Chloe frowned and remained confused. "Employers? You didn't say you had a new job..."

"Phil is now a member of an organisation," Kenneth chose his words carefully.
"A club, if you like. Unique and still in its infancy."
"What - like the Masons?"
"You could say it's something like that. However, our ideals and dealings are of a far more serious nature. Our organisation has a very limited, elite, number of members."

Chloe intently leaned forward and quizzed, "You mean ... you're not a recognised organisation? You're an underground group? Unlicensed. Are you Illegal?"
Kenneth hesitated.
"You're not like the Mafia are you?" Chloe persisted.
"In a manner of speaking... yes," confirmed Maurice.
"We're not publicly recognised. Our purposes are not the sort of work that your average man or woman can do using Yellow Pages."

Chloe smiled nervously.
"What do you do then?"
Phil coughed quietly. Maurice eyed Kenneth.
"I cannot tell you that. All of our members take a vow of silence upon joining the organisation."
"Oh, I see. So you hurt people? You must be outside the law! People don't usually hold guns to women's heads. I couldn't miss that, could I? I had it shoved in my face for ten minutes..." Chloe ranted.
Phil tried to calm her down. "It's okay. It's all my fault. I'm sorry you had to get involved in all this," he appealed for her to listen.
"You're SORRY! So that makes it alright? Dragging me out of bed at five in the morning! That makes everything fine, does it?"

Kenneth and Maurice exchanged glances of growing concern.

"I'M LEAVING!" Chloe stood up suddenly with her eyes flashing.

"I'm sorry Mrs Lee but I'm afraid you cannot leave," Kenneth said gravely.

Chloe raged on, "Excuse me! I have a trial to attend. In case you don't know, my daughter's murderer is getting his just reward today. I intend to be there at ten this morning, so don't tell me I can't leave!"

Phil nodded, "She's right. There would be questions asked if she failed to show up today. Me too. We're already too involved in this case."

"We're aware of your circumstances, Phil... Chloe... You'll both be in court in good time. You've my word on that. Melvyn, your lawyer, is a member of our organisation," Kenneth stated.

Phil's eyes widened.

"Pike! A Brother?!" he exclaimed.

Chloe looked at Phil quizzically.

"Did you say 'Brother'?" she asked quietly.

Phil looked at Kenneth and his expression was one of despair.

Maurice spoke, "We've got no choice Ken. She has to know. We've got to tell her now."

Ken lowered his head slowly. He nodded to Mo; deep in thought. They hesitated. "Chloe... please sit down. Now listen to me - very carefully..."

****

Chloe found her mind wandering throughout the second day's proceedings in Court One. The morning had been a tense, fraught affair. Her reactions to the revelations of Ken, Mo and, to her surprise and shock, Phil had been a series of mixed emotions. By the end of two hours she was a physical wreck. The Brothers of Justice, however, had a new female member.

On reflection, she was disgusted to find herself agreeing with the men's aims and ideals. However, she instantly felt an affinity with their views on crime and punishment. The one thing that rankled with her was Phil's inability and refusal to tell her about these activities. Ken and Mo had explained everything slowly and concisely. Phil sat and listened while they told Chloe everything he knew and everything he had already accepted.

Nevertheless, by the end of the meticulous conversation, Chloe knew that she wanted to identify with The Brothers too. Even with the violence for justice. Had the death of Janice lessened her threshold for accepting that this sort of solution could possibly work? The word 'vigilantes' cropped up time and again. Ken and Mo were at pains to inform Chloe that they were in no way a vigilante group. They were merely people who were fed up with a society which accepted crime as a part of everyday life. They saw their group as an elite cleansing force. A force for the innocent, the good and the victims. So, with this in mind, she joined.

****

She left the isolated country farmhouse with Phil. Their sense of impending doom when they had arrived evaporated and was replaced by a confident air. Phil negotiated the loan of The Brother's BMW to get them back to the court on time.

They arrived early. The street was again awash with people; scurrying like ants around the entrance, placards waving and voices raised. The press and TV crews surrounded them again as they pushed their way through the crowd. Phil's lack of tact was evident as he brushed the heaving mass aside on the steps, while closing his ears to the barrage of questions which assailed them from every quarter.

"Are you happy with the trial so far, Mrs Lee?"
"There's a rumour he'll get off!"
"Picture please! Smile please – over here..."

Each time, Phil responded to the intrusive interrogation with, "No comment," or a terse, "Piss off!"

They sat in the same seats as the previous day. Chloe's head felt as if it was full of cotton wool and a nauseous wave swept over her every few moments. The lack of sleep and the bright court room lights were a hellish combination. Phil did his best to comfort her, even though he was suffering the same symptoms too. He explained to Melvyn Pike why they were in such a fragile state and the attorney nodded.

"The Brothers have lost none of their subtlety," he whispered with a smile. "Welcome to the club," he added as he gave Chloe a friendly wink.
She stared back with her mind uncertain of what he'd said. The judge entered the court.

The morning passed slowly. Edwin Moore made a few more patently dismal attempts to pass Hart off as some kind of saint to the obvious disgust of two of the jurors. Mrs Hart came forward to give evidence. When asked if her son could kill, she explained in a half-hearted fashion that Gary had always loved animals and he'd never harm his pet. When asked what relevance a pet dog had to the murder of a young woman, she had broken down in the dock and was unable to reply. Gary Hart had remained unmoved at his mother's distress and he had his usual sullen expression on his pasty face. Chloe tried to find some mite of compassion for Hart but his reaction to his mother's plight only reinforced her original opinion that he was a young thug without any redeeming features.

Hart's headmaster came forward to offer a character assessment of the miscreant. It's a catalogue of petty offences, bullying and truancy. When asked if he could perceive any redeeming facets to Hart's nature, he shrugged and smiled nervously with the comment, "I'm afraid that Gary has never impressed me, either as a pupil or a person. There are a lot of people, who could not honestly say Gary was innocent or guilty. My own feeling is that I regret that his education could not instil some sense of right and wrong in him."

Chloe's eyelids drooped with weariness. In spite of herself, she felt her head drop on to Phil's shoulder. The heat in the room was stifling and she fought to stay awake. Phil nudged her.
"Not long now love."
His time in the forces had inured him to long hours without sleep but even he felt wiped out.

The judge spoke, at last. Her plummy tones droned on and Chloe's mind closed down as she fell asleep Phil supported her as he realised she was out of it. He silently implored Judge Coombes to wind up the session.

Pike glanced at the couple. "Your honour - may I approach the bench," Pike's voice boomed across the court. Judge Coombes nodded with a questioning look on her face. Pike crossed the court and spoke in an undertone, while nodding in the direction of Chloe and Phil. The judge also nodded as she listened. Pike returned to his seat. "Bingo!" he murmured to Phil.

"The court will retire for today. We shall reconvene at ten o'clock tomorrow when I will hear your closing statements. Thank you."

As she rose to leave, Phil smiled gratefully at Pike and ruefully commented, "Not a moment too soon!" Chloe's snoring was becoming louder by the second...

****

BARNCHESTER HOUSING ESTATE - SATURDAY 10.00am

Dave Bramhall, 'Tiny' to his peers, stared out of the kitchen window. He held the remains of a cigarette in his left hand and a half-drunk can of strong cider in his right. Stubbing out the butt in the grimy sink he exhaled the final dregs of smoke. He looked at his watch and belched loudly. 10.15am.

Today was the big one. Town versus Athletic. The only match in Dave's book which really mattered. He didn't care if they (Athletic) got relegated. A four-nil thrashing away at Norwich or Forest paled into insignificance when levelled against today's adversaries. They must WIN!

Athletic - scum!
Athletic! To lose was unimaginable.
To win was the best feeling in the world. Better than the birth of his daughter, Chelsea. Better than a blow job off Madonna! (*Well, almost!)*

He smiled his lop-sided smile, the one that had first turned Carole, his long-suffering wife, on.

Dave had always been small; five foot five in his loafers. Nevertheless, he was built like a prop-forward and then some. He had not grown upwards since he was eleven years old but he sure had grown outwards. They say you can't grow in both directions at the same time.

He was nicknamed 'Pitbull' by the time he was nine. He had a quiet demeanour belied by his looks. He had the face of an angel. Alcohol disagreed with him but he liked a drink and a fag. Two of life's pleasures. Football and sex came a close third and fourth. Chelsea came about eighth.

"Dave. Your mates are 'ere!" Carole shouted.
He turned away from the sink, crushing the empty can and dropping it into a black plastic bin liner in the corner of the room.
"Comin' love," he replied in his thick Northern accent.

Carole stood by the front door, leaning against the rotting wooden bannister, chewing a spearmint gum. She wore a cheap denim skirt and white stilettos. Her 'shopping kit' Dave called it.
She craned her head to kiss her husband's neck as he passed. She was barely five feet, even in her shoes.

"See you love - behave!"
Dave smiled. "Of course - Scout's Honour!" he dib-dibbed at her.
"Piss off!" laughed Carole, playfully slapping him on the side of his head.
"Giz a kiss sexy," Dave invited as he pulled her to him. Her thin blouse stretched and her full breasts almost escaped from their confines. She never failed to arouse him, even after six years of arguments and torment.

Someone knocked the door.
"Fuck off, we're shaggin'!" shouted Dave laughing.
A voice answered. "We'll come back in thirty seconds then - give you time!" Uproarious laughter accompanied this jibe from the street.
"Bastards," whispered Dave as he released his embrace and opened the front door.

"Hope they win," said Carole.
"Say bye to Chelsea for me."
"OK. She's still asleep though. That school trip knackered her yesterday."
"Love you!"
"Love you too!"

With their ritual farewell complete, Dave turned to face his pals.

The terrible twosome - Spud and Jud. Dave's best mates.
"Hi, sex bomb!" greeted Spud as he blatantly eyed up Carole's ample chest.

Carole thrust her fulsome bust towards the pair of jokers. "You two probably have more interest in these than him," she said with a chuckle and tossed her head at her husband.
"We wish!" responded Spud.
Jud blushed and shyly turned away.
"How's things lads?" asked Dave, "Long time - no see."
Jud found his voice, "I'm back on t' dole and Spud's shagging a nigger."

Everyone collapsed into shrieks of laughter. Subtlety was not Jud's strong point.
"You bastard! You said you wouldn't tell!" Spud thumped his side-kick between his shoulder blades and sent him staggering.
"Go on! Piss off, you lot! You'll be late for t' game," grumbled Carole. "I've got washing to do and Chelsea will need her breakfast."

Dave grinned. He and his mates knew each other inside out, especially when they were having a laugh. Like now...
"Thought you had a garage job Jud?"
"Yeah I did, 'til the boss caught me with me hands in the till," Jud replied self-consciously.
"Prat!" commented Spud, soullessly.
Jud glanced at him and said, "At least I stick to white women."
"You're only jealous!" Spud was rising to the bait.

"How big are her tits then?" Dave asked slyly.
"That's it! Clear off to your match cos I've heard enough already!" shouted Carole as she pushed them down the steps into the street.

They all strolled away down the street and she watched them go, as she always did. Dave, Spud and Jud. She loved them all for their gutsy humour. They were like brothers. Inseparable!

As they reached the corner, Dave turned and blew Carole a kiss. Spud called him gay.

Carole smiled, waved back to Dave and closed the front door.

****

They'd gone through school together. Dave, Cliff Edwards and Terry Judge. 'Spud' Edwards and 'Jud' were nicknames born in their primary school years. They all supported Gailey Town, even when they were relegated. Even when Pete Wall arrived from the scum. They had swopped stories about their first kisses and cried watching ET. They'd learned about condoms in the same class talk with matching blushing faces. Soul mates forever! Any outsiders would get a good kicking. Growing up in an inner-city slum meant learning to look out for one another.

Spud was jack-the-lad. He told the jokes; the one-liners and put-downs ready for anyone threatening their little clique. His mop of mousey brown hair hung over his brown eyes. He was like an urchin from 'Oliver

Twist' - the eponymous Artful Dodger. A brilliant impressionist and his voice could conjure up any person or a sound. He had a tattoo of an eagle on his forearm with a scroll reading 'DAD'. Sadly, he'd never known his mother who'd died of a stroke when he was only two. His father was a feared man on the estate, but a gentleman too, and respected for bringing up Spud alone.

Jud was the quiet one. He had six O-Levels and wrote poetry. He also boxed. His nose had been broken and he looked like a ruffian but the boxing had disciplined him. Nobody crossed Jud if they knew what was good for them. He'd already had lost two teeth; a legacy of a school playground fight when he was sixteen. Jud won! His hard reputation and the poetry meant female company was never far away. He lived respectably with his parents and sister, Julie, who worked in a travel agency in the heart of the city.

"So, shall we hit the Old Legion?" suggested Dave. At twenty seven he was the acknowledged leader, married with a 'rug-rat'.

Content, they caught the bus into the city centre. The Saturday crowds milled like ants. Normally they would be wearing the 'colours'; their chosen shirt for the day. Not today. Today was Derby Day!

Any self-respecting supporter did not wear their colours against the scum. Wearing colours meant you didn't want trouble. It meant you were going to see 'the game'. Derby Day was about more than the game. It was about the hatred that ran through their veins. For years, Town had played second fiddle to Athletic. Athletic won and Town lost. That was it.

The last time Town had won something, Churchill may have been in power and so the taunts went on.

They'd supported Town since 1984. They'd won at Wembley and it was the best day of their lives with more to come. Or so they'd hoped but it didn't happen. Chance after chance of winning a 'big one' came and went. Year after year so 'hope' typically turned into embarrassment.

Today things would change. It was always 'today'.

They purposefully climbed off the bus with their hands in their pockets. Four hours to kick-off.
"In 'ere?" suggested Dave.
The huge pub bristled with men and women. The noise was deafening and they all talked the same language. This was a Town pub.

"Oh, aye, I remember Doyley. He used to shit all over Jonah 'til 'e bust 'is leg, poor sod."
Cliché after cliché resounded around the bar.
"... got a tenner on a 2-0..."
"They won't live with us today..."

A young boy aged about six took a sly swig of his father's lager. He wore a scarf and a T-shirt with a picture of a sixties idol across the front.

"Colin Welling - fuckin' artissst," slurred a fat man as he pushed by the young lad. His wife followed in his wake, clutching a short glass. The contents slopped over as she was nudged by another raised elbow.

Her lipstick was smudged and the mini-skirt did little for her spreading hips.

Spud nudged Dave as they glanced around the seething scrum.
"Fuck me, it's packed!" he muttered while he tried to signal an order to the harassed barman.
"Yeah," replied Dave with a wink.
"They've all come out for this one!"
Jud nodded. "There's Mad Dom over there – look."
A six foot skinhead stood next to the bar entrance. He held a pint glass in one hand and his latest female companion with the other. They both sported identical donkey jackets and white jeans.
"Not many colours in here today," commented Spud.
"Nah, they must be expecting some hassle."
"Never – 'the Reds' should never come near here. Not ever," slurred Jud as the half a can of imported beer hit his senses.
"Still can't take your beer. Fuckin' boxers can't take it," laughed Dave.
"Too much trainin' thassall," replied Jud thickly.
"Give it up and get pissed you twat," joined in Spud. The chink of glasses and the general revelry all but drowned out his voice.
The jukebox shook the floor with 'A Little Respect' by Erasure. *(80s heaven!)*
"Put some 'Take That' on!" screamed a female voice.
It was twelve minutes past midday.
"Fuck off! Put some Town on!" said a drunken, thick set, bald man.
Everyone cheered.

The atmosphere held a tension which was tangible. People leered warily at everyone who entered the bar. Some were recognised immediately, with much back slapping and laughter but all strangers were scrutinised constantly. There seemed to be no real threat thought Dave as he downed his fourth can of cider.

A lone voice started to chant, "'We love you... To-o-own...we do'!"
Then the whole pub took up the chorus, "We love you... Too-o-own, we do! O-o-oh, To-o-own, we love you!"

The barmen and women joined in; some out of tune.
"Fuckin' Ace!" Spud shouted maniacally.
Dave just nodded and swayed to the rhythm.
Jud leaned across to Dave with his eyes glazed.
" 'ere, Dave, why don' you bring Carole to the match then?"
Dave put his arm around Jud's muscular shoulders and said, " 'cos she 'ates fuckin' football me ol' mate. Simple."
Jud's eyes struggled to focus and he hiccupped loudly.
"Ahh...," he nodded sagely.

Dave turned to Spud and probed, "What's this new bird like then?"
"Who? Claire?" Spud's eyes lit up. "She's fuckin' gorgeous!" Spud yelled back at Dave, "And she ain't black neither. You've got it all wrong cos she's a half-caste."
"Off-white, you mean?" snorted Dave above the uproar.
"Yeah and she's horny as hell!" countered Spud.
"Stick with her then. My Carole still turns me on!" slurred Dave.

Spud looked shocked as he said, "Really? You mean she still shags and gives blow jobs after ten o'clock?"

Dave suddenly looked around. "Where's Jud gone?"
Spud looked around and pointed. "He's over there chattin' up the leggy, blonde barmaid. Bet he cops off. He always did. Lucky sod!
Dave laughed. "Jud's such a charmer but p'raps it's his broken nose that brings out their maternal instinct."
"More like his ten inch cock!" joshed Spud.
They both broke out into guffaws at their wit about Jud's pulling progress. One minute Jud was talking, the next he was kissing the prettiest as she passed him to clear the glass laden tables.

The landlord separated the embracing twosome. "Save it for later Janine!" he spat with his face turning purple.

Perhaps he's pissed off with the increasing demands of punters thought Jud.

Jud returned to the fold looking very pleased with his latest conquests.
"Nice one Casanova!" greeted Dave with not a hint of jealousy.
"Yeah, what's her mate's name?" asked Spud.
"Dunno but think I'm in love," murmured Jud.
"Seein' her again Jud?"
"Nah Spud."
"Why not? She's a scorcher mate!"
"Fuckin' married to the boss!" blurted Jud.
A sudden silence fell on proceedings.

Time stood still for a split second when the first brick smashed through the pub's window. Heads turned in slow motion. Another brick suddenly hurtled across the bar, through the shattered hole in the glass. Then another...
"Christ!" someone shouted.
A skinhead's girlfriend screamed and their child began to cry. Her boyfriend's horizontal body lay just inside the entrance and his blood was pouring from a large gash wound above his eye. He was unconscious.
"It's the scum!" yelled Dave.
Spud's eyes widened in horror. "Oh, no!"

The doors crashed open. About fifteen huge men surged in. One of them, obviously the leader, held a small box and a lighted match. The skinhead lay at his feet.
"Wha's he doin'?" slurred a voice.
Silence hung over the bar apart from Take That singing 'It Only Takes A Minute Girl' on the jukebox.
"Masks on!" the leader screamed. He then struck a match to its box.
Spud looked at Dave. "Eh?"
Jud moaned incoherently, "Tell 'im to fuck off Dave."

In one concerted movement, the group at the door put on their gas masks. The match fizzed into life as it contacted the CS canister. The leader grinned to himself, beneath his mask.
"Fuckin' hell - they're gonna gas us!" a man screamed and made a dive for the door but two burly figures blocked his path.
Pandemonium broke out as the canister flew through the air. As everyone took breath to scream, the noxious fumes hit their lungs.

"Get out!" yelled Dave as he realised their danger. He threw his large frame towards the entrance. Bodies blocked his way as panic ensued and people collapsed into a thrashing mass.

"Athletic!" chanted a menacing masked figure.
The sound of retching and vomiting filled the room as people blindly tried to get out. Tears streamed down their faces from the toxic air.

Then, the violence started. The group carried baseball bats and knives. People fell as the bats found their random targets. Knives slashed indiscriminately. Jud was trying to fight back instinctively but he couldn't see his opponents through his bloated, bleary eyes.

A fist caught Dave full in the face. The pain was diminished by his survival instincts. He lashed out in a rage, fuelled by his hatred. "Fuckin' scum!" he yelled.
He never saw the baseball bat coming from behind. It split his skull with a sickening thud and he collapsed onto the vomit-spattered lino. Death was instantaneous. He would never see Town's 2 - 0 defeat...

****

'TWO MINUTES OF HORROR!'
The newspaper headlines grabbed public attention for twenty four hours but the actual cost of the madness affected only the families of those who were unfortunate enough to be in the Old Legion pub.
Four men died along with two children. Three of the men were hardened criminals and well known to the authorities.

Spud had multiple stab wounds but survived.
Jud wasn't so lucky. The life support machine was switched off after eighty-three days in coma.
Town and Athletic play on. Families sit together, more out of pity than any friendliness between the groups. The charity record reached Number One and it raised more than three million pounds.
Athletic still hate Town and vice versa.

None of the attackers were traced. Police arrived five minutes after the riot. People lay in the street, either vomit-ridden or unconscious. Passers-by were affected by the gas too.

The pub became a shrine. Scarves and favours lay scattered for weeks until the council wound it all up.
"They've grieved enough," said one official.

When a referee was stabbed to death on a playing field two weeks later; nobody took much notice.
"It's getting out of hand," commented an F.A. spokesperson.

****

Chapter Forteen

Vanguard II

The Ten sat once more around the long oak table. Smoke rose into the air. The low murmur as they spoke among themselves gave the room the air of a mystic ritual.

The Head sat motionless at the far end of the table; simply watching and waiting. At eight o'clock precisely he rose from his seat. The murmurs subsided.

"Gentlemen – welcome," said the Head in a low monotone. He stood ramrod straight. "You're obviously wondering why you've been summoned so soon after our last meeting. The truth is that it's time to branch out. Time to increase our membership," he explained.

The room was silent. The faces of his audience registered their attentiveness.

"Our 'Brothers' and supporters will march in three weeks. We'll, as it were, 'go public' for the first time. It's time to show the do-gooders and weak-minded parliamentarians that there's choice. A choice between being the punished and the punisher or being threatened and doing the threatening. It's my intention to show those in power that the people have had enough!"

Murmurs of approval greeted his words.

"I want to march on London. The Home Secretary is presently totally unaware of this. However, I intend making certain people within the cabinet au fait with our intentions. Furthermore, the police are under strict orders not to intervene."

A lone voice interrupted, "Do you think that's wise sir?"

The Head sought out the speaker. "Wise? I think it's very unwise but that's the reason for doing it."

With no further comment coming from the assembly, the Head continued, "Victims of crime will assemble in Trafalgar Square. They will not demonstrate. They will be passive and peaceful. This will show the support we have and the vote of confidence in favour of our movement will become a visible fact."

"How many people are expected to attend sir?" another voice queried.

The Head nodded and answered, "Our underground connections have informed me they expect a turnout of massive proportions. Approximately half a million people."

"Good grief, that's incredible," came another disembodied voice at the far end of the room.

"Exactly. This is no anti-fascist lobby. This is not just a couple of hundred students campaigning for more grant cash. This is the biggest show of strength against the criminal fraternity in British history. I'm not going to Number Ten to hand in a petition. Those have been ignored too many times before. Names on paper carry no weight. This will be people power - ordinary people. The Home Secretary will have to act in the interests of public order - and act quickly!"

"What else? How many dissenters are likely to be present?" another Brother asked the Head.
"Very few since the march has been planned in total secrecy, so any dissenters will be outnumbered and will be dealt with on the spot. The police will not intervene."

"What do you mean - on the spot?"
"Wait and see my friend, wait and see..."
"Will you be there?" a distant voice asked the Head.
"Yes, but only as an observer. I don't intend being interviewed on the steps of Number Ten."
Laughter broke out briefly.
"Is it possible 'The March' could get out of hand? asked a small man, seated next to the Head.
"Yes, but the incidents will be contained by our own people who are specifically tasked to deal with them."
"No police then?"
"No, as I've said, they're already under strict instruction not to respond to any incidents."
The murmuring broke out again as the implications of the news were realised by the company around the table.
"What about TV and media coverage? Are they aware of this event?"
"One of our Brothers in the communications business is making certain our message is transmitted worldwide. Satellite coverage will be extensive.
The march will hit the Prime Minister and the government where it hurts.
His only course of action will have to be swift and decisive. Any inability to grasp the seriousness of our intentions will be detrimental to his prospects of continuing in office."

"In other words, if he doesn't act, he's in the shit!" chipped in another voice; to the accompaniment of laughter.

"Very succinctly put my friend." The Head allowed a slight smile to soften his message. "If he won't act, then we will. He certainly will not have the right to remain silent!"

More laughter emanated from the brotherhood. Animated gestures could be seen as they discussed this momentous news.

"So there you have it my friends. The time has come to put ourselves on the map."

The Head rapped his gavel to gain attention over the rising hubbub. The voices ceased and they gave him their full attention once more.

"Now - to recent activities. I know it's not long since we met, but I am sure we've all seen and heard about the Hart teenager accused of rape and murder. Hart's just the sort of person I could personally snuff out for no reward. We should keep our eyes on this case and one of our own is directly involved in the outcome. Phil Queen arrested the accused and is awaiting the sentence.

His girlfriend is the mother of the victim. They're both now members of the Brotherhood. If, by any remote chance the accused youth is let off on a technicality..."

"A loophole," someone shouted.

"Yes - a loophole," continued the Head, "Then it's my intention that this little runt will be eliminated."

"Hear, hear," came the approving reply in unison.

"Queen shall have the tasking if it becomes necessary. The boy looks like being sentenced but it'll be interesting to see what transpires tomorrow. We may yet have more ammunition to throw at our wondrous government."

The Head resumed his seat as the clock chimed the half-hour.

One by one the Ten departed from the room. The Head remained impassive. He sipped at the remains of his glass of red wine, while he listened to the rhythmic ticking of the clock...

****

The country was on tenterhooks. All thoughts were on the coming events in Court One. The trial of Gary Hart had gripped the nation and beyond. Tourists camped outside the old grey buildings of the court. Many brought garish, cheaply-made placards which leaned against the railings alongside the figures rolled up in their sleeping bags like maggots or huddled in blankets. Newsmen and women mingled with the public. A hamburger van did a roaring trade and its empty paper cups were discarded in the gutters. A stray dog with its ribs showing through its quivering skin, sniffed hopefully in a plastic bag.

Four a.m. and the expectant ghouls were awaking. Gary Hart was a blessing to the media.

Phil's sleep had been disturbed by an assortment of visions. As a child he had suffered from nightmares, and the recurring one where he walked unsteadily on a high wire above the earth had resurfaced last night. He would always fall from the wire and wake with a jolt on impact. A cold sweat covered his body as he sat bolt upright in Chloe's bed. Was the nightmare an omen? He hadn't dreamt it for over twenty years. He breathed erratically and wiped his streaming face on the sheet.

He'd played the verdict over and over in his brain – guilty! He tried to smile but all he managed was to bite his lip and frown.

The bedside clock's red digits clicked closer to judgement time. 5.36a.m. and counting...

Chloe lay beside him and she breathed low and steady. She'd dozed fitfully only dropping into a deeper sleep as dawn was breaking. Phil's nightmare jolt had no effect on Chloe as she dreamt of Janice. She saw her daughter running towards her in slow motion across a field of corn. When she just reached touching distance, Jan's image disintegrated. Low clouds hovered across the cornfield and Chloe was alone. She heard a low chuckle behind her and as she turned she saw Gary Hart sitting on a gate. His eyes were black holes and his hair had grown longer. It began to rain and his echoing laughter mingled with the swish of the wind across the field. He'd disappeared in the damp air too.

They didn't talk much over breakfast. A black coffee each was all they could manage. Chloe wiped a silent tear from her cheek as she made herself presentable to face the day ahead. A framed picture of Janice lay on the bedside table and it made her heart turn over again. My beautiful Janice at seventeen years old and holding her pet rabbit, Thumper.

Phil wore his suit. He felt as if he'd just done a four-day patrol in Belfast without a break. His head felt as if it was stuffed with cotton wool and his reactions were blurred. He'd shaved carefully visualising Judge

Coombes. She mouthed the word 'guilty' over and over. He fancied he could even hear her gavel as she tried to restore order to a tumultuous public gallery... When they were ready to face the world and the media hounds, they embraced.

Phil held Chloe close. Their eyes met; moist with emotion.

"Remember, I love you whatever happens," he said tenderly.

"You big softie," she replied as she broke away to make her way out into the hall.

An envelope lay on the mat. Chloe bent and picked it up. Inside was a card. Everyone in the village must have signed it. On the front read – 'GOOD LUCK!'

Chloe's fragile composure dissipated and tears filled her eyes.

"I can't believe how kind everyone's been."

"Bloody marvellous!" said Phil gruffly and continued, "Come on now - you know you've got them all backing you!"

"Yes - let's go," said Chloe squaring her shoulders. She tucked the card into her handbag like a talisman.

They walked down the flower-strewn path to the car. The big day had begun!

****

Melvyn Pike was waiting for Phil and Chloe in the corridor outside the courtroom. His large hand enveloped Chloe's, transmitting confidence and support. "Are you awake today Mrs Lee?" Pike's voice boomed, as the heavy scent cascaded over her from his expensive suit.

"Yes, yes - of course... I'm sorry about yesterday's performance," she smiled at his joke.
"Well, no problem. I sometimes wish I could curl up in a ball and disappear sometimes too!"
That would be a good trick thought Phil, as he contemplated the bulk of the barrister.
"We've run the gauntlet again outside and we're getting the hang of it now."
Pike laughed out loud. "Oh, the media scrum - yes! What a palaver eh? You'd think the Bay City Rollers were in concert, wouldn't you?" he boomed. Some heads turned at the hilarity.
"There's only one person who will get in without any hassle. The runt who caused all this bother," Phil said bitterly.
"I'm afraid you're right Phil, but I guess he'll have more on his mind than a few nutters with pieces of cardboard."

Pike laughed a lot thought Chloe, as the barrister enjoyed his own joke again. She considered him quietly as Phil and he chatted. A professional to his heel tips, obviously in love with his work and himself. All this trauma was meat and drink to him, yet he didn't come across as unfeeling. She liked him in spite of herself, whereas if he'd been in different circumstances she felt she'd have loathed his bonhomie.

The court doors opened and people began to file in. Phil and Chloe sat behind the prosecuting counsel and Phil turned around to survey the gathering crowd in the public gallery. They were a mixed congregation and ready for the ritual. People craned their necks to get a better view. Stewards and officials did their best to keep order . An impossible task. Extra seats had been brought in. It was like a Cup Final!

To their right, Brenda Hart sat chewing gum and gesticulating wildly at the defence solicitor, the puny Edwin Moore. He looked even more like a scared rabbit, thought Chloe. She compared him to Melvyn Pike and smiled inwardly. How could Hart hope to win with a defence like that?

The newspapers had been having a great time with numerous editorials by psychologists and counsellors who all propounded various theories about Hart's state of mind. Politicians sat on the fence, not wanting to alienate thousands of potential voters by taking sides. Even the criminal fraternity had been espoused for their opinions. Billy Nogan, himself serving time for the rape of a sixteen year old epileptic, stated from his cell in a letter to one of the more lurid tabloids that Hart should be incarcerated with him and they could swop ideas! The lunatics were taking over the asylum and the press...

At one minute to ten the final round began.
"All stand!" called a disembodied voice.
All talking stopped. People coughed.
Judge Coombes took her seat and 'Queen of the Castle' sang in Phil's head.
Chloe reached for Phil's hand.

Gary Hart entered Court One to hear the last battle for his future life. He wore a collar and tie and his hair had grown slightly in the past two weeks. It was greased and combed; giving him an air of respectability. This was

totally at odds with the dishevelled figure that Phil had arrested.
"He looks like flaming Marlon Brando," Phil hissed in Pike's ear.
"Just a pitiful attempt to make him look human," Pike remarked unmoved.
Hart sat in the dock, flanked by two male police officers. He looked across at his mother with a half-smile on his lips. Hart is as cocksure as ever, thought Pike.

A low rumble of comment arose from the public gallery, as the watchers took in the scene below in excited anticipation. Heads bobbed and excited glances passed among the crowd. They were, after all, THERE! One up on the crowd outside.

With the preliminaries over, Judge Coombes announced the procedure for the summing up of the evidence by the Defence and Prosecuting Counsels.

Silence fell as Edwin Moore stood to persuade the jury and the world that Gary Hart could not, and did not, kill Janice Lee in cold blood.

He looked like a fly caught in a jar thought Phil as he began his peroration.
"Your' here Honour," Moore said nervously, while genuflecting towards the bench as if to a deity and taking a sheet of paper he approached the jury box.
"Ladies and Gentlemen of the jury - your job... your duty is to ascertain beyond reasonable doubt that a thirteen year old boy..." he gestured awkwardly at Hart, "...Did or did not murder a defenceless lady."

Moore coughed timidly. The jury regarded him impassively.
"Gary Hart is not a very nice young man. He's coarse, obnoxious, immature and aggressive," Moore continued. Then Moore's voice rose shrilly, "Is he a KILLER?"
Silence...
"You can walk down any street, in any town, in any area in Britain today and you'll find any number of Gary Harts. They're everywhere and they're called 'teenagers'!" said Moore.
Gasps emanated from the public gallery at this blatant generalisation. Pike tutted under his breath.
Chloe's grip tightened on Phil's arm.

Edwin Moore continued, "Gary Hart has no doubt that HE did not kill Janice Lee. If he did not, then who did? Who knows? Certainly, all the evidence pointed at Gary Hart." Moore paused and turned to face the defendant. "You've heard his story - he was let in. He admits that he followed her back to her flat and that he intended to frighten her, but what happened when she opened her door to him? She screamed. He lost his nerve and ran away. Flimsy facts. He was there, he doesn't pretend he wasn't, but he says he did not kill her. She was alive when he fled from her flat."

Moore walked back to his desk and took a sip of water and paused for his words to take effect.
"Look at him, ladies and gentlemen. A thirteen year old boy is big for his age, but could a thirteen year old boy kill?" continued Moore.
Gary Hart's eyes never strayed from the jury's faces. He was no longer smiling. His face was expressionless.

"If you think Gary Hart slaughtered Janice Lee in cold blood, then go ahead and convict him. However, if you have the slightest doubt in your mind at all that this most horrific crime was committed by him, then I implore you to show him some mercy. He could have pleaded guilty but he didn't. Why not? Because he's innocent of this murder!" said Moore.
Moore turned to face Judge Coombes, nodded his conclusion and resumed his seat.

"Bollocks!" screamed a voice from the gallery. An official swiftly moved across to remonstrate with the offender and silence again engulfed the court.

Judge Coombes rapped her gavel and affirmed, "If there are any further interruptions I shall clear the public gallery. There will be civility during these proceedings!"

Melvyn Pike rose and acknowledged the judge with a brief nod. As he moved across the floor, Chloe caught another whiff of his aftershave. She couldn't place the heavy musky aroma.

Thirty seconds passed. Two jury members fidgeted and glanced at each other.

"Ladies and Gentlemen!" Pike's mellow voice reverberated around the court. "The question is not 'Could a teenager kill in cold blood?' The question is 'Could a teenager, called Gary Hart, kill in cold blood?' My learned friend, Mr Moore, tarnishes all teenagers with his remarks in his summing-up of this case. This is a grave error of judgement. All teenagers are not aggressive murderers roaming our streets seeking whom they may devour! I have two teenage sons whose only association with violence is the odd Batman video!" declared Pike.

Laughter rolled down from the gallery. The judge's gavel sounded again. "Mr Pike..." she warned.

"Yes, your Honour," he acknowledged his levity but continued in a sterner tone. "The question is, having weighed up the evidence which undoubtedly does point to Mr Hart - did he do it? As Mr Moore says, he admits he was there, that he had attacked Janice Lee earlier in the park. He actually followed her with intent back to her flat. His hat was found at the scene of the crime. His prints match. What more do you want?"

Pike's authority far outweighed Moore's, thought Phil. It was like comparing lager with champagne. He watched the response of the jurors. One young woman was staring at Pike, unblinking. She looked like a convert who had found God. Go for it Pikey!

"You, the jury, have a duty! That duty is to lock up this little monster so that the next Janice Lee can walk home in the evening, watch TV and sleep safely at night without the threat of assault or murder. You must return a verdict of 'guilty' on Gary Hart. Thank you!"

Melvyn Pike turned his back on the jury and returned to his seat.

Applause broke out from the gallery and feet stamped in a display of approval.

Phil's gaze found Gary Hart. No smiles now. His face looked like a piece of stale cheese. The cocky facade had gone. He was obviously shaken by the force of Pike's words. He stared down at the floor in silence.

Judge Coombes addressed the jurors.
"You have heard all of the evidence in this case. Murder is the ultimate crime. I ask you to take your time to consider all you've seen and heard, however obvious or basic it may seem, and return here with your verdict. The court will rise," said Judge Coombes.
"Short and sweet," commented Phil to Pike.
"Yes," murmured Pike slowly, as he watched the judge leave the court. "I'm afraid it's out of my hands now Philip. I've done my best," Pike expressed.
"You were superb," Chloe interrupted. "Twice the professional of Moore," she gushed.
Pike frowned momentarily. "I thought he did quite well, actually..."

****

The jury was out for three hours and twenty minutes. The court rapidly reconvened for the verdict on Gary Hart. Most people resumed the places they'd had earlier in the day. Judge Coombes sat like an eagle on her raised dais. Phil and Chloe held hands and waited as Gary Hart was led back into the dock. His six foot frame belied his age. He looked worldly wise; confident even.

"Foreman please stand," said the clerk of the court.
A small man in a checked lumberjack shirt and jeans got to his feet and shrugged his shoulders tensely. He held a small piece of paper and looked ready to pray.

Judge Coombes' voice broke the expectant silence, "Have you reached a verdict on which you are all agreed?"
"We have your Honour."
"Do you find the defendant, Gary Hart, guilty or not guilty of the charge of murder?" A short pause.
"Guilty, your..." the foreman's reply was drowned in a deluge of cheering and stamping feet.
Phil and Chloe turned to each other; their eyes wide with relief as they hugged each other. Melvyn Pike stood up and watched the reaction of Gary Hart. He was shaking, white-faced and a look of total disbelief had overtaken the confident leer he'd shown most of the week to the assembled court. His mother collapsed into her seat and was being supported by Edwin Moore, who was shaking his head and mouthing soundless words at her.

Judge Coombes gavel was drowned out by the ecstatic roars of approval from the public gallery, as people began to stream out and down the stairs to break the news to those outside the court. Officials tried to restore order and restrain those leaving so that the Judge could announce the sentencing.

A young man in a blue suit, impeccable before the fracas broke out, was fighting with a policeman in the gallery. It would be reported next day in the national press that he was an ex-boyfriend of Janice Lee. He would sell his story of his passionate clinches with the dead girl in the storeroom of the supermarket where they worked. He'd be made richer by £20,000...

Judge Coombes at last made herself heard and she said, "Gary Hart, you have been found guilty of murder. You will be remanded in custody, pending sentence Monday week. Court is adjourned."

Melvyn Pike turned to Chloe and Phil as the judge left the court and uttered, "A good decision by the jury, I think. I must admit, however, that there were one or two points on which I thought Moore would have a stronger case, but evidently he saw fit not to introduce them. I feel justice has been served here today."
"Thank you so much for all you've done," said Chloe clasping Pike's large warm hand, "and I hope I can start to get my life together again now," she continued.
"I'll be around to help with that," Phil assured her, "but let's get out of here for now. I've had my fill of this place and we've got to get through the mob outside again!"

The scenes in the street resembled a fair on a traditional celebration day. Flags were waving and placards lay in shreds in the gutter as the crowd waited for the prisoner to emerge from the court. The rent-a-mob section always squeezed out the last drop - the ritual banging on the sides of the closed van. Few people noticed Hart's bereaved, sobbing mother as she left Court One alone.

****

Chloe and Phil slept peacefully that night. Their lovemaking had a new urgency; a new release. No nightmares invaded their sleep...

Gary Hart spent his first night of captivity in a state of black despair. His cocksure demeanour had deserted him; to be replaced with a normal teenager's terror of what lay before him. Every time he closed his eyes all he saw was Janice Lee's terrified face as she had lain on her bedsit floor screaming at him...

****

A phone was ringing. It echoed through his subconscious like a nagging tooth... Ignore it, you're dreaming...

Phil's eyes opened slowly. The early morning light shone through the half-open curtains. Chloe lay still beside him; her breathing even and calm. The purring mobile had not disturbed her sleep.

Phil remembered the phone was reassuringly by the bed, and he closed his eyes against the brightness of the day as he reached out to silence the noise.

"Hello," he croaked into its mouthpiece.
"Phil, is that you?" Melvyn Pike's unmistakable tones sounded urgent.
"Yeah," Phil murmured, as his brain vaguely recognised the caller.
"Phil, wake up! It's about Gary Hart!"
Phil sat up with a start.
"Hart? Why? What's up?" he replied; now wide awake.
Chloe turned over as his movement disturbed her.

Pike's voice was grave, "Yes - Hart... He's dead! Suicide."
Phil swallowed and his stomach churned.
"Suicide? How on earth...?"
"Wrist job. He'd got a piece of glass. Lord knows how and there's a heck of a stink blowing up."
Phil looked at the clock. It was seven-forty. He could hardly comprehend what Pike was saying.

"He left a note. They'd let him have a newspaper, he'd torn out letters and arranged them on the floor. A sort of message – 'not me – sorry'.

"That's all?" queried Phil.
"Yes, except he'd spelt 'sorry' with one 'r'."
Phil smiled wanly; thinking of the young truant. "I almost feel sorry for the little bastard myself," he whispered.
"Is that with one 'r' or two?" chuckled Pike.
Phil let out a deep sigh at the weak joke.
"Well, it'll save the taxpayers a bob or two I guess," Pike added.

Chloe stirred again and Phil stroked her hair as she squinted up at him.
"Who's that?" she asked nervously, "It's early, isn't it? Is it one of your 'Brothers'?"

Phil put his finger to his lips.

"It's okay," he indicated as he winked to Chloe.

"Sorry I had to disturb you so early Phil. I just thought you should know," concluded Pike.
"Yes - thanks, I'll be in touch. It may be a blessing. Cheers." Phil switched off his mobile and lay back on the pillows. Chloe was fast asleep again.

His mind raced back over the past few weeks. Gary Hart trying to escape from his flat when Phil arrested him, Brenda Hart's condemnation of her son and the school reports of the uncontrollable lout.

"Good riddance!" he murmured and relaxed against the warmth of his lover.

****

Gary Hart's death was big news for all of two days. The trial was a distant memory to the tabloids whose lead stories reverted quickly to the latest royal scandal or celebrity hype, such as **'PRINCE PHILIP INSULTS JAPS!'** or **'EMMERDALE STARLET IN THREE-IN-A-BED ROMP!'** Gary Hart was a forgotten man. Old news!

Chloe placed her hot mug of coffee beside Phil who was hunched over the kitchen table. In the three days since the verdict, he'd grown a dark stubble on his chin and resembled a young Richard Branson.

"Aren't you going to shave darling?"
Phil looked up and smiled. "Are you complaining?" he frowned.
"Er... nope," replied Chloe, as she wrapped her arms around her lover's broad shoulders and she tenderly kissed his ear lobe.
"It tickles when you kiss me...especially..." oozed Phil.
Phil lifted the mug to his lips and sipped tentatively at the steaming coffee. He indicated the newspaper he was reading.
"Interesting piece here. Did you know that it's possible that many women have been raped by their future husbands without realising it?"
Chloe nodded. "Oh, yes. Of course!" she glanced at him, expectantly.
"'Many women have sex before marriage through pressure, not for love, according to 'experts' *(he really emphasised the word)* in Sweden,"' Phil quoted.

"Oh really, perhaps I should call the cops then?" Chloe replied mockingly.
She reached for the telephone, teasing him.
"They'll be telling us sex is bad for us soon," Phil commented sarcastically as he tossed the paper across the room.
"These are the same people who tell us brown bread is better than white, semi-skimmed milk healthier than pasteurised - blah, blah - bollocks!"

Chloe nudged him on his shoulder and declared, "Get off your soapbox Queen! You sound like Adolf bloody Hitler!"
Phil looked up with a sheepish gaze.
"Do I?"
"Yeah and you SMELL like him! Get in the shower PDQ. I'm coming too!"

Phil leapt to his feet, ran out of the kitchen and up the wooden staircase calling, "Come and get me sex fiend!"

Chloe followed him and laughed playfully. Peals of laughter echoed around the cottage.

Neither of them noticed the envelope lying on the mat inside the front door. It lay face up with no stamp. It was addressed to P.C. Queen.

****

PART TWO

Chapter Fifteen

Phil picked up the envelope almost casually. Another well-wisher, he thought.

He whistled shrilly as he made his way along the sunlit hallway of the cottage towards the kitchen.

Opening the envelope, he absentmindedly banged his head on the low door frame. He winced. The radio played Whitney Houston's 'I Want To Dance With Somebody' in the background as he lowered his lean frame onto the sofa. He took out the plain white note folded neatly down the centre.

Phil frowned and stared at the message 'YOU GOT IT WRONG! I DID IT! It was written in red capitals. He was confused. This one's definitely not a well-wisher.

He reached for the envelope. It contained something else. His fingers poked inside and he felt something like wool. He froze with revulsion as his fingers brought out the enclosure. It was a small clump of matted brown hair.

****

It was an hour since Phil had opened the envelope. He sat in a daze on the settee; unable to comprehend this latest turn of events.

After Phil discreetly vomited, he immediately tried to hide the note and refused to believe what was happening.

Chloe noticed the change in his behaviour as soon as she came downstairs from getting dressed.
"What's wrong Phil?"
Phil backed down in minutes. "No more secrets," he whispered.
"None," she agreed and he handed her the note.
Chloe shrieked, dropped the envelope and ran back upstairs.
Phil followed her with the envelope.
"You'd better look at this..."
Chloe's face drained of all colour.
"It's Janice's... It's her hair!" she moaned in agony and turned away with her hands over her face.
"We can't be sure of that darling," Phil reasoned, "It could be anyone's. I'll get it over to forensics."
"You'll do no such thing! The last thing I want is all this dredged up again!"
Her eyes were flooded with bitter tears.
"Who could DO such a thing? Is it someone's idea of a joke?" she wept.
"I don't know..." Phil felt helpless.
"Well - it can't be Gary Hart cos he's dead!"

Phil stared at the note and the clump of hair. His head throbbed and nausea tugged at his stomach once more.
"I must tell 'The Brothers'," he said finally.
"What?" exclaimed Chloe.
"Phil stood up. "They can help. We must tell them."
Chloe was silent.

Just as he picked up the phone, Phil had a startling flash of deja vu. He recalled the envelope he'd received a few weeks earlier. It contained an identically written message too. Similar envelope, same red capitals and no stamp. Had it been from Maurice and Kenneth? His mind raced. Don't be stupid, they're on our side. Snap out of it!

Beads of sweat appeared on his forehead. His hands were cold and clammy as he tapped out the digits on the handset. His breath came in short gasps. He got a tone... It went on for what seemed an eternity.
"Hello."
Phil responded hoarsely as he acknowledged the answer,
"Hello - Moss? Ken?"
"It's Moss. Is that you Phil?"
Phil was sweating profusely now. (*Calm down!)*
"Er yeah, it's me."
"Hi pal! How's life? I can't tell you how chuffed we are about that little runt. How's the gorgeous Chloe?"

Phil frowned.
If they'd sent the envelope, Moss was doing a good line in acting normally, he thought. He relaxed slightly.
"Oh - yes. I know. We're both very relieved."
"Actually Phil, I'm glad you phoned."
Moss's Geordie accent came over as reassuring to Phil all of a sudden. There was no hint of any antipathy.
"Oh?" queried Phil.
"Yeah - we're having a big meeting here tomorrow night. Sorry for the short notice but there are things that need sorting. The wheels are turning and gathering speed now."
Phil frowned again.

"What do you mean exactly, Moss?" asked Phil. (*Tell him about the note!*) "I can't say over the phone. Be at the house - our house - tomorrow night at seven sharp. Bring Chloe too, if you wish, but not a word to anyone else. Is that clear?"

Phil nodded; still frowning. "Well, yes, no problem. There are a couple of matters I need to speak to you about. It concerns Gary Hart."

"I see. We can do it all tomorrow evening."

"Okay."

"Shame about him dying," said Moss matter-of-factly, "Pikey was on the phone to me straight off. Did a wrist job, didn't he?"

"I believe so," mumbled Phil.

"Tough shit. Deserved it, though - little bastard. Ken and I downed a couple of celebratory whiskies. A toast to you and Chloe!"

"Cheers!" responded Phil, though he didn't sound happy. All he could see was the envelope and those strands of hair.

"...tomorrow then. Seven o'clock," Moss was still talking.

"Oh yeah - sure. See you then Moss. I'll bring Chloe. She could do with a change of scenery."

"Don't we all mate..." Moss cut off the call in mid-sentence.

Phil sat, staring at the bedroom wall. (*You should have told him!)*

He wrung his hands; shoulders hunched.

"Tomorrow... I'll tell them tomorrow," he whispered to himself.

****

Ken and Moss sat in the rear garden of their imposing mansion. Ice tinkled in the expensive crystal decanters. The trees rustled as the warm summer breeze flowed through their flowered boughs. Birds sang and danced from branch to branch.

Ken folded the edition of The Times and placed it beside Moss's copy of the Daily Mirror. Every newspaper of that day covered the table; even The Sun was not exempt from their urgent attentions.

"There's a cracking article on teenage solvent abuse in the Mail," said Moss.

"I know. It seems it's becoming fashionable to peddle the stuff on the streets. Superglue will be as popular as hash in two years."

"That's what they get for tightening up on shop sales."

Moss nodded and asked, "How's the leg?"

"Fine. Had a twinge last night. A mile too far."

Moss grinned, "I wish I was as fit as you with two legs."

Ken smiled. "You've never had to keep fit. String bean!"

Moss sipped thoughtfully on his iced Cola. "Mmm... lovely."

Ken leaned forward.

"So! How's Phil and Chloe?"

"Fine, fine. They're both coming tomorrow." Moss nodded.

Ken raised his eyebrows. "Both? Good! I like Phil. Admittedly, I had my doubts about him but Clive certainly picked a good 'un there."

Moss nodded again.

"Tomorrow night's meeting is important. Preparations for 'The March' are well underway. London won't know what's hit it!" said Ken.

"I gather they have a couple of paedos under scrutiny for the flogging?" said Moss.

"Yeah," agreed Ken. "One of them is from North London. He's been under surveillance for five weeks. Nasty bastard. We intend to nab him the night before. One of 'The Brothers' has infiltrated his pervert haven. Apparently he's into all sorts of weird shit."

Ken turned his head and spat a trail of phlegm into the newly-mown lawn.

"Waster!"

"Another of our targets for a bit of fun is a Game Warden from Kent."

"Name?"

"Terence Gordon."

"And?"

"He's raped seven women and children. Two of the women were pregnant.

Luckily, the babies survived the trauma. However, the mothers will be under medication and need counselling for some time yet. Tragic!"

Ken shifted in his white chair.

"Is he out?"

"Yep and we're going to give him a trip he won't easily forget."

Ken stared across the garden.

"When will 'The March' commence?"

"At daybreak," said Moss drily. "People will be arriving at Trafalgar the night before. The cops have it all under control. People will be invited to join in on the same evening, with their only parameter being that they're sober," he continued.

Ken grimaced.

"It could get out of hand..."

"No chance! We have twenty six groups of security experts in attendance. Each group has forty eight highly trained personnel, equipped with all the trappings necessary to quell any uprising. They're trained in various defensive disciplines from karate to origami. I don't think they'll have any problem with the odd skinhead or socialist freak."

"And the Police?"

"They will simply 'observe'," said Moss bluntly.

Ken stretched in his seat.

"At the last count, we reckoned we had over a quarter of a million people attending. Should give someone up Whitehall something to think about," Ken commented.

Moss nodded approvingly.

"What happens at Downing Street?" asked Ken.

"That's yet to be decided. We have it on the agenda for tomorrow's meeting.

The last thing we want is for something to happen that the public will find intolerable.

I don't think teaching people like Gordon a lesson will be in that category, do you?"

"No...no, of course not," Ken agreed.

Moss smiled in anticipation.

"Certain people are going to get the shock of their molly-coddled, sheltered lives," said Ken.

"Fuckin' historic! It'll be fuckin' historic," grinned Moss.

The silence was satisfying.

"More Cola?"

****

Phil and Chloe found the second envelope at two-thirty in the afternoon. Early closing of her shop meant they could relax and spend the half-day together alone.

Phil opened it and stared bleakly.

The envelope had been blank. The message was written in identical handwriting to the first.

"Blue Biro this time," whispered Phil as he looked at Chloe earnestly, whilst trying to gauge her reaction.

"What does it say?"

Phil swallowed, "It says 'I AM NOT A CRANK! IT WOULD BE DANGERUS TO THINK THIS! IM WATCHING YOU! Punctuation isn't his strongest point though."

Chloe's eyes widened slowly. She sat down on the settee.

"He's HERE Phil! He's in the village!"

Phil was silent. He nodded, as he clenched his fists and crumpled the note in his grip.

"It seems so," he said finally.

Chloe picked up the envelope.

"Phil, wait!"

Her fingers felt inside the envelope.

"Oh my God!"

Phil was at her side as she began to shake violently.

In her hand was a tiny red earring.

He caught her as she fainted.

****

"Souvenirs."

"What?"

"Souvenirs. He keeps souvenirs of the victims. It's a common trait with serial killers. They like to keep a memento of the moment," said Phil.

Chloe sat opposite him across the kitchen table; coffee in hand.

After the initial shock of finding one of Janice's earrings in the envelope a sudden icy calm had come over her. Realisation and resignation replaced the trauma.
"Poor Gary Hart," she whispered.
"Poor Gary Hart - bollocks!" spat Phil, "He started all of this!"
Chloe nodded swiftly and apologetically, "Yes, yes I know darling but he is..."
"Dead!" Phil's tone held no emotion.
"What can we do?"
Phil fingered the earring.
"Whoever is doing this knows where we live."
Chloe nodded.
"That's number one. Two – he's in the village, or very near. Three - he's confident and sure of himself. Four - he's taunting us... Five..."
"Five? What's five Phil? Tell me."
"I know him!"

Chloe started. "No! How on earth could you know who did this? They convicted... You convicted Hart!"

Phil put his arm around Chloe. She began to sob quietly.
"Sssh - I know it's hard to believe, but I feel sure he knows me. He's goading me. I've seen this sort of thing before in other cases. He likes the feeling of power," Phil whispered, "He has waited until now and he's having his bit of fun by taunting me."
Chloe's eyes were wide with terror.
"He would do it again, wouldn't he?"

Phil's face was a mask. The clock ticked into the silence.
"Yes, I'm afraid so."

A sudden knock at the front door made them jump.
"I'll go. Stay here," said Phil.
"Be careful."

She heard him take the latch off and speak in a low monotone; his words inaudible. There was a pause... then , "Cheers pal!"

No danger, phew.

She sipped the remainder of her tepid coffee.
Phil returned to the kitchen.
"What was it?"
"Postie - van delivery."
He held a brown package in his hand. He looked at the address.
"Funny..." he murmured while frowning once more.
"What's up?" asked Chloe.
"There's no stamp on it but he didn't ask for..."
Realisation hit him.
He ran from the kitchen. Flinging the front door open he sprinted down the garden path and into the street.
The van was nowhere to be seen.
"Shit!" spat Phil breathlessly.

****

Chapter Sixteen

He was playing games again. His favourite pastime. It was weeks since he killed her. That stupid cop didn't have a clue!

She was his seventh victim. He had followed the news coverage avidly. The previous six still remained unsolved. Two in Spain while he was 'on holiday'. One in a French chalet. One on a car ferry. One in the Lake District buried next to the big lake. Last, but not least, the little girl from Scotland; presumed missing. Just another name on file.

God, he was clever! His teacher had said that he's too clever by half. He'd eight 0-levels and five A-levels, a good opening bat and a dab hand at chess. What a star!

He felt no remorse for Gary Hart. Just another victim - just another game. As he sat in the park, he stared down at his tatty, weatherworn plimsolls. An old man walked slowly past with his walking stick clicking on the tarmac.

"Mornin'," the youth grinned and his eyes only saw a silhouette. The sun would be warm today.
"Hi son," answered the old man; not even turning his head to look at the figure on the bench.
"Ignorant old fart!"

His eyes darted from scene to scene. The park was busy today with kids everywhere. Their mothers too.
Lunchtime was a good time to hide. After all, he was only half a mile from the cottage.
When he'd delivered the envelope, he had power. He had looked the enemy in the eye. Stupid bastard hadn't even realised.
Typical! Not fast enough Queen! No promotion for you. No more tea and biscuits with the boss.

He thought about them opening the envelope. He saw their shock, felt their disgust, tasted their fear and enjoyed every second...

A high-pitched scream made him look up. A little girl had slipped in the playground. Adults rushed to her aid. Other children began to cry in sympathy.
It reminded him of Scotland... (*Stifle the scream then finish it!*)
It reminded him of the lake. (*Buried alive - died of boredom!*)
And it reminded him of the flat. (*I heard a noise; don't be frightened I can help... Be QUIET!*)

He wiped a tear from his eye and contemplated his next move... and his next victim.

****

One of the few times Phil Queen had been physically sick was after his second go on the waltzer at an out-of-town fair in 1983. He hated throwing up.

When he opened the buff envelope, a wave of nausea was so strong that he had to sit down. The envelope

was 10" × 8". It had been stuck down with Sellotape. No saliva, nor prints. Clever!
The black and white photographs were poor. An amateur in the journalistic stakes.
It didn't take much to fathom out what the scenes depicted. Six murders. Six women and children.

In the first picture there were two bodies of naked female teenagers. They lay entwined on a bed in what looked like a hotel room. Phil could not make out any wounds. On the reverse of the photographs, Phil found brief descriptions of the scenes in red Biro and in capitals, such as 'Two Spick, Majorka '89, Shit beer'!

The second photograph showed a grassy hillock. No people. Puzzled, Phil turned it over and it read, 'Wick '91. It rained a lot, poor girl'!

Phil retched silently.

Number three was a large expanse of water. A lake or inlet. Scotland? Wales? The reverse read 'She's under there somewhere. Nice legs, Kendal '92'.
The fourth showed a Belgian ferry, docked in port. Phil could just distinguish the words 'Oostend' and 'Limited' on the side of the ship. Blurred. The message was blunt and malicious as it penned 'Dutch. Poor Fuck. Strangled and dumped overboard. Sorry. Dover to Ostend '93'.

"'Sorry?" whispered Phil, disbelievingly, as he turned to the next horrific picture. He felt awful.
Five was the worst. A parlour maid lay in what looked like a barn. Her eyes were open and mouth constricted

in rictus. Her skirt was pulled up above her waist; her black stockings torn and shredded.
Phil closed his eyes and reversed the picture. "Christ!" he muttered.
The red capitals on the back of five were 'She looked like my neffew. Didn't struggle much, Normandy '94'.

There was a separate note again. Phil unfolded it, as he prepared himself for more mocking lines. He wasn't disappointed as he read 'Got enough clues yet? Didn't photograf Janice. Too dark. You're too slow Queen! Be back soon'.

"Bastard!" spat Phil. He sat on the bedroom floor surrounded by the photographs. They almost pleaded with him. He'd come straight upstairs from outside. Chloe was making more coffee.
He heard her voice from below.
"Phil! Coffee?" Chloe asked.
"Yeah - thanks love," he answered quietly.
He placed the photographs back into the envelope and made his way to the bathroom. As he retched (*again*) he caught his reflection in the mirror.
He hadn't shaved in four days. "You're a mess," he murmured as he turned on the cold tap.

They sat at the kitchen table once more. Chloe eyed Phil warily.
"What did he look like Phil? Can you recall?"
Phil wiped a stray hair from his forehead.
"No, I didn't even look at him really. All I saw was the van. A white Transit. I signed the pad and gave him his pen back."

Chloe fidgeted in her chair and quizzed, "Well, was he young or old? Tall?"

"... young, I think. He wore overalls. Blue ones. Like a tyre fitter, you know."

Chloe toyed with a biscuit and continued, "His voice. Did you recognise it?"

Phil thought back through his every movement. He closed his eyes to remember what had happened.

(*He opened the door...*)

'Mornin' sir, delivery!' It wasn't a local dialect. (*White van!*) 'Yeah, cheers pal.' Phil remembered.

"Long hair," Phil said placidly.

'Nice day eh?' (*Plimsolls, overalls...*)

'Yeah, great.' (Then he gave me the envelope!)

"I signed the pad but mine was the only signature!" Phil recalled.

Chloe's eyes widened.

"Ours was the only delivery?!" she exclaimed.

Phil nodded furiously. He stood up rubbing his forehead, trying to recall... (*Warts on his fingers!*)

"He had warts!" said Phil.

"Where?"

"On his hands!"

"Right," Chloe was jotting down notes on the buff envelope.

She hadn't seen the photographs and didn't wish to.

As she wrote, something caught her attention.

"Phil, come here. Look!"

Phil spun round and nearly fell as he stepped back to the table.

"What is it?"

"Look..."

Chloe's index finger pointed to a small yellow price sticker.

"Piper's 17p. Piper's! That's the corner shop in the village! Old Ted Gavin runs it!" said Chloe excitedly.
"So?" queried Phil; not cottoning on to her train of thought.
"So, he's been in Ted's shop! Don't you see? He's bought this envelope from the shop!" Chloe explained.

****

Old Edward Horatio Gavin was getting on. Time wasn't on his side no more, he'd say.
Seventy-three, hearing aid and a walking stick. The NHS did a great job. He voted Conservative and he always wore a tie.

He was a gunner in the Second World War and he'd been hit by stray shrapnel at Monte Casino. It was always his party piece. He'd tell his story a thousand times over but it was always interesting.
Good old Ted!

His little corner shop had been a thriving business for as long as villagers could remember. A family concern. His daughter and son-in-law would look after it at weekends or when Ted knew he was in for a bad day.
The shop sold everything from batteries to baby food. Newspapers, groceries, tinned food, fresh bread - the lot. The villagers didn't need a supermarket. Ted sold it.
Ted called it 'Pipers'. Why? Because Ted loved the sound of bagpipes. Simple! He had served with the Black Watch and learned to play during his time in the Army. They could have called it 'Gavin's Cabin.' That's what Minnie wanted. Ted's persuasive powers were considerable and

she had backed down. He only had to smile at Minnie. Darling Minnie.
She had died in 1990. Cancer. What else? Her last words had been 'Whatever you do, keep the Cabin open!'
Ted smiled at the memory. He smiled often. He hated dull people. Life was meant to be lived - that was his motto.

He sat next to the till as usual. It was busy today. First, the papers. Get them delivered. Kerry was always on time. Seven o'clock on the dot. There were only fifteen papers to be delivered. Most of the people in the village were retired and preferred to walk to the shop and have a chat. Then, there's the school kids at eight-thirty for a chaotic fifteen minutes. Oh, the petty little arguments but he loved it all!

It always calmed down around ten o'clock. With the morning rush over, he'd make himself a cup of tea and read the headlines. Perk of the job. He hadn't bought a newspaper for over twenty nine years.
The headlines had become progressively worse in recent years, he thought. Where had good manners gone? It was all scandal, death and perversion. Such violence. He recalled the outcry in the '60s at the first 'Page Three Girl' and smiled.
He remembered when teams like Derby or Huddersfield won football trophies and money didn't really come into it.

How times changed. Time for a cuppa. The kettle boiled silently. He still used gas. He put his one sugar lump into the mug and waited for the tea pot to brew.

As he poured the tea into the mug, he heard the shrill ring of the shop door bell.
Customer...
"I'll be right there!" shouted Ted with a smile in his voice.
"That's OK Ted, no rush!"

It was Chloe. Lovely Chloe. He knew all his customers by their voices.

Chloe and Phil stood at the counter.
"Artillery eh?" commented Phil, eyeing the crest above the counter.
"Oh yes, Ted's proud of his military past," answered Chloe.
"And rightly so," smiled Phil. "We wouldn't be here but for people like Ted."
The door to the rear kitchen opened wide and Ted emerged, carrying his mug of tea in one hand and leaning on his stick with the other.
"Hello, Chloe...er..." Ted eyed Phil curiously; a smile on his lips.
"Oh, I'm sorry Ted. This is Phil Queen," Chloe said as she ushered Phil forward towards the counter.
"Pleased to meet you sir," said Phil confidently. His military bearing was not lost on the old soldier.
They warmly shook hands.
"A soldier too eh?" enquired Ted, as he sat on his stool.
"Well - used to be. Military Police."
"Ah – Redcaps, Monkeys - remember 'em well!" Ted teasingly replied.
"I'm out now. Helping Chloe come to terms with a few things, you know."

Chloe interrupted, "Phil helped catch Janice's killer." She spoke flatly, trying not to think of the recent turn of events.

"Oh, a policeman too?"

"Yes, only until recently," replied Phil rather sheepishly.

"Not anymore?" Ted's eyebrows raised.

"Er, no. Had enough. I want a quieter existence now."

"Don't blame you lad. You've done your time."

Phil smiled at the old man. "You must have some stories to tell?"

Ted bristled with pride.

"Too many to mention - too many. I bore folks to death!" he laughed.

"Now, what can I do for you? A paper?"

Chloe spoke quietly, "Well Ted, we're trying to do a bit of detective work actually and we think you could help."

"How exciting! What do you want to know?"

Phil offered him the buff envelope.

"Well, it's a person we're trying to trace. A young man. Teenager possibly.

He bought this envelope here at your shop. Look, there's your sticker."

Ted picked up his spectacles from the counter.

"Let's put me peepers on. Now then," he took the envelope and looked at the writing.

"Ignore the writing on the back, It's just me making some notes," said Chloe.

"Mmm... yes, I remember him. He's been in a couple of times."

Phil's hand grasped Chloe's. "Did he buy anything else Ted?" she asked urgently.

"Let me see..." Ted gazed out of the window thoughtfully.

Phil could sense his mind ticking over like a primed incendiary.

"It was a couple of days ago. Scruffy individual. Smiled a lot but..."

"Yes?" urged Phil.

"It wasn't a 'nice' smile. More like he was putting it on to make an impression, if you know what I mean?"

Phil looked at Chloe and nodded.

Ted continued, "He bought a packet of smaller envelopes and a couple of pens."

"Sellotape?" prompted Phil.

"Yes, Sellotape! I remember because I directed him to the post office for stamps."

Chloe groaned, "He doesn't use them."

Ted looked confused. "I'm sorry?"

Phil assured Ted, "Oh, nothing – please carry on Ted."

"OK, he spoke with an accent. Northern... Yes, that's it. I had a pal from Leeds once. He reminded me of him funnily enough."

"That's him!" said Phil, elated.

"Did he say anything else?" asked Chloe; ecstatic at their detective work.

Ted frowned.

"Well, no, not exactly. I must admit though there was something about him. He never looked me in the eye. Never trust people who can't look you in the eye. That right, Phil?"

"Sure - spot on Ted!" Phil replied earnestly but tried not to sound patronising.

Chloe pressed on, "Sorry to push you Ted but is there anything else? Can you remember what he wore?"

"You said he was scruffy," prompted Phil.

"Yes! The usual T-shirt, jeans, pumps... you know."

"Anything on the T-shirt? A design or wording? A slogan?" pursued Chloe.

There was a silence as Ted pondered. A car drove past the shop slowly.

Ted announced, "It was a black shirt, I think. Dark at any rate. Oh, and he left in a van - a white van. Yes, definitely white."

Phil punched the air. "Yesss!"

Ted looked at Chloe and asked, "Is he a relative, this lad?"

"In a manner of speaking yes," she replied coldly.

Ted smiled. "It's so good to be of assistance. I hope I've helped you."

"You sure have," said Phil as he leaned forward eagerly, "Now, could you do us one more favour?"

"Of course." Ted nodded.

"If this lad comes into the shop again, phone us straight away but don't let on. We want it to be a nice surprise for him. Here's Chloe's number."

Phil wrote Chloe's eight digits on a price tag before he handed it to Ted.

"Of course, it'll be a pleasure. I like to help when I can."

"Thanks Ted," said Chloe. Her cheeks were flushed and the old man glowed with satisfaction.

"Think nothing of it. Nothing at all. I'll ring as soon as I see him again."

"Be very careful though," Chloe urged earnestly.

Phil and Chloe left the shop hand in hand. Ted waved and smiled them off the premises.

He returned to his customary station by the till, turned the 'Daily Star' over and scanned the sports headlines as he awaited his next customer.

****

He'd seen them enter the shop. Seen them exchange shitty pleasantries. Saw the envelope.

They were asking too many questions, far too many...
The old man knew too much.
Too alert for his own bloody good. It would be his downfall.
Too helpful by far old son...

****

The phone was ringing when they got back to the cottage. Chloe answered it.
"Ted! Hi, that was quick!"
Phil stared as Chloe spoke. She nodded slowly. "I see!" she exclaimed.
Phil frowned.
Chloe raised her eyes and mouthed, "It's Ted... In the park, you say?" She went on listening and nodding.
Phil sat down waiting for the message.
"Great, I'll tell Phil. Thanks Ted. See you soon." Chloe replaced the receiver.
"Well? What's he say?"
"He forgot to tell us something."
"What?" urged Phil in frustration.
"He says he saw that youth in the park this morning."
"In the park?"
"Yes - that's all. He was just sitting in the park."

****

Steven Kennedy sat next to the lily covered pond, thinking...
The shopkeeper was now a threat. He had to be eliminated.
Steve didn't like the word 'killed'. Too basic and boring. His educational prowess meant that he could always think of better, longer words to use. It was part of the game. His spelling needed some work though.

He didn't know what had been said in the shop. All he'd been able to see were the animated movements and laughter. Laughter? Were they mocking him? If they were; they would pay!

Steve eased a dandelion out of the freshly mown turf, thinking... They must have warned the old man. Of this he was certain. Why spend so long buying absolutely nothing? He'd seen the envelope as they entered the shop and they still had it when they left.
"Oh, we just thought we'd pop in and talk about the weather, show you this incriminating evidence and leave," he whispered and imagined scenario to himself with a wry smile.

A couple walked past and stared at the figure muttering on the grass.
Just another drugged-up teenager...

No, the cop was on to him... (*Could he remember you?)*
Very doubtful! Photographic recall was the stuff for science fiction movies, Marvel comics or the late night chat show when everyone came home pissed and believed anything!

Ah but the copper was clever. He had found the sticker - the pissin' sticker. (*You should have noticed that. Idiot!)*
So - why wasn't the village crawling with uniforms? He frowned to himself as he slowly dismembered the dandelion.
Yeah - this was personal. The cop wanted to do it alone and get all the glory...
They've locked all the doors and windows, loaded the shotgun and now they're waiting for the showdown. No way.
To attempt anything too soon would be fatal. Too quick. too soon. They would be ready. Wait a while... A few days. Give them time to relax once more.

(Change your appearance!) The thought came to him. Yes - they know me now, so time to disguise and disappear. There was a hairdresser in the village. A crew cut would make all the difference...
Coincidence happens. Just like the weather...
The dandelion was being uprooted while Chloe was spreading margarine on slices of wholemeal bread.
"You'll have to clean yourself up for tonight's meeting!"
"I know, I look as if I've been in a trench for a week," answered Phil from the study.
Chloe smiled as she sliced a cool tomato for the salad.
"What is it you army types say, 'A shower, shave...?"
"Shit, shower and shave!" shouted Phil; interrupting with a laugh.
"You need all three - twice!" came her rejoinder.

Phil stared at his reflection. His black stubble was getting out of control.

He eyed his lengthening hair with a grimace. He didn't usually let himself go.
"Time for a haircut," he murmured.
"You need a haircut too!" yelled Chloe from the kitchen.
" I get the message! You don't fancy my trendy image!"

****

'Short back 'n' sides' stood next door to the butcher in Rattigan Street which passed for the High Street of Knotton. It was a barber shop and had a regular male clientele. Mainly villagers in for a trim.

Jeremy Woodley charged £4.50 for a regular trim. Nice price; not too steep. Kids under ten got a quid off. He was a slight man in his late forties. A bachelor. His own hair was long gone. Bald as a coot. Some advertisement!

The locals called him either Jerry or Woody. Teenagers liked him. He was harmless enough, though his sexual preferences had often been debated in the pub on the corner.

"Bent as they come..."
"Just a loner."
"Mummy's boy."

They liked him though, he was part of the village and lived in the flat over the shop for ten years. Content. Secure...

The young lad was his fourth client that morning. A new face in the village. Small talk was part of Jeremy's service unless the customer was dumb or Tunisian!

"Just passing through?" he offered as an opening gambit.

The stranger stared back at him through the mirror.

"Yeah," came the monosyllabic response.

Jeremy persevered. He hated long silences. "Where are you from then?" he asked as he combed through the long, mousey locks.

"Up north. Near Leeds."

"Oh, I see - a travelling man then?"

"Could say that."

Jeremy was conscious that this was not going to be a conversational client.

"How would sir like his hair?"

There was a pause. The youth's eyes had an unnerving quality, as if he was hiding something.

"All off! Skin!" snapped the figure in the chair.

The sudden, clipped response made the barber a touch uneasy.

"Is that a crew-cut sir, or a total skinhead?" he asked, while trying to maintain a cool professionalism.

"All off. Skin it!" came the cocky retort.

"Fine."

Jeremy Woodley plugged in the electric clippers to the socket on the wall. He began to cut swathes off the youth's hair in sweeping motions. He was enjoying himself. This was a welcome change from touching up the sideburns of crotchety old fogies.

"A bit drastic don't you think?" commented the stranger, as he stared directly at Woodley. The northern accent was noticeable.

Woodley paused, leaned on the chair and said, "Well to be honest, it'll suit you young man. I'm sure of that."

The youth smiled. A strange smile, thought Woodley. More of a grimace. He continued his attack on the remaining hair.

The bell rang as another customer entered the salon. Woodley clearly felt the figure in the chair stiffen under his hands.

"Morning Mr Woodley?" Phil Queen greeted the barber.

"Yes, take a seat. I won't be long," Woodley answered with surprise. He felt a sense of relief that another client had arrived.

Steven Kennedy swallowed silently. (*Calm, calm, calm, a voice said in his head.)*

"Nice day. Busy?" Phil commented.

"Fair, I suppose. Midweek is pretty quiet," responded Woodley, concentrating on Kennedy's scalp.

Phil picked up a 'What Car?' magazine and he quietly flicked through it.

From time to time, he glanced up at the master at work. The youngster in the hot seat was having a rather fearsome demolition job on his cranium. All Phil could see was the back of his head. There was about a quarter of an inch of stubble left. In a few more moments, the lad was as bald as Woodley himself.

Phil lost interest as the haircut ended so he returned to the magazine.

"Is that enough sir?" Woodley queried as he switched off his clippers.

No reply but Kennedy nodded silently in affirmation through the mirror.

"Let's just tidy you up," Woodley purred and dusted the stray hairs from around the youth's neck. In a practised movement, he held the rear view mirror but the youth was already on his feet.

(Don't look up, you bastard!)
Phil idly flicked the pages of the magazine; oblivious of the final ministrations of the barber.
Kennedy handed over five pound coins, opened the door and was gone.

"Well and thank you too!" commented Woodley as he turned to Phil who was removing his blue bomber jacket.
"Mmmm?" queried Phil as he sat in the chair.
Woodley lowered the chair to a convenient height.
"Strange lad. He forgot his change," said Woodley shaking his head.
"In a hurry eh?"

Woodley picked up his broom and deftly swept away the pile of hair.
"Yes - it seems so. Can't say I'm sorry to see him leave."

Phil looked down at the huge amount of hair.
"Such a lovely head of hair too..." murmured Woodley absently.

Phil frowned slightly as a ripple of suspicion crossed his mind. "That lad - just now. Did you know him?" he casually asked.

Woodley leaned on his broom, stared out of the window and answered, "Nope, never seen him before. Said he was just passing through. Ignorant little bugger."
"Ignorant you say? How d'you mean - ignorant?"
"Well... He was just a little strange. Very jumpy. Nervy type," murmured Jeremy.
Phil sharply rose out of the chair. "What did he say to you? This is important!"
Woodley replaced the broom beside the sink and stepped back at the urgency in Phil's tone.
"Not a lot really. Can't say I got to know the blighter! He's only been in for a skin-cut."
Phil headed for the door. "I'm sorry. I must rush! Oh - one more thing... Where did he come from? Had he got any accent or dialect?"
"Sure! Up north! Manchester or somewhere I'm certain!" he responded.
"Thanks! Thanks a lot!"
And Phil was gone.

****

As he jogged down the main street, he caught glimpses of himself in glass partitions or doorways. His new bald head made him look a right nasty piece of work.

That's how he wanted it. It gave potential victims less chance. No hair to grapple with. No hair in his eyes to block his view of their final moments.

The bitch in the flat had grabbed him by the hair, just before he covered her face with the pillow. Little cow had just made him more angry, more powerful...

He stopped jogging and slowed to walking pace as he entered the park. He sat down on a bench to consider his next move.

Go back to the pad, get some rest, change of clothes and choose a weapon. Then it's time to find another one to snuff... Wasn't life a breeze? He closed his eyes and waited for the voices in his head to return...

****

"He's changed his appearance. Crafty sod," said Phil in a matter-of-fact manner.

Chloe sat opposite and her face was drained of colour.
"He obviously means business by the very fact that he's still here," he continued.
Chloe gripped a white handkerchief while her eyes welled up with tears.
Phil stood up, frowned and walked across the room to peer through the net curtains. He was frowning a lot these days...

The phone interrupted his musings. He reached across and lifted the receiver. Chloe saw his expression change immediately.

****

Ted was a weak bastard. No bottle. Old soldier or not; it was easy.
He hadn't recognised the lad standing at the magazine rack. Hadn't seen him lock the door as he had entered the shop. And, he hadn't prepared himself for the savage attack that followed.

Without warning, the thug vaulted the counter. His knife had punctured Ted's lung in one easy movement. Death came slowly but surely. As he choked violently, the youth sat on the shop's counter.

"Ten, nine, eight...hurry up!" screamed Kennedy.

He grinned at his victim. It had taken two minutes.

****

"Ted says come quickly; he's dying," spat the disembodied voice.
Phil threw down the phone and ran. Chloe was frantic.
"What is it?!" she shouted as Phil darted out of the room.
"He's got Ted!" screamed Phil
Chloe froze in horror.
"Oh no, not Ted!" she yelled and the door slammed behind Phil's retreating figure.

The shop was locked.

"Fuck!" spat Phil. Sweat rolled easily down his furrowed brow.

People looked on incredulously as he elbowed the glass and shattered it easily. His hand reached in and flipped the lock. The sign still read 'OPEN'. It swung crazily as Phil crashed through the door.

A foot could be seen sticking out from behind the counter.
"Ted!" yelled Phil.

It was too late. The wound was deep and accurate. He had died in agony and his face was contorted. His walking stick lay alongside his body. Phil tentatively picked it up between thumb and finger, noting the splashes of blood across the floor.

Turning to look around he saw the envelope on the counter. He ripped it open and took out the note. Red ink. Again. 'Too late as usual... Bye' it read.

Phil sank to his knees and wept.
The bell rang as someone entered the shop.
"Is there a problem?" asked an ageing man in a quavering voice.
A crowd had gathered outside; necks craning to see what was happening. Phil passed out.

****

Chapter Seventeen

The inner sanctums of the 'establishment' are viewed only by the privileged few who work there, by workmen, media moguls or the odd unwanted trespasser. The latter normally find themselves splashed across the tabloids for a couple of days. Their fifteen minutes of fame or shame recorded for posterity.

Kenneth and Maurice Jamieson were there by appointment. Their passes had been prepared weeks earlier. The Brothers had contacts. Contacts who, if made public, would cause much unease in the corridors of power as well as outside them.

The moles had been painstakingly selected through surveillance, interview and background. Such checking was normally associated with persons working in high security areas within the Armed Forces or the Foreign Office.

Clifford Hulme was one such case. Hulme began his career humbly in the Civil Service. He then progressed through a distinguished transfer into the Army, reaching senior rank, and through higher echelons of officialdom he'd now reached the pinnacle. He's Chief of the Defence Staff no less.

Married to Lady Eleanor, with two sons, the high life was theirs. They lived in unadulterated splendour in the Hertfordshire countryside, walking the dogs and hosting the occasional high society party. The parties always got a mention in the 'Tatler' naturally.

Hulme was to meet the Jamieson brothers today. 'The March' on the capital would take place in a matter of weeks. Trying to balance his bona fide work with his usual problems was a trial in itself. Since joining The Brothers of Justice, his temper was frayed and his sex life non-existent apart from the occasional visit from his twenty-two year old mistress, Holly. Eleanor knew about Holly but she did not make any waves. The parties and the boys came first these days...

Ken and Mo climbed the hard, cold, concrete steps. The entrance was a familiar backdrop to television news reports. They showed their passes and were nodded through. This was their fourth visit to see old Clifford. He was, after all, the Head of the Southern area activities for The Brothers and had been instrumental in recruiting them down from their home base in Sunderland. He had sorted out the house, the rent and the security aspects of their move. His office was a bastard to find.

"I hate this place," said Mo as they waited for the lift. The grey silence of the hushed corridors pressed in upon them.

"Yeah, it's such a shithole," agreed Ken.

Smartly dressed in dark suits, they didn't look out of place rubbing shoulders with Armed Forces advisors and officials from different nations.

Ken carried a black briefcase so he looked every inch the young politician. If only they knew...

The lift arrived with a dull thud. As the door slid open, a tall naval official stepped out and looked resplendent in his uniform. Ken stepped aside to let him pass.
"Most kind," murmured the figure.
"No problem," answered Ken but his Geordie accent sounded oddly out of place.
The twosome entered the lift.
"Which floor is it Ken? I canna remember."
"Eight or Nine," replied Ken.
"Let's try eight then."

Mo pressed the plastic console confidently and the lift began its slow ascent.
"I couldna work here man," said Mo quietly.
"I know, boring or what?" answered Ken as he stared down at his highly polished black brogues.
The lift stopped suddenly at the fifth floor. The Brothers watched silently as a young man entered carrying a buff folder marked 'Secret'.

"Mornin,'" said Mo. His ginger hair shone in the strobe lights.
The young man nodded uneasily.
"Which floor?" asked Ken.
"Er... nine please," said the youth.
Mo interrupted, "You couldn't tell us where the CDS' office is, could you mate?"
"General Hulme? Er, I'm going there now."
Mo looked at Ken with a smile and whispered, "Bingo."
The lift juddered onward and upward.

"You like it here then?" asked Ken. He'd broken the stilted silence which always seemed to prevail in a MoD lift.

"Nah, it's shit," came the sullen reply.

This surprised the Brothers. The youth had visibly relaxed.

"I was in Northern Ireland before this rat-pit. Chief Clerk in a Londonderry infantry detachment. It's much more lively and no crowded tube trains!"

Mo smiled. "Yes, I can see your point mate."

The lift stopped once more on the ninth floor.

"Interesting file then?" Ken nodded at the buff folder in the clerk's hand as the door swung open.

"Dunno. I'm not allowed to look in this one. 'Judicial/ Various' is one of seven for CDS' eyes only."

"I see," Ken winked knowingly. Old Hulme had his finger right on the button.

"They're coded so I can't get in. Look..."

Mo saw the digital entry system which had been recently employed by The Brothers. It's a

godsend! It meant that the only people having access to the files were accredited Brothers.

"Interesting, I've never seen that before," he lied with his most passable 'haven't a clue' frown.

The threesome walked along the dull, featureless corridors.

"I can never remember the bloody way!" cussed Ken.

The clerk nodded. "I know, it took me weeks to get my bearings. They should issue a map or a ball of string at the door!"

"Where're you from then?"

"Coventry."
Mo nodded. "Shit team!" he laughed.
"I know, they'll never match Newcastle will they?"
"Or Sunderland!" said Mo defiantly.
"Shit team!" laughed the clerk.

They turned yet another corner.

"Here we are then," said their guide and he knocked on a huge solid oak door.
"Come in," called a faraway voice.
"Could you wait?" asked the clerk brightly.
"Certainly son," agreed Ken.

They listened as he entered Hulme's office.
"Ah, Sergeant Clifton. Good day."
"Sir! Here's the file you requested and you have two visitors outside. Mr Jamieson..."
A short silence ensued as the file was handed over.
"... Right, send the buggers in!"

Ken grinned at Mo. "Same old Clifford," he whispered as they entered.

Sergeant Clifton stood to the left of the Chief's large mahogany desk, awaiting his next exciting mission.
"Coffee please Sergeant. Oh, and see if you can rustle up some Peek Freans from the kitchen!"
"Sir!"

Clifton braced himself, left the office and nodded at Ken and Mo as he left.

Mo winked and smiled, "Cheers!"
"Kenneth old chap. Take a seat. And how's younger brother, Maurice?"
"Thanks Clifford, we're both fine. No hassles."

The brothers sat in plush chairs and Ken placed the briefcase beside his seat. The office was liberally hung with photographs of the General's military past. Twenty three years in the Devon & Dorsets. A full life. Ken and Mo were in awe of Clifford. He's a man's man, make no mistake.
"So!" Hulme's voice boomed, "How's life?"
He eyed the two brothers over horn-rimmed spectacles, clasped his hands together and leaned forward awaiting their reply.
"Great," answered Ken confidently.
"As you know Clifford, 'The March' is definitely scheduled to take place in three weeks. Preparation is well under way and we are optimistic that the day's events will have the desired effect on certain people and their uncivilised activities."
Hulme shifted in his seat.
"Yes... Good! I called you here because, unfortunately, I cannot be at tonight's meeting. Much as I love your company, will you please pass my compliments to the other nine heads."
"Of course." said Mo with a questioning glance.
"Regimental dinner I'm afraid. Old boys' reunion. Loads of war stories and alcohol, you know."
Ken smiled. "Bet you can't wait."
Hulme shook his head and feigned distaste.
"Absolutely hate it!" he boomed while laughing loudly.
The brothers gave each other a sidelong glance.

There was a knock at the door.

"Yes?" called Hulme.

The door opened slowly. Crockery tinkled as a young female entered carrying a tray of cups and saucers. Sergeant Clifton brought up the rear with a large pot and a jug.

"What, no biscuits?" queried Hulme.

"Sorry Sir, none left," Clifton replied timidly.

"Oh well, we'll get a McDonald's." Ken smiled in an attempt to smooth the lad's predicament.

The young girl set up the cups on a small table beside the window. The distant rumble of London's traffic could be heard.

"Thank you Private Adams."

"Sir." The pretty young girl smiled and turned sharply.

"Thanks Sergeant. We'll do the rest. Get back to your office and bury your nose in a file!" teased the Chief.

The two young staff left the room quietly.

"Nice lad," commented Mo.

"Yes, he's good. Got a sense of humour too - that helps. By God, you need one in here!"

Ken nodded. "I can imagine."

"Right, let's get down to business! What's happening in the world?" asked Hulme.

Ken picked up his briefcase and clicked it open on his knees.

"These are the first proofs of the leaflets we intend to circulate during the week prior to 'The March'."

He handed a copy to Hulme.

"Larger posters are being prepared for the day itself,"

Ken continued intently, "Placards will be carried by the majority of our marchers."

Mo looked on silently.

"What time is 'kick off'?" asked Hulme as he scanned the leaflet on his desk.

"The March will convene in Trafalgar Square but people are expected to arrive the night before. The police will be monitoring movements without getting involved. Clive Badger has seen to that."

"Good old Clive! He's a vital cog in all this. How's his latest recruit, Queen, doing lately?"

Mo spoke up.

"Fine. We managed to get him to quit the police and he's now becoming a vital Brother - slowly but surely. We're carefully preparing him for a higher position in the organisation."

Hulme coughed. "Didn't he move in with the mother of that poor girl?"

"Yes, that gave us a small problem at first but now she's also with us and Queen seems well settled since they caught the murdering little bastard and locked him away."

"But didn't he commit suicide soon after?"

Ken nodded. "Yes. One night into his sentence. Wrist job - with a little help from a contact we had in the cell block."

Hulme frowned. "How unfortunate!"

"He's attending tonight's meeting and we're constantly monitoring him - and numerous other new recruits' efforts," said Mo excitedly.

"Excellent!" remarked Hulme while opening the buff file which the clerk had delivered to his office. "Look at this," he murmured handing Ken a photograph. Ken studied the picture.

"Who is it?"

Hulme stood up slowly. "That's the chap who'll feature on many front pages the morning after 'The March," he said sternly.

Mo took the photo from Ken. "Isn't this..?"

"Terence Gordon – paedophile." Hulme stood at the window, staring out at the busy centre of London. "He will be made an example of at 'The March'."

Ken looked up. "In what way?"

There was a brief silence as Hulme sat down again.

"Execution!" he stated flatly.

The word hung in the air.

The three men were silent and their eyes avoided each other.

"But... I thought it was going to be just a set of stocks?" said Ken.

"It was but it has since been amended to get the maximum shock effect.

The final decision is yet to be made on whether to have a lethal injection or a hanging... in public."

"Fuck me!" muttered Mo.

"Fuck me twice!" added Ken. Another silence ensued as they all contemplated the significance of this information.

"I know it's a shock," murmured Hulme, "but the 'Brothers' are of the opinion that we must maximise our chances at this event of shocking the public into an awareness of the situation."

"Will it be shown on TV?"

"Of course and it's all part of the Brothers' intention. If this doesn't get the scum of society and the do-gooders thinking then nothing will."

"It could cause panic!" suggested Ken.

"No, the vast majority of the marchers will be aware of what will happen."
"Who'll pull the chair form under the bastard - or do the injection?"
Hulme sighed. "One of the parents of one of his victims is looking forward to his opportunity to redress the balance."

A shrill ringing interrupted their conversation.
"Excuse me," said Ken as he lifted his portable telephone from his briefcase.
He pushed the reply stud eagerly. "Hello?"
Mo watched his brother calmly. Hulme replaced the photograph in the file.

Ken's expression suddenly changed. "When?"
Mo shifted uneasily at the tone of his brother's voice and Hulme glanced up.
"Is he all right?" continued Ken with a frown.
Mo and Hulme eyed each other and waited.
"Thank you Chloe. We'll be in touch."

He pushed the aerial back into the mobile and replaced it in the briefcase. "Bad news I'm afraid. It's Phil Queen. He's collapsed. Could be a breakdown. That was Chloe his girlfriend. Phil's in hospital and he's under sedation."

****

Chapter Eighteen

"Mr Queen? Mr Queen, wake up!"
He opened his eyes slowly and blinked in the half-light. A figure stood over him. It was just a shadow; a blurred mass.
"Where ... Where am I?" he croaked.
The voice was low and gentle.
"It's all right, everything will be fine. You're in hospital."
"Hospital?"
"Yes, you had a nasty fall."
His mind raced. Hospital? Fall?!

He made an effort and managed to raise himself up in the bed. The cool crisp sheets felt like silk on his bare skin. As his eyes became more accustomed to the room, he was aware of a dull, steady ache in his temples. His finger traced across his brow until it found the tender spot where he'd hit his head.

The nurse, immaculate in her pale blue uniform urged him to stay still.
"Now, now, Mr Queen, don't be too adventurous..." she scolded.

Phil could see her now; his vision was improving and clearing. She was plump but very pretty; the way nurses always looked on TV. Brunette, nice teeth...

"How long have I...?"
"Been asleep?" she interrupted him.
Phil nodded.
"Three hours."
"Jesus!" he murmured, almost inaudibly. "What... where was I?"
The nurse sat on the edge of the bed. "Don't you remember?"
"Vaguely... The shop..."
Then the memory hit him like a sledgehammer. He saw the body on the floor - then nothing.
"You fainted. Banged your head on a shop counter."
"Of course..." Phil whispered as his mind began to recall the events.
"The police want to question you but we put them off. You're in no fit state at present."
"Thanks," he replied and rested his head back on the pillows. His head throbbed incessantly. "Can I have a drink of water?"
"Sure, I'll get you a jug."

The young girl left the room. He was in a single ward. He tried to focus on the view from the window next to his bed. All he could see was part of the car park.
His thoughts turned to Chloe. Did she know he was here? Where was she?
The nurse returned with a covered jug of water.
"What's your name?"
"Siobhan."
"Hi, Siobhan." (*Explained the Irish lilt, thought Phil*).
"Hi, er..."
"Phil - call me Phil."

"Phil." she grinned whilst taking note of his returning faculties. She filled a beaker with the cool water and handed it to him. Phil sipped it carefully.

"Where am I?"

"St. Paul's. In town."

Phil nodded silently.

"My girlfriend..."

"Mrs Lee? Oh, yes. She's been in and gone back home. She said she'd phone in later to see if you were able to have visitors."

Phil sat up suddenly.

"I must speak to her!"

He had a wild look in his eyes and the nurse stepped back in alarm at his sudden movement.

"It's okay Phil. She'll be fine. She had two men with her. They said they would look after her. Calm down now."

"Two men?" Phil's mind raced.

"Yes, they were very concerned. A bit rough I thought but..." Siobhan frowned slightly as she remembered the three people.

Phil sighed. "Ken and Mo," he commented, relaxing visibly.

"They're friends?"

"Yes - no problem."

"Are you hungry?" Siobhan asked.

"No - actually I feel a bit queasy."

"Right. Just try and get some rest now then. I'll come back and see you in a while."

"Cheers." said Phil gratefully closing his eyes. The sedatives were having an effect and he drifted off into semi-consciousness.

As his thoughts dissolved, he heard a sharp click.

Immediately his eyes shot open but there was nobody in the room.

He sensed that the noise had been the door latch. Someone had been in the room!

He couldn't have been asleep for more than a minute, could he?

The nurse had left the door slightly ajar but it was now tight shut.

He sat upright, intently listening. Nothing.

Panic suddenly seized him.

"Nurse!" he shouted, "Nurse!"

Siobhan came back hurriedly. "Phil, what is it?"

"Someone was in here... just now!"

Siobhan stepped up to the side of the bed and smiled gently.

"Now, now. Don't be silly. I've been your only visitor in the last hour. I left you about twenty five minutes back. Remember?"

"Twenty five minutes?" Phil was taken aback.

"Yes. You must have been dozing. Maybe you've had a dream or something?"

Phil relaxed slightly as his hunched shoulders were slackening.

"Oh - you drank all your water?"

Siobhan retrieved the water jug from his locker. As she turned away from the bed, she paused.

"Hello, what's this?"

Phil's eyes opened,

"What is it now?"

"It's an envelope."

She handed him a small white envelope. Phil felt his throat contract again as he took it from her.

"Give it to me!"

She noticed what little colour had returned to his cheeks had now receded. He looked as if he'd seen a ghost. She watched him with a sense of unease. He's been in the same room, thought Phil. His mind was in a turmoil. He's getting really cocky to risk coming in here!

Siobhan watched as he opened the envelope and drew out a single sheet of paper. Red ink, as usual. The familiar handwriting.

He spoke in a whisper. "It says get well soon."

"That's nice then. Now, try to rest," said Siobhan as she absently smoothed the sheets of his bed into order.

Phil's eyes closed in desperation. Siobhan stepped silently across the room again to the door so she didn't disturb her model patient...

****

He could've finished me off there and then! No, he wants the game to continue. He was enjoying it now. The thrill of the chase; the hunter and the hunted.

It was too easy to get into the hospital. He simply walked in. Security was a joke. Nobody even approached him. He approached them. So confident, but not over-confident. Another little note. Another dig.

He'd watched as the ambulance arrived at the corner shop. Too late mate! Then he'd been surprised to see a stretcher carried out and being lifted into the vehicle. The prone body was not enfolded in a body bag but had drips protruding and a bag was held high by one of the emergency personnel. Blue lights were flashing as the stretcher slid onto the runners and two ambulance staff leaped in after it. People stared as the vehicle sped off with its siren wailing. Mr Policeman had collapsed. How sad!

The crowd of ghouls and passive onlookers had slowly dispersed leaving the forensics, SOCOs and a young constable to tidy up the mess. Lots of white tape and to-ing and fro-ing as usual.

It didn't take long to find out where they'd taken the unfortunate Mr Queen. He'd simply played the inquisitive youngster.
"What's happened officer?"
The constable played the game.
"Just a bit of an accident son," came the stock answer.
A bit of an accident? I wouldn't call the punctured lung a bit of an accident.
"Oh I see, how unfortunate," he replied.

Queen's girlfriend had been there too. Her tears had been plentiful again.
She'd been shepherded away by two minders.
Relatives? Maybe, maybe not.
He'd have to put his next plan on ice. Just for a while...

****

"You look like death," murmured Phil.
Chloe sat beside his bed with her eyes red raw from her constant tears. Her hands clasped his.
She sniffed defiantly. "I'm fine. You're the one who looks ready for a coffin."
"Rubbish!" Phil placated her.
Ken and Mo stood by the door with their faces austere.

"Do you want to be alone?" asked Ken with a serious frown.

Phil shook his head slightly. "No, we're fine. Thanks for your help chaps."

"No problem." Mo smiled. "The sooner you're out, the better."

Phil took Chloe's hand. "He was here this morning!"

Chloe's eyes widened. "What?!"

Ken and Mo stepped forward.

"Chloe has told us about the letters," said Ken earnestly.

Phil nodded. "Good. You had to know sometime."

Ken pulled up a chair closer to the bed.

"It's someone very clever. Someone very clever and very close. He obviously does this for a living."

"He does," said Phil flatly. He felt Chloe start at his words.

"What do you mean?" she asked; clearly shaken.

Phil hunched himself up in the bed.

"I've had another envelope."

"And?"

"It contained photographs of previous victims."

Ken looked anxious. "He's killed before?"

Phil nodded with his eyes closed.

"How many?" asked Mo.

All eyes were on Phil. He stared down at the bed sheets.

"Could be double figures," he sighed heavily.

Suddenly, the door opened and the nurse poked her head in.

"Another five minutes, then It's time up I'm afraid," she murmured with a quick smile as she closed the door again.

"I think Chloe should be under guard," said Ken.

Chloe turned sharply. "Me?!"

"Yes, I agree," said Phil, "Ken's right. We're dealing with a clever bastard here."

Mo nodded in agreement. "It's a fact. I think you're his next target."

Chloe moaned.

Phil looked at Ken and asked, "Could she stay with you while I'm in here? I should be out by tomorrow with a bit of luck."

Ken smiled to lighten the atmosphere. "Sure, it'll be nice to have a lady about the house."

Mo grinned. "What's your cooking like?"

Chloe began to sob.

"Ssssh – it's alright darling. You'll be in safe hands with Ken and Mo. Don't worry," urged Phil.

"I'm scared Phil and I thought it was all over after the funeral," she answered tearfully.

Phil offered her a tissue and she gratefully dabbed at her eyes and face.

"We'll look after her Phil," Ken assured him.

"Thanks lads. I owe you one."

"Two!" said Mo as Ken stood up.

"Are you going to tell the police about all of this?"

Phil shook his head.

"No!" he said firmly.

"I think you should!" said Chloe.

"No, I want The Brothers to help me, not the police. If he wants a war, he's going to get one!"

Mo shrugged. "So be it. Anyway, we are the police..."

The visitors moved towards the door. Chloe hung back for a while as her hand gripped Phil's.

"See you soon."
"You're beautiful," whispered Phil.
"Good luck at tonight's meeting lads," Phil called after the departing pair.
"We'll mark you Absent With Out Leave," laughed Ken.
"Thanks a lot!"

They all left. In the silence, Phil's sleep came swiftly...

****

BEVAN GARDEN ESTATE, PECKHAM - 5.30pm
Terence Anthony Gordon wasn't expecting visitors. The slight knock at the door distracted him from the TV screen. He pressed the red button on the remote control and lumbered over to the curtained window which separated his disgusting existence from the outside world.

He pulled the thin cotton aside. It was a dull grey outside; dusk had enveloped a typical desultory British afternoon. A man stood on the doorstep. He was immaculately dressed.

Gordon frowned. He wasn't expecting anyone.
The figure knocked again, more urgently.
"Fuckin' salesmen..." he muttered under his breath. His breath stank of curries, half-eaten kebabs and chip fat. He lived on takeaways and lived alone in his dank council flat.
His recent past had been spent in prison - Section 47 inmate. Solitary Confinement. Kept well away from the more stable prisoners. Being head of an international paedophile ring meant special treatment. Two attempts on his life had been futile. He'd been attacked within

twenty minutes of entering the prison. It took five officers to pull Higgins off him.
Later, having failed to snuff out Gordon, Higgins had committed suicide in his cell.

The second attack had been by an actual prison officer. The young lad had been tipped over the edge by his stories and taunts. 'Mind Games' they called it. Near strangulation. He'd been a strong boy but once again Gordon survived. The officer was suspended and dismissed after an inquiry. How unfortunate!

He'd won again... The parole board had been very sympathetic.

"I'm comin' - hang on!" he shouted, as the third knock echoed through the empty hall. He zipped his trousers up as he went to the door.
"Who is it?" he shouted while undoing the latch.
"Environmental Health sir!"
Gordon opened the door.
The young man looked up at him from the step. His aftershave smelt expensive thought Gordon enviously.
"Good afternoon - Mr...er... Gordon?"
Gordon nodded slowly. "What's up?" he snapped impatiently.

The visitor held a clipboard.
"The council is doing a poll to ascertain whether the local public are satisfied with hygiene control in the area. Rats are becoming a constant menace and..."
"Yes! Yes - I'm quite happy..." exclaimed Gordon as he interrupted the smart young representative. "Now, if

you'll excuse me, I'm very busy," he added frantically. He was enjoying his latest video before this inconvenience.

The council official took a step forward.
"I'm sorry sir but if you'll just answer a couple of questions, I'll be on my way."
Gordon grimaced, "Oh, all right get on with it."
The man shot a Biro and poised it over his clipboard.
"Question one. How often are your bins emptied?"
"Every Wednesday mornin' - except Bank Holiday weeks," snapped Gordon.
The young official painstakingly ticked the sheet.
"Question two. Is there ever any cause for complaint with regard to the behaviour of council employees?"
"No."
"Question three. Do you..."
"Oh, do get on with it!"
"Er, this is your final question sir."
Gordon stared at the floor, clearly irritated by this officious little prick in the sharp suit.
"Do you still hanker after little boys?"
There was a short silence.
Gordon flinched. "Eh?"

In one swift motion Gordon was thrown violently back into his hallway.
The kick to his solar plexus winded him momentarily.
The shock of the attack was instantaneous. He heard the assailant shout, "GO! GO! GO!"
Footsteps thudded up the driveway. Scrabbling about on the floor, he heard more shouts. "It's him! We've got the bastard!"

Shadowy figures appeared through the doorway. Three? Four?
He hid his face in panic. “What’s happening? Who are you?!”
No one answered. A rag was stuffed into his mouth. It tasted of oil, dry and soiled.
A balaclava enveloped his head. Rough hands tied him up unceremoniously while dragging his arms round to his back. The pain was excruciating.

Then, all went silent. He leaned against the wall on the hall floor.
“Wh...mmm...?” he moaned through the gag. Struggling was useless.

He listened. They were in the study! Someone had turned the video on. Voices whispering. Police?
The sounds of the film were clear and strident. He felt the familiar stirrings of an erection.
“Dirty bastard!” someone murmured in disgust.
Footsteps... coming out of the study.
They stopped. He sensed someone standing over him in the darkness.
The silence was threatening. Brooding.
Fully thirty seconds passed...
There was only darkness when the punch connected with Gordon’s head.

****

Vanguard III

They sat around the table once again. This was the third such meeting in as many months. There had been no time to place a message in The Times. Word spread in strict secrecy by telephone, letter or personal visits.

The Brothers of Justice were joined by others tonight. Outsiders in reality.

Chloe sat with Ken and Mo in seats positioned around the perimeter walls. About twenty five other men and women did likewise. This was their first time too.

The central figures were the Heads of Districts.
Waitresses carried trays bearing a miscellaneous choice of drinks. Chloe took an orange juice, Ken a dry martini and Mo had a beer. All very cordial, he thought to himself.
The scene had both shocked and excited Chloe. There was a definite undercurrent of power in the room. When they entered the house, she and the other guests had been ushered into the main chamber by a tall gentleman in a tuxedo.

"That's Cliff Marsh. He's in charge of East Anglia district," whispered Ken.

"Ex-mercenary," added Mo dully.

Chloe followed the throng into the large conference room. The seats were arranged so that people sat directly opposite or as close as possible to their Area Head. Name cards were placed on each seat.

"Snazzy!" said Chloe as she took her own seat.

Ken smiled in agreement.

"I wish Phil could see this," she whispered.

"Who's he?" Chloe continued and pointed discreetly at the figure in front of her at the table.

Ken leaned over. "That's Clive Badger, Head of District Four - our District."

Chloe frowned. 'Badger'? That name rings a bell, she thought.

Mo put his finger to pursed lips. "Ssssh!"

He nodded as another figure entered. The clock struck nine.

"All rise," a voice boomed and resounded around the huge chamber. All present stood stiffly.

Chloe couldn't resist a giggle. Mo nudged her and shook his head slightly. She tried to compose herself. It's like a royal visit, she thought.

A man took his place at the head of the table.

"Welcome, Brothers and Sisters! Please be seated!"

As she resumed to her seat Chloe stared at the speaker. She knew his face from somewhere; she felt certain of it. There was a hushed silence as he began his introduction.

"May I say a special thank you to the organisers of tonight's meeting. I realise that, at such short notice, there are a few notable absentees."

Chloe noted there were two empty seats remaining at the table.

"These past weeks have been the busiest yet. Countdown to 'The March' begins in earnest today."
"Eh?" queried Chloe but Ken motioned her to stay silent. This was serious.
"As you all know, plans are afoot to rock the foundations of Parliament." Glass tinkled. There was no other sound in the expectant assembly.
"The Brothers of Justice is only just beginning. In the last year, our Brothers have systematically removed dozens of the criminal fraternity. We're not talking about burglars or traffic regulations violators."
Chloe leaned forward intently.
"I'm talking about rapists, murderers and drug dealers. Bullies are being scared witless. I want this country cleansed. With your help, Brothers and Sisters, we shall put our activities on a world stage in weeks!"
"Hear, Hear!" responded a lone voice but the Brothers and Sisters murmured in agreement.

When the commotion faded, the figure at the far end of the table sat down.
A small, tubby gent in an identical tuxedo to the usher then stood up.
"Des Pardoe - Welsh District," whispered Mo.
"Ladies and Gentlemen. I have personally ensured that 'The March' will be strictly monitored by my highly trained and highly motivated personnel."
More murmurs of approval broke out.
"Police are under strict orders not, I repeat NOT, to intervene if things look like becoming, shall we say, difficult."
A few people chuckled approvingly.
"Disruption will be dealt with. There are bound to be various factions who, once word gets out, will want to

jump on the proverbial band-wagon. They won't stand a chance." Cue applause.

Pardoe sat down while he was on top. Wise move, thought Chloe. It was turning into a mini back-slapping session.

The commotion subsided and another man rose to his feet.

"Garth Madeley - South East representative," murmured Ken under his breath.

Madeley looked impeccable in his three piece suit. He wore glasses but they didn't detract from his menacing presence. He stood fully at six foot five and had a jaw of granite appearance. His voice, however, was almost gentle. Chloe was transfixed. He'd only said three words.

"We have Gordon!"

The whole room erupted. Ken and Mo did 'high fives' over Chloe's head.

Chloe and other obvious newcomers looked totally perplexed at this spontaneous outpouring of excitement and emotion from the assembled mass.

Chloe stood up. "Who's Gordon?" she shouted above the din.

Mo was grinning maniacally. "He's been our main target for seven months! One of the most vicious paedophiles in the country, Europe even. And we've got him!"

He punched the air triumphantly.

The atmosphere was electric, thought Chloe, and she was a tad concerned.

Eventually, the room became silent again. The main figure at the top of the table spoke again.

"Where is he?"

Madeley spoke and remained seated. He'd made no move during the uproar.

"He's in a safe house and under guard."

"Underground?"

"Of course. A shitty little cellar."

Applause rang out again.

"We snatched him from a council flat in east London this evening. He sustained a few minor bruises in the struggle."

"Were there any witnesses?"

"Just him."

"Good, well done!"

Chloe nudged Ken. "He's been kidnapped?"

Ken nodded. "Yeah, for a reason but I'll tell you later on pet," he whispered.

Chloe nodded. She was enjoying herself now and she felt secure in the company Ken and Mo.

When another speaker rose, she thought of Phil in hospital. Just wait till you hear about this she thought, smiling smugly to herself...

The meeting lasted another forty minutes. Once it was over, people began to disperse. Chloe chatted to a few of the new arrivals but she was surprised when a vicar shook her warmly by the hand. There were all types of people there. Butchers, journalists and firemen. Just about every conceivable member of the public. Just ordinary people who were fed up with a weak, pussyfooting justice system.

Ken and Mo had been in deep conversation when she tapped Ken on the shoulder. She felt relaxed as she drank another orange juice.

"Ah Chloe! Please, I'd like you to meet our very own Area Representative – Clive Badger." Ken smiled warmly as he ushered her into the group to join their conversation.
Chloe smiled and shook Badger's hand. It was a firm friendly handshake, not a limp introduction. She liked Badger immediately.
"Mrs Lee, isn't it?"
"Yes, I'm glad to meet you...er... sir," She stifled the urge to curtsy!
"Oh, please just call me Clive. I get enough grovelling at work!"
"Of course, sorry, Clive," Chloe responded as she released her hand almost apologetically.
Mo interrupted, "Clive recruited Phil to The Brothers."
Chloe smiled again. "Oh - I see."
Badger nodded. "Yes, Phil's a fine man. How is he, by the way? I hear he had a bit of a situation yesterday?"
Chloe's face fell. "Yes, it was awful. He's been through the mill recently and yesterday tipped him over."
"I do hope he'll make a full recovery very soon. I was hoping to speak to him tonight."

Badger placed his glass carefully on a passing tray.
"Why don't you get in touch with him? He should be out tomorrow. Here's my phone number and address. If ever you're in..."
Chloe offered Badger one of her business cards.
"Oh, no. I much prefer to speak to Phil face-to-face. I haven't seen him since he left the force."

Chloe started. "You're a policeman?"
"Yes I was Phil's last boss, just prior to his recruitment to the 'Brothers'."

Realisation hit Chloe like a blow in the face.
NOW she knew where she had heard Badger's name! This was the man who had crushed her lover!
Trying to cover up her feelings of distrust, she probed a little further.
"Am I to understand that Phil knew that you had recruited him for this organisation?" she asked, trying to sound as non-committal as she could.
Ken glanced at Mo; a sharp glance unseen by Chloe.
"Well..." Badger's expression betrayed his discomfort.
"I think it's time we left," Mo suggested suddenly and his hand cautiously grasped Chloe's elbow.
"Hang on!" said Chloe urgently.

Badger smiled. The pleasant demeanour was slipping. "So nice to have met you, Mrs Lee."
He nodded and departed; swallowed up in the melee of departing members.
Chloe stood rooted to the spot. "What's up with him?" she asked; her eyes wide.
Ken smiled tactfully. "He's got a very full diary I'm afraid Chloe."
"But I wanted to talk about..."
"I know," said Mo gently, "but Clive is a very important part of this jigsaw. He has lots of big fish to fry."
"So, I'm only a bloody small fish?" Chloe spat.
Ken smiled again at her anger and attempted to smooth things down.
"I'm sure you'll meet him again soon."
Chloe's eyes blazed with suppressed fury.
"He's the bastard who lost Phil his job isn't he?" she ranted. Heads turned as her voice rose.

Ken's composure had disappeared. This was getting embarrassing.
"Now come on Chloe. We'll leave now."
"Too bloody right we'll leave," she muttered under her breath.

Mo smiled apologetically at the surrounding guests. They moved towards the front entrance of the house.
"Wait till Phil hears about this. He'll be ecstatic!" she continued.
Mo and Ken were getting edgy.
"Excuse me boys, I need the toilet!" Chloe snapped and suddenly left them standing.

"Bloody hell, that was close!" said Ken.
Mo pulled Ken close. "I didn't realise she knew who Badger was!"
Ken frowned. "Neither did I. The last thing we want is Phil finding out at this stage."
"I know."

They watched Chloe collect her coat from an attendant. She was still fuming as they walked down the gravelled drive to the waiting BMW.

"Phil's going to be well chuffed when he hears Badger's a bloody Brother as well!"

Ken spun and faced Chloe. Mo was silent.
"And who's going to tell him?"
"Me, of course. As soon as he gets out."
"Do you think that's wise Chloe?" he asked with a rather quizzical look on his face.

"I don't care. I think it's a bloody farce! He loved the police. It was his true vocation. Not a tin-pot vigilante group! Are you threatening me Ken?" Chloe's face was inches from his.

Mo smiled. "Come on Chloe, let's go. You're upset."
"Too right, I'm upset," Chloe retorted. She shrugged off Mo's hand and quickly walked away with her shoulders hunched. She stood with her arms crossed beside the BMW.
Ken and Mo followed her at a distance.
"She's a bloody liability..." Ken whispered to his brother.

****

Chapter Nineteen

The morning was bright. A cascade of light shone into the room. A nurse was tidying up when Phil awoke. His eyes took seconds to become accustomed to the harsh rays.

"'Morning." he croaked as he shielded his face with his forearm.

"Hello Mr Queen. How are we today?" the Irish lilt was evident in her voice but she did not look him in the eye.

Phil swallowed. He'd slept for twelve hours.

"Great... I think," he whispered.

"Let's raise your pillows then," the nurse responded as she crossed the room to plump up his three cushions.

Phil eased into a more comfortable sitting position.

"And what would you like for breakfast?" she asked as she stood with her hands on her hips.

"Cereal please and some black coffee. Thank you."

"Oh - very healthy."

As she turned to go and prepare his meal, Phil spoke, "I want to be discharged today. Tell Sister will you?"

The nurse smiled and nodded. "Shouldn't be a problem. You seem fine to me."

Phil sank back on the pillows. He hated hospitals. The smell of them made him feel ill and there was the constant noise. Luckily, they had put him in 'solitary' as he called it in the forces. He hated being in a large ward. So public. No privacy.

Suddenly, he jerked into full consciousness. Had he been visited last night? His eyes scanned the bedside table. There was no envelope.

He leaned over and tugged at the drawer to the dresser. The top drawer was empty. The second contained a paperback novel and a pen. The bottom one stuck as he tugged at it whilst hanging out of the bed.

"Mr Queen! What ARE you doing?"

Phil looked up in alarm. Siobhan stood holding his breakfast tray.

"Oh sorry. I was looking for a tissue. My nose is bunged up."

The nurse tutted impatiently. "All you have to do is ask. That's what we're paid for."

"Yes, of course..." Phil feigned sincerity.

No visitor. No envelope and no Chloe.

"Were there any messages for me last night?"

The nurse was pulling the bed table over the bed for him. "Not that I know of," she frowned slightly.

Chloe would have gone to the meeting with Ken and Mo and then gone home. Surely, she would have phoned?

"Could you check at reception for me? I'd be very grateful."

The nurse nodded.

Phil noticed her white bra strap as she leaned over him. Her slight aroma of perfume was gorgeous.

"You smell nice," he commented as he slyly looked up at her.

"It's Givenchy," she offered happily.

"Really?" said Phil, trying to sound knowledgeable. "It suits you."

"Thanks - my husband says it turns him on. He loves it!"

Phil's face flushed. "Have I got Ricicles or Coco Pops?" he asked to cover his embarrassment.

"Neither – it's Cornflakes!" replied the nurse laughing as she turned to leave the room again.

Phil winked at her as she departed. "You would look good in high heels," he managed the last word as she closed the door.

Smiling to himself he ate his breakfast. The coffee was cheap but hot. The paper cup was no substitute for the comfort of a mug at home.

Minutes later he heard familiar footsteps. The nurse put her head around the door.

"No messages I'm afraid Mr Queen. Not a sausage..."

Phil sank back on the bed, frowned silently and stared out of the window.

Where was Chloe?!

****

BASINGSTOKE TRAIN STATION

It wasn't his fault he was bored. He needed a fix. The money from the till would last him for a couple of weeks. He could go anywhere he liked. The train would be a good option. Lots of opportunity on a train.

His next victim had to be soon. Boredom made him frustrated.

He was becoming famous. The old codger's death was the lead story in the papers.
"SHOPKEEPER IN STABBING HORROR!" screamed the local rag.
"VIOLENT BRITAIN!"... 'Police have refused to comment on reports that a serial killer is at large..."

That's you, Stevie-boy. Fame at last!
In the Express, a map of unsolved murders was splashed across the centre spread. The little girl in Scotland got a mention but they were miles away from Steven Kennedy. You've only been at it for a few years. Must try harder.

He sat on a bench on the station platform. The Inter-City sleeper would arrive in minutes. Lots of single compartments to choose from. He scanned the platform. Young students stared at timetables. Nubile females strolled arm-in-arm with their boyfriends.
"Wankers," he whispered.
He felt for the knife in his sock. Still there. Good!
A Transport Policemen strolled past, oblivious to the scruffy shaven-headed youth on the bench to his right. People milled around in confusion.

His eyes darted from scene to scene. A pair of teenagers wrapped themselves around each other as the train pulled in. A girl was in tears, although a young lad with her kissed her on the nose and forehead. His hand squeezed her backside tenderly. She wore a tartan miniskirt, black tights and high heels. Her tight top only just about contained her heaving chest. They were heedless of the any onlookers.
"Slapper," muttered Steven Kennedy enviously.

His eyes closed. He pictured the girl with nothing on. She was asking for it! Her long, blonde hair swung as she sat astride him, willing him on.... (*Harder! Faster! Deeper! Pleeeease..!*).
His erection was uncomfortable. He stood up and stretched. She'll do for today he thought.

The necking couple didn't even notice as he clambered aboard the waiting train. He still had his hand on her arse! Sitting next to the window, he could just about hear their parting words.
"Love you Lisa."
"Me too."
The whistle blew shrilly. Slamming doors heralded the departure of the train. The girl climbed in quickly. She leaned out of the door, still kissing, as the train began to move. The engines hummed and groaned when they reluctantly parted. Her boyfriend waved, becoming a distant speck on the platform. Blowing kisses, she excitedly waved back.
He saw all of this.
Then she entered his carriage, sniffling into a tissue.
Sit there! he implored.
She sat down opposite to him in the corner seat. Yes!!
He looked out of the window at her reflection in the glass.
She blew her nose silently. She was gorgeous close to.
He stood up to put his bag on the overhead compartment.
They were the only people in the carriage.
Don't get carried away now! As he sat down, the girl looked across at him and glanced away as strangers often do.
Go for it!

"Hi!" he said amiably.

The girl didn't answer. She stared out of the window as the train clattered on.

Ignorant cow!

"Where you goin'?"

She shifted slightly in her seat. She's heard you all right but she doesn't want to know you.

His knowledge of body language was primitive but he knew when the going was tough.

She wasn't interested.

His hand went to his jacket pocket. (*She's watching you through the window*!)

"My name's Neil," he volunteered again.

No answer.

"Polo?" he offered her the opened packet.

Her eyes found his.

Smile you bitch!

"No. No thank you." she said nervously and turned away. She chewed her nails as she watched the trees and fields rushing past.

The door suddenly crashed open.

"Tickets please!"

Shit!

He looked up at the inspector standing over him. Handing over his orange ticket, he turned away in silence. The girl was rummaging through her handbag as the large uniformed figure studied the orange stub.

"You're on the wrong train son," he said without expression.

(I know…)
"Am I?" he lied.
"Oh no! I'm goin' to be well late," he continued.
The inspector studied his timetable.
"If you get off in two stops you can catch a return to where you got on."
"Okay, cheers mate."
The inspector turned away but the girl smiled at him across the carriage.
(Feel sorry for me do you? That's a start, I suppose!)
"Three stops, change at Staines."
"Thank you," said the girl as she took back her ticket.
The inspector departed and closed the door behind him.

The fantasies started again as the train hurtled on, rocking him gently from side to side.
He imagined his hands on her breasts and teasing the nipples to erection, her arms pulling him down on top of her, her legs wrapped around the small of his back, eyes shut tight and her moans as they climaxed together.

The train's horn sounded. It was approaching the tunnel. He could just see it in the distance around the curve of the track.

The girl had closed her eyes, her arms crossed and her head leant against the window.

(It's always noisy in a tunnel so now's your chance…)

His hand went to his ankle. He withdrew the knife surreptitiously and concealed it alongside him on the seat.

As the girl snoozed, her skirt had ridden up her crossed legs. Shapely thighs - there for the taking.

Again, the horn sounded. The train entered the tunnel and its noise blasted and echoed.

She didn't have time to scream. He was upon her in an instant. In the darkness he fumbled wildly, his left hand smothering her mouth. She tried to struggle but his frustration doubled his strength.
His right hand undid his fly. She was rigid with fear and blind in the darkness as his hands clumsily grabbed her breasts. She heard his breathing in the black hole of her panic. The tunnel was endless and the noise easily obscured the sounds of their struggle.
He tried to force his penis into her mouth but she resisted, turning her head, realising his intention dimly through her horror.
"Suck it you bitch!" he shouted. In her panic she did but gasped.
It took him seconds to ejaculate.
The blackness and the disorientation added to her terror of this merciless attack. She retched from his seed and sobbed wildly. Her body was totally numb with terror.

He felt for the knife he had lodged in his back pocket.
Suddenly, the train emerged from the tunnel in a blaze of light!
The reverberating noise abruptly ceased. Time stood still.
He kneeled over her on the floor of the carriage. Her eyes were wide and dazed. His flecks of semen dripped from her long, blonde hair. Her mouth was wide open as she coughed and sobbed.

Then she screamed. It was an ear-splitting howl.
"Shut up you dirty cow…!"
The knife came down in an arc, entering her just below the rib cage. As he withdrew it to strike again, blood spurted across the narrow gangway.
"Oh my God!" she whispered.

He calmly sat back on his seat and watched as her breathing became more and more difficult. This was his favourite bit… He watched in silence as she faded away. Her eyes stared silently back at him while her head banged on the seats. Her top ripped during the attack so her breasts remained exposed too. The bra strap was completely broken and crimson blood seeped onto the floor beside her, slowly creeping up to her attacker's foot. He stood up in disgust. The train rumbled on.

As she sighed her last desperate breath, he placed his mouth close to her ear, "It's not your fault..."

****

Chapter Twenty

As he sat in the rear of the taxi, Phil pondered the last two months of his life. His resignation, Chloe, The Brothers, murder and mayhem.

He'd found happiness with a beautiful woman. This would be many people's idea of heaven. However, other events had conspired against him.

Chloe was the most important factor in his life. Together, they could easily get by in the shop, living and working with each other. The village was a serene 'picture post-card' place and their neighbours were friendly without being too overbearing. It was perfect!

As Phil stared out of the window, he thought back to his father's words when he was a teenager.
"It's your life so do what you want with it."
He had been given so much freedom and taught very little parental discipline. A so-called factor as to why kids grew up to be villains.
Joining the Army had been a natural progression. He was out on his own. Success was up to him, no one else. All he ever wanted was to be independent. He'd made a few friends in the forces. Oh, and he was popular, very popular. However, his pals were distant ones, acquaintances, that's all.

He realised at that moment that he didn't know anybody from his time in the Army. He'd lost touch. He couldn't pick up the phone and talk about 'old times' like thousands did. Not for Phil Queen the 'old boy' network and the British Legion. No thanks!

The driver cocked his head as he drove.
"Which end of the village sir?"
Phil leaned forward.
"The centre please. Drop me by the pub. Do you know it?"
"Yeah, no problem. The White Hart?"

Trees sped by. Summer was approaching. The green leaves would turn to brown of autumn, then nothing. Just skeletons again in winter.

The taxi entered the tiny enclave. An old couple walked hand-in-hand across the green and a Jack Russell snapped playfully at their heels.
He was home. Back home to Chloe. He couldn't wait to see her, touch her and simply smell her.

The vehicle pulled up outside the pub. It was four-fifteen. Chloe would be at the shop but it would soon be closing time and then she'd back at the cottage.
He hadn't phoned her from the hospital. It wasn't often he surprised her.
"That's just twelve pounds sir."
Phil handed the driver fifteen pounds. "Cheers, ta!"
"Keep the change. Get a pint or two in on me," the driver nodded and grinned.
"You'd get two pints for a quid fifteen years ago," he added mockingly.

Phil laughed and slammed the rear passenger door. He slapped his hand on the roof of the taxi as it pulled slowly away from the kerb.

He approached the shop carrying the large box of dairy chocolates and the bunch of pansies, bought from the hospital shop as he left.

The first thing he noticed was the bottle of milk on the step. Hmm, Chloe always collected the milk first thing, as soon as she opened up, thought Phil. Phil frowned slightly. On trying the door he found it locked and he could see no sign of movement when he peered through its window.
The sign hung still - ‘Closed’.
He knocked on the pane. It was Thursday so it was not early closing time. Chloe always worked on Thursdays. Not today it seemed thought Phil uneasily. He resisted the slight frisson of anxiety. Don’t panic!
She’s okay because Ken and Mo were looking out for her.

He made his way back and into the pub. A couple sat at a round wooden table eating a club sandwich. He smiled as he caught their attention. They nodded; chewing like a pair of contented camels without a care in the world.

“Hello? Shop!” Phil called as he propped on the bar. He placed the chocolates and flowers on a stool beside him. Pauline, the young barmaid, emerged from the rear kitchen. She had a cheerful freckled face, devoid of make-up and ginger hair.
“Hi! Paula isn’t it?”

"Close – it's Pauline actually. What would you like?" she said with a grin.
He urgently leaned forward.
"It's Chloe. Have you seen her this morning?"

Pauline stared into the distance momentarily in concentration.
"Nope. Not today. The last I saw of her was about two days back. She popped in for a couple of hours to tidy up at the shop. Said she was going to see you at the hospital."
Phil examined the beer mats on the bar as he assessed all the information.
"Oh, I see."
"Are you okay now?" asked Pauline breezily.
"Yep. I'm fine thanks," murmured Phil with his frown deepening by the second.
"Fancy a bite to eat? A beer?"

Phil suddenly turned and ran out of the pub.

The couple in the eatery stared as he shot past them.
Pauline remained still yet open-mouthed. "'Charming, I must say!"
"He's forgotten his flowers and chocolates," the elderly lady pointed out as she sipped on a gin and tonic.
Pauline lifted the bar entry flap and picked up the intended gifts from the stool. As she hoisted them over the bar a small tag fell to the floor. She bent down and picked it up.
"To Chloe. I'm back to stay. Love you. Phil xx"
"Aaaah, how sweet." she smiled as she placed them beneath the counter. The old couple continued to eat

their club sandwich in silence. They were lost in their own thoughts...

****

He hadn't run this fast in years. That time, he'd come third in the two hundred metres and knackered his hamstring into the bargain. It didn't take long for him to become short of breath and covered by a sheen of sweat.
(*You're too unfit buddy!*)
Still he ran and gasped for more oxygen. It was a good half mile to the cottage. Being fully clothed and wearing black leather brogues meant he eventually had to stop, slow down and walk briskly for the last three hundred yards or so.
His mind whirled about Chloe as he wiped the beads of sweat from his brow.
(*She's fine. She's at the cottage with Ken and Mo. They'll have made sarnies for your arrival.*)
My darling Chloe! He cursed himself as he pictured her lying on her duvet, legs apart and urging him into her.
(*Stop it! Is that all you can think about?!*)

Finally, he reached the garden gate. It was shut. Birds chirped merrily in the trees surrounding the picturesque little building. The road was silent. He flicked the catch on the gate and walked purposefully up the path. His car stood in the road where she usually parked.
He knocked on the old wooden door. It was surrounded by a brilliant array of summer flowers in hanging baskets. It's the archetypal village cottage. So British! Bees buzzed amid flowers and birds sang on, oblivious to Phil's feelings of foreboding.
No one came to the door.

(*Was she next door with 'Miss Marple'?)*
He walked as slowly as he could, without panicking, around the cottage.
The plants hung over on to the path. He trod gingerly, not wanting to damage them. A huge glistening orange slug sat in a dark recess at the side of the path. He side stepped it, with revulsion. He hated slugs. The smell of fertiliser and freshly mown grass assailed his nostrils.

Opening the rear entrance gate, he noticed how long the grass had become. Chloe was always mowing the lawn. She called it therapeutic. The rear lawn stretched away a good twenty yards from the cottage.

A cat sat on the fence, cautiously staring at him. It yawned, pawing at its ears as he closed the gate behind him. The sound of a lawn mower could be heard from further along the village street.

His shirt collar felt cool and clammy as his body temperature lessened after his short jog.
He knocked on the back window.
"Chloe! I'm back. It's me Phil!" he shouted.
Silence.

He squinted and peered into the scullery. There was nothing in the sink. Three mugs sat on the table. He noticed that the jar of teabags was open. A spoon protruded from the sugar bowl.
She'd had visitors. Two, by the looks of it. (*Ken and Mo. They brought her back and had tea. Stop fretting!)*

Phil suddenly remembered the spare key. He ran to the garden shed. Cobwebs cocooned the lock as he opened the rickety old door with a tug. A spider ran down the side of the frame. The key was under the second plant pot on the left. Lifting the pot he breathed a sigh of relief. Taking the key, he pushed the shed door shut and jogged back down the path, dodging the ornamental pots and small statuettes. He felt himself beginning to sweat again. The sun was getting warmer by the second.

The key turned the lock of the front door easily and he smiled as he entered the cottage.
Then he stopped. (*Something's wrong!*)
The telephone table lay on its side and the cable disappeared into the living room.
Phil swallowed silently as he followed the cable.
On entering the front room, his vision blurred slightly. Sweat trickled into his eyes. The heat was oppressive now. He wiped his eyes with his forearm. His white shirt was stuck fast to his shoulders.
A fly buzzed high in the corner of the curtain. Chairs lay on their backs. Chloe's assortment of
figurines were scattered in abandon all over the floor. His foot hit something hard. Looking down, he saw it was the framed picture of Janice and her rabbit. As he picked it up, shards of glass fell to the carpet.

Then he saw the mirror. The words were written in lipstick. Red lipstick!

'SHE'S UPSTAIRES' The spelling mistake unnerved him and Phil's eyes widened in horror.

"No," he whispered in total disbelief.

He turned and hurled himself out of the room. He took the stairs three at a time, shouting with every bound. "Chloe! Chloe!"

The first door he faced was her bedroom.
It was empty. Apart from...
The mirror! More red lipstick. His eyes dazedly took in the words - 'WRONG ROOM'.

Panic now seized him. The silence was deafening and he couldn't breathe.

There were only two more rooms! The spare. She's got to be in the spare! He kicked the door open in a white hot anger.

"Chloe?"

Nothing! Just boxes full of rubbish and jumble. A cabbage patch doll mutely looked up at him.
Then he saw the envelope. Propped up on the window ledge directly opposite the door.
He snatched it up and read 'OPEN ME' in red ink.
He ripped it open. The note was the usual size. Three words....
'IN THE BATHROOM - SILLY!'

Phil screamed and fell to his knees. Tears blinded him as he sobbed, crunching the note into a tiny ball.
"No! Please..." he moaned; swaying on his knees with his head in his hands. He hauled himself to his feet and groggily made his way across the landing to the bathroom door.

He didn't want to look inside. This was not happening. (*I'm still in hospital.. . I'm dreaming... Please God, let me wake up!*). His hand gripped the door handle. He stood for what seemed an eternity, staring at the door, inches from his face.

He twisted the brass knob and the door swung open, creaking slightly.

Phil closed his eyes and muttered, "Oh fuck!"

As the door swung back, Chloe stared at him serenely.

She sat on the toilet seat. She wore stockings, stilettos and a red summer dress. Her eyes were open but seeing nothing. Her hands rested on her knees as she leaned back against the cistern.

In her left hand was another envelope.

Phil could feel his heart pounding as he took in the ghastly scene. He knelt before her in the shocking silence, hearing his own laboured breathing.

He took the envelope from her limp fingers and forced himself to open it. 'BINGO' he read. There were a dozen flies buzzing now in the fetid room.

His gorge rose and he vomited uncontrollably into the marble tub. Tears coursed down his face as he leaned over the turned on the cold tap. He splashed his face and watched the vomit disappear down the plughole.

He forced himself to turn again and look at Chloe.

"You didn't deserve this." he sobbed.

The indignity of her position in death impelled him to embrace her cold body, as if to offer her some last comfort. He lifted the dead weight and carried her gently through into her bedroom. Carefully laying her on the bed, he parted her hair and closed her wide eyes.

Trying desperately to pull himself together; he sat on the bed and gazed at her prostrate form.

Slowly, his professional training began to surface through his pain. (*You shouldn't have moved her. Well, I have so it's too late now!*)

He examined her face and saw dull bruises below her jaw and lesions on her neck.

"Strangled," he murmured.

There were marks on her wrists where the skin had been pressured.

He recalled the note. Him again. He had to know...

Gently parting her legs, he inspected her labia. No contusions. Resisting the urge to be sick again, he inserted a forefinger into her vaginal passage. (*Forgive me, my love.*) His finger came out dry.

"Thank God." he sighed dully.

Pulling the duvet over Chloe, he returned to the bathroom and washed his hands.

Chloe's shoes lay on the floor next to the wash basin. His trained eyes inspected everything. A tampon floated in the toilet. Looking up, he saw the shower pilot light was switched on. He bent down and felt the shower tray. It was dry.

"You were going to have a shower, weren't you?"

"He came in while you were undressing," he mused.

He spoke to himself and it calmed him somehow. He sniffled. His tears had abated. He felt he would never cry again. No more tears. Just hard, cold, inner fury radiated now.

"So, how did he get in? The house was locked."
Phil frowned as he leant back on the sink.
"You didn't let him in, so he must have broken in somewhere. Where?"

He left the bathroom and went downstairs. He methodically checked every window pane and frame. No sign of a forced entry.
"So - you've gone for a shower. Did you leave the front door unlocked?" he muttered.
He shook his head where he stood. "No - no way. You've got more sense than that."
He struggled to come up with a solution, as he slowly walked towards the scullery with intense concentration. Though the sun was still brightly shining outside, the scullery was shadowed and almost gloomy.
Phil sat on the edge of the table and stared at the three empty mugs. There were tea dregs in them all.
"Ken and Mo.. They must have been here, then left," he muttered.
"You must have seen them off, and then shut the door. You always do." (*Did - you always did. Past tense - she's dead remember?!*)

Wearily, he closed his eyes once more. The room was cool. No flies down here.
"Fuck it - have a cup of tea!" he spat.
The bastard had waited for Chloe's return and seized his chance. Another notch on his deathly bedpost thought Phil as he dropped a tea bag into the rinsed mug.

Something caught his eye.
It was a small card, lying by the sugar bowl. He picked it up and turned it over. Just a phone number. Below it was scrawled 'Anytime' in grey pencil.
Phil left the scullery and returned to the living room. He retrieved the phone from the floor and tapped out the number on the card. His frowning face stared at Chloe's photo on top of the television set. He looked away quickly.

"Hello?"
Phil spoke, trying to sound as normal as anyone who has just discovered a corpse sitting on a lavatory.
"Who's speaking please?"
"It's Maurice. It that you Phil?"
Phil's shoulders relaxed. He let out a sigh of relief.
"Mo! Yeah, it's me."
"How are you? Are you out yet?"
"Yes - I'm at Chloe's cottage."
There was a silence at the other end.
"Hello? Mo? Are you there?"
"Yeah... sorry, a bit of interference on the line mate. Sorry, where did you say you were?"
"I'm at Chloe's cottage."
"Oh, right. How is she? Bet she's glad to have you back eh?"
Phil swallowed as he felt tears prickling his eyes again. He squeezed them tight shut for a moment.
"Mo... I've some bad news. Terrible in fact. Are you sitting down?" he asked quietly.
"Why? What's up? You forgot to post a winning pools coupon?" Phil could hear the tease in Mo's voice.
"No - No, please listen to me. It's Chloe... she's," Phil gathered his wavering voice, "... she's dead."

Another silence.
"She's DEAD - did you hear me?"
"Sorry Phil, I didn't catch what you said."
"Chloe's dead! Murdered. I found her half an hour ago. Strangled."
There was only the crackle of static. Phil heard the kettle switch itself off in the kitchen as it came to the boil.
"Fuckin' 'ell mate!" Mo breathed down the line.
Phil spoke again. "There were messages too. The same. It was him again. He got her."
Mo interrupted, "I knew she should have come with us. We offered but she refused point blank. Ken will be beside his sen'."
"It's... it's not your fault Mo. She's always stubborn," said Phil forlornly.
Mo's voice rose, "Phil! Are you still there?"
"Yeah?"
"Stay put! We're comin' over. Stay right where you are. Don't call the police 'til we get there and we're on our way now." The connection clicked out.

****

Chapter Twenty One

Steven Kennedy hadn't reckoned on the ticket inspector coming back up the train so soon. If he had done, he might never have been caught.

On the train's arrival at the next station after the tunnel, he had got off the train. He walked slightly faster than the other two people who had also left the train. He feigned a casual indifference.

He'd spent the three minutes after the killing of the teenager in the stinking toilet, which was two carriages further down the train. This gave him the opportunity to wash the flecks of blood from his hands. The black cotton of his T-shirt effectively hid the stains across his belly. He'd smiled to himself in the mirror as the train rumbled into the next sleepy stop-off point.

Rural England was the perfect hiding place. He was getting good at this. Or so he thought...

Ian Perry had been a ticket inspector on the same route for ten years. He still enjoyed it. He liked people. Too much, his mother said. At thirty five, he was still single. His mates called him 'Fred' after a once-famous tennis player. Ian hated tennis but he loved trains. Indeed, any form of public transport thrilled him. His ambition as an acne-covered teenager was to drive a double decker bus.

It was not to be. His colour blindness, inherited from his dead father William, meant he couldn't drive. Full stop to that ambition.

Ian Perry was your actual train-spotter. Girls were a boring encumbrance. He'd only ever been intimate with two women. The first was a girl from Wales who he met on a Club 18-30 holiday in Corfu. She'd given him a hand job behind the hotel after a drunken binge in a local taverna.

Romantic it wasn't. He couldn't even remember his conquest's name. Sharon? Kim? Kelly-Louise? It was one of those. She was as common as muck. He'd come all over her hot pants and she'd mocked his two minutes staying power.

Sex didn't interest him. Just trains, buses or ferries. He would have swopped a swinging sex life for a trip on the QE2 any day.

He paid to lose his virginity in the red light district of Antwerp. A buxom lady called Trixie had done him thirty minutes for a hundred pounds. She didn't laugh. She just nodded and kicked him back into a Belgian side-street. Ian had brushed himself down and returned to his pals in the bar on the corner. They had greeted him with ironic cheers.

"By George! He's done it!" they sang as he smiled wanly. He was thirty one years old.

The train was nearly empty today. He had only checked about seven tickets, including the lad who was on the wrong train. Quite a common occurrence he mused. The number of people who got lost on a daily basis was unnerving. They should be issued with maps and a ball of string he smiled to himself.

As he walked back along the almost deserted train, he smiled at each passenger. Most of them stared straight through him or turned away. Typical Brits.

The train clattered on.

It had just emerged from the Tunnel and the sudden light disorientated him. The swaying of the train always made it difficult to keep a balance even after ten years' experience. Few people could manage a perfect gait on a British train. He enjoyed watching passengers as they were wildly thrown about, lurching over those in the seats trying to read their papers.

It was quiet today, though. Midweek. No real pressures today so take your time Fred.

As he entered the next carriage he stooped to pick up a discarded sweet box. He was puzzled to see that it contained a few uneaten jelly babies.
His frown deepened when he turned the box over in his hand. A thick, viscous red smear stuck to his thumb. His breath instinctively stopped short.
Surely not? He turned to his left as the train roared onward.

"Oh my life!"
His legs gave way. He grabbed for the seating frame and sank down on to the seat, hardly daring to look. He had

never experienced a dead body at such close quarters. There had been the odd suicide on the line but he had never got a look. Never wanted to!

The blood was everywhere. Then he noticed a footprint... Two or three footprints led away from the girl's motionless form. She stared glassily at him with her mouth slackly open.

He retched violently.

"Don't panic," he whispered; struggling with his thoughts.

He glanced up at the emergency chain. The train was about a minute from the next stop.

"Don't pull it!" He found himself talking to himself.

This was incredible! The killer was still on board! It was scarcely five minutes since he'd checked the poor girl's ticket for God's sake.

That youth! Skinhead. Lost... He had sat opposite to her. He had done it!

Ian Perry - detective - more like Perry Mason, he thought.

The horn sounded, jerking him back to the present. The train was slowing down. The girl still stared sightlessly at him. He resisted the urge to stare at her breasts that were so cruelly exposed.

He sprang up and hurtled along the carriage.

"Don't be a hero. This bastard's dangerous," he whispered as he pulled himself along, seat by seat. Outside the windows, the blurred green mass became trees and buildings as the train groaned into the station.

He positioned himself opposite the station exit and waited. One lone figure stood waiting to get on the incoming train.
"Don't get into the mid-section," he implored quietly.
If someone else found the body, his plan was done for.
The train stopped smoothly.

Perry lowered the window and waited.
"Come out, come out, whoever you are..." he murmured.

The new passenger climbed on two carriages along and the door clunked shut. "Phew!"
Then the door at the far end opened slowly.
Ian Perry smiled. "Come on down..."

His excitement threatened his composure. He was shaking with combined fear and the thought of being a media hero.
"Easy...eeeasy..."

Steven Kennedy came down the platform between a couple of middle-aged men carrying briefcases. He walked steadily and confidently.
Ian Perry knew why. "Cocky little sod!" he frowned.
He watched silently as Kennedy strode closer to the exit and yards from his hiding place.

"Where are you going now?" he thought as Kennedy strolled through the exit.

Perry opened the passenger door and jogged briskly along the platform to the driver's compartment. He tapped on the window.

"Here Colin. Give me a couple of minutes. Must make a quick phone call."

The driver nodded and looked bored. "No problem Fred. It's quiet anyway."

Perry literally sprinted to the telephone kiosk at the end of the platform.

He dialled three digits diligently. He didn't want to mess up. He felt like Bruce Willis in 'Die Hard.' Sweat prickled his forehead.

"Hello? Police? Listen carefully..."

****

Steven Kennedy made his way through the subway across to the opposite platform. He whistled a nameless tune and sat down awaiting the departure of the train he had just left. His bad deed for the day was done. Another superbly executed operation.

"You're the man," he murmured, leaning back. Hands clasped behind his head. Legs open.

The platform was deserted. He checked his watch. Four minutes to the next return train. Perfecto!

He scanned the train, trying to work out where he had snuffed out the slag.

The body would be bound to be found soon. Possibly in about fifteen minutes he reckoned.

By then he would be miles away. Free to plan his next move. He was invincible!

Steven Kennedy, you'll go down in history. He couldn't wait to read about his exploits again...

Ian Perry replaced the receiver. He jogged back to the waiting train and blew his whistle. Its shrill whine was so perfectly British.

He didn't get back on the train as it pulled slowly away...

Kennedy closed his eyes as the train chugged away. He could not see Perry in the waiting room opposite.
Waiting...
Perry needed a crap. Pronto.
(*Heroes are always inconspicuous*!)

Perry had told the police about the murder. He had told them to get to Redwood station, like now, because the killer was actually there!
"No sirens. You'll scare the bastard off!"

Kennedy checked his watch again. He stretched and arched his back on the old wooden bench.
Ian Perry just watched...

The train was coming.
Perry breathed in slowly. He had phoned central office as well. He wasn't stupid. The train would be delayed. That wouldn't shock too many people. Trains often stopped short of stations and everyone just sat and waited never querying why. It's the English way...

Kennedy's eyes opened as the train turned the corner about seven hundred yards down the track. He smiled his 'you're safe' smile again and stood up his hands in his jeans pockets.

The three squad cars had pulled into the tiny rural car park moments before the train pulled up to the platform. Unmarked. Manned by the crack Special Operations unit.

Eight plain clothed figures clambered out; microphones set invisibly in their ears.

Deployed within seven minutes; they were the best. Kennedy climbed into the waiting train. Oblivious! The 'King' was about to lose his crown...

Perry darted out of the waiting room; unseen. He bounded down the exit steps towards the new arrivals.
"He's just got on. I can hold the train."
A huge man with a moustache nodded grimly.
"Well done son. You'll be fuckin' knighted for this!"
Perry blushed furiously.
"All in a day's work. Come on!"

Kennedy settled into his seat, reaching into his pocket for his Polo mints. He stared across the platform at the advertising hoardings and chewed his sweets. After lifting his feet on the seat opposite, he closed his heavy eyelids and drifted off to sleep.

Perry climbed aboard. The eight-man patrol had split. The big one with the moustache followed him along the aisles and an unseen nine millimetre pistol was strapped against his kidneys.

Two policemen climbed on at the front of the train; two on the rear. One stayed by the station exit, ostensibly reading the Daily Express. It was all too easy really as they found Kennedy asleep in compartment Six.
Perry had said simply, "Tickets please."
Kennedy hadn't even recognised him. All ticket bods looked alike didn't they?

When the big bloke with the gun entered the compartment, he didn't have time to register any surprise. It took seven seconds to overpower him.

A few expletives later and the situation was contained.

The twelve other passengers were unaware of what had happened until the following morning.

'I was on that train!' they'd say disbelievingly.

Lisa Bloors' body was removed by police at the next stop. She was seventeen waiting to go to college to study law. She'd died from a punctured spleen. Another vital statistic. Another meaningless death but Kennedy's spree was at an end.

Ian Perry would be a household name for a week. The whole world knew he was a train-spotter now. The girl who gave him a hand job in Corfu didn't get in touch though...

****

When Phil Queen saw Steven Kennedy's face on the front of the Daily Mail, you could have knocked him down with a feather. He sat studying the newspaper with his head in hands.

He knew that face... but where from? Where?!

"I know you... " he whispered as he stared at the photograph.

He stood up and went over to the fridge. The magnetised door opened with a sigh. It needed a fair tug. He took out half a carton of semi-skimmed milk and drank some of the cool liquid, concentrating his mind.

The cottage was silent, except for the flapping curtain at the scullery window.
He'd spent the last two days phoning all of the people listed in Chloe's extensive personal address book. He'd broken the horrendous news to her friends and acquaintances as far apart as London and New Zealand.

Many of the calls were not necessary but he made them just the same. He felt it was only right. The majority of people had learned of Chloe's death from newspapers or TV reports. It didn't take long for the hacks to suss it out. A few people had phoned the cottage.

In their short time together, he'd met some of Chloe's friends and relatives briefly. She had no grandparents and Phil was glad of this. He wouldn't have been able to face telling them. Flowers and cards littered the sitting room; many unopened. Phil's grief was not assuaged by the sympathy being expressed.
'She will be missed'. (*She will!*)
'Chloe was wonderful'. (*She was!*)
'A well-loved friend, above all'. (*Can't argue!*)

Phil had been mentally drained by the last 48 hours and the coming funeral would be an added stress.

Ken and Mo had left him to his thoughts. They knew what he was going through. He'd slept two hours out of the last thirty six.

Police were linking Chloe's killing to that of a young teenager on a local train. The constant TV bulletins and newspaper reports made Phil want to curl up in a ball and hide. The last five months of his life had been a roller coaster of emotional turmoil. He needed a holiday.

He drained the carton of milk, wiped the residue from his lips, kicked open the waste bin and dropped the cardboard container into it. Then, he went back to the newspaper and that photograph.

It showed the suspect. Steven Alastair Kennedy from Leeds.

"Leeds..." he murmured, closing his eyes. Who do I know from Leeds?

The picture showed a sullen youth with lank greasy hair, astride a motor bike, unsmiling. He wore a heavy metal T-shirt with an undistinguishable logo. The shirt was black.

Phil knew the youth.

He thought back to the visit from the delivery boy. The envelope. The photographs.

"It was you wasn't it?" he muttered dully as he stared at the photo once again.

Reading the text, Phil tried to sort out some clues. Where had he met him? Phil had only ever arrested a couple of men of that age. Neither from Leeds, at any rate. It was not a professional con.

"You didn't have a grudge against me then," he mused, "You just enjoyed it."

"TRIANGLE OF DEATH!" screamed the headline.

Phil nodded slowly to himself.

He thought about Ted, the shopkeeper. Chloe and the girl on the train. All snuffed out. For FUN!

He closed his eyes and leaned back in the chair. The face of Steven Kennedy burned into his brain.

He still had the envelope and the photos and now it's time to give them to the police. He had to meet Steven Kennedy too. He needed to know why and where he knew him from.

He also knew something else. He knew he wanted to kill Steven Kennedy because that's what he deserved.

Phil picked up the telephone and dialled the police.

****

Chapter Twenty Two

The cellar was tiny. He could feel the walls around him. It smelt of stale beer, old newspapers and rotting food. His captors were, as yet, unseen. When he regained consciousness he was still blindfolded.

"Hello?"

Silence. Darkness. And the smells.

The balaclava was itchy. His hands were bound double, as were his ankles. He couldn't move.

Now he knew how the children had felt. Alone.

He refused to panic. His muscles screamed for release.

Who were these people?

They weren't police that's for sure.

His mouth was dry. He could taste the gag they had stuffed in earlier.

His head ached. A stubborn, dull thump, heightened by the oppressive silence.

He rolled his closed eyes under the woollen mask. Sweat trickled down his back. He had never known such discomfort. He swallowed without saliva and felt his throat constrict. He needed water.

"Is anyone here? Can anyone hear me?" he mumbled through the hot hood.

His ears strained for the sound of any movement.

Nothing.

They're going to let me die here...
I could be miles from anywhere. I may even be buried alive!

He shook his head in the darkness; fighting of the terror of negative thoughts about what may become of him. He kicked out in panic, his ankle caught a sharp object and he winced in agony.
"It's no good," whispered the voice inches from his ear in the darkness.
"Who? Who is that?"
Silence returned and with it his inner panic.
"Who are you? Where am I?"
Nothing.
No reply.
"I know you are there..!"
"How observant of you," came another whispered reply.
"It's no use you bleating. You're goin' nowhere fat boy," the quiet voice continued.

The voice was quiet but menacing.
"I need water – please."
"Tough!"

He heard a slight scuffle, and then he was aware of light behind his mask. A door opened, a lock unbolted and he heard movements close at hand.
"Water! Please - give me some water," he pleaded with his voice rising in terror.
The clank of metal could be heard.
"Here, have some then!"
The shock of cold water hit him as someone emptied a bucketful over his head! It was freezing. His discomfort

doubled as icy water seeped into his clothes and stuck his shirt on his back. He frantically stuck out his tongue to the wool of the hood, hoping to find some droplets to assuage his thirst.

Then, the door shut with a loud clang!
He was alone again. Cold and clammy, he shivered in the darkness. He gritted his teeth as an ague claimed him and his body began to shake uncontrollably.

It was silence and darkness once more...

****

Chapter Twenty Three

Clive Badger sat at his office window, staring pensively at a group of six teenagers. They all sat on the far wall of the Police HQ. Busy doing nothing; like thousands of others. Baseball caps and jeans - the uniform of youth. All mouth and trousers!

He smiled to himself; his fingers caressing his pursed lips. Life was busy lately. Too busy! Trying to juggle his high profile position in the modern police force with the underground tribulations of the 'Brothers' was becoming a little too much. And not just for him...

His dear wife was showing signs of being distinctly hacked off with the hours he spent away from his 'slippers and tea' existence he had accepted before his elevation to 'The Brotherhood', as she called it sarcastically.

"You're supposed to do less the higher you get," she would moan in that high-pitched whine of hers.
"Yes darling but you love the parties don't you?" he'd replied with an oblique smile. The ones where you get to wear your little black dress. Where you flirt with all my associates, he thought bitterly. Where you literally take over the whole show and then belittle me when we have to leave.

"Oh yes you love the bank account - can't wait for the end of the month and it's off to M & S to splash out on all your expensive essentials."
He was now talking to himself again.

The recent few weeks had been a trial. He didn't have the stamina anymore. It was becoming a struggle to put his uniform on some mornings, especially after his flirtation with the odd call girl.

His position in the 'Brothers' meant he was not questioned too closely about his leisure time. He was aware that most of the other members did the same. They all had their cake and were eating it all right. Why not? He worked hard and the rewards were good.

His thoughts turned to 'The March' just as the intercom buzzed. He swung his feet off the desk and pressed the red button.
"Badger... Mr Badger, there's a visitor for you," Karen spoke from another office.

"Yes, who is it Karen?"
"It's a Mr Queen."
A short silence ensued.
"Mr Badger, shall I send him in?"
Clive Badger frowned.
"Yes..." he paused. "Please do. Tea, as well, please Karen."
"Will do."
The intercom switched out.
Badger stood up in readiness. Phil Queen no less. What did he want?

There was a knock at the door. This was going to be tricky.
"Come in..." said Badger.

Phil didn't really want to see Clive Badger. When he had found out where Kennedy was being held, it had taken him an hour or so to decide whether or not to bother. He detested Clive Badger although he hated Steven Kennedy more. But what was important? Swallowing pride and asking a favour of the man who'd sacked him, or having the opportunity to meet the person who'd murdered the most important person he'd ever known? No contest! So, Phil stood still and found himself knocking on Badger's door once again.
As the door swung inwards he had the creepy feeling of deja-vu as he stepped once more into the spacious office, where months earlier he had faced his own personal firing squad.

"Phil, do come in and sit down. There's a pot of tea on the way." Badger greeted him with a hypocritical smile. They shook hands speculatively with neither certain of the other's thoughts. Their slack grasp confirmed their mutual embarrassment and distaste.

Phil unbuttoned his dark suit jacket and eased himself into the leather chair. It squeaked as he positioned himself casually.
"New chairs?" Phil commented to his ex-boss who sat hunched over his neat desk.
"Oh, yes. I spent some of the police funds. I've always liked leather. Tasteful, don't you think?"
Phil didn't answer. Silence hung between them. Badger coughed, uneasily, glancing at the door. Where's that

tea? All this false bonhomie was uncomfortable in the extreme.

Phil crossed his legs slowly.

"So, how's life Phil?"

Phil shrugged. Their eyes hadn't met since he entered.

There was a knock at the door. It ended the uneasy stalemate.

"Ah Karen, thank you!" Badger motioned to his secretary to place the tray next to Phil. Nice legs, thought Phil.

"Thanks," Phil winked; noticed by Badger.

"Always were a ladies man weren't you Phil?" smarmed Badger with his cheesy grin.

The secretary left the office; blushing profusely.

"Nice lass?" said Phil finally.

"Yes, she's great. What a body eh?"

Phil exhaled in muted disgust. He reached over and poured himself a cup of tea.

"Two sugars in mine please," said Badger as he leaned back in the chair.

"Make your own. I don't work here anymore remember?"

Badger stood up and came round the desk and his face suffused at Phil's response.

"Look here Phil, "I didn't have to let you in here so cut me some slack. I realise you must still be sore about your dismissal..." Badger's tone showed that he was trying to grasp why his ex-sergeant had reappeared on the scene.

"Petty, stupid, dismissal!" spat Phil as he sat stirring his tea deliberately.

Badger coughed again and sidled round the desk and poured his own tea. Then, he leaned down close to Phil's right ear.

"I didn't want to dismiss you Phil but I didn't have any choice." he whispered flatly.

Phil frowned.
"Eh?" he exclaimed.
"It's a long story."
"So shorten it!"
The atmosphere was becoming more strained by the second.
Badger resumed his seat and pressed the intercom button.
"No calls Karen. I could be a while."

Phil leaned forward intently. "Explain!"
Badger shifted in his plush expensive chair.
"This may come as a bit of a shock to you Phil," Badger expressed gently.
"Just get on with it!" Phil was becoming more agitated.
"First of all, can I ask why you're here?"
"I would have thought it's obvious," snapped Phil.
"No?"
Phil's hands were clasped together, as if in prayer.
"It's Kennedy."
"What about him?" asked Badger
"I must speak to him," pleaded Phil.
Badger leaned back. "You realise that shouldn't happen Phil? He's being held in custody and you're no longer..."
"Yes, but I've good reason to want to speak to him. Let's throw the rule book out for a change eh?"
"Indeed but tell me why I should."
"One – I think I know him."
Badger raised his left eyebrow but made no comment.
"Two - you owe me a favour."
The silence returned. They sat at an impasse; facing one another.

"Tell me Phil. How do you know Steven Kennedy?"
"I can't answer that really. All I know is, I've met him somewhere before. I can't recall where. I just know..."
Badger sat and stared. Waiting.
Phil continued, "He's been following me, sending me notes... photographs. He's killed my girlfriend too."
"Mrs Lee?"
Phil started, "How did you know...?"
"I saw all the files."
Phil fell silent. Badger stood up.
"These photos... letters. You think Kennedy sent them?" asked Badger.
"I know he did," said Phil flatly.
He reached into his jacket.
"Here," as Phil spoke the envelope landed with a thump on Badger's desk.
"It's all there - take a look – please!"
Phil bit his lip. A bit of buttering up didn't matter as long as he got to Kennedy.
Badger sat down again. He took out the contents of the creased envelope. He spread the photos and notes over his desk.
"Christ, he's sent you all of this!" he murmured and his shock was obvious.
"Happy now?" Phil interjected.
"Really, has he sent you everything?"
"All of it!" Phil leaned across and pointed to the notes. "These were regular. The envelope was a one-off and hand delivered by Kennedy himself."

Badger shook his head slowly.
"You're one hundred per cent certain it was Kennedy?"

"That's why I want to see him," said Phil nodding. "When I saw his picture in the paper this morning, I knew I'd seen him before. What I don't know is where. I have to know. Can you understand that?"
Badger nodded slowly his agreement. "Yes. Yes, I can." He mopped his brow with a stark red handkerchief. "This is vital evidence. You do realise?"
"Yes, I know."
"He'll go down for life and it should clear up a number of cases with these photos," Badger declared.
"About ten or twelve in all, I reckon, but there could be more we don't yet know about though," said Phil.
"I must have all of this and you'll testify of course?" probed Badger
"If I must!" replied Phil.
"The bastard's only eighteen for fucks sake," spat Badger; staring at his paper-strewn desk.
Phil sat down again. "So, can I see him?"
"Yes, I'll see to it straight away. He's down in the cells," replied Badger decisively.
"I can't wait," said Phil grimly.

Badger pressed the intercom.
"Sergeant Phipps?"
Phil smiled. *(Phipps!)*
"I need access to Kennedy in a few moments. Please get it sorted."
Terry Phipps answered, "OK, no problem sir."
The connection clicked off.

"So - let's go and see our friend," said Badger as he moved towards the door.
"Hang on a minute!" Badger turned. "What's up? You were going to tell me something earlier. What was it?"

"Oh - that can wait. Let's go. I'm very busy. I can speak to you again soon I'm sure," stressed Phil.
"But...? Do you want to see Kennedy or not?"
"Well, yes but..."
"Let's go!" Badger followed Phil into the dimly lit corridor; smiling wanly.

****

Steven Kennedy is not so famous now. He sat on the bare wooden bench staring at the barred window. His knees were drawn up to his chin. He was caught. End of story. How was he to know the ticket inspector was a closet detective?
Graffiti stains smeared the bare walls of the cell:
"Tiny 1987"
"Ginger woz ere. May 1991"
The list was endless...
The walls looked as if they had been painted and washed hundreds of times. The stink of disinfectant and the constant banging of doors assailed his senses and his stomach churned again.
He squeezed his eyes shut and exhaled slowly. Meditation would make all his troubles disappear.
He heard footsteps. And voices!
"Wait here - he's in Number Three..."
More footsteps - one person.
The viewing hatch slid open. Kennedy looked up. He stared at the eyes of Sergeant Phipps.
"Visitors Kennedy! Smarten up now!"

The door suddenly swung open. Phipps was a big man, burly and imposing. His thick beard gave him an extra air of authority.

"Come on, let's go!"

Kennedy slid off the bench.

"Who is it then? Me mam?"

Phipps smiled. His keys jangled as he walked the corridor.

"Not quite son. Not quite."

He was led into a large room. One side of the room was dark, double-sided glass. He couldn't see through it but he sensed someone was on the other side.

He waved a desultory hand in greeting.

"Hi y'all," he smiled as he sat down beside a plain table.

Phil Queen watched as Kennedy entered. A whole rush of memories assailed him as he stared at the cocky, sullen youth.

"That's him."

Badger put his hand on Phil's shoulder.

"I realise this is difficult. Just don't do anything stupid. Do you want to go in alone?"

Phil nodded sharply and affirmed, "Yes."

"You will be constantly monitored. Should anything happen help will be at hand."

Phil recalled the delivery boy. He stared intently at Kennedy. He knew him for sure. The face was so familiar and so were the trainers...

"Where?" he thought to himself.

"Problem?" queried Badger; eyeing Queen quizzically.

"I can't remember where we've met before but I know him from somewhere."

"They call it déjà vu. You've got ten minutes," stressed Badger.

Badger opened the heavy door.

"Sergeant Phipps? That's fine."

Phil smiled as he entered the interviewing room.

"Hi Terry! How's life?"
"Phil!"
They shook hands warmly.
"See you later, OK mate?" said Terry with a grin; not asking why Phil was there.
"Thank you Sergeant. That'll be all," said Badger impatiently.

The door closed behind him with a click.
Badger sat and observed through the glass as Kennedy turned to meet his visitor. Phipps left the room silently.

Phil entered the room warily. He couldn't dismiss a shiver of fear as he stood over Steven Kennedy.
Kennedy stood up and offered his hand; inches from his visitor.
"You've got two hopes!" spat Phil as he rejected the overture. His head was thumping with a mixture of hatred, anger and disdain while Kennedy smiled sardonically.
"How nice to see you again Mr Policeman, or should I say Sergeant?"

Phil halted his approach. "Sit down Kennedy."
"Of course," drawled Kennedy winking and his northern voice echoed within the confined space.
Kennedy resumed his seat on the bench and shrugged and turned his palms upward in supplication.
Phil frowned as he stared at the young man.
"What's up? Confused?" asked Kennedy slyly.
Phil nodded. His lips pursed on upstretched fingers.
"Where do I know you from? That's all I want to know."
Kennedy lazily stretched his arms above his head.
"The final piece of the jigsaw is it?" he sneered and his eyes narrowed.
"You could say that."

Phil was trying to contain his fury. He realised he was shaking and sweating profusely. His shirt stuck to his back. (*Calm down!)* He suddenly thought of Anthony Hopkins' face. Hannibal Lecter made flesh. This was no movie and you are no Clarice Starling he thought...

Kennedy whistled the theme to the 'Twilight Zone' under his breath. Mocking.
"Cut the shit Kennedy and just tell me!"
"Put you out of your misery you mean. Do you remember the first couple of notes?" he replied.
Phil nodded. He felt dizzy.
"I said you'd got the wrong guy in Hart didn't I?"
Phil nodded again as he wiped beads of sweat from his brow with the back of his hand.
"So?"
"So - Mr Policeman, I must have known who killed Janice Lee, mustn't I? I must have known, because..."
Phil interrupted. "YOU killed her..."
Kennedy clapped his hands slowly. He grinned sarcastically.
"Exactly!"

Phil slumped down on the bench. His mind whirled with a confusing mass of thoughts.
"Hart ran off - just like he said!" Kennedy shouted.
Phil gazed in amazed realisation. He felt sick too.
"You? How...?"
Badger leaned forward in his invisible cell watching the scene through the glass. "Christ, " he whispered.

"THINK man!" spat Kennedy as he visibly enjoyed his power over Phil. He recalled the clipped Leeds accent... the trainers...

"Remember when you found the supermarket slapper's body?" whispered Kennedy suggestively.

Phil nodded bleakly. His eyes were tight shut as he visualised the horror of that scene.

"I... was there."

The words hung in the air.

Phil's eyes shot open as realisation dawned. Kennedy grinned.

"I made the coffee. Remember?"

"Neil?" muttered Phil.

Kennedy's arms shot into the air. "Hooray! You've cracked it! Ten out of ten for observ..."

"NO!" screamed Phil.

"YES!" countered Kennedy.

Phil felt like a drowning man. The scenes flashed before him - Janice Lee spread-eagled on the bed, the legs splayed, the blood... Chloe on the toilet seat... the corner shop - Ted, his legs sticking out from behind the counter... it was all too much!

Phil was on Kennedy in a flash. The knife he'd concealed slid easily into his hand.

Clive Badger was too shocked to react. He was rooted to his seat as he witnessed the scene as if in a movie. The violence was silent and immediate. The mirrored glass was smeared with blood as Kennedy's jugular vein was slashed. Phil's unarmed combat skills easily overpowered the unprepared youth.

"This is for Chloe!" he shouted while he slid the knife along Kennedy's left wrist. He'd held him in a vice-like grip. Kennedy's screams of terror filled the room.

"How does it feel Neil or is it Steven?" Phil's rage was totally out of control.

Kennedy's eyes bulged as he tried in vain to stem the flow of blood from his throat. Slicks of thick viscous blood covered his hand.

Phil stood shaking over the collapsed youth, already in his death throes. "Take your time..." Phil whispered; his breath coming in gasps. Kennedy slowly beckoned Phil over to his upturned mouth.

The youth's lips moved for the last time. "I didn't kill Chl..." he choked.

The door of the room was flung open. Phil could hear an alarm going off somewhere in the distance. He was roughly manhandled out into the corridor. Clive Badger stood at the door as he was led out by Phipps and a young constable.

"What have you done?!"

"Call it revenge..." snapped Phil, "... and the bastard didn't deserve another minute alive!"

They led him away up the corridor in silence.

Badger entered the interview room and saw Steven Kennedy breathe his last. Another young constable tried to stem the blood but his efforts were futile. He turned to Badger and his face was ashen.

"Don't bother son. He did a good job." Badger remarked, as he turned and walked slowly away along the corridor.

****

Chapter Twenty Four

Rough hands pushed down on Terence Gordon's aching shoulders.

"Sit!"

He was still blindfolded. How many hours had passed? He slumped in the cold, dark recess.

They'd come for him and manhandled him up some stairs. He imagined about eight. He obeyed every command while trying to work out who was holding him prisoner.

The shackles that bound his wrists were removed. He could only see darkness. The balaclava was itchy as hell and was the most infuriating thing he'd ever experienced. Movement in the confined space had been virtually impossible. He tried stretching his legs. Cramps set in immediately. Gasping with the pain as his muscles tightened through lack of use. It's no use moaning, he thought wildly. These bastards know who you are and they don't like you.

His tied ankles were suddenly freed. He let out an audible sigh of relief as the constricted veins expanded and the blood began to flow again.

"Make the most of it wanker," said a voice. A different one from before.

Suddenly and in one swift movement, the balaclava was snatched from his head and the blindfold was released. Light assailed his startled eyes. He instinctively ducked his head down on to his chest and squinted furiously. The harshness of it all shocked him.

"Happy?"
He raised his head slowly while trying to take in as much information as possible.
"Y..Yes..." he replied.
As his eyes became accustomed to the light, he could make out three figures standing in front of him. They presented a black mass. Each one wore black overalls and balaclavas. He stared blankly at his captors. They were big men and tough with it. He could see their eyes through the slits but nothing else. They also wore gloves. Loads of info there...
"Who...who are you?" he whispered and his fear was palpable. His attempts to sound in control were useless.
"Holiday reps!" sniggered one. His voice was indistinguishable. It could have been any one of the group. They just stood over him menacingly. Brooding and silent.

He swallowed. There was no saliva. This was scary.

There was a table behind the threesome. It was a plain wooden table.
One of the trio turned and picked something up. He took a couple of steps forward and held the object inches from his terror-stricken face. He felt beads of sweat form on his temples. He licked his lips as the figure spoke abruptly and shoved a grainy, old photograph into his view.
"Claire Weekes. Name ring a bell?"

He nodded. He recognised her immediately. The pale blue eyes, the turned up nose, flowery skirt...
"We know what you did to her fat boy."
He needed a shit...
"I...I..."
"Don't make excuses! We know what you are! Sick."

He felt his genitals contract. The urges were always there. He pictured Claire's face, smiling nervously, as he had taken her panties down.

The smack caught him on the side of the head. Thwack! The pain was incredible.
He toppled sideways on to the cold wooden floor. Head swimming and tears in his eyes, as he attempted to climb back on to the chair.
"Don't move!" snapped one of the figures.
He froze on the spot because he didn't want to risk another blow.
"Stay there! That's where you belong - in the gutter!"
As he curled up into a ball, he began to retch violently. He hadn't eaten for more than a day. He liked his food. God, how he needed a kebab...
"Trying for the sympathy vote are we?"
"Too late I'm afraid," gestured another.
The balaclava was replaced over his head with a jerk.
"No, not again!" he pleaded and his voice rose in a plaintive whine.
"Is that what little Claire said before you fucked her again? Time for bed..."

****

Chapter Twenty Five

Phil Queen sat in a holding cell; staring almost nonchalantly at the opposite wall. A young constable stood motionless by the exit door. Phil drew in a long breath. Ten minutes earlier he'd killed a man yet, as he sat, he was filled with an incredible urge to laugh out loud. He resisted the impulse. He didn't want the Constable Turner thinking he had a raving loony on his hands.

He looked down at his shirt. Flecks of drying blood had clotted on the chest area. Constable Turner followed Phil's gaze and coughed quietly. Phil looked him squarely in the eye and winked slowly.
Then the door opened and Clive Badger entered. His normally pristine appearance was gone. The top button of his shirt was undone and his tie knot was tugged down. He looked as if he'd been dancing for two lively hours at the Policemen's Ball. Phil again resisted the urge to smile. He was resisting a lot of urges, he thought.

"Thank you Constable Turner. Please leave us," Badger spoke impatiently and he left the cell in a hurry.

Badger circled the small table and chair where Phil sat waiting.

An uncomfortable silence fell.

Phil breathed slowly. He felt elated; the adrenalin was still pumping when Badger broke the silence.

"This is very serious Phil."

"I know. I ain't sorry though," replied Phil.

The silence returned.

Badger stood opposite and he didn't look at Phil as he spoke. He was looking at an invisible spot on the wall behind Phil.

"You have put this station in an unfortunate position," Badger remarked. "Me too," he added after a pause.

"Tough!" responded Phil contemptuously.

Badger looked directly at his ex-colleague at last.

"Covering up your how shall I put it, altercation, will be no problem," said Badger. Phil frowned slightly. (*Covering up?*)

"However, I'm sure the Brothers will view your actions as admirable," continued Badger.

Badger smiled while Phil shifted uncomfortably in his seat.

"Come again?" queried Phil.

Badger walked closer to the table, placed his hands flat on the surface and he leaned down inches away from Phil's face.

"I shall need to explain how Steven Kennedy died whilst being held in custody. A few well-chosen white lies should do the trick. The body is already in the mortuary Phil. You have no need to worry."

Phil swallowed. His mind swam as Badger's words sank in.

"You... you know... about the Brothers?!"

Badger nodded and his smile was conspiratorial.

"I am one. Just like yourself... Sergeant Phipps too."
Phil's eyes closed. Beads of sweat began to form on his brow. This was a real nightmare!
Badger's gentle voice whispered, "Phil... listen to me. I recruited. No - recommended you to the Brothers."
Phil shook his head slowly. His hands bunched into fists. "NO!"
"Yes, 'fraid so my friend."
"But?"
"You don't honestly think that knocking over a dustbin is a disciplinary offence do you? You were a top-grade sergeant Phil. One of the best in my humble opinion. When I joined the Brothers, I was under orders to recruit as many top notch personnel as possible. I earned twenty grand commission when you resigned and joined the brotherhood."
"Now hang on!" spat Phil.
"Let me finish Phil please."

Phil nodded urgently. Badger sat on the edge of the table. He drew his tie from around his collar, unbuttoned his shirt further and winced at his own discomfort.
"Now - I know you think Ken and Mo were responsible for recruiting your excellent talents don't you?"
"They did, didn't they?" asked Phil.
"No, I did. I recommended they should approach you," mumbled Badger.
I knew you were vulnerable and angry after your resignation. You were an easy target. The fifteen grand must have seemed like manna from heaven after having your pension terminated."
Phil nodded, yet he was still in disbelief at these revelations.

"So 'Mr Know It All', how did you figure I would resign?"

"Pride. Simple as that," commented Badger. "I knew your psyche. I also knew you disliked me. I knew you would kick against the system and I was right," Badger concluded in calm tones of deep satisfaction.

Phil simply silently stared at Badger.

"Oh, now - come on Phil! What do you take me for?" chided Badger. "OK - I get the best of both worlds I admit it. My police status and sizeable chunks of cash from the Brotherhood. Would you argue? Now - be fair, Phil..."

Phil stood up suddenly.

"'Be fair' you say!?" Phil shouted.

Badger flinched noticeably.

"You single-handedly, deviously strip me of my job for a poxy little mistake. You make me a laughing stock and for what? To get me into this organisation, to get your commission as you call it. You sit in your little ivory tower playing God! Fuck you Badger! My future's up the spout thanks to you! I don't give a toss about your station's reputation. I enjoyed killing that bastard in there! He didn't deserve to sleep another night on this earth. Do you hear?"

Badger stood up.

"Phil. Please sit down. I can understand your anger."

"Bollocks! You only understand two things! Power and money so fuck you!"

Phil leaned against the cell wall and stared at the floor. His head spun. He began to cry and loud sobs echoed around the small room. He fell to his knees as all of his energy drained from him. He felt a hand on his shoulder. As he looked up through a blur, he saw Badger standing over him.

"It's going to be OK Phil. Trust me..."

Phil closed his eyes and gave in to the racking sobs.

****

Chapter Twenty Six

"Terence Gordon - Paedophile! Here's your breakfast!" The light hit him and he squealed. The plate rattled as it was slammed down in front of him. Another clunk and he saw a torch next to the plate. Then the door closed again and it shut out the light.

He grappled for the torch. His fingers felt the rubber handle and he found the switch button. He clicked the light on.

His eyes hurt as he became accustomed to the sharp light. It was a shock to his system after the all-enclosing darkness of the last few long hours. He saw his surroundings for the first time. A tiny cellar about six feet by six.

He turned his attention to the food - the first he had been offered. A spider scurried by over his cold hand. He flinched away. The torch beam revealed a sausage and a baked potato. He grabbed them both and thrust some of the tepid food into his mouth. Christ! He needed a drink. The sausage went down in one, the cold potato clung to his teeth but his hunger cancelled out the unpalatable taste. Make the most of it. Take your time, he thought.

He shone the torch up and around the cramped prison. Who were these people? Extremists? Political Lobbyists? Why him?

They knew his past and that was obvious. He felt a shiver of apprehension.

Nobody liked what he did. His life wasn't normal. He had never had sex with a woman, just kids and the odd homo. What did they want? Money? When would they let him go? He had been locked up before but never beaten. At least then he had regular meals. He was missing his kebabs and curries. He needed to masturbate too.

They must have found the video collection... Oh no! Not the one with little Kelly...

The door crashed open again. Light flooded in.

"Finished?!"

"Yes thanks."

A kick to his kidneys made him scream in fright and pain. He fell down and vomited the food he'd so recently consumed all over the filthy floor.

"Tut tut! What a waste," sneered his visitor.

Gordon writhed as his hand fell into his own vomit; making him retch again.

"You'd better clean this up before I get back you animal! Got it?"

The door closed with a thud.

The smell of sick assailed him and he felt his gorge rise again. Where was the torch? He frantically felt all around. It had gone!

His screams went unanswered. He had lost all sense of time. He didn't even know what day it was.

It was June 5th.

****

"He's looking like shit," said Rattigan.

"Good," answered Guy Winters. They sat in the kitchen. The kettle whistled shrilly.

"Tea's up!" said Clive Rattigan, ex-mercenary. He'd fought in Zaire and Kuwait. The money was good and death was just lurking in the shadows. As an ex-Para, he knew only two things: good beer and action. Lots of it! A hardened criminal from Glasgow prior to signing into the red berets, he had the hard, lean, good looks of your average psychopath. Romance wasn't high on his list of priorities.

"Sugar?" he asked, in gruff Glaswegian.

"Two and a touch of milk darling," minced Winters affably.

Guy Winters, a bare-knuckle fighter from Hackney in London sat trying to negotiate The Sun's crossword.

"Two across - nine letters and ends in ED. A slang term."

"Knackered!" laughed Rattigan. His smile resembled a snarl.

"Spot on! Fuck me - you can finish it!" Winters flung the newspaper across the table.

They'd been guarding Gordon for forty eight hours. A bit like guard duty but without the bullshit, thought Rattigan.

They'd joined the 'Brothers' together. Since their meeting, during a spell with Securicor where their boredom thresholds were severely tested, they'd shared a fragmented life. It was a wage and that's all you could say.

Winters could watch Arsenal regularly and Rattigan found a prostitute to shag twice a week.

A radio played in the background.

"Remember this one? 'Mad World' - Tears for Fears - Classic!" commented Winters.

"Mad world. They got it right even then but I preferred Madness meself, 'One Step Beyond'," Rattigan replied as he sipped the hot, strong tea.
The pair smiled at the memory.

They stared out of the windows at the bright sunlit street.
"Nice day again. We're wasting it in here. Should be out in the park leching the women."
"Yeah - all those skimpy tops and tight shorts! And the women too!"
They both laughed at the implication. It broke the monotony.
"Bastard puked on me shoe," snarled Rattigan.
"Is he ill then, poor wretch?" asked Winters in mock sympathy.
"Nah, I gave him a dig after breakfast. Didn't mean to. It just happened yer know."
He winked slyly at Winters.
"Yeah - I know."
The radio droned on.
"Good one this – Genesis - 'I Can't Dance' Mega!"
"I bet Gordon won't dance much after 'The March'!"
Their cackling laughter rang around the small kitchen.
Terence Gordon was oblivious to it all.

****

Posters and placards had been prepared in readiness for almost two months prior to 'The March' on London. They left nothing to the imagination.
'NO MORE INNOCENTS KILLED - CLEANSE THE COUNTRY!'
'JUSTICE FOR THE PEOPLE!'

'NO SUSPENDED SENTENCE - SUSPEND THE KILLERS!'
'BROTHERS UNITE! DEATH TO THE DEATH DEALERS!'

The posters starting appearing all over London on June 1st. In the dead of night, two hundred volunteers pasted up five thousand notices across a forty square mile area.
'JUNE 6th - DAY OF RECKONING!'

People at first walked past. Then, as newspapers and media broadcasting picked up the first threads of information, recognition began to dawn. The word spread.
June 6th had some significance. A 'big thing' was in the offing but what?
'JUNE 6 - BE THERE!' (*Where?*).
'THE MARCH - JUNE 6th - DO IT!' (*How?*).

Only the chosen few of the 'Brothers of Justice' knew. Sky News rolled on and on pontificating endlessly about what may happen. Jeremy Paxman on 'Newsnight' was getting his knickers in a twist as per usual.
There were now two thousand members. By June 7th there would be millions. Out with the do-gooders and in with the new regime. The people had had enough. On the sixth of June, the world would know in no uncertain terms. The world was about to change forever...

****

Chapter Twenty Seven

Ken received the phone call from Clive Badger approximately twenty minutes after his confrontation with Phil Queen. Badger's tone told Ken that things were looking grim in relation to Phil's ability to continue as a Brother.

"So - he's cracking up is he?" said Ken sternly.

"It looks that way. He wasn't exactly chuffed when I filled him in on my association with the firm," confirmed Badger.

"Is he a totally lost cause do you think or could he be rehabilitated?"

"I'm not certain. In fact, I feel a bit sorry for him. The poor bastard's been through a lot recently. Many blokes would have thrown in the towel long ago. By rights, he could have been in Rampton by now."

Ken stifled an urge to laugh at the weak joke.

A brief silence was broken by Badger, "He thought Kennedy killed Chloe. You and Mo did a very professional job there Ken."

"Cheers, but don't think we enjoyed it Clive. Chloe was a beautiful woman and the envy of many. However, the Brothers' cause must be paramount in all our minds now," muttered Ken.

"I know it must have been difficult for you both. I certainly thought she was an ideal convert to the cause," replied Badger.

"Yes, but then she found you out and you're not exactly everyone's flavour-of-the-month now are you?" remarked Ken.
"No - I realise that. Perhaps it's as well I've got a hard exterior."
Another pause ensued.
"Where's Phil now?" Ken asked.
"Still in custody. We've given him some sedatives and he's out like a light."
"Then what?"
"I'm going to get him into your local hospice for rest and recuperation tomorrow."
"Good thinking Clive. Well done."
"You should make sure there is a watch on him too," cautioned Badger.
"Yeah, he may be a wild card where 'The March' is concerned," implied Ken.
"Have you contacted Heads of Sheds yet?"
"No, but I shall."
"How's our friend Gordon the paedo?"
Badger laughed.
"He's in a shit state according to his guards."
Ken laughed in unison.
"I bet he hasn't got a flaming clue where he is."
"He hasn't."
"Are they feeding him?"
"Just scraps - fit for the dogs."
"He won't be any expense on the Sainsbury's bill after Saturday. Have we found a suitable executioner yet?"
Badger's voice rose slightly. He sometimes couldn't believe what he had got himself into here.
"Oh, yes! A parent of a victim. He's travelling down from Carlisle to kick the box away."

"Super job! The TV crews won't have a clue what's hit them. Sky will come in its pants!"
"They'll all be warned off when things get interesting. Interrupting the Test Match should get maximum impact eh?"
"Great! The Lords Taverners will have a seizure!"
"I'll see to it personally," Badger assured his partner.
Ken smiled.
"It'll make the Embassy Siege look like Tom and Jerry. If the clones at Westminster don't take notice of this lot then I think we may as well pack it in."
"They'll notice Ken. I guarantee it. They'll notice like they've never noticed before! Power to the victims!"
Then, the phone clicked off.

****

As soon as Badger left the cell, Phil sat upright on his bare wooden stool. He stared at the four sedatives on the table. A glass of water stood next to the white pills.
"Trust me!" he whispered and he smiled to himself.

His ability to feign hurt had been one of his talents since schooldays. It was a sure-fire winner with the prettier teachers. The bullies saw him as an easy target but it was all an act. The Army taught him how to fight pain, grit the teeth and stick out the chest.

Interrogation training was a favourite. They never broke him. His act today had been spot on. He considered the last few hours and something was wrong.
Badger was a Brother. That had come as a shock no question but something didn't fit.
Chloe's murder. It was perfect. Too perfect.

He'd had to kill Kennedy. He had started all of this with the attack on Chloe's daughter.

Phil walked over to the table. Picking up the four tiny pills, he crossed to the far corner of the cell. He removed his left shoe and placed the pills on the floor. Using the heel of the shoe as a pestle, he ground the sedatives easily into a fine dust, resembling talcum powder. He took a deep breath and blew. The powder dispersed in a light cloud; invisible against the pale linoleum tiles. He stood up, took the glass beaker from the table and drank the contents in one gulp. He replaced his shoe and lay down on the hard wooden bench. Simple.

"Trust me," he whispered and smiled slightly.

His eyes closed as he crossed his legs at the ankles. He didn't need the pills to drowse. They'd be back in a while to check on his condition.

He planned his next move and thought about Chloe.

****

"Phil! Wake up!"

He opened one eye. It was Sergeant Phipps.

"Terry, it's been so long." Phil smiled up at him.

Sergeant Phipps was unsmiling. (*That's not like Terry thought Phil.*)

"Phil - wake up. They're taking you away. Did you take your pills?"

"Pills?" responded Phil quizzically. (*You'll get an Oscar!)*

"Oh, yeah -those. Knocked me out they did. What were they for?"

"Dunno. Sedatives I suppose." answered Phipps disinterestedly.

"Oh - right. I see. Christ, my head!"

Phipps grasped Phil's shoulders. "You all right mate?"
"Never felt better Tez," Phil replied drowsily.
"Your shirt's a disaster," commented Phipps.
"Cost me thirty five quid from Burton's," slurred Phil. His acting was taking on a new lease of life.
"Badger's comin' back in a bit. Tidy yourself up!"
"Fuck off Terry. I'm a murdering bastard and 'they're coming to take me away - ha ha"'
Terry Phipps frowned. "You've flipped mate," he whispered.
"What's the time Tez?"
"Ten to four."
Phil frowned. "How long have I been out for the count?"
"'bout half an hour. The tablets won't have taken their full effect yet."
"Oh dear." Phil sat and swayed on the edge of the bunk. Phipps knelt down in front of him and looked up into Phil's face.
"Phil, listen to me! They're goin' to pack you off to some fuckin' hospital or somewhere. I heard Badger chatting to some bloke on the phone."
"The men in white coats eh? And about time too." Phil's pretend slur was becoming more pronounced.
"I heard him say they're going to put a guard on you."

Phil's mind snapped into alert mode at these words. He continued his simulated slide into oblivion. The tablets had to be seen to be working.
"What? A guard of honour - for me?" His head lolled. His eyes rolled glassily.
Then, he heard footsteps.
"Badger!" said Phipps hoarsely.
Phil was ready. The door opened with a thud.

"How is he Sergeant Phipps?" queried Badger as he looked down at the floppy figure on the bench.
"He's high on the sedatives I think sir. He's been singing his head off."
"Good. Let's get him to the ambulance then son."
"Fine, I'll need a hand though as he's like Banana Man."

Badger rolled up his sleeves and nodded.
"Come on Queenie-boy. Time to go."
They lifted Phil roughly. His arms wrapped limply across their shoulders.
"Be gentle wi' me," he moaned with sagging knees.
Badger smiled grimly as they dragged their cumbersome patient down the corridor to the rear entrance of the police station.
Phil's eyes darted to left and right but this was unseen by his supporters.
They were putting him out of harm's way. Why? What were they hiding?

An unmarked ambulance waited near the exit doors. The driver leapt down from the cab and opened the rear doors of the vehicle.
Sergeant Phipps' beard rubbed against Phil's face as they bundled him inside. He smelled of mint. Been eating Polos? Covers up the whisky chasers thought Phil.

The radio played in the driver's compartment. Louis Armstrong's 'Wonderful World.'
Bollocks thought Phil as the doors slammed shut behind him.
He strained to hear what Badger was saying to the driver.
"Tell them to keep him well sedated and well-guarded.

Let him think he's in a bad way and don't let him out through next week. Tie him up if need be. Got it?"

Phil closed his eyes and grimaced to himself. He could smell antiseptics.
"I'm a prisoner now." he thought and his mind raced. Where were his mates, Ken and Mo? He looked down at his clothes. Blood was drying on his shirt. His trousers were torn and sweat ran down his back profusely.
Keep calm he told himself. Alert. Calm. 'Play the game. They think you're cracking up.' He found he was talking to himself...
Pull yourself together! Talking to yourself is the first sign of madness.

The ambulance lurched as it left the station. He heard the driver whistling.
Phil lay back on the stretcher bed. All kinds of pictures came into his head. *(You should've taken those pills. Put you out of your misery once and for all).*
He saw Chloe. She was sat on the toilet seat again but this time she was smiling her most beautiful smile. 'Come in darling, I'm nearly finished.'
Phil's eyes shot open. *(Stop it! You're hallucinating!)*
He saw Steve Kennedy on the stairs of the flat. He dropped the cups of coffee but there was no coffee in the cups! 'Do you want milk or blood?' Kennedy sneered.
Phil squeezed his eyes shut again. He saw the pain in the eyes of each of Kennedy's victims...
The little girl buried alive.
The waitress. Eyes wide and legs akimbo.
Then, he saw Kennedy in his death throes, clutching the gaping wound in his neck. His lips were moving and his

words were croaking out in a hoarse whisper – 'I didn't kill Chl…'

What?!

'I didn't kill C…'

Phil sat up suddenly and stared at the darkened glass of the windows.

"You didn't kill… CHLOE!" he screamed.

Then he fainted again. This time for real.

****

A bleary vision floated in front of his eyes. Phil struggled to focus. He was in a bed. His sight cleared and he saw it was Mo.

"Hi Phil," Mo's Geordie accent was no comfort.

Over Mo's shoulder, Phil could see Ken and a young woman. She was the Irish nurse from his previous hospital visit.

"Don't I know you?" he slurred, without realising he wasn't acting this time.

She smiled. "Yes. You said I'd look good in heels remember? I'm Ken's wife."

Phil stared at the ceiling. "Ah Siobhan but…"

Ken interrupted abruptly.

"I know this will seem strange Phil but it's all for a purpose."

Phil tried to sit up. He was tied to the bed!

"What's all this? Colditz?" he yelled.

"Ssssh…" the Irish nurse remonstrated with him.

"You've had a breakdown. You need rest," Mo smiled.

"I know this seems harsh Phil but the sedatives make people do all sorts of funny things."

"Fuckin' strap me in for God's sake? Don't treat me like an idiot! Get me out of this shit!" shouted Phil with his eyes were bulging as he fought against the restraints.
"You need rest and you've got to keep a low profile while the Brothers sweep Kennedy's murder under the carpet."
Phil struggled. "I'd get better treatment in Strangeways you bastards! I thought we were mates?"
"You'll get chicken for tea you ungrateful sod," replied Mo with a smile.
"We're just under orders Phil," added Ken.
"Who from? I thought you two were the big fish!"
"There are bigger fish," murmured Ken but his eyes did not meet Phil's.

Phil was suddenly assailed by a sense of dread. A prisoner of the people he was supposed to be helping? Something was amiss but he was damned if he could put a finger on it.
Then, he thought of Kennedy's dying words. 'I didn't kill Chloe.'

He stared at Mo and Ken.
"What have I done wrong? All I did was snuff out a low life. That's what our organisation's all about isn't it?" delved Phil.
Ken nodded sagely. "Quite right Phil, but right now you're drugged up and about as stable as a horse in an apple cart."
"You're a liability for now so we just need to keep you under wraps until 'The March' is over," Mo pointed out.
Phil shrugged. "At least give me some dignity. I feel like an animal waiting for the experiment to begin!"

Mo looked at Ken. Phil saw a flicker of sympathy.
Ken nodded. "Untie him and give him some more sedatives."
"Mmmmm - yes please," Phil mocked them sarcastically.
Mo grinned. "You know we don't want this mate," he whispered as he loosened the straps holding Phil to the bed.
"Silence of the Lambs Two," answered Phil. His joke caused Mo to laugh out loud. Ken looked on soberly.
"Get us a drink Siobhan," he ordered his wife.
'Nurse Paddy' left the room. Phil's eyes followed her plump buttocks rolling under the tight uniform.
"Make mine a lager!" he grinned and he was visibly relaxing.

****

Chapter Twenty Eight

"God! I'm bored," said Gary Winters.
Clive Rattigan sat opposite, hands clasped behind his head and his feet hung on the kitchen table. He chewed gum.
"So am I," he replied.
It was eight o'clock and dusk was falling.
"There's only so much you can do in our position isn't there?" he murmured while staring at the open window dully. "We used to watch vids in the army. Always some sprog with a porno movie or the latest blockbuster," he continued.
Walters nodded "I suppose it helped the time pass."
Rattigan smiled sagely. "The number of lads I've seen going out on patrol with hard-ons was incredible!" He laughed as he reflected on the past.

Winters stood up and stretched. "It must be a bit weird watching a porn vid with ten strapping squaddies," he frowned. "If you had a girl on either side - I could handle that," he added enthusiastically.
Rattigan grinned. "Yeah, steam used to come out of the player after about an hour or so. Always a permanently engaged toilet as well."

The two guards laughed heartily.
"Pity we ain't allowed a telly then, innit?" grumbled Winters.

"Tyson's fightin' tomorrow on satellite," commented Rattigan.
"Bastard!"
"I 'spec' they think it'd take our minds of the fat bastard down below."
Rattigan nodded, "Oh yeah. What would you rather do gents? Be paid twenty grand for watching TV or kicking hell out of a scumbag?".
"No contest!"
"Only two days and we can go on holiday."
"Yeah - what you doin'?"
"Seychelles. Or maybe Jamaica for coupla weeks."

Winters sat down.
"I'm married with two little 'uns."
"Disneyland easy!" suggested Rattigan.
"I didn't say happily married," replied Winters.
"Oh – sorry."
"'s okay. Been eight years. She's there but no love lost. We stick it for the kids really."
Rattigan nodded slowly. "I see, so come with me to Jamaica then!" He grinned suddenly.
"I'd love to but I'd miss the kids. Love 'em too much."

A bump caught their attention.
Rattigan picked up a large baseball bat and opened the kitchen door.
Another muffled thump emanated from the cellar.
"It's him but fuck 'im. He can't go anywhere," muttered Winters disinterestedly.
Rattigan disappeared in the direction of the noises. He kicked the cellar door twice.
"Shut it wanker!"

A slithering sound came from behind the pale wooden door. The baseball bat fell from Rattigan's grasp. His keys jangled in his hand as he inserted the largest one into the lock. He turned the key and tugged the door violently.

He wasn't prepared for the sight which greeted him.
"Shit!"
Gordon had managed to take off his sweat-sodden shirt and tie it in the darkness around the handle of the door. He had then put it around his neck and knotted it. His face was turning puce as Rattigan opened the door.
"Terry, come quick! Bring a knife!" Rattigan yelled.

He lifted the huge bulk of Gordon off the stairs which led down into the cellar as best he could. The huge stomach defied his grasp and the strangling paedophile gurgled.
"You ain't gonna get out of it this easy you bastard," grunted Rattigan as he struggled to release the garrotting shirt.
Winters was at his side with his eyes wide in astonishment.
"Cut the shirt!"
"Fuckin' 'ell!" gasped Winters sawing at the sodden fabric. It parted, fell away from the door handle and released the tension. Gordon and Rattigan toppled sideways together.
Winters tugged at the shirt around Gordon's neck and said, "Come on! Come on!"
Suddenly Rattigan laughed hysterically.
"I can't believe it! We're trying to save the life of a fuckin' nonce!"

Gordon choked and heaved as air flooded his throat. His breathing resumed spasmodically.

"Why?" he gasped, "Why did you save me?" his eyes rolling in his head.

Winters knelt beside him and whispered close to his ear, "Wait and see matey. Just you wait and see."

****

Chapter Twenty Nine

"Right! I'm off," said Ken kissing his wife on the forehead tenderly.

"I should only be a couple of hours. Just tying up the final itinery for the big day."

Mo stood on the doorstep and sipped beer from a can. He watched his brother depart. Ken limped uneasily to the stationary BMW on the curve of the gravelled driveway.

"See you mate," he called and lifted the can in salute.

"Keep your eyes on Phil. He mustn't escape," Ken reminded them as he lowered himself carefully into the driving seat.

Siobhan waved and smiled. Mo stood behind her. As Ken slammed the car door in the distance, Mo leaned forwards slightly and whispered in her ear.

"Have you got your stockings on nurse?"

She nodded as she continued to wave. "Of course," she muttered out of the side of her mouth; unseen by Ken as he switched on the engine.

"Can't wait!" Mo nudged his crotch against her back.

Siobhan didn't respond and continued to wave until the car meandered out of sight into the adjoining country lane. Then it was gone.

She turned to Mo. He crunched the beer can and left it on the door ledge. His taut arms encircled his brother's wife's waist as their lips met in a long lingering kiss.

"Naughty naughty," whispered Siobhan, the Irish lilt in her voice was always an aphrodisiac to Mo's animal instincts.

"Upstairs - NOW!" he urged her.

They almost ran hand-in-hand. As she did so, she tugged a hair grip and released her long brunette locks. Mo heaved off his T-shirt as they entered the bedroom.

"SSssshhh.. We don't want Phil hearing up!" hissed Siobhan.

"Don't worry, he'll think I'm Ken. How's he to know otherwise?" gasped Mo with his breathing laboured. "Anyway, he's a little tied up at the moment."

Siobhan sat on the edge of the huge king-size bed. She lowered her blue skirt slowly and lifted her long legs in their sheer stockings above her head. Mo's jeans came off in one easy movement.

For over three months and at every opportunity, Mo had been servicing Siobhan's desires, which had been badly neglected since Ken's injury. It meant Ken's athleticism between the sheets had been curtailed. The pains in his lower back had reduced his sex drive considerably.

Mo had seized the initiative one night after a house party. Ken had retired to bed early, well primed for sleep by alcohol and his pain killers, leaving his wife and brother to clear up the mess from the revelry. They had ended up making love on the cold kitchen floor. Since that night, or whenever Ken was otherwise occupied or out of the house, they'd taken every chance which presented itself.

"Hurry up! I want it in me - now!" cried Siobhan hoarsely. She lay back on the soft pink duvet with her legs apart. Only her black stockings remained. She sensuously toyed with her huge breasts whilst her hips writhed.

Mo was having trouble with his socks.

Siobhan giggled. "What a stud!"

Mo climbed astride her as his erection bobbed up and down.

"Wait!" Siobhan.

"Eh?" Mo gasped as his face was turning crimson.

She rolled over on her stomach and raised her buttocks. Her voice came, muffled from the pillows, " 'n mmmm.m...ere."

"No hassle madam," Mo muttered as he moved forward. Siobhan let out a low moan as he inserted his manhood into her moist haven. She pushed backwards as his searching hands cupped her swinging breasts.

"Christ, you're hot today!" he panted.

The bed creaked as they thrashed wildly together.

It did not take long for Mo to climax. It never did. "I'm comin'!" he croaked hoarsely.

Siobhan heaved her body away from him. "Not inside me!"

Mo lay over her buttocks, his teeth gritting in the anticipation of his release and the warm milky fluid spurted along her back and past her bowed head on to the satin-padded headboard of the bed. They both sank like deflated balloons into the dishevelled bedclothes. Siobhan resembled a wild harpy and her hair was in tangled knots. Mascara streaked her face and the pillows.

"Fuck me Si, that was the best!" Mo's voice was fragmented as his heart beat resumed a normal tempo.

She turned to face him; a beatific satisfaction was evident in her dark eyes.

"I came too," she gloated as he leaned over and licked her nipples.

They kissed deeply and their tongues entwined.

"I'm knackered."

"I'm not. 'Please, sir, I want some more.'" Si giggled.

"Not today. Maybe Phil could help out?" Mo suggested slyly as he lay back on the duvet.

"Now there's a thought! Mmm.... he's a real looker isn't he?" She toyed with the hairs on Mo's chest as she glanced at his face.

"I don't think that would be a very wise move," cautioned Mo.

"He wouldn't have any cause for complaint during his captivity anyway," joked Siobhan. Her expression became pensive. "Ken hasn't a clue poor sod. I've had to bring him off anyway these last two months. He can't manage in any position now. He's in so much pain and nothing seems to help and it's not much fun for me too," Siobhan concluded.

Mo frowned.

"I hate doing this to my bro but I see it as a favour to you Si. At least it's in the family as they say," muttered Mo.

"I'm not complaining big boy," commented Siobhan. She stretched like a lazy cat. "Any more for any more?" she moaned in his ear.

Mo grinned.

"Wouldn't say no to a cuppa tea," he answered flatly.

****

Phil was bored.

He sat in his makeshift prison and stared at his reflection in a mirror on the bedside table. He'd slept without the aid of tranquillisers. Ten hours! His solitude during the day had given him time to think and logically evaluate his current position.

Ken and Mo had fed him twice that day. The treatment he was having was relaxed but serious. Ken's wife, Siobhan, was absent though. Probably at work.

He decided he wasn't in any immediate danger. Not physical danger at any rate. He was just being kept under wraps and out of harm's way.

'The March' was just days away. He wanted to be part of it a couple of weeks ago but now all he wanted was to escape from the nightmare world in which he had become embroiled.

The Brothers would cover up Kennedy's messy death. He knew that at least. The self-satisfaction at his impulsive actions in the police cell the day before had now given way to doubts.

He had lain in his 'bed-cum-prison' for most of the day; re-running the events of the past few weeks like a video through his brain. The conclusions he'd reached had shocked even himself.

Steven Kennedy had not killed Chloe. He was sure of that. He had a good idea who were the real killers now. He had carefully pieced together the happenings of the day of Chloe's death.

It had to be Ken and Mo.

Two things had led him to this conclusion. The first was the fact that Chloe had not been sexually assaulted. The note had read 'She enjoyed it' but the absence of any semen traces indicated there had been no sexual behaviour during the fatal attack. Chloe had been seated on the lavatory when he had found her. Someone had positioned her there.

It was too perfect.

Why would Kennedy have bothered with the note on the mantelpiece? Surely any attacker would have left the house immediately.

Another aspect occurred to Phil. The messages on the mirrors were unusual too. The punctuation was spot on. Kennedy's notes were always mis-spelt, almost illiterate, hurried scrawls in poor English. His was a graffiti-style. 'She's in the bathroom' the note had read.

Kennedy would never have used apostrophes. Never!

Phil's mind raced as he'd mentally re-run the moments he'd spent in the cottage up to when he found Chloe's body. There were no signs of a forced entry. No broken glass, no broken door or window frames. Nothing!

Chloe would never have let in anyone she didn't trust. She always latched the door chain when she was alone in the house.

It was too perfect by half! It had to be Ken and Mo. There had been three coffee mugs in the kitchen. Chloe, Ken and Mo. It was so obvious he almost laughed. All three of them had gone back to the cottage after the meeting. They said they would look out for Chloe. She had impressed them. So, why kill her? What possible motive was there? She was a beautiful, soft, caring woman. Something must have happened after the meeting.

Phil sat on the edge of the bed by the locker. His hands drooped between his knees and his shoulders sagged. His face had aged considerably in recent weeks. Dark circles were present under his eyes and he'd become unshaven with heavy jowls.

"You look like a bloody refugee," he whispered to his reflection in the magnifying mirror next to the lamp.

He glanced at his watch. At about eight o'clock he had heard a car pull away from the house. He couldn't see the car but he heard the low moan of the powerful BMW.
Someone had left. Perhaps all of them. There was no sound.
Siobhan, Ken and Mo. Which one had taken the car? Had he gone alone?

Perhaps he was alone in the house? A chance to make his move? He lay down on the duvet and gazed at the ceiling.
Then he heard a thump, some more bumps and laughter. A woman's laughter.
He heard running feet. They came up the stairs and a door banged shut. (*Ken couldn't run!*).
His ears strained for further noises. The silence rang in his ears.
He closed his eyes and concentrated. He was sure he heard more dull bumps and intermittent voices. He couldn't be certain.
(Hallucinations?)

Half an hour passed and he began to drift in the silence. Then, more voices and a door clicked. Laughter followed again.

He got up off the bed and went over to the door, putting his ear against the painted wood panelling.

Silence.

He knelt down and looked through the tiny keyhole. His view of the landing and the bannisters rails was restricted. He blinked in concentration.

Then Mo came into his line of vision. He was carrying a tray. Nothing especially strange about that except that he was wearing only a pair of cotton boxer shorts!

Phil swallowed and blinked again.

Mo disappeared from his view to be replaced almost immediately by another half-clad person. The large buttocks were unmistakable. Siobhan!

She wore the top half of a man's pyjama, pale blue with a tiger leaping up the back. Her hair was flowing down her back and her feet were bare. Then, she was gone too.

Phil sat back on his haunches and grinned to himself.

"Well, the sly sod!" he murmured.

Mo was shagging his brother's wife!

Life was certainly never dull around this lot.

****

"Hi," Phil greeted Siobhan as she came into his room carrying a tray.

"Here's some tea Phil. Do you want sugar?"

"Two please."

Siobhan had a pair of pull-ups covering the anatomy he'd so recently witnessed through the keyhole. Phil eyed her up and down slowly as she poured.

"You look better with your hair down," he said quietly.

Siobhan flushed as she dropped the sugar lumps into the cup.

"Oh... er,.. yes... thank you Phil."

She sounded flustered and began to stir the tea. "I only put it up for work," she commented.

"As the actress said to the bishop," grinned Phil. (*He could use his new-found knowledge to some advantage here.)*

"Phil, you are a tease!"

(So are you kid, so are you!)

"Where are the boys?" he continued with his tone feigning a disinterest.

"Oh, er, Ken's out at a meeting and Mo's fixing the lawn-mower."

(A likely story. Changing the bedclothes more like!)

Phil leaned forward slowly.

"You look great tonight," he murmured tentatively while stroking her forearm.

"Phil! Please stop!" she scolded and withdrew her arm away. "Drink your tea.

Come on now," she pleaded as he held her wrist while turning to look at the open door.

"What's the matter? I'm just complimenting you, that's all. I haven't seen you in your 'civvies' 'til now," said Phil.

Siobhan stood up and made to leave.

"Don't you get many?" asked Phil.

"Many what?" She turned to face him.

"Compliments."

"That's none of your business!"

"Oh - come on now. Ken's limp must get him down. Bet your sex life is no great shakes either."

Siobhan's face blazed scarlet and her eyes flashed angrily.

"You on top all the time now is it?" Phil pursued her.
"Cheeky bastard!"
The door slammed shut.
Phil sipped his tea. He smiled to himself smugly.
"One-nil," he whispered.

****

Oblivious to the fun and games back at his house, Ken had been to visit Badger and his wife. The large house sat away from any outside intrusions. The driveway must have been twice as long as Ken's and it was shrouded by trees and shrubbery.
He had pulled up next to Badger's Land Rover. The hall light was on as darkness was falling. It was nine o'clock.

As he struggled out of his car, the front door opened and he saw Hilary silhouetted against the light.
He limped up the steps and greeted her with a kiss on either cheek.
"Hi Hilary," he greeted.
She wore sensible brown shoes and a chunky, checked skirt.
"Good evening Kenneth. Do come in. Clive's in the study."
Hilary always observed formal greetings.
"I hope he's not too busy," asked Ken as they entered the large hallway.
"No, not at all. He's been watching some old Chelsea videos so nothing too drastic."
"I'm a Sunderland man myself."
"I would never have guessed. Your accent is hardly noticeable," Hilary replied with gentle sarcasm.

"Ken, come in!" Badger rose from the leather sofa and switched off the TV. "Just catching up on some football nostalgia. I've followed Chelsea since 1970 when they won the Cup."

Ken smiled. "I remember it well. They stuffed dirty Leeds in the replay, didn't they?"

"Spot on! Come to think of it, your team won it around then as well didn't they?"

"Yep. Seventy-three. Beat dirty Leeds one - nil."

"Oh yes, Bob Stokoe and all that."

Hilary smiled at their enthusiasm and waited for a space in the chatter to ask, "Tea or coffee?"

"Oh, coffee please," replied Ken with a grin.

"I'll have a whisky darling," ordered her husband. His wife beamed them a bright smile and she left the room.

Ken sat down and clipped open his briefcase.

"How's Phil?" asked Badger earnestly.

Ken grimaced slightly. "Pissed off but he's fine."

He took out a sheaf of documents.

"He should be bloody grateful Ken." Badger shifted uneasily in his seat. "I've covered up a very messy situation for him so a bit of gratitude wouldn't be amiss."

Ken nodded.

"I know but he's very confused. I wouldn't give too much credence to anything he says or does after all he's been through lately."

Badger frowned.

"The men at the top need to know whether his position in the Brothers has been compromised," Badger insisted.

Ken nodded again. "He's a bloody good bloke from that point of view but if ever he found out exactly what happened with Chloe I wouldn't be answerable..." His voice tailed off.

"Yes, I agree. Things could take a nasty turn if he got wind of that little business, but we're watertight aren't we?"

"Yeah, I'm sure of it. He doesn't suspect a thing. He's so clapped out at the minute; I reckon he would laugh off an invasion by friendly aliens offering him a contract."

"Even if they offered him hard cash?"

"Yeah even then Clive. He's a straight-up bloke. They're thin on the ground at the best of times."

The door reopened and Hilary reappeared with their drinks and some biscuits.

"Perfect darling. Thank you."

"I'll leave you two to your deliberations." she smiled her bright hostess smile and the door closed quietly behind her once more.

"You're a lucky chap Clive."

"She's okay," Badger agreed. "A bit lacking in the looks department but she's got a heart of gold. You're married aren't you Ken?"

"Yeah - Siobhan. Irish lass from Belfast. Very pretty and she's an ex-nurse."

"I must meet her sometime."

"Of course, you're always welcome. She works at a local hospice. Old People with cancer. It's pretty tough."

"And is your brother, Mo, married yet?"

Ken smiled. "Oh no, he's still a wild card with women. He's so independent it's frightening."

"You're close though eh?"

"Oh yes, I love him like a brother." laughed Ken.

"Let's hope he can settle down. The Brothers like their members to be stable and responsible - you know?"

Ken nodded. "Could be a while with Mo. He's quite happy living with us at the minute."

Ken reached for his papers. "Right! The March!" he declared as he got down to the business of their meeting.

Badger leaned forward.

"We're ready. It's all systems go for Saturday," said Ken.

"Yes."

"The TV coverage starts at midday. It'll be pretty sporadic at first.

The odd news flash during the sports programmes then the frequency will pick up as things begin to happen."

"Are we still on for the big finale?"

"Yes, that's scheduled for five o'clock. Terence Gordon will go live at five. Dead at five plus ten. Police and security will not intervene as planned. This will bring it home to the people that the 'Brothers' really do mean business."

Ken looked at Badger intently.

"The Prime Minister is in the country, isn't he?"

"Yes."

He's going to be knocked sideways by this. He's completely oblivious to everything we've planned."

"Christ!" said Ken as he contemplated the full implications of Badger's words.

Badger swallowed a mouthful of his whisky as if sealing their plans.

"With a bit of luck we'll have forced the Government's hand by Saturday evening. Public outrage will be at its highest. Support for our cause will give us total control over future proceedings."

"What do you mean Clive?"

"I mean that the Government will have to realise that its lost control. The Government will have no jurisdiction over justice - the 'Brothers' will!"

Ken swallowed as he felt the hairs on his neck rise.

Badger's eyes glistened.

"The streets will be full of people begging to follow our regime. No more do-gooders. No more pandering to the criminal fraternity. No more parole. Justice will be justice for the victim. The 'Brothers' will ensure a united country."

Ken shifted uneasily in his chair, at the almost messianic tone of Badger's voice. He sounded like Davros, leader of the Daleks!

"This is what you and I have worked for Kenneth!"

Ken realised some response was expected.

"The criminals will be quaking in their boots after Saturday."

"Oh, yes! I can guarantee that most certainly! Once they see the power of our organisation, crime will slowly be eradicated. The support of the masses will override the impotence of the police and the judiciary and the chickens will come home to roost - no mistake!"

"Will you be there on Saturday?" asked Ken.

"Yes, I'll be on the fringes."

"Low-key, I take it?"

"Yes, it wouldn't look good if it was discovered that I was a member of the police and the Brothers. Not at this stage, anyway" Badger assured him.

"No, I see your point completely Clive."

"Most of our members are ordinary people who've been waiting to do some good. They want to root out the bastards in our society who spoil life for the nation. Saturday is THEIR day. A day for the PEOPLE to say 'Enough'!" Ken leaned back in his chair while sipping his coffee contentedly.

****

Chapter Thirty

The car returned at about ten thirty. Phil was propped up on his bed. He was listening...

His ears strained to hear every nuance from the other side of the door. He heard footsteps in the distance. The gravel underfoot gave away the fact that it was Ken. His uneven tread. Once again, the sounds of talking, mingled with laughter, muffled by the locked bedroom door.

"Hi darling," Ken greeted his wife as he placed his briefcase on the reproduction table near the staircase.
"How did it go?" asked Siobhan with her eyebrows raised.
"Fine. Everything is ready. The countdown has begun..."
"Thunderbirds are Go!" shouted Mo.
Mo rested against the architrave of the sitting room door. His eyes were glazed and his gait unsteady as he clasped a wine bottle.
Ken glanced at his brother and laughed ironically.
"Been on the vino again eh Maurice?"
Siobhan flashed an angry look at Mo who lurched over to his brother.
His breath stank of stale wine.
"How's Badger then, Ken? Still a superhero?"

"He's fine mate," smiled Ken; refusing to rise to his brother's facetious enquiry.

Mo swayed visibly.

Siobhan took Ken's coat and draped it across the table.

"Run me a bath, there's a love," Ken turned to his wife, "I'm as stiff as a board."

Siobhan nodded and gestured towards Mo, "He's plastered. Been knocking it back since you left."

"That's OK. He's harmless. It's the pressure of work, that's all."

Mo turned and wandered back into the sitting room whistling 'Two Little Boys' in breathy fits and starts.

Ken smiled at his wife and patted her rounded hips, kissing her on the tip of her nose. "Go and run the bath please."

She nodded and started up the stairs. Ken limped after Mo. He needed a drink too.

****

Phil had not heard the greetings in the hall but he knew he had to escape. He'd spent his evening working out his strategy. Siobhan was the weak link. She fancied him. He could tell. He had to get to her then he could get away.

He heard footsteps coming up the stairs. He clambered off the bed again and knelt down to the keyhole. He could hear taps being turned on and steam began to drift along the landing from the bathroom. Phil saw Siobhan coming into his view and her hair was once again neatly piled on top of her head and she was fully dressed. He saw she was coming to the bedroom.

"Shit!" spat Phil as he scuttled backwards, realising he was wearing only a pair of brief cotton pants.

The key turned in the lock and Siobhan entered.

Phil had thrown himself face down on the bed, feigning sleep. He heard the faint rustle of her nurse uniform as she walked past the bed. He smelt her perfume.

She opened a large cupboard and took out two large towels and a man's night-gown.

Phil opened one eye. "Hi," he murmured, as if he had been disturbed from slumber.

Siobhan jumped. "Gosh, you startled me! I thought you were flat out!" she exclaimed.

"I was but I'm a light sleeper. Slightest noise and I'm ready for action," Phil explained. "It comes from night exercises," he added with a hint of double entendre.

Siobhan's eyes scanned Phil's muscular frame.

"I apologise for my state of undress. It was hot earlier."

He allowed her gaze to linger a few more moments then he slowly drew the duvet over himself.

"I see you have tattoos," she remarked as she folded some towels over her arm.

"Yeah, I was pissed up in the Army and thought why not?"

"I like a man with tattoos."

"So do I," Phil laughed. She coloured up slightly as Phil leaned forwards and his eyes met hers. "Come back later and I'll show them to you in more detail," he suggested almost inaudibly.

"Mr Queen, how dare you!" she spat.

Phil watched in satisfaction as she stomped across the room to the door.

"I bet you give a good bed bath!" was his parting shot as she slammed the door and turned the key in the lock.

Phil smiled to himself and was surprised to find he had an enormous erection between his legs. He laughed out loud then turned on to his stomach and closed his eyes once more.

It was eleven o'clock precisely. He closed his eyes and dozed.

****

He knew she would be back. His eyes clicked open as he heard the lock turn. It was one fifteen. The room was pitch black but he was used to it. He had not slept since she left two hours before.

He sensed her approach as she came across the carpet towards his prostrate form. He made no movement or sound.

Brace yourself...he smiled to himself in the darkness.

He closed his eyes and waited. The duvet was half on and half off his body.

He could smell her perfume. It was stronger now. She must have prepared herself for this encounter.

"Phil..." her whispers barely reached his ears, "...Phil, are you awake?"

He shifted on the bed as if merely disturbed in his sleep. He mumbled an incoherent response.

"Phil, it's me – Siobhan."

In the darkness he smiled again. Still unseen.

He felt her hand reach out and stroke his chest. Slowly it moved down towards his groin. She leaned over and kissed his stomach. Phil groaned. He was going to enjoy this no matter what the consequences. She pulled at his pants and his erection bounced upwards.

Feigning shock Phil gasped, "Bloody hell!"

"Sssshh..." whispered Siobhan. "I know you want this."

"But?"

"No arguing. Just lie back and think of Ireland."

Phil grinned in the darkness. This was much more than he'd anticipated. Siobhan's soft mouth closed around his straining manhood.

"Oooo...oh, my gaaa..." he moaned as the smooth silky movements of her experienced mouth sent wave after wave of electric sensations through his body. His back arched in response.

She was leaning over the edge of the bed. He reached out and cupped her breasts and teased her nipples to erection. He suddenly flicked the side lamp on.

"Take your gown off!" muttered Phil.

She climbed over him onto his cock. "Fuck me," she whispered; throwing back her head with gusto.

God this was good, he thought. He was slowly losing sight of his main objective. *(Concentrate, you idiot! She's just a one off.)*

Escape!

She slid up and down, leaning forward with her hair flailing over his face. She was tantalisingly him for sure and she smelled divine.

"You're damn good," she gasped as her body arched wildly.

"Keep the noise down love. Ken might hear. Or Mo!" suggested Phil.

"Fuck them! They're both pissed. Suck my tits!" came her blatant comment.

Phil raised his face into her twin mounds. "Chri...I'm going to c..." she moaned.

"Do it. I've got all night," Phil urged her.

She groaned as she thrust down on the bed and seconds later she was visibly relaxed. *(This is a nice send-off!)*

"More?" asked Phil with his erection still intact.

"Oh yes please soldier-boy!" laughed Siobhan as she lay at rest.

This was his chance.

The door key was lying feet away on the bedside table.

Siobhan lay, eyes closed, momentarily sated.

"What do you want next?" Phil asked his willing partner.

"Whatever you like except buggery. That hurts!"

Phil had to stifle a laugh. (*Must be Catholic!)*

"Well, I've always fancied bondage..." Phil suggested.

Siobhan laughed excitedly. "Go for it! There's some handkerchiefs in the bottom of the locker."

Phil grinned. (*Perfect!)*

He lurched off the bed led by his aching erection. He needed to relieve it soon. She was a real turn-on.

He opened the locker and found for the hankies.

"Put your arms up sexy," he instructed.

"I'm all yours," she conceded.

Phil flicked off the bedside lamp.

"You're gorgeous," he grinned as he tied Siobhan's left wrist to the bedhead.

"Not bad yourself! You can't see me now though you kinky sod."

He could smell her sex. It emanated from her vagina. He leaned over and caressed her with his tongue.

"Ooooh," she wriggled and squirmed on the duvet.

He tied her other wrist. His erection was enormous.

"Just a sec," he whispered. He returned to the locker and found two more handkerchiefs, banging a toe on the drawers in the dark. "Bugger! Let's keep the light on eh?"

He returned to the bed and gazed down on the prone figure. She was a beautiful woman. Slightly overweight but her creamy skin and deep mass of wild hair gave her an almost feral quality. Her breasts rose and fell; her breathing had a ragged sound. Her blue eyes searched for his crotch.

"Now! Fuck me again," she said matter-of-factly.

Phil entered her and began slowly and sensuously to pleasure himself.

Siobhan struggled. Her hands strained at the knots as he pounded her body.

Her legs locked him closer.

"I'm going to come forever," he muttered and nuzzled her neck. His thrusts were more urgent. Faster!

"Please! Now!" she implored.

Phil grinned. His head went back and he shot his load. It seemed to last a lifetime. His head swam and his knees buckled.

"Oh my God!" Siobhan screamed at the culmination of their coupling.

"Yeah!" shouted Phil as his release cleared his brain and he could now sense the triumphant conclusion of his plan. His body satiated, he fell alongside Siobhan, sweating and gasping.

"Wicked!"

"Dead on," she replied with a huge grin. Her eyes closed and her body seemed deflated after their exertions.

Phil sneaked a quick glance at the clock. Two fifteen. He rose from the bed, stretched his body and toned up his muscles from his shoulders to his knees.

"That was some work-out!" he grinned.

"Mmm..." came the lazy reply.

He picked up his trousers from the chair and started to dress.

Siobhan's eyes gradually took in the scene.
"What are you doing?"
"Things to do. People to see," winked Phil, reaching for a t- shirt lying over a chair.
Siobhan stared at him uncomprehendingly.
"OK, the joke's over. Untie me Phil," she urged in an edgy tone.
Phil winked at her again as he pulled the shirt over his head. The label at the neck read 'Versace'
"Is this Ken's?" asked Phil.
Siobhan was struggling with her bonds.
"Nice fit don't you think?" queried Phil jokily.
"You bastard! Untie me this minute!" Siobhan's voice rose shrilly.
"Sorry, I've outstayed my welcome me thinks," said Phil simply.
He bent and tied his shoelaces slowly and calmly. He was in control now.
As she struggled in vain, Phil noticed a trickle of sperm from her vagina, staining the pink bedclothes.
"Tch tch, you've soiled the linen. Ken won't be too chuffed."
Siobhan's expression betrayed her terror now. Her face was crimson with the effort of trying to free herself.
Phil approached the bed and pulled the duvet over the struggling figure.
"In case you catch cold," he remarked quietly and then unceremoniously he stuffed one of the spare handkerchiefs into her gaping mouth.
"Sleep well; you've earned a nap dear. Resistance is useless. I know all my Navy knots."
He kissed her nose, picked up the key from the table, walked over to the door and turned to look back at

Siobhan. She'd stopped struggling now but this was replaced by tears which were rolling down her white face.
"You were truly wonderful," was his parting shot.
He closed the door and locked it leaving the key in the lock.
The bathroom light was still on. From another room he could hear snoring.
Mo.
He went on downstairs and in the main hallway found a notepad by the telephone. He leaned over and wrote:

THANKS FOR YOUR HOSPITALITY BOYS
SIOBHAN WAS GREAT (MO SHOULD KNOW!)
I KNOW YOU KILLED CHLOE
SEE YOU ON SATURDAY
LOVE - PHIL XXXX

He propped the message against the telephone.
"Revenge is sweet," he whispered to himself.

Taking his time, the urge to run was difficult to suppress as he made his way to the kitchen.
"Keys.. keys," he murmured. Then he spotted them, hanging on a special rack next to a Sunderland F.C calendar. (*Very efficient household! Security poor!*)
"Yeah," he crowed gleefully. He'd never driven a BMW before...

****

PART THREE

'The March'

Chapter Thirty One

They came for Terence Gordon at 3a.m. It was four hours since his abortive suicide attempt.
There were more than two this time. Something was going on. He covered his face with his forearm but he could smell the tart odour of his armpits. He hadn't showered in three days.
They handled him roughly and efficiently. No one answered his pleas and his panic-stricken demeanour only exacerbating their treatment of their captive.

"Where're you taking me?" he whined. His gritted his teeth and expected a harsh blow from one of his captors at any time.
When the light assailed his eyes he had to shut them. He'd become used to the darkness. Pins and needles crept up his legs from his shins to his knees. They grasped him, half-pulled and half-carried him, and his feet were dragging behind him as they went through the flat.
"Walk!" The voice was clipped and angry.
Gordon obeyed. He was terrified that he might incite them to further violence upon him. His eyes remained closed as he heard a door open. Fresh air hit his face and he breathed the coolness into his stale lungs with vigour. A light drizzle clung like a film over their clothes as they pushed and goaded him down some steep steps.

Another door opened, sliding sideways. His bleary eyes saw a white transit van standing in a dimly-lit street.
"Get in you twat," a guttural voice ordered.
"Just tell me where...wh..."
A fist thudded into his stomach and it winded him. He doubled up. He was lifted bodily and thrown into the back of the van.
"Don't talk! Sit!" spat another voice.
He sat on a bench seat running the length of the van. Silence enveloped him. He nervously glanced around at his surroundings. There were three figures. One opposite, legs crossed, and the others were alongside him. They all wore balaclavas and they were all big men.
(*Four-to-one. Unfair!*)

He shuddered. The chill morning air crept through his flimsy T-shirt. The fine rain stuck to his hair and clothing in minute beads and were now soaking through. He realised he was still barefoot and his teeth began to chatter uncontrollably as another ague took hold.
The van lurched forward and Gordon was thrown sideways in his seat.
A radio snapped on in the driver's compartment. Someone lit a cigarette and the familiar acrid smell was a much-needed fillip to his senses. He could hear a familiar song but couldn't recall the title.
But he was scared. Where were they going? To the Police? Court? Another hiding place?
He listened intently for the radio. It took his mind off his situation for a few moments. The newscaster's voice cut in and droned on...
'Here are the headlines. The body of a five year old boy has been found next to railway sidings in Camden. Police

say the boy had been strangled, sexually assaulted and battered with a heavy instrument. His parents are said to be distraught and under sedation...
Riots in South Africa have caused the suspension of the annual elections. Police have quelled unrest in virtually every large township. A spokesperson reported looting, violent unrest and groups of teenagers fighting on the streets...'.

Gordon concentrated as a further item began. 'All eyes are on Trafalgar Square in London at this moment as people arrive for the highly publicised 'Day of Reckoning'. It is not known quite what is meant by this. However, a low police presence and the good nature of the participants is sure to allay any fears of another 'Poll Tax type fiasco'. A spokesperson at the event has commented on the joviality of the atmosphere and the good-natured banter between early arrivals. It's a joy to observe...Radio Paramount will be visiting the scene throughout the day's events to keep you informed of the progress of the activities.
And now the weather...'.
The radio clicked off. Someone spoke.
"It's going OK," the gruff voice behind the balaclava could not disguise a suppressed excitement.
"Apart from the drizzle," another replied.
"No hassle, it's only water."
Terence Gordon leaned forward and held his head in his hands as the van rumbled on through the rain.

****

TRAFALGAR SQUARE - LONDON Saturday 6th June
They met as strangers. They came from the north, east, south and west. Ferried in by sea and from abroad.

They arrived on flights into Heathrow and Luton and on the special trains into the capital's centre too.

Trafalgar Square. Six fifteen a.m.

The fine rain fell upon the early arrivals. Typically, British drizzle seems to suspend itself on fabric and plastic yet insinuated itself through to the flesh, creating a moist cocoon.

Some found it comfortably warm but those without good circulation soon became chilled.

Dark figures ambled around drinking coffee and tea. Dawn was creeping up behind the surrounding buildings. Men, women and children sat in groups on walls and steps talking in monotones. The odd laugh linked nodding heads as people greeted those they knew or introduced themselves. The cooing pigeons fluttered down from their overnight roosts. For them, it was just another average day of people, traffic and noise. However, this would become no average day.

The Brothers, Sisters and Children of Justice were at last mustering for their day of revelation to the world. The Day of Reckoning had begun.

By seven o'clock their numbers had swelled into hundreds. Milling groups, pointing fingers, anecdotes and stories were swapped. People shook hands. Recognition made friends of total strangers. All 'Brothers' together.

"Hi! I'm Keith Thomas from Derby. This is my wife, Janice, and our kid, Thomas. Where are you from?" said one 'Brother' as he welcomed another.

"Ayrshire. It's taken us a day to get here but it's worth it. I'm Colin Baxter and I own a farm. It's looking really good, isn't it?"

Those who knew each other hugged on meeting. Nelson gazed impassively from his column, as he had over so many similar gatherings. The lions, in their sphinx-like pose endured the climbing children. They'd witnessed so many rallies: the suffragettes, unemployed, miners, nurses, gay activists and political orators. They all came and went. However, this cross-section of humanity had a different undertone. There were miners, lesbians, nurses, gays but all there for one common cause.

A lone figure walked towards the fountains. He carried a large long package. On reaching the steps, he unfurled a huge flag. He called for assistance and people rushed forward, eager to help.

A few yards to the left of Nelson's column stood a large wooden dais. Behind the dais was a large metal stand that had been erected with ladders on either side. A microphone had been set up in the middle of the platform. At present, it was covered with a plastic bag to protect it from the fine drizzle that persisted.

The flag was laboriously hoisted to cover the stand. It measured some forty by twenty feet and had small flags of all nations around the edge. In the centre of the design was a mother sheltering a small child. Above them a clenched fist punched the air. People turned to read the message which arced over the fist: **'JUSTICE FOR THE VICTIMS!'**

Spontaneous applause filtered through the throng. Whistles and whoops drowned out the pigeons for a full minute.

"It's like when the wall came down!" an onlooker remarked to his wife. His accent was unmistakably German. They hugged each other and smiled.

Then, the man responsible for hoisting the flag switched on the public address system. Feedback screeched through the loudspeakers. People cheered and fell silent as he stood at the microphone.

He was just an ordinary man. His name was Clifford Parsons. He was a supermarket manager from Grantham in Lincolnshire. Two years earlier he'd found his wife throttled with the telephone line in his detached cottage, just off the High Street. The murderer had been caught. A fifteen year old youth and his two years' suspended sentence was Clifford Parsons only solace. He related these details solemnly and deliberately and his words touched chords throughout the crowd. Murmured comments floated back to him as he looked down with his head bowed.

It was seven thirty. The drizzle hung like cobwebs in people's hair.

"Welcome, Brothers and Sisters - and to your children. I know it's early. I know you've had some troubled journeys to reach us and some more than others." His arms opened in supplication.

"This is... OUR day!"

People clapped and whistled.

"This is... YOUR day! Your children's day and your children's children!"

Still people filed into the square as he spoke. In the hour that had passed the numbers had trebled.

"Today will not be forgotten. Today we shall show the world..." he waved an arm "...what this flag, you and I stand for!"

Applause rang out again. Polite applause. It was too soon for rebel songs.

"Thank you."

The figure stepped down from the stand and was lost in an instance in the milling hordes.

Coaches and taxis drove around the square, dropping off more people like lemmings. Children skipped and screamed. Some had brought family pets: dogs, cats, a pony or two and even a parrot in a cage. It was a family day.

A hamburger van wound its way along the concourse.

"What's goin' on 'ere?" shouted an excited taxi driver. "I ain't seen so many people 'ere since the Coronation!"

The taxi driver's distinctive Cockney accent continued and it brought smiles to those within earshot.

"We're here to make a point!" shouted a young girl.

Then the hamburger van driver pulled over slowly and said, "Bloody 'ell! It's like a Pavarotti concert!"

He looked at his wristwatch. "It's only just gone seven. I was on my way to Tottenham for a football Open Day but I think I'll set up 'ere!" The crowd whistled and shouted.

"You'll make a killing here today mate," shouted a tall, bearded figure.

"Too right mate but where are the cops? I've got my licence to think about."

"They're under orders to stay low profile."

"Eh? Under orders? Whose orders?"

"Ours!" someone yelled back at him.
The van driver shook his head disbelievingly.
"I've heard it all now," he said and laughed.
A small boy ran up to the van with his mother in tow.
"Can I have a hot-dog please?"
"Certainly can son - you certainly can. Just give me five to get up and runnin'."

An observant spectator would, by now have noticed on the periphery of all the activity some figures at strategic points, circling the square. They wore fluorescent jackets and jeans. On closer examination, it was apparent they had small black earpieces and radios inside their jackets. These were the specially trained co-ordinators. Their job was to deal with troublemakers, infiltrators and obvious yob element. Their general demeanour was that of a casual onlooker but woe betide anyone causing a scene.

The other unusual feature was the total absence of police. Those who had attended other such rallies were accustomed to the silent presence, but not a single uniform was in sight. They had their orders for this day.

The vast flag fluttered gently as people continued to pour into the famous London landmark.
The drizzle continued to weep down upon the assembly of the victims. The minutes ticked by...

****

CHAPTER THIRTY TWO

"What the hell is going on?" stormed Jeremy Dawlish. He gripped the phone in his right hand while he supported himself against the wall with his left hand. His eyes were wild, darting up and down and from side to side, as if following some imaginary fly.

"I don't give a flying shit what it's all about. I didn't KNOW Alan!" His voice rose in pitch as he paced uneasily around the room. "How the hell am I to govern this nation if I don't even know what's going on in my own backyard? A pretty big backyard don't you think? Bloody Trafalgar?!"

He stared at the wall opposite as he waited for a reaction from the caller at the other end of the telephone. The muscles of his jaw tensed visibly. The Prime Minister was still wearing his nightgown, an expensive one from Harrods, and he remained barefoot.

"You'd better find out Alan, and quick, for your sake and mine," he stated flatly. The veiled threat in his voice was unmistakeable.

The crackle of a voice made him pause.

"What do you mean? You had no idea! You're the blasted Home Secretary for God's sake!" He slammed down the receiver. His eyes closed in exasperation. Saturdays were

usually such quiet affairs. He'd risen at five-thirty as usual. When he heard the six o'clock news report he'd been drying himself after a bracing early shower.
"Day of Reckoning?" he whispered then frowned.
He had sat on the edge of his bed and listened intently to the broadcast. It was when he had phoned his Chief of Police, Dermot Breen, that things began to look a little difficult.
"Dermot! Good morning! Yes... I know it's early old friend. Listen, what's happening over in Trafalgar Square this morning, only..." The smile had faded slowly when he was interrupted.
"Just run that by me again, Dermot..."

Jeremy Dawlish, Prime Minister. Conservative. Former Minister for Defence. Former Tory candidate for the Colchester constituency. Essex man made good. He'd been schooled privately. His parents were big in publishing and still were. His interests included cricket (Essex CCC in particular. He was friendly with Graham Gooch, the highest scoring English Test batsman in history, no less).
A big fan of classic opera, he was often photographed attending gala nights.
The fight for his tenure as Prime Minister was his finest hour, beating off the threat of 'grey man' Arthur Millington (Sussex Man) with ease.
His victory speech had eclipsed Thatcher's first attempt hands down. Maggie was said to be 'quietly pleased' for Essex man.

He was immediately made a Freeman of Colchester. Three years before, however, no one had even heard of him. His rise had been meteoric. His forceful, no-nonsense nature had endeared him to the British voters. Even the Scots liked him; no mean feat in itself!

Six months into his term as PM, things started to slide. The euphoria of his victory was soured by a 'dirty tricks' campaign by the Socialists. Crime was at its highest level for ten years. Cabinet ministers were being caught regularly with their pants down and the final insult, Essex came third in the County Championships. Bad form.

A bad time for all. The nation was beginning to turn to others for guidance.

His wife, Miranda, was his tower of strength. She'd even bought him some colourant for his rapidly greying hair. No matter how the tabloids portrayed him, she was there always smiling and waving. The calm in the storm. She wasn't here this morning however...

He replaced the handset slowly. As he sat at his desk, he could hear traffic in the distance. Horns and voices. London was waking up.

The phone rang loudly which aroused him from his thoughts with a jerk.

"Yes?" His face softened noticeably.

"Oh Miranda... Hi love. Yes, I know. I've heard." he smiled.

He leaned forward slightly.

"No, I didn't."

His voice was a low monotone, expressionless. Two frown lines appeared on his forehead. He blinked twice.

"How many...? Did you say - sixty thousand people?"

He visualised the famous square.

"What do you mean ... you're going?" He shifted uneasily in his seat.
"I forbid you!" He paused listening to his wife's tinny chatter.
"I don't care if Jenny's going! It's not a fucking funfair!" His eyes blazed with anger. It was eight thirty a.m.
"She can say what she likes! YOU are not to go! You'll have the TV and press swarming around you like flies!"
He stared incredulously at the phone as he held the receiver away from his ear. "Put Jenny on!" he screamed into the mouthpiece.
There was a pause. He struggled to regain some sort of control over his voice.
"Jenny? What the hell's going on?"
He stared at the large clock on the opposite wall for a full thirty seconds.
"... Justice? Justice for whom, for God's sake?"
Beads of sweat began to form on his greying temples.
"... How many people? One hundred thousand?!"

Jeremy Dawlish slowly replaced the receiver, slammed his fist on the mahogany desk and rose to his feet. Walking across to the window, he stubbed his toe on a chair leg. His cry of pain sounded like a wounded animal... a cornered, helpless animal.

****

It was eight-forty when the van reached Trafalgar Square. Five minutes earlier a blindfold had been placed over Terence Gordon's eyes. He remained silent throughout the near-two hour journey. The small talk of his captors had failed to give him any idea of where the van was heading. Earlier, he'd spotted a couple of London landmarks through the van's rear window but the film of rain on the glass had made it difficult to make out exactly what route they were taking.

His breathing was normal under the circumstances. One of the figures seated opposite shifted slightly in his seat.
"A good turnout or what?"
The driver of the van answered without taking his eyes off the road.
"Better than good. About seventy thousand at a guess already."
"Pity about the weather though."
"Yeah. Still, they reckon the afternoon will be brighter."
"For some..." murmured the voice.
Gordon fidgeted conscious of a veiled threat.
Where the hell was he?
He recalled the news report some hours earlier. A rally of some sort...
Trafalgar Square?

He heard voices outside. Lots of different accents. Whatever was happening there were certainly a lot of people present.
The driver spoke once more. "Where are we going for the morning?"
"Take the next left," came a response.
The van lurched suddenly. Gordon grasped the edge of the seat. A gnawing fear was building inside him. Whoever these thugs were, they weren't acting in an official capacity. He was there for a reason. His mind raced. A violent nausea hit him as he tried to come to terms with his situation.

"It's just here," another voice said. The van stopped. There was a slamming of one door and then another opened. Rough hands tugged at his thin shirt. His body tensed in apprehension as unseen figures hauled him unceremoniously out of the vehicle. He heard voices but the words were indistinguishable.

A door opened and closed with an echoing thud as they stumbled into a building.

He sensed darkness and a disquieting silence.

He sensed people all around him but no one spoke.

He shivered and waited.

"You can take your hood off now," said an emotionless voice.

He tugged nervously at the thin cotton but his eyes remained closed. He didn't really want to open them. When he did look around it took a few seconds for his eyes to adjust and take in the scene. It was a warehouse of some kind. He stood at the top of a flight of steps. At the bottom, stood five figures shrouded in the gloom.

He could smell oil. A factory smell. No rotten fruit today.

The figures moved back into the dark recesses of the warehouse.

"Come down the steps, Mr Gordon. Don't be afraid."

There was no threat in the voice this time. He hesitated, then took a faltering step forward. Just as his foot touched the second step the lights came on, blinding him temporarily.

"Welcome!"

He shielded his eyes from the harsh glare.

"Who...Who are you?" he whimpered gingerly as he made his way down, one step at a time.

He waited when he reached the ground floor, his eyes searching for some person he could identify. None were visible.
He inched forward slightly. Afraid. Very afraid!
"Stop!" He stopped in mid-step, almost falling over. He waited. Someone spoke.
"We are... the Brothers of Justice." stated the disembodied voice flatly. The monotone unnerved Gordon. The words echoed in the sinister atmosphere drifting into the vast expanse of the warehouse.
"I...I don't understand. Why...?"
"You don't need to understand anything Mr Gordon," the voice interrupted him once more. "Suffice to say, you are here today for a purpose. As an example to others like yourself. Those who prey on the weak and the innocent. Those who take from them and frighten them, so that they have no freedom to walk the streets of our great country."
Gordon licked his dry lips. His mouth felt like sandpaper. Another voice started, "You are our lamb to the slaughter Terence."
"Slaughter? What do you..."

Suddenly, a picture appeared on the wall to his left. He heard a low whirring sound. A click.

"Do you recognise her Terence?" enquired the silky voice.
He did. "Yes, he replied, almost inaudibly. He swallowed drily, his saliva was non-existent.
"Kelly Louise Abraham."
"Yes... I know. I knew her," Gordon continued with his eyes wide open.

The picture showed a little girl holding a teddy bear. A picture of innocence.

Terence Gordon fought a sudden urge to wet himself.

"Yes, you knew her," a voice commented.

"We know something too. We know what you did to Kelly Louise," the tone suddenly changed to a malevolent threat.

The whirring sound and another click. This time it showed a male in his mid-twenties. He wore flared jeans and a football shirt with an England badge on it. He was smiling.

"Bet you don't know him Terence," teased the voice.

Gordon shifted uneasily. "No - I don't," he replied and his eyes trained on the image above him.

Silence hung in the air.

"You'll see a resemblance in a tick."

The picture changed in a second. This time, a man held a little girl in his arms. They were at the seaside and it was a sunny day at Blackpool. Both were grinning at the camera.

"Mister Tambling..." whispered Gordon.

"...and Kelly Louise! Top marks for observation!"

Applause echoed around the warehouse.

"Spot on Terence! Well done!" shouted a voice above the noise.

Gordon could not tear his gaze away from the picture. He stood as if in a trance. Memories came flooding back. The day he'd first seen the little blonde girl in the playground. The way her hair kept tumbling into her eyes. Her white ankle socks and the smell of soap on her face... It had all happened twelve years ago.

Twelve long years.

He found himself sobbing. "I'm so so..."

"Sorry?" boomed a voice.

He nodded slowly as tears flowed down his plump, unshaven face.

The monitor whirred and clicked again. He strained to see the next slide. Rubbing his fist across his eyes, he forced himself to look.

It was a young girl, blonde again, in some sort of uniform.

He knew the smile. She stood next to a huge aeroplane hangar.

"It's her isn't it?" murmured Gordon.

"Yes, she's now nineteen. An air stewardess. Thanks to counselling and years of loving support from her family, she leads an almost normal life now."

Gordon bowed his head.

"She still has the occasional nightmare of course. She hates men. She shares a flat with a girlfriend. No thanks to you, she can never bear a child of her own."

Gordon sank to his knees sobbing. "I couldn't help it!" he screamed.

"She was so beautiful. I'm so sorry!"

"Spare us the theatrics Terry!" the voice boomed.

"We've seen your video collection. You haven't got a remorseful gene in your body. You're beyond help. That's why we've chose you. Society won't miss you Terence. You're no use to anyone are you?" another voice stated.

The sobs echoed around the dank, dark domain of his captors. Footsteps came nearer. Their pace quickened and the lights went off once more.

The hood came down again over his straining head. His screams went on disregarded.

They tied his wrists and ankles and left him alone and terrified, in a box of rotting apples...

****

By ten thirty the crowds of milling people, young and old, had swollen to a massive throng. Incidents were small. The usual ignorant hangers-on stood on the periphery and watched, spellbound, as still more folk arrived. Many were greeting old friends enthusiastically.

The hamburger van had sold out by ten-thirty and the owner, delighted with his good fortune, had closed the serving hatch and secured his van in a nearby office parking area. He then returned to join the masses. He wasn't going to miss this. He would risk a ticket.

TV camera crews and media moguls began to arrive, disgorging equipment and miles of cable from vans. 'SKY News', 'CNN', 'British Broadcasting Corp', 'ABC' and 'Carlton'. They were all there by appointment only. Every available vantage point was covered. Cameras panned the crowds for any violent disruption or disorder. There was little and what there was immediately got nipped in the bud in its infancy. Scuffling teenagers got a clipped ear and short shrift from the minders on the perimeters. News reporters talked into cameras on every corner.
"Bored or what?" moaned one ITN cameraman to his boom operator.
"When does it start?"
"Dunno. They'll be puttin' up a bouncy castle next!" laughed one of the technicians.

At five minutes to eleven something happened...

"Who's that?"
"Dunno,"
"I know the face... it's... you know – what's-name."

All talking died away as the slight figure climbed on to the podium. The huge flag behind him made him look more imposing. Powerful. It fluttered and flapped in the breeze, drawing people's attention.

The drizzle of the early morning had given way to a hazy sunshine. Steam rose from the damp paving slabs and the clothes of the crowd, creating an air of fantasy in the suddenly eerie silence.

Thousands of faces stared as one at Alan Percival. Confusion gave way to recognition and slowly but surely, word spread. Cameramen and media reps strained to close in on the man of the moment.

"That's Percival innit?"
"Yeah - 'ome Seccertery."
"I don't believe it! What's he doing here?"

More scuffles broke out as the assembled hacks and paparazzi jockeyed for better positions. Alan Percival looked slightly fazed by the vastness of the sea of faces below him. His eyes darted from side to side as he tried to compose himself ready to speak.

He coughed slightly and smiled. "Good morning ladies and gentlemen! Brothers and Sisters!"
Some people called in reply. Others were too surprised at this new development. Someone applauded briefly but it was soon lost in the general murmur of puzzled response.

Percival continued, "I suspect ... a good many of you are a little shocked to see me, your Home Secretary, standing here before you!"

More murmurs of assent filtered through the cool morning air.

Somewhat haltingly, Percival carried on, "I, like yourselves, have become sick and tired of the apparent inability of our country to control those, shall we say criminal elements, that are ruining lives for decent people."

"Hear, hear!" came a lone cry. The crowd silently absorbed the unexpected content of Percival's remarks.

"For far too long we, in this great country of ours, have been impotent against the steady rise in crime and violence around us! We have witnessed an inexorable erosion of decent values and morality. Daily, we read of assaults and murder on the weak and helpless, those unable to defend themselves. More decadence! More drugs! More death! All meaningless and cruel..."

People whistled and applauded shrilly.

"My friends! NOW is the time to call a halt!" Percival's voice rose and became more strident and confident.

Percival continued, "Prison is too good for these vicious cowards. Thieves, drug dealers, rapists, murderers - the list goes on and on while decent, law-abiding people suffer and have their lives destroyed!"

Supporting shouts rang out as people began to get the drift of the minister's speech.

"BUT..." He paused to scan the crowd. "These people are no longer safe!"

He raised a pointing hand to the flag behind him, which showed a huge clenched fist. "And this is why!"

A crescendo of applause rang out. The large flag to his rear flapped wildly as if in affirmation.
A TV cameraman a few yards from the podium grinned, not knowing why.
"You tell 'em, Percy-boy! Go for it!"
Percival opened his arms in an expansive gesture.
"YOU are the future! The people of this nation have had enough of the do-gooders! I admit, and I'm afraid to say, my policies have not done enough! Just as those before me failed too. The Brothers of Justice are here to offer you a new future. A new vision for society."
A wave of noise and approval swept across the ancient square which had seen so many protests and riots in the past.
Percival waited for the sound to die away as the crowd awaited his next words. "In this past year, The Brothers of Justice have seen fit to snuff out some of those dregs of society. You may not have read about our successes in the tabloids but I can tell you today that no less than over forty known violent criminals, such as rapists, murderers or just plain vicious thugs, have met their maker!
No more cushy prison for them! The Brothers of Justice have seen to it. They've been removed from our midst!"

More cheers, more applause...
"The Brothers of Justice are only just starting my friends! The future of generations is in their very capable hands."

Percival turned to face the nearest camera and smiled slyly.
"Are you watching Mr Mugger? Do you see the demonstration here Mr Drug-Baron? Does your stomach clench all you paedophiles? All of you out there - this is

our message! We KNOW you. We don't like you and we are YOUR bogeymen. Who may be behind YOU or at YOUR door? You now have something to fear... not just your beat bobby who you know you can subvert and ignore. We are not the spineless judiciary who disregard the victims in your favour of clever points of law. NO! We, the Brothers of Justice, are the future of this country, the new law and order. Look around us here... which ones ARE the Brothers? We know you but you don't know US!

Percival's eyes glittered as he turned away from the camera eye and people cheered and waved.

"Kill them all!" someone yelled.

Percival called for calm once more. Someone started singing 'Jerusalem.'

****

At the Prime Minister's official residence, the television screen shimmered with the scenes taking place a few hundred yards away. The Prime Minister sat transfixed as his wife flitted from room to room. She had lasted only twenty minutes in Trafalgar Square. Her best friend and confidante, Jenny, the wife of a Liberal councillor from Morecambe, had stayed on to support the rally.

"Coffee darling?"

A grunt was her husband's brief reply. He stood up briskly.

"I don't understand it! Alan never mentioned a bloody thing to me about this. I've been betrayed by my own right-hand man. This will get out of control. Mark my words," he groaned.

"They'll want me to speak in the next hour or so. What the hell do I tell the House? 'Oh, by the way, my Home

Secretary is a closet vigilante'? For God's sake, Miranda, what do I do?" he continued to groan.

There was a knock on the door.

"Yes!?" he snapped.

George, his batman, put his head around the heavy wooden door. Miranda let out a sigh.

"Ah - Prime Minister - the press are congregating outside. Will you speak?"

A phone warbled in the distance and was silenced.

"Yes... Yes! Thank you George. Give me half an hour."

George nodded grimly and closed the door softly.

The television picture showed Alan Percival still holding the rapt attention of the crowd. He was describing the capture of a child molester. People cheered at some comment he had made.

"They've even interrupted the bloody Test Match," murmured the Prime Minister grimly.

"It's already out of control. What are you doing to say to them darling?" whispered Miranda with her eyes never leaving the TV screen.

Dawlish suddenly remembered with a sinking heart, that his Press Secretary was away on vacation...

****

Chapter Thirty Three

Phil Queen stood next to Nelson's Column. His head was covered with a black cotton hat. He wore a black bomber jacket and jeans. His training shoes looked shabby. He looked shabby.
Unshaven. Unkempt. All for a reason.

The rally was going superbly. The Home Secretary was a real coup. Never in his wildest dreams had he expected a cabinet minister to be in the 'Brothers'. Phil was impressed but it wouldn't deflect him.

He stood surrounded by a group from Cardiff. They were all craning their necks to get a better view of the speaker. Their Welsh dialects cut through the general noise like a knife.
"Isn't it brilliant?"
"He's a star!"
"I can't believe it. The bloody Chancellor is on our side!"
"It's the Home Seccetery, Bevan," corrected a young female, as her arms linked with his.
"Oh, whatever," agreed her companion.
Phil smiled at their naivety.
He slid away from the Welsh mob and concentrated on the larger crowd. People were agog with excitement.

He could almost feel the electric atmosphere being generated by the rally. It was a good cover.
His escape from Ken, Mo and the rampant nurse from hell had been perfect. He'd driven up to his cousin's house at Luton, sold the car and got a make-over. A crew cut at his local barber had given him a new image.

The return journey to London by British Rail had renewed his lack of confidence in public transport. Four hours late due to a horse on the line. It was a better excuse than the wrong snow...

He had booked into a seedy hotel behind Waterloo Station and waited...
Phil weaved in and out of the heaving crowd. He noticed there were still people arriving. Coaches and London buses disgorged hundreds more into the seething cauldron.
Smiling, he noticed a clown on stilts.
"Ooooh - look! The Chief of Police has arrived!" shouted a wag, which brought whoops of derisive approval from his mates. The clown grinned, waved and plodded on.

Ken and Mo were here. He knew it. Probably Badger too. But where?
His eyes scanned faces constantly and furtively. He recalled the times he'd been on leave from the Army, when he'd bumped into old friends on the street.
A couple of seconds of recognition, brief flashes of memory of old times shared, then the smiles and backslaps. There would be none of this if or when he spotted Ken or Mo on this day.

Only bad memories - of death, sadness and betrayal. Of Chloe.
The mission today was to search and destroy. Search for Ken and Mo. Destroy Ken and Mo.
As they'd found and destroyed him...

****

"Good move that," murmured Mo.
"What?" snapped Ken, still smarting from finding his cold, naked wife splayed on their supposed prisoner's bed the morning earlier.
"The Home Secretary making a speech. This is what it's all about. It'll make Kennedy's assassination look like a picnic."
A small black and white TV flickered high on a wall near the counter in the small cafe in Holborn. The street outside was full of people all moving in one direction; excitement was rising by the minute.
"You needn't try worming your way back into my good books, you bastard!" Ken's face reflected his anger.
Mo flushed at his words.
"We're only here on business then you're OUT - soonest!"
"But..."
"No buts! I can handle my wife fancying a bloke like Queen but my own brother!"

Ken rose from the table and limped unsteadily across to the counter. He took a sachet of sugar and resumed his seat.
"Your leg hurting?" asked Mo sympathetically.
"What do you care?" glared Ken as he stirred his tepid coffee. Their eyes never met. "I'm more concerned with Phil's whereabouts."

"He took the bloody car didn't he?" Mo shrugged his slight shoulders.

"It could've been worse. At least we're alive. He could have murdered us in our beds what with all the training he's had."

Ken glowered silently. His thoughts were a maelstrom of possibilities.

Where was Phil Queen? Would he be in Trafalgar Square? Was he likely to be still committed to the Brothers or was he now on his own personal mission?

****

As Jeremy Dawlish urinated, a frown played over his normally calm features. He zipped his fly unsteadily. Turning towards the mirror, he washed his hands slowly, staring at his reflection in the stained mirror.

His mind whirled as he prepared his next move. The vultures were out in Downing Street. Journalists, cameras, the full media works were guaranteed to be on duty.

"Fuck!" he said, drying his hands underneath the automatic heater. The noise was oppressive.

He'd changed into his suit. A blue one, with the paisley tie and black shoes. Now he was girding himself symbolically for the coming jamboree.

"Time to face the music, I suppose..." he muttered to himself.

He strolled down the corridor of power. Number Ten. The pinnacle of his career.

Maids and administrators never found his gaze. He was alone. Deserted and uninformed by his Home Secretary - for what purpose?

Vaguely, he heard voices from TV and radio .... 'In turmoil. We await the Prime Minister's response but first, some music...'
Dawlish stifled a wry smile as 'Lily the Pink' played on.
"Bloody Radio Two - subtle as ever."
He plodded down the stairs past portraits of former premier's: Thatcher, Heath, Wilson...
As he approached the front door of 10 Downing Street, he could hear the gabble in the street. It was normally such a quiet place these days since the erection of the security gates but now the press awaited a statement.

Not even during the elections had he felt such an atmosphere. The world would soon witness today's events through the miracle of instant communication. The world would watch his every move. Every flicker recorded and pored over for significance then judged and used.
He felt a momentary sympathy for the people who were missing the Test Match transmission. It was twelve noon, precisely...

****

At one minute past twelve the rain started again. It was a light summer drizzle, warm and wet.
At one and a half minutes past twelve, the Prime Minister emerged through the famous black door in Downing Street and began the most critical speech of his career. He hadn't had time to consult his spin doctors and fawning assistants so there were no prepared texts. He was the last batsman in.
He was on his own and didn't they let him know it! Like baying hunt hounds the garbled barrage assailed him as he stepped across the threshold.

A far cry from the victory speeches and post-war rhetoric. The easy life was over.
He blinked at the camera flashes as the photographers jockeyed for the best angles. Trying to smile confidently, he stepped up to the familiar set of microphones, yards from the steps of Number Ten. The dark blue suit and sober tie emphasised the serious tone of the pronouncement.

"Please, ladies and gentlemen - a little decorum, if you don't mind," he gestured and raised his hands trying to placate the mob.
They ignored his remark. The babble of questions became more insistent. Beyond the media merchants, the world watched.

Inside Number Ten, his loyal wife, Miranda, sat rapt and clasped a large neat whisky. She didn't normally drink during the day but today was different. She stared at the large TV screen and struggled to contain the tears that were welling up in her eyes. She nervously bit her lower lip.

"Be brave darling," she whispered at the TV.

Events were unfolding literally thirty metres away, outside their safe haven of ministerial power.

The questions were shouted, incoherent, gabbled noise and a solid wall of inquisition.
"One at a time!" Dawlish called; with a frown of distaste for the situation. The noise abated slightly.
A small fat man, near the front of the assembled morass of shifting, nudging bodies spoke up confidently, "What's going on Prime Minister?

Did you not know about today's event in Trafalgar Square?"

Still the cameras whirred and clicked.

"No! I didn't!" stated Dawlish flatly.

Gasps of astonishment greeted his response.

Miranda Dawlish wept openly inside Number Ten.

Dawlish eyed his next questioner like a cornered villain.

"How do you explain your own Home Secretary's defection to an underground vigilante group?"

Dawlish shrugged.

"I cannot explain it," he replied. A muttering amongst the group replaced the loud interrogations, as this reply permeated their consciousness.

Dawlish bowed his head slightly.

"The Home Secretary, Alan Percival, has betrayed his government and his constituents. I am very shocked and disturbed at these events."

Another disembodied voice rang out.

"Who are The Brothers of Justice Prime Minister?"

Dawlish frowned once again. He stared in to the faces in front of him but saw no one.

In the distance, a police siren wailed mournfully.

"From what I have seen and heard this morning, I believe they are, as you have so quaintly put it, an underground and illegal vigilante group."

Another question.

"They seem to have enormous support from the general public sir. Are they the backlash against the government's inadequacies and apparent legal impotence to deal with the escalating criminality in our midst?"

Dawlish nodded recognising the authoritative tone of the broadcaster's question. He paused to add some gravitas to his reply.

"I believe that in this country we uphold the belief that justice is generally seen to be done."

Someone shouted, "Rubbish!"

"Days past have proved that crime is being curbed," continued Dawlish doggedly," proving that my government's hard-line policies and our crack-down on violence and the drug culture are bearing fruitful results!"

"So, why are rapists given suspended sentences or allowed bail?" a voice yelled from the rear of the crowd.

"Yeah! Why are convicted murderers released after serving only half of a life sentence? Why isn't life for life?" spat another voice.

"I...I only know that we, in Britain, have a policy on crime that is regarded as one of the most effective in the world..."

Inside Number Ten, Miranda was willing her husband to maintain his grasp of the situation. "Hold on darling... don't crack. Don't give in!" she whispered; wringing her hands slowly.

Dawlish continued by quoting figures and percentages on recent victories in the crime statistics but his only reward was more derisory howls of protest from the mob opposite.

"What is your next step then Prime Minister? Are you powerless to halt today's rally?"

Dawlish shifted slightly.

"So long as the rally is peaceful, I shall not intervene. We do still live in a democratic state, after all. I am not a judge."

"Hear, hear!" shouted a female voice.

Dawlish was visibly shocked by the attitude of the normally respectful people who assembled outside

Number Ten. As he scanned today's crowd he could see only anger and spite reflected in their faces, coupled with not a little bewilderment.
This unnerved him. If the Prime Minister was not in control, then who was? Who, at this moment, holding the upper hand? Another sharp question jolted him from his whirling thoughts. A foreign accent - Irish? *(Don't panic, stay calm!)*
"Does the Prime Minister agree that his position as an authority is this morning being undermined by today's events?"
Dawlish flinched. They were sniffing blood here.
"No! No... not at all. As I said earlier, there is democratic rule in this country."
He struggled to muster a more coherent and convincing reply.
"There have been demonstrations before and there will be others in the future.
I think the people will decide. Their sense of fair play is legendary in this great country of ours."
"But it IS the people who are demonstrating Prime Minister - not a Left-Wing faction!" The frail voice was almost inaudible but it reached Dawlish's ears. He turned in its direction and saw an aged lady, wearing a tweed suit and a red hat.
He was looking at Miranda's mother...

****

Forty million Britons saw the Prime Minister's collapse on live TV.
In some pubs and houses, people actually clapped and cheered.

In Conservative strongholds, in Berkshire and Windsor, Essex and Hampshire viewers collapsed with him, as did their careers.

Jeremy Dawlish had to be physically dragged back into Number Ten Downing Street by a policemen and his official minders.

Fleet Street went into overdrive. Editors held not only their front pages but suspended editions whilst the news was frantically re-hashed to absorb the momentous tidings.

Spectators at Lord's, oblivious to the happenings around Westminster, applauded a rousing half-century by India's precocious young talent, Billy Nawaz, at the moment Jeremy Dawlish fell. The stoppage of play as drizzle began to impinge on the safety of the players meant that news of the rally began to filter through via those who carried personal stereos.

Fifty miles away in Oxford, Labour leader, Robert Frewin, sank another midday vodka before phoning his main office. His hand shook slightly, reflecting mixed emotions of excitement and tension.
"Terry? Have you seen?" He nodded frantically, absorbing the response of his secretary.
"No!? I don't believe it? I was doing the weeds, when Helen called me in to watch..."
The line crackled. He smiled.
"Yes. Yes, I know my friend. We won't need a bloody manifesto after this morning!"

****

In Holborn, Ken and Mo had watched in growing suspense as the Prime Minister's inert form disappeared into his official residence and the black doors closed in the faces of the press.

"This is more than victory," whispered Ken temporarily forgetting his feud with his brother.
Mo nodded.
"This is the end of this government's power - or any other," Ken continued.
Mo's eyes widened.
"Badger for PM!?" he laughed, clenching his fists comically.
Ken just stared at the TV screen. They were showing the talking heads in some studio, somewhere in Shepherd's Bush.
"Experts! What do they know" he snapped.
"Zilch!" grinned Mo. His pudgy face was relaxed now that his brother had apparently resumed normal communications.

A gaggle of young student types nosily entered the café. They were laughing and singing some old tune. 'Ding dong - the PMs dead! Ding dong, the wicked PMs dead...'

Ken looked deadpan at Mo and said, "Wizard of Oz wasnit?"

****

Terence Gordon was cold. The tears had long since dried on his masked face. He needed a piss.
All he could smell was fucking apples. Rotten ones at that and he could feel the sickly slime from them seeping through his thin clothing.

He'd always preferred oranges. He shuffled as he tried to make himself comfortable in the wagon-load of fruit.
His ears picked up odd sounds. Creaking metal, dripping water. An icy draught cut across his legs. He seemed to be in some sort of derelict factory.
He was alone and his mind replayed the words of his captors. He realised he was to be used for some purpose later. Some statement or something they'd said.
They're nuts he thought, but they knew him. They knew his past. They also knew his future...

****

Dr Lawrence Leek arrived at Downing Street within ten minutes of the call out. It was fortuitous that he was spending Saturday at his apartment in Chelsea and not at his country retreat. His highly lucrative Harley Street practice supported a satisfactorily comfortable lifestyle but he was 'on call' every sixth weekend for the House.

Saturdays in summer were a nightmare with the tourist traffic, let alone the congestion of the rally taking place in the muggy drizzle in the Square.

He was ushered into the large reception room, where Jeremy Dawlish was slumped in a large winged chair, surrounded by his anxious staff. He was pale and sweating. It's a far cry from his electioneering days, thought Leek.
"Good morning Lawrence," whispered Dawlish through tight lips.
"Prime Minister..." Leek knelt down and opened his bag of tricks.

"Magic sponge time eh?" joked Dawlish wanly.
Leek shook his head as he listened through his stethoscope. He spoke in short sharp bursts and a slight Scottish accent was just detectable.

"No - blood pressure first."
"Then what?"
"Well, from the look of you, a holiday in Barbados and then retirement!"
Dawlish sighed.
"Oh, come on doc. I'm as fit as a fiddle. Only yesterday I beat a young strapping graduate at squash!"
Leek silently continued his examination, as he rolled up Dawlish's shirt sleeve and wrapped around his blood pressure cuff.
"Where's Miranda?" asked Dawlish lethargically.
"Upstairs scolding her mother," came the reply from one of his staff.
"Good. Bloody in-laws!" snapped Dawlish.
Leek completed his cursory tests and replaced his equipment in his bag.
"Well? What's the damage?" asked Dawlish.
A large figure in a flak jacket, wearing an ear piece, looked on impassively from his position near the window.
"You need to rest sir."
"Some hope," commented Dawlish as he fastened up his shirt. His voice seemed somewhat stronger.
"What's the Test score?" he added brightly to the grave-looking medic.
"Can't say. Hate cricket. Rugger's my game." replied Leek.
Dawlish fell silent.

"One fifty eight without loss. Rain stopped play," murmured an aide hesitantly.

"England or India?" asked Dawlish.

"India."

Dawlish slowly shook his head. This was becoming a very bad day indeed.

****

Chapter Thirty Four

Phil Queen sat next to the podium where history was being made. The rain continued to soak into the expectant crowd milling around the fountains. All the talk was of the collapse of the Prime Minister and speculation as to the subsequent situation.

The atmosphere of the rally was now electric. A queue had formed of people wanting to address the crowds. People jostled for better positions. As he sat listening to the rantings of various Brothers, Phil struggled to control his anger. The last couple of months had been like something out of a ridiculously plotted spy novel. From the day he'd interviewed Janice Lee to the death of Chloe - from being in love to being betrayed. It had all happened and his life was overturned. For what?

The noise around him was incredible. People danced, sang, argued, ate burgers and chatted. But he heard nothing.

All he wanted was revenge. Ken and Mo had murdered Chloe. All for their cause. His cause? The only woman he had loved had been snatched away. For what?

How could he find Ken and Mo? He could wander all day around London, looking, searching but all to no

avail. Something drastic had to be done. They must be looking for you too, he thought suddenly.
Exactly!
Draw them to you! (*How?*)
Make your own speech!

Phil laughed out loud. People turned to look at him.
"It's okay. I'm nuts." he smiled. They turned away from him, all except one.
An attractive girl in jeans and an anorak came across and sat down alongside him on the stone step. She offered her hand.
"Hi! I'm Sue Longstromm."
"Phil. Phil Queen."
They shook hands gravely among the seething throng.
"I'm nuts as well," smiled the girl.
"Join the club."

She had piercing blue eyes and straight blonde hair.
"Are you a natural blonde or bottled?" Phil grinned.
She caught his humour and replied, "Born like this. I'm Swedish." She tossed her hair as if demonstrating the veracity of her remark.
"Sue's a strange name for a Viking," Phil continued to send her up. He liked her spontaneity.
"Oh, I changed it three years ago. Helga was a pain and gives some people strange ideas - especially men. I came to England to study thirteen years ago from Stockholm."
Phil sized her up and felt a melting of his anger and frustration. She was beautiful and uncomplicated. He relaxed and smiled.
"How about you?"

"Oh, I'm in between jobs at present. Ex-Army, ex-police - just ex I guess."
"Ooh! A soldier. Men in uniform..." she grinned back.
"Yeah, yeah. I know. Now who's got strange ideas eh?"
"Oh come on Phil. Are you telling me you hate nurses, French maids? We all have our secret fantasies or fetishes."
Phil blushed. He hadn't blushed in weeks. Not since Chloe...

"Coffee?" asked Sue suddenly; producing a flask from a holdall.
"Great - prepared for this picnic were you?"
"I have salmon too."
"Does that mean you're a Pisces?"
She studied him seriously.
"It was a joke," he remarked.
"No - Gemini - two faced - happy, sad, that's me!" she replied philosophically.
"And what did you study?"
Sue frowned and sipped her drink.
"Psychology."
"Ah, I see now. You've sussed me out already then have you?"
"No - not at all. It takes time - if you've got it?" she turned and smiled directly into his eyes.
"All the time in the world."
He had forgotten Ken and Mo.

****

The doors thudded open. Darkness was all around him. He heard footsteps coming down wooden steps.

More than one person – two or three? Their movements were rougher this time.
"Oi, steady on!" shouted Gordon, as firm hands gripped his body and dragged him to his feet.
"Shut up - or you may die early!" whispered a hoarse voice.
(Die?)

The smell of fruit receded as he was led outside and fresh air assailed his nostrils through the fabric of the hood. He could hear distant traffic, horns and voices. The sounds of the city.
Then he heard the familiar noise of the van door being thrown back and he was pushed headfirst into it once more.
Dare he speak? *(No!)*

He was seated between two other bodies and they all swayed as the vehicle started up. One of his captors lit a match. He could smell the sulphur. He had never smoked but he would have gladly taken a cigarette now, if only to take his mind off his present situation.

The van lurched from side to side. It wasn't going very fast. You couldn't break speed limits in central London unless it was World Cup Final day and England were playing.

He gradually became aware of people outside. Many people.
His muffled hearing caught the sound of amplified voices. Someone was making a speech.
One of his guards spoke.

"Head for the podium. The police know we're on our way."

Gordon's eyes widened behind the mask. (*Police?*) (*Podium?*)
Suddenly, fear and panic gripped his mind. Things became clearer. Remarks he'd heard fell into place.
He was being taken to be made an example of.
Why were there crowds? Was it in public? (*Die - they had said 'die', hadn't they?*)
His mouth dried up as realisation began to dawn...
"Help! Help me!" he screamed, trying to get to his feet but the same hands grabbed him and restrained his frantic struggles.
Fists rained down on his head and torso.
"Fuckin' 'ell, he's flipped." gasped one of the captors.

Their thrashing bodies caused the van to lurch as it cautiously weaved through the crowds into the Square. The windscreen wipers cleared the weeping drizzle.

Gordon's bonds chafed his wrists and his breath came in gasps. His head throbbed from the vicious beating.

"No more Terence. We're here," said a stern voice in his ear. He could smell stale coffee on his captor's breath.
The van stopped.

****

Phil and Sue had seen the van pull up across Trafalgar Square and they watched as it disgorged seven figures.

They were all dressed in blue overalls, balaclavas and industrial boots. Phil shivered. One word occurred to him. Sinister.

Sue tugged at his jacket.
"What next? Tap dancing?" she giggled nervously.
Phil looked at her sternly.
"No - no. I don't think so," His mind was working overtime. One of the uniformed figures clapped his hands once. The other six circled the van and waited.

All the singing, chattering and frivolity ceased. A fearful calm descended on the multitude.
"They're waiting for something. Or someone," Sue muttered.
He stood up and strained to see more of the crowd.
They heard voices and a low shuffling noise. The crowds began to thin and separate allowing several people to approach the podium.
"I guess Lady Di," chuckled Sue.
Phil was grimly silent.
The voices got louder as the crowd made its way and some words became more distinguishable.
".... our time! Now! ... No going back..."

Phil felt the hairs on the back of his neck rise. He knew the voice.
Badger!
Sue murmured, "Mmm?"
Phil had not realised he had spoken.
"I know him! It's Badger!"
His eyes never left the three figures who now mounted the dais.

No need to search any more. It was Badger, Ken and Mo together!

Badger stepped up first. Ken had to be assisted by Mo as his old injuries hindered his progress.
Phil tutted.
"All friends again..."
Sue nudged him.
"Who are these people?"
"You don't want to know," answered Phil impatiently.
Sue frowned and looked confused.
The thousands upon thousands stood silently. Waiting...
Badger approached the microphone. He shook hands with the previous speaker, an ageing man in cords and a combat jacket.
"Thank you Brother Kelly."
The man stepped down with pride and waved to a group of friends nearby and they cheered.
Phil spat on the floor. Sue looked at him.
"What's up?" she whispered urgently.
"Murderers! These people are murderers," Phil replied harshly.
Badger tapped the microphone somewhat tentatively.
"Can you hear me at the back?" he called stridently.
A huge roar of sound greeted him.
"Yes!"
"Good!" came Badger's response as he nodded.

The crowd settled again as Badger surveyed his audience. Ken and Mo had taken up positions behind him and their faces were expressionless as they scanned the crowds.

"Welcome, Brothers and Sisters and your children!"
Badger's loving this, thought Phil.
"Today is YOUR day! The future is YOUR future!" began Badger. "No more giving in to violent scum, to fear, to drugs, muggers and rapists!" he continued.
People cheered in different groups. Little cliques and parties but they'd all assembled with a common goal.
"Justice - for the Victim - not the guilty criminal!" screamed Badger and he raised his clenched fist, mirroring the flag behind him.
"We all have a job to do! There are thousands more ready to join our cause today! Our politicians are impotent. Crime and violence have escalated for the past forty years and no amount of statistics, flippant argument or spineless justice can cover up the cracks in our society!"
A huge roar rolled up to the dais.
"It is time for change! Time for you, the decent law-abiding majority of people in our country to join forces and say, enough is enough!"
The air was crackling with expectancy. It was electric.
Sue frowned.
"It's like a Nazi rally," she whispered close to Phil's ear.
Phil nodded. "No – it's worse than that. He has the nation already on his side - not just a few crazy fanatics."
Sue's face registered her shock at Phil's words.

Badger's voice moderated; making his words even more authoritative.

"He's been practising," murmured Sue as she recalled her psychology training. He's going to start working on them now, whipping them up. Look at their faces!"

Phil eyed the people crushing up nearest to the podium. He realised they were almost swooning, in a sort of ecstasy of excitement; more like religious fanatics.

The speech continued.

"This morning, our own Prime Minister was made aware of the situation. He knows he is a beaten man. The Home Secretary has defected to join us all. The government is spent! The Brothers of Justice have arrived! We will not go away. We are here to stay!"

Phil shook his head, as he absorbed the message of Badger's words and another wave of sound assaulted his ears. Sue was applauding too. He heard her shouting above the general confusion, "This is why we are here! Why are you looking so unhappy?"

Phil's face was grave.

"I came to stop all this!" he shouted back.

Sue ignored his answer. She put her fingers in her mouth and let out a piercing whistle of triumph. She didn't see Phil leave her side.

He eased his way through the milling throng of different accents, coloured people, Chinese, Irish, German and Scots. These were people from anywhere and everywhere. Still the speech went on. Badger raised his arm and the crowd listened again.

"Ten days ago, the Brothers captured someone!" Badger paused to let his words sink in.

"Terence Gordon is a convicted paedophile."

"Shame!" People started hissing.

"Today he's our prisoner!"

Cheers rang out all around Trafalgar Square. The pigeons circled above, unable to alight in their usual haunts. No feeding bags today.

Phil turned to watch the circus unfold. He was some sixty metres from the stage. There was a lull in the proceedings and then Mo slowly stepped forward. Badger stepped aside.

"Bring him out!" Mo's North-east accent brought memories flooding back.

Phil bowed his head. He heard a door open. The van door. There was a short, scuffling sound and the odd expletive floated across the heads of the watchers.

Terence Gordon was manhandled on to the dais. The hood still shrouded his head and his hands were tied behind his back. The flag to their rear flapped on lazily.

Phil swallowed silently. The tension was incredible. A silence descended.

Mo spoke again.

"Ladies and gentlemen. Meet a child molester!"

Screams of hate and derision, a terrifying stream of abuse cascaded forth. The figure on the dais stood stock still, too scared to move. In one swift movement, Mo stripped off the hood.

"Meet the enemy!" Mo stated flatly.

Phil watched in silence, as missiles flew through the air, some of which struck Ken and Badger. Mo put up his hands firmly, "NO!"

Gradually the objects ceased flying. A stray banana cannoned off a wooden support.

Phil moved forward to get a better look. He managed to get within ten yards of the dais. He could no longer see Sue where he'd left her.

Tears ran down the paedophile's face. He wore an expression of abject terror.

"This man raped and tortured a little girl. His favourite pastime is watching videos of such unspeakable acts!"
People screamed. Women were crying. Phil felt a twinge of pity for the man but it was swiftly replaced by disgust.
Mo continued, "He was jailed for fifteen years. He was released this year after nine years and now he's back in our community."
The crowd booed and hissed.
"Is this justice? For the children he attacked? For their families? No - it is not!"
Gordon swayed and moaned audibly.
"Today justice will be SEEN to be done!"

There was a sudden hush.
Phil frowned. The figures surrounding the van approached the stage.
Mo turned to Badger and said something but Phil could not make it out.
Another figure joined the group on stage. He looked about sixty five and had greying hair and he walked with a slight stoop. He shook hands with Ken, Mo and Badger and nodded.
The uniformed figures disappeared behind the huge flag. A few bumps and a dragging sound. They reappeared, carrying a large wooden structure.
There were gasps of recognition around the square as the hanging gibbet was hoisted upright behind the unsuspecting Gordon, whose head was once more covered with the black hood.
"Christ! No!" muttered Phil.
TV commentators and cameramen gabbled excitedly, more in shock and horror than in their professional capacity.

"Get in closer!"

"We're going live!"

"Get me a link-up - now!"

The giant structure now stood stark against the backdrop of the National Gallery's grey facade. Nelson looked on approvingly, as if judging the show below him.

Ken stepped up to the microphone.

"Hello," his voice sounded somewhat nervous.

The older man stood to his right, stock still, and he stared ahead over the massed heads.

Ken placed a hand on his shoulder.

"I want to introduce to you Mr Abraham Willis of Carlisle. An ordinary, hard-working man. All of his life he served his locality as a fireman. He was loyal, courageous and compassionate in his work."

Applause broke out as the people listened intently.

"Abraham's daughter was five years old when she bumped into Terence Gordon. Five years old. She liked horses and wanted to work in stables when she grew up."

Women were openly crying now. Grown men bit their lips nervously.

"Kelly Willis never rode a horse," Ken continued.

Phil felt a lump in his own throat and his eyes welled up.

A man next to him dabbed his eyes with a handkerchief.

Terence Gordon himself began to shake and sob.

"Bastard!" someone cried far away.

"Shame!"

Ken spoke again as he leant heavily on his walking stick.

"It's time for justice to be done and to be seen to be done."

This time, no one cheered. The silence was infinitely more sinister.

One of the dark figures threw a rope up through the frame. It snaked down and held taut; the noose now clearly visible. It hung threateningly from the oak gibbet.

Gasps of astonishment and a low muttering rippled around the crowded area. The drizzle continued unabated. Things happened as if in slow motion.

"No! This is anarchy!" shouted a lone voice in the distance.

There was a short scuffle and then silence again.

Phil's nostrils twitched. He turned towards Gordon.

"He's crapped" said a voice flatly.

People gagged as they witnessed the almost unreal scene unfolding before them. A woman vomited. It slapped on a pavement in front of a group of children, some of them were crying.

"They won't really..."

"Where are the police?"

Realisation began to turn to incredulity. Terence Gordon was screaming.

"I don't want this!" shouted a young girl. She had a pushchair with a young child. Some people began to move away and the shock was beginning to sink in.

"It's obscene," said a youth as he smoked his spliff.

"Fun though." Grinned his spotty faced friend, as he stared at the events unfolding before him.

Gordon didn't struggle as he was lifted on to a wooden stool. He'd given up the fight. A pool of water and flecks of excretion were left where he had stood. His hands were stiffly tied behind him.

Phil wiped his hand across his mouth. His tongue felt like sandpaper.

He was powerless. If he intervened, he too would become a target. The rope noose dropped over Gordon's head and it tightened within seconds.

Then Abraham Willis stepped forward slowly, almost shyly. The world was watching.

"Are you OK, Mr Willis?" asked Badger. His righteous anger was totally undiminished. He was on a high at the culmination of all the plans.

"Never better!" came the strong reply as Kelly's father stepped forward and without further ceremony he kicked the stool away from beneath Gordon's feet. It shot across the dais and fell down into the crowd snapping on impact.

Those who fought for the souvenir missed Gordon's last moments as violent summary justice ended his life. The huge torso wriggled and kicked for fully thirty seconds and his head was at a strange angle to his body.

People cheered again, but more in a release of the tension of the preceding moments. Gordon's body swung, thrashed and turned in mid-air. Someone screamed shrilly in the distance.

As the movements dissipated, the feet finally twitched, and the body hung still. Lifeless.

Abraham Willis calmly left the stage, climbed into a waiting car and he was gone. There was no remorse from him. The gibbet creaked slowly in time with the body's movements. Slower and ever slower...creak, creak. Creak. Then, all was still.

Badger returned to the microphone.

"That was justice - for the victim!" he boomed.

The response was muted. People were weeping openly now. No one cheered. No one clapped.

They were in shock. The crowd seemed to swirl as people began to leave.

The truth was out. Badger eyed the milling crowds without speaking a word.
Phil smiled grimly.
"You've lost" he whispered to himself.
On the stage, Badger's face looked grim as he searched for more inspiring words, more sound-bites for the cause. However, nothing would come.
The giant flag fluttered in the breeze, its design indistinguishable as if in anti-climax.
Badger gestured almost angrily at his entourage.
"Get him down and clean this shit up!" he snapped.

Phil approached the stage, without apprehension. He stood, looking up at Ken and Mo who were trying to justify the proceedings to an American news channel.
"Hi boys," he called out to attract their attention.
Ken and Mo turned sharply.
Phil eyed them. Their surprise gave Phil some much needed confidence.
"Sorry to have to say it gents, but I think you really messed this one up today."
Ken's eyes widened in anger.
"You little shit!" was all Ken could say.
Phil smiled.
"Shouldn't you be keeping an eye on your wife Ken?"
"You abso'…!" Ken exploded and he almost overbalanced in his anger.
Mo jumped off the stage and gestured furiously at Phil.
"You think you're so fuckin' brilliant don't you Queen?"

Phil merely shrugged yawning in mock boredom. The van doors slammed twice in the near distance.
"Cool it Mo. You know I could do you with one hand tied behind my back if I wanted to. Perhaps it's you who should be keeping an eye on his wife?"
Mo lunged forward aggressively but his arm was instantly caught into an agonising arm lock.
"How about a bust arm to go with your brother's bust leg?" Phil whispered.

A small crowd had gathered now to watch this new circus. The TV cameras had also turned in their direction.

"Leave it Mr Queen," said Ken.
"Oh, it's Mr Queen now is it?" laughed Phil.
"You're out in the cold now Phil. You've got nothing - no one."
"He's got me," said a voice behind Phil.
He turned. It was Sue.
"Where did you go?" she asked smilingly as he put a hand up to his face.
"Nice one Phil. You're never at a loss eh!" remarked Mo suggestively.
Ken's face flushed with anger.

On the dais, Badger was supervising the dismantling of all the props of the execution. Phil's eyes scanned the scene.
"I think it's you lot who have nothing. Just what did you achieve today?" Phil commented.
Ken looked at Mo.
"Nothing! You were no better than the people who you claim you've wasted these past months. You disgust me!" exclaimed Phil.

Sue grasped Phil's arm as she sensed his anger and urged him to leave.
Mo stepped forward sneering, "You're all bull-shit Phil. You should be a politician - all words and no action!"
"We could snuff you out just like that!" Ken snapped his fingers.
Phil bristled.
"Oh yeah? Where are all your supporters now then?" he gestured to the practically empty square which had cleared dramatically after the sickening spectacle of Gordon's death throes. Nelson gazed impassively down on the scattered litter and the pigeons now restored to their usual spaces.
"You've shot yourselves in the foot boys. This isn't the French Revolution! People haven't got the stomach for the guillotine style of justice anymore.
By going public, you've ruined everything."
"Bollocks!" spat Mo.
Phil smiled. "I was taught one thing when I was in the Army. When dealing with the enemy..."
"What? General Queen!"
"Surprise is the key but you've no surprises left after this little show. You're all marked men. All your faces are known. Your little circus has proved nothing at all," spat Phil.
Sue tugged at Phil's sleeve.
"Come on Phil, let's go...now!"
"Yeah. Okay, I've said enough."

He turned to leave, his anger started to subside into a feeling of anti-climax and rueful despair. Handled differently, he thought, things could have been achieved quietly. Too late...

As they walked away, footsteps came running after them. Phil turned, instinctively preparing for confrontation. It was Mo.

"Phil!"

Mo offered his hand.

"Here - have this... I'm sorry."

Phil took the object from him. Sue watched quizzically as Mo departed. It was Chloe's necklace.

"The Twins of Gemini..." he murmured.

He looked at Sue.

"Do you like jewellery?"

"Depends..."

"Then wear this - for me. For us..."

He placed the chain around her neck reverentially.

"Let's go," he whispered. He firmly took her hand and they walked arm in arm up the steps in the direction of Covent Garden as sirens wailed in the distance.

The rain continued to fall relentlessly in drizzly swirls and it enveloped the couple as they disappeared into the distant crowds.

****

Vanguard IV

JULY

They sat, as always, with their decanters full, the lighting subdued and wreaths of expensive smoke circled their heads.
The meetings were still a success.
The Brothers of Justice had only just begun...

The tabloids had had a field day. Banner headlines screamed the news of the rally and its culmination.

When the Head rose to speak, a full three minutes elapsed before he could be heard. He waited for the approving applause to cease. Waiters scurried to the side of the room and stood to attention.
"Thank you gentlemen."
He leaned forward on the huge oak table and scanned the assembly.
"The world saw the future of Justice in Trafalgar Square recently."
Hands clapped or banged on the table in agreement.
"Already, as a result, we have recruited sixteen Tory and five Labour Members of Parliament to our cause.

The Home Secretary should be applauded for his support and tolerance."

"Hear, hear!"

"The Houses of Parliament are in turmoil but we shall not waver!"

Murmurs of agreement greeted his statement.

"We - you - us - are the future!"

The Head raised his glass in triumph.

"No more victims!" he boomed and he resumed to his seat.

Everyone stood and confirmed the toast. As they sat down again, one man remained standing.

"I think one man deserves our applause more than most on this occasion." More murmurs agreed with him.

"Gentlemen, please rise again and I give you a toast..."

They all raised their glasses as one.

"I give you Dermot Breen of the Metropolitan Police, our inspiration and our Leader!"

"Dermot Breen!"

"And Justice to all victims!" The familiar refrain of the National Anthem filled the room. They sang with gusto. Brothers. United as One.

Their new world was just beginning...

****

EPILOGUE

WESTON SUPER MARE SEAFRONT – JULY 2034

The old couple sat on the bench, staring silently at the approaching yellow surf. It would soon be time for curfew. The time that all people, young and old, must return to their respective pods. Malingerers or refuseniks are at risk of arrest or worse in the world they now inhabit. The sea is a dull yellow sludge.

The great earthquakes and tremors of 2015 were a taste of things to come. Whole cities in the southern hemisphere disappeared overnight. Weather systems changed in the following months. Vast swathes of the earth are now uninhabitable. Millions of people died and thousands now live in vast desert shanty towns, lashed by electrical storms and unpredictable temperatures.

In 2017, forty five thousand people simply walked into the sea in Japan. The biggest mass suicide in history. It was pre-planned in the two months beforehand.

The new world order, created by the Brotherhood in 1995, created what they believed would be a new and better existence. They were wrong. In London, England, the austere conditions thrust upon its people were, at first, greeted with relief by the populace. Criminals became virtually non-existent within a few years as their activities were curtailed by the introduction of a selection of simple yet incredibly effective solutions.

The reintroduction of summary justice in June 1996 meant that murderers and the like were not sent to prison. The first unfortunate victim, a David Millward from Camberwell in London, was killed by hanging within a day of being caught. The majority of the public supported this. The Brotherhood grew. Its two founder members, Kenneth and Maurice Jamieson, recruited millions of like-minded supporters. The scum of society had no hiding place anymore.

Phil and Sue Queen stare out at the incoming tide. Their wedding in 1994, just three weeks after their first meeting, was a very private affair. Phil is now 64. Sue is 62. The sea swells towards them, giving off its familiar sulphurous stench.

"Put your mask on honey. It looks bad tonight. The forecast is for another night of acid rain. Do you remember the day we came here to live? It was 28 degrees. We had ice cream on the pier and you got bitten by a crab!" Phil smiles at Sue as he clasps her hand tightly. His greying hair is still full and healthy but his skin is now sallow.

The sun stopped shining in 2027 after the sky turned black. No stars shine in the sky anymore. The world is dying.

"Yes darling," says Sue, who is blind and bald. Her blue eyes see nothing now and the cancer that ravages her body causes her to wince at every sudden movement. She smiles at Phil and as tears roll down her cheek and she says, "I really love you Phil."

"Love you too hon. You're still the most beautiful woman in my life."

"That's because I'm the only one!" Sue replies. She coughs suddenly and her body is racked with pain.

"Masks on! Now!" shouts Phil loudly.

Sue leans forward and quickly places her face protector over her nose and mouth. The oxygen rush is a blessed relief. Phil follows suit, checking the position of both their respective visors.

"I fucking hate these things!" snaps Sue.

"Needs must my sweet, needs must," replies Phil flatly. They huddle together closely and the sea is now feet from their feet.

"Can I ask you something?" says Sue, her voice muffled by her mask.

"...Course, go ahead," replies Phil matter of factly.

"Do you think of Chloe often? I mean, do you miss her?"

Phil is momentarily silent. The name Chloe takes a couple of seconds to register with him, as his oxygen rush has affected his memory for a few moments.

Chloe. Darling Chloe. He pictures her, leaning on the cottage gate with her summer dress swirling in the breeze. She smiles and blows him a kiss. Then just as quickly, she's gone...

"Not a lot. No my love. She died years ago and I don't even dream of her now," he lies with his eyes closed.

Sue shuffles in her grey overalls. Her name tag is pushed up under her chin. She turns to Phil slowly. His eyes are still closed, protecting him from her staring, sightless eyes.

"So when you scream her name at night in your sleep you are thinking of someone else?"

Sue smiles. "Gotcha!"
Stony silence from Phil...

"Liar, liar pants on f..."

"Okay, okay... you got me!" Phil grins shyly. "She's dead darling. Anyway, who is Sven? You have been crying in your sleep for years over him!"

Sue grimaces. "Aaah, Sexy Sven. He was my masseur..."

"Wha...?"

"Only kidding darling. Sven was my cousin. We were very close. He also died. Motorcycle crash in Denmark in 1990."

"Oh, I see...I'm sorry."

"Why the Chloe interrogation then?"

Sue leans into Phil and hugs him.

"I don't know. I just want you all to myself my love. I know you wanted children and she could have bore them for you. I am just a cancer addled, barren old cow."

Phil kisses Sue and their masks clicked.

"We could only have one anyway. The law says so. When that was legislated I was glad we had none because I would have wanted two or more! The Brotherhood law machine meant we would have only one child."

"Ssssh Phil they may be listening!" whispers Sue quietly, pointing upwards slightly.

The overhead camera and listening post stares back at the couple. The black box hums dully. The Brotherhood monitor all conversations and dissenters are severely dealt with.

"That one's broken. Gareth told me. I bumped into him the other day at the cull. He has had a promotion. He wishes he was coming up for retirement like me. The light isn't flashing on it. It's kaput."

Phil gives the camera the middle finger. He hasn't been brave like this before. Sue doesn't see this very dangerous behaviour.

Sue coughs. A guttural, animal sound.

"At least we are the right height and weight," says Phil.

"The obesity police have almost finished rounding up the last few thousand over eaters,"

Sue chuckles. "I could murder a burger and fries. I had my last one thirty years ago, they were awesome."

The Weight Freight wagon trundles past as they speak. The shouts of fear from the latest internees are a normal sound nowadays.

"Too many pies and chips eh?" murmured Sue.

The driver of the truck is a drone. Scarlet robots that move of their own volition. When public transport became obsolete the robots took over the driving of all vehicles. The petrol dried up years ago but scientists created the new wonder oil called 'VISCEX'. Driving your own car is now banned and all travel to foreign countries has been outlawed.

Phil and Sue have not left Weston for eighteen years...

The correct height and weight must be adhered to. Failure to comply means two years at the huge Starvation and Vitamin Control Station in Birmingham. The station is run by the same red robots. Selected members of the Brotherhood oversee the operation. Billions have been saved and ploughed into luxurious living accommodation for the top echelons of the ruling class.

Food is rationed for the majority. A maximum 2,000 calories for women aged over 18 a day. 2,599 for males.

Obesity has all but been eradicated. It is 4 years since Phil has seen an overweight person. A close friend, Paul Abraham, was interned at the SVC IN 2030. He lost 8 stone in 3 weeks. He committed suicide on his last day. His mind was erased by the strict regime.

Phil had warned him for years about the pounds he was piling on, but to no avail.

Sue suddenly nudges Phil. “Come on. That smell is really doing my noggin in.”

The yellow sea slaps against the sea wall. A thick grey steam rises from the thick, viscous sludge. Phil stands up slowly with his walking stick by his side.

“Someone’s coming. Make sure you smile!”

A tall figure approaches the couple. He wears the same grey uniform as Phil and Sue, however he wears the insignia of the Brothers on his lapel and chest area. The green badge states the letters J.D and the number fourteen. J.D14 is very close now.

“You have three minutes to vacate this area thank you.”

Phil smiles. A rictus grin. Sue does the same.

“Yes sir. No problem. Thanks for the warning,” says Phil, holding Sue’s hand tightly.

Justice Department Fourteen at your service,” replies the tall figure. He smiles and carries on walking along the deserted promenade.

There's a sudden clap of thunder then the rain starts.

"Fuck…it's acid. Come on my love, let's go," murmurs Phil, as he pulls the collar of his uniform.

Sue strides alongside Phil, into the rain. His stick clicks on the road. It stings the skin if they are in it longer than five minutes. Thousands have been burnt to death in the wastelands over the years. Their bodies ignored. Rotting in the dark.

The couple reach their pod in less than a minute. Houses are obsolete. The pod is a single room with a bed and furniture. A large screen on the wall shows old films and historical documentaries. There is no more sport. Today's film is 'Ann of Green Gables.' Violent films are banned and the internet is only for the use of Brotherhood members. Phil and Sue are not members.

"What I would give for an old western or a Bruce Lee movie!" says Phil.

A buzzer sounds and the evening meal appears on a tray set into the wall.

"Oh no. Salad and pasta again! I'M BLOODY SICK OF THAT!" shouts Sue.

Phil takes the tray. Sue's acute sense of smell means she knows the meal instantly.

"Lucky the Brotherfeed is dead. You would be in deep shit for that kid," smiles Phil.

His smile fades suddenly at a knock on the window at the pod entrance. Phil recognises J.D14...

Sue stands stock still. "Shit. They heard me!"

Phil bites his lip as he opens the pod door. The rain has eased considerably. J.D14 smiles that unnerving grin.

"Dissent will not be tolerated. You have one Behavioural Warning left according to my records,"

"Sorry officer, my wife has cancer and has had a tough week. We will contact Unit 100 and apologise immediately, it's a horrible night isn't it?"

The grinning man outside nods slightly. His eyes are black pools. The smile fades.

"One more B.W and she will be tagged ready for Personality Pooling sir, have a good evening," then the smile returns.

Phil grins back. "Of course. I understand. Thank you. Goodnight."

Sue is weeping when Phil returns to her side. She mouths silently at him. Phil lip reads her words.

"I thought the feed was broken!" her eyes are wide.

Phil replies "So did I. Fuck!" he whispers.

Sue slumps on to a plain wooden chair sobbing.

"I'm not hungry anymore, you have it."

"You must eat. It's the law remember?"

Sue mouths silently, "Fuck the law, I've had enough! I hate this pod and I hate the life I have!"

"Careful hun else he'll be back," whispers Phil.

Sue stands and walks to a square pad on the floor. The weighing slab flickers and a voice states flatly "One hundred and three calories consumed today. EAT!"

"Told you," whispers Phil. "You need more calories inside you for today."

Sue sits at the table and silently starts to eat. Phil joins her and eats his plate of salad.

He has an extra four potatoes and a serving of meat on his plate.

"Yummy. Wonderful," says Sue sarcastically. Looking in the direction of the Brotherfeed in the wall recess.

Phil puts his finger to his lips and grins. "Sssh..."

With dinner finished, they retire to the living area. The acid rain drums on the roof. Distant claps of thunder can be heard in the distance, a low growling sound. Lightning splits the darkness outside and makes patterns in the sky. Beautiful yet utterly terrifying.

The clock reads 2215 hrs, yet there is only darkness, day and night. One day runs into the next. Monday? Tuesday? They don't exist anymore...

"Shall we go down to the park tomorrow Sue," asks Phil as he changes into his issued nightwear.

"I have to attend a Memory Meeting."

Sue nods and smiles. "What is the subject?" asks Sue.

"I think it's 'The Death of Maurice Jamieson and the Lessons to be Learned.'

"Didn't his brother kill him? Kenneth wasn't it. Around the time of our wedding?"

"Yep. They created this wonderful existence and I was privileged to know them," said Phil flippantly. His mind wandered back to Trafalgar Square many years before.

"You remember them don't you, at Trafalgar, the day we met?"

Sue frowned. "Vaguely, it's so long ago darling," she murmured yawning.

"We'll need the torch as the weather looks terrible for tomorrow," said Phil as he lay on the bed. He put his stick next to the table.

Sue lay down next to him. She exhales loudly, coughing heavy bursts into the night air.

"I have not got long left darling, I can feel it."

Phil wraps his arms around Sue tightly and kisses her on the forehead. "Every day is a bonus my love," says Phil quietly. He reaches round her neck and grasps the necklace he gave her in 1994. The Twins of Gemini. Then their eyes close.

Phil is quickly asleep. He dreams of the long ago. The nightmares vary. People from the past drift in and out of his thoughts. Chloe in the shop. The two school bullies he beats up outside the school. A lifeless body hanging from a tree in a park. The football riots and the dead bodies in the bar. The two joyriders casually snuffed out beside the road. Chloe in her stockings beckoning him to bed. The judge's wife that got murdered. The dreams are regular and vivid. He has them every night...

He twitches spasmodically on the bed with drops of sweat appearing on his hot forehead. Clive Badger stares at him from behind a desk. He is frozen in fear as Badger stands and grins maniacally at him. "You must obey us Queen!"

Then, he's awake! Sue is asleep beside him; snoring as usual. The storm lashes the windows and he stands up. He walks over to the window and stares at the unbelievable weather outside. The sea lashes the wall across the road. Steam rises from the ocean and it crashes over onto the road. The rain is heavier now and lightning bolts stagger the darkness.

Phil Queen sits on a stool and closes his eyes. He's an old man in a mad world? Or a mad man in an old world?

He watches the storm with eyes of glass. Is this it? He thinks to himself. A tear trickles down his cheek onto his grey Brotherhood Issue flannel nightwear. The never ending storm continues to rage on outside.

The woman he loves will die soon, and so will the world. Phil falls back to sleep next to Sue again, but only to wait for his nightmares to return once more...

THE END